The Marcella Fragment

Edited by Meg Dietrich
Cover design by Jeff Raby: Creatis Group http://creatisgroup.com/

Cover art: Six-winged Seraph (Azrael)
By Mikhail Alexandrovich Vrubel [Public domain],
via Wikimedia Commons

Newcal Publishing
http://newcalpub.com

Trade Paperback Edition
ISBN-10: 0985016817
ISBN-13: 978-0-9850168-1-4

This book is set in Palatino Linotype and is printed on acid free paper.

For Bob

"[Miracles] . . . seem to me to rest not so much upon faces or voices or healing power coming suddenly near to us from afar off, but upon our perceptions being made fine, so that for a moment our eyes can see and our ears hear what is there about us always."

Willa Cather

Contents

Cast of Characters

The Council of Pelion

She-Who-Was-Ilena, Fourteenth Mother
She-Who-Was-Vena, Fifteenth Mother, "The Outsider"
Beal/Belwyn, Master of Mysteries, "The Wanderer"
Stanis, Master of the Voice, "The Panther"
Luxor/Lycus, Commander of the Legion, "The Wolf"
Nerissa, Instructor of the Maze, "The Dove"
Ladon, High Healer of Pelion, "The Hound"

Mission Helpers

Rhacius, Commander of the Cavalry
Maenon, healing partner to Chloe
Chloe, healing partner to Maenon
Carmanor, Commander of the Infantry
Phylas, former ernani, member of the Infantry
Grasos, Tyre's guard in the Maze
Zelor, son of Luxor, Head Trainer of the Maze
Gelanor, Master of the Hetaera Guild
Grudius, Master of the Horse, Legion Cavalry
Idas, Healer to the Legion

Citizens of Pelion

Melos, Iron Master of the Forge
Lukash, translator for Stanis
Nomia, mate to Phylas, member of the Hetaera Guild
Evander, mate to Megera, Master of the Weavers Guild
Megera, mate to Evander, Mistress of the Nursery
Kara, daughter of Evander & Megera, "Moon Child"
Thalia, rejected from Preparation

Ernani and Women of Pelion

Brimus / Minthe
Dino / Dias
Suda / Chione
Rama / Varuna
Pandar / Tessa

Land of the Lapith

Ariod, Tribal Chieftain, Clan of the Running Horse
Tyre, son of Ariod, "The Golden One"
Hourn, friend-in-blood to Tyre, mated to Nephele
Stheno, the Mouth of Sturm
Llyr, friend-in-blood to Ariod, Tribal Elder

Servants in the Maze

Eris
Baldor

The Marcella Fragment

by

Anna LaForge

Book One of Maze

Prologue

The First Day

SHE COULDN'T FATHOM it, the brilliant blue of a sky that belonged in a painting or a photograph from a former age. The skies of her youth, of her middle age, of her old age, roiled as brown and dirty as the seas. Sad, she thought, sad to know your world was dying.

"Does it please you?"

He was here, but not here, shimmering in and out of focus, beside her but not beside her, part of him here on the top of this hill, another part on the ship hovering above this strangely empty world. Other parts of him existed in places beyond the power of her imagination.

"We intend to please you. All of you."

She wondered how many had survived the exodus. More than that, she wondered how long she had slept. A year? A hundred years? A millennium? How long had it taken them to find this world with its single moon and golden sun? How long to grow forests and populate these hills and valleys with flora and fauna similar to that of old Earth, including the eagle riding the thermal currents high above her head?

"You are full of questions."

That she was, although she knew from long experience he couldn't be pressured into answering. He had lived inside her thoughts for so long that it felt unnatural to form words and speak them aloud. Odd as it was to communicate in this manner, she understood that he could not lie to her, nor could she lie to him.

Why had he brought her here? That was her first and foremost question. He seemed to be asking for approval of some kind, but for what reason? Were others being awakened or was she the only one? And what was this place in relation to the new life she was to live?

"This will be home to you and others like you. We found you in a place like this. We return you to a similar place."

She almost laughed out loud. When the last days came, with an unexpected offer of transport for any who survived the final paroxysms of the dying planet, she was stranded in Bavaria, near Oberammergau, in the foothills of the Alps. If she hadn't gotten the study grant, she would have perished with everyone who lived and worked in Southern California.

The book she was writing had both saved her life and determined the geography of her new existence.

"We have your books."

She was immediately alert, focused. The precious few books she traveled with survived? Those, too, that other people brought with them as they rushed to the transport sites? She mourned the world's great libraries, treasure troves of human creativity, lost now and turned to rubble, until she thought to wonder if they, too, might have been rescued.

"We will help you begin. When we leave, you must help each other."

A hard lump of fear formed inside her. When this voice inside her head was finally silenced, she would be horribly alone, more alone than she had been before she knew what it was to share her thoughts with another being.

"We have given you a gift."

You've already given us a second chance, she thought. Transport to another world as well as help beginning a new civilization. What did we do to deserve this?

In answer, he began to sing to her the songs of Puccini, Mahler, Berlioz, de Falla, Ellington, Bernstein . . . .

Her eyes growing heavy, she closed them on the sky of brilliant blue, remembering as she tumbled back down into sleep something he told her the first day, the day she was rescued.

"We call ourselves Sowers."

The Marcella Fragment

. . . until the time of the great Transformation which shall be known by the signs. One shall come from desolation, unknown and unknowing; she will behold the night but fear it not. They will be gathered unto her, the silent panther, the ravenous wolf, the cooing dove, the clear-eyed hound; and all will lie down and delight in her service until the time comes that they must go into darkness . . .

. . . a Maze is formed in the belly of the earth and lo, a great voice calls from its depths, "Come!" and from the points of the compass come the chosen ones, brought by the hands of a wanderer. And from the north and the west a sun will move across the sky of day, and from the south and east a moon will travel on the sky of night. And so they shall meet at the place of the sacred fire and the Path will be revealed. And the elder days will pass away, and that which was black will be white, and that which has been, will be no more, and that which has never been, will be.

Marcella, Scribe of the Great Library, wrote this

Chapter 1

Land of the Lapith

SQUINTING AGAINST THE glare of a fiercely burning sun, Belwyn wished briefly for his headgear. "You are not old," he reminded himself, annoyed at his growing fixation on encroaching age. Upon reaching a crest that rose above the plain, a sweeping survey of his surroundings revealed a lone horse and rider moving over a shimmering mirage of water-covered grass.

When his mount unexpectedly shifted beneath him, Belwyn's smile became a grimace. The last time he'd occupied a saddle the resulting soreness in his backside stretched well into the following week. Shaking off that decidedly uncomfortable memory, Belwyn concentrated on observing the rider at work.

The horseman rode bareback, disdaining the use of reins now draped across the animal's neck. He rode as Lapithians had ridden for generations, at one with the animal, his forearms upraised, elbows level with his waist, his fingers pointing skyward, schooling his equine student in the basics of battle. His upraised hands held no weapons now, but in time they would, by which time the horse would be capable of executing commands through subtle shifts of weight and the tightening of the rider's buttocks, thighs, and knees.

Her white-stocking legs flashing as she moved in ever-decreasing circles, the horse, a trim chestnut filly, stopped, reversed her lead, then continued her circles without varying the rhythm of her strides. Next were a series of figure eights, elegant serpentines woven in an unbroken pattern of nearly heart-stopping perfection. Even an amateur like Belwyn, who never sat a horse until well into middle age, could appreciate the skill of the rider. White specks of foam along the filly's neck and withers attested to the difficulty of the rider's demands as well as the dry heat of a morning already unseasonably warm considering the chill of approaching autumn nights.

Recognizing the end of the lesson, Belwyn raised his voice in a shout, causing the rider to lift his head and wave in acknowledgement. In the next breath, man and horse turned toward the crest, the filly sparking into a gallop, the rider low on her neck, her mane whipping in the wind, blending with the streaming hair of the rider. Five paces in front of Belwyn, she skidded to an abrupt halt, sides shuddering, nostrils flaring, eyes showing white.

"What's all this?" Belwyn demanded, "No one questions your skills where horses are concerned. Better to spend time on your studies."

Despite his best intentions, Belwyn's lips curled up at the corners as he addressed his pupil, betraying his attempt at severity. Lifting his leg over the filly's head, the rider slid to the ground. Pulling a cloth from his belt, he went to work wiping down the horse's sweating flanks, establishing a soothing rhythm that soon had the filly flicking her tail in silent contentment.

After his own, far less graceful, dismount, Belwyn's expression changed to one of rapt assessment. Had his pupil bothered to turn his head, he might have been startled by the keenness of his tutor's gaze. Sun-bleached hair, several shades lighter than the horse he now groomed, hung well below his shoulder blades; a bronze circlet worn horizontally across his forehead kept it clear of his face. Dressed in the informal garb of a Lapithian warrior, his tall, spare frame was covered from throat to toe in a tunic, breeches, and soft boots fashioned from chamois leather.

As a native of more southern and less modest climes, Belwyn was continually amazed by the amount of clothing worn by both genders in Lapith. To this day he had never seen a Lapithian woman without full-length robes and seemingly obligatory layers of veiling over her face. If, he thought grimly, he had seen one at all. The few times he did, what he remembered were their hands, roughened and callused from milking sheep and cattle and countless household tasks that kept them busy in the confines of the women's compound.

In his twelve years of service in Ariod's household, Belwyn virtually lived with Tyre as he oversaw his education, yet in all that time, he had seen the boy unclothed only once, when, during his sixteenth year, he was inducted into the warrior clan. Part of that initiation included a dunking in a pond hacked out of the frozen lake that provided water for Ariod's tribe and their herds. Granted the honor of assisting the chieftain's son (an unheard of favor considering his position as an outsider) Belwyn held the fur robe around a shuddering body as it emerged from the freezing water, observing the thin angularity of an adolescent body that promised the sinewy strength necessary to a warrior who must hunt and fight on horseback. In the years that followed, he watched the boy grow to manhood, although Belwyn suspected he had still not reached full growth. Tall and strong as his pupil might be, Belwyn wondered about his stamina. Pushing that thought away, Belwyn started as his pupil swung around to address him.

"What brings you here, old man? Sturm knows I've spent enough time studying that infernal tongue you insist I learn. Can't I have one free morning to train for the races? Freena is fit enough, but we must train together if we're to win again."

Despite these complaints, his pupil's expression revealed neither rancor nor guile, but regarded his tutor with teasing affection. In a characteristic gesture Belwyn recognized from his first meeting with his young charge, Tyre of Lapith, son of Ariod, brushed several loose strands of hair from his shoulders and settled them onto his back. With that familiar movement of sun-bronzed hand through wind-swept hair, the figure of the tall man before him shimmered, shrank, and Belwyn stood as he had so many years ago, meeting Tyre, the boy he recognized from dreams of what might be.

Having heard a rumor that a tribal chieftain was in need of a tutor for his son, a boy reputed to possess the golden hair of those loved by the god Sturm, Belwyn hurried to find this particular tribe. Here, by the shore of a shallow lake, he introduced himself to Ariod, the tribal chieftain. When Belwyn requested an interview with his prospective pupil, Ariod objected. Accustomed to instant and unquestioning obedience by boys and men, Ariod assured Belwyn that his son would heed his father's instruction without comment or complaint. Baffled by Belwyn's insistence that the boy be consulted concerning the selection of his tutor, Ariod capitulated to Belwyn's steady resolve and directed him to a nearby paddock. Even though Belwyn's conversation with the young prince was to be private, three household retainers lounged against a nearby fence. Belwyn noted that a powerful chieftain with only one son need be a very careful man.

Brows knitted in appraisal, twelve year old Tyre regarded Belwyn with frank curiosity as dirty hands pushed a tangled mass of fair hair away from his face. Despite his youth, there was nothing childlike in his bearing; no awkwardness or timidity usually associated with a boy of a mere twelve years was evident. Instead, there was a quality of imperiousness about him, as if he understood that childhood was a luxury not granted to those who would lead.

"My father tells me I must study with you. What do you have to teach me?"

The boy's gaze was direct, his inquiry serious. Belwyn recognized the challenge behind the question.

"Ariod tells me his son must be trained in the ways of a ruler. We will begin with reading and writing . . ."

His prepared speech was quickly interrupted.

"My father, his father, and his father before him, ruled without such things."

"Yet your father sees the wisdom of it or I would not be here."

The boy considered him gravely for a moment. Refusing to be intimidated by one so young, Belwyn shifted strategy, judging that this one would never be won by docility. To the boy's challenge, he offered one of his own.

"Law, mathematics, languages, and healing will be our major course of study, with the addition of war and defense. I will need assistance from your warriors with the latter, since my people defend themselves somewhat differently."

The young face showed a rapt consideration of his explanation, brightening with interest as his last words were spoken.

"How do your people fight?"

"Without horses."

The boy's eyes widened in amazement. As surprise faded, he hooted with laughter, his hair falling back into his face with the shaking of his shoulders.

Belwyn, comfortable with improvisation, didn't hesitate. In a simple move every boy on his street had mastered by the age of six, he grabbed the boy's hair with his right hand, shifted his center of balance, and threw the boy over his left hip, sending him sprawling facedown into the sandy loam of the paddock. Raising his head from the dirt, the boy screamed "No!"

Belwyn frowned. He had not anticipated a fractious brat who would take the fall with such little grace. In the next instant he found himself locked in a punishing embrace, his neck pulled back almost to the breaking point, six strong arms holding him motionless. Taking care not to struggle, he assessed the rage of the three men holding him. Before he could begin sending messages of appeasement and submission, his eyes caught the gleam of metal. Again, he heard the treble cry of the boy.

"Don't hurt him! I forbid it! Do you think everyone fights as we do? I must learn all the ways in order to defend the tribe!"

The knife vanished; hands released him slowly, grudgingly. Belwyn stood stock still, feeling the unabated fury contained in the three fast-breathing guards.

A dirt-smudged face scowled up at him, demanding, "Teach me how that is done!"

Wordlessly, Belwyn repeated the maneuver in slow motion, cushioning the boy's descent, admiring the way the young body slapped the ground in order to absorb the force of the fall. Belwyn chided himself for his earlier concern; it was likely that this boy had taken far worse tumbles since he sat astride his first pony.

Without moving his eyes from the now laughing boy, Belwyn gauged the minds around him, noting the ripples of humor quickly replacing the killing rage of a few moments ago.

"Ah," he rejoiced silently, *"I have found one who loves his people and is loved by them."*

The first lesson over, they walked toward the long earthen structure that served as Ariod's great hall. Belwyn looked down at the boy who was to be his life's work.

"Your hair will prevent you from ever becoming a good wrestler. Wrestlers have short hair so there's less chance of a grip."

A grimy hand moved swiftly to the tangled hair in a protective, almost violent, gesture.

"I follow the ways of Sturm. A warrior's hair is never cut. Only slaves have short hair."

Registering Belwyn's short dark curls in that moment, the boy's face relaxed into a smile.

"Slaves and tutors."

"Old man, I'm waiting for your answer! Has the sun fried your brain?"

The voice might have dropped an octave but the teasing lilt was unmistakably Tyre's, a full-grown warrior now and a man to be reckoned with.

Belwyn hastened to relay the message with which he had been entrusted.

"Apologies, young lord. Stheno asks, nay, commands, your presence in the lodge."

Tyre frowned and turned on his booted heel, striding up the crest toward the earthen structure that commanded an unobstructed view of the surrounding plain. The filly, bred, delivered, and trained by the sure strong hands of her rider, followed her master without a lead, nosing him in the back to beg for a treat from his never-empty pockets. Belwyn picked up the forgotten blanket and led his horse up the sandy bank. Pausing to offer a palm of grain to the persistent filly, Tyre waited for Belwyn's approach.

"What's the problem?"

Weighing his words with care, Belwyn replied, "It seems Hourn's mate has given birth to another girl-child."

Tyre's tanned face lost its color. Lifting his eyes, he viewed the sprawled arrangement of low tents surrounding the great lodge. As Belwyn finished, Tyre's jaw set and he jerked into a swifter pace, his long legs forcing the filly into a trot.

Unable and unwilling to keep up with Tyre's rapidly retreating back, Belwyn paused, wiping perspiration from his brow with the back of his hand. Would he ever accustom himself to this land without shade? Narrowing his eyes, he viewed the village as he had seen it that first day, after so many years spent wandering.

Having volunteered to undertake the role of Searcher, he accepted with equanimity, if not enjoyment, the nomadic life the position demanded. Even so, his travels seemed endless, taking him further and further north until he reached this Land of the Lapith. A sun-worshipping people, they seemed to fulfill the requirements of his mission, especially when he discovered that his arrival coincided with an ambitious chieftain's search for a suitable teacher for his son. All signs seemed to reveal the rightness of his choice until the day Belwyn asked Tyre about his family. That particular memory still made Belwyn flinch.

It had been an afternoon of gentle rain dripping on the leather roof of the tent, Belwyn recalled, a rarity in this climate of rapid shifts of temperature, when thunderstorms sent downpours to flood ravines and trap sheep, cattle, and horses in dangerous flash floods. He and Tyre were working on plans for increasing the tribal herds: counting stock, discussing possible breeding lines, figuring weight gains, and examining a crudely drawn map to find alternate market routes to the south.

The boy was interested, but easily distracted, the energetic young body fidgeting restlessly in the close confines of the tent. After waiting several minutes for a response to a question that was easily answerable by his bright pupil, Belwyn cleared the papers from the low table with a sweep of his arm. Settling himself onto a comfortable pillow on the richly carpeted ground, Belwyn remarked, "Since you're unable to concentrate on your studies, I'll be the pupil for a change."

The boy threw him a look of pure astonishment, then brightened as he considered the prospect of reversing roles with his often too-serious teacher. Enthusiasm vanished to be replaced with chagrin.

"What could I hope to teach you? My father says you've seen sights no Lapithian can imagine."

Belwyn settled into training mode.

"Never feel apologetic about your life or your people. Everything that lives is precious. I'll never be able to ride as well as you do, and your people's knowledge of curing, tanning, and working leather is unequaled in my travels. Choose something at the heart of tribal life and I'm sure to learn something."

Belwyn studied the boy as he settled to the assigned task, watching as he propped a pillow under his stomach and leaned his head against his bracelet-covered arm. Probing delicately into a mind Belwyn was only beginning to know, he sensed the boy's eagerness to please, his respect for the knowledge of his teacher, his bewilderment at trying to assess a way of life he rarely, if ever, questioned.

Belwyn went to work, soothing the young mind, mindful that he was forbidden to control the thoughts or emotions of his charge. His instructions were all too clear: *"Though he lifts his hand to strike you, you will not stop the blow."*

All adepts could receive thoughts to greater or lesser degrees. Belwyn's mastery included the sending of images and the subtle transformation of thought patterns. His purpose was to help Tyre achieve his natural potential, not control him to the point that he became someone else. Intent on his task, Belwyn waited as the boy's mind sorted through possible topics. Recognizing the image of the sun, Belwyn gave a gentle nudge to reinforce the boy's choice.

"I've decided. I will tell you about Sturm."

The boy's face radiated confidence. Too late, Belwyn remembered that Stheno, the priest of Sturm, had taught Tyre earlier that day. Belwyn knew little of this religion, except that it revered the sun and held the highest regard for individual bravery and tribal honor.

The treble voice began its instruction.

"Sturm is a demanding and a jealous god. He gives us the winds, the rains, and victory over our enemies. To live for Sturm is honorable; to die for Sturm is divine."

Wincing inwardly at Stheno's fanaticism, Belwyn honored his teacher with a question.

"This Sturm, does he have a mate?"

"A mate?" the boy repeated blankly.

"A mate. A woman. Your father has a mate . . ."

"My mother died."

"Even so, someday you, too, will mate. That is the way of all things. There must be mares as well as stallions if the herds are to grow."

During this exchange, the boy's body tensed, his mind knotted, his emotions jangled.

"Of what use is a mate to Sturm? He is complete in himself. I know that I must . . . must . . ." try as he might, he could not stop stammering, ". . . must do what you say. If I were not my father's only son, if I had brothers, I would never . . . ever . . ."

Unable to finish the sentence, the boy clamped his mouth shut, a faint sheen of perspiration over his upper lip.

Dismayed as he was by this adolescent's sexual anxieties, Belwyn was even more troubled by the seemingly misogynous nature of Tyre's religion. Quickly, he cast about for information concerning the women of Lapith, realizing too late that in the fortnight he'd spent among Ariod's people, he had only seen women from a distance, and had seen very few of them at that. Cursing himself for ignoring such an important factor in the boy's emotional and social development, Belwyn remembered making an assumption that the voluminous robes and head veils were worn because of his presence, to protect the women from his view. As a stranger to the tribe, he could not yet be trusted, but in time he would be allowed to associate with Tyre's female relatives. A knot formed in his stomach as he realized he had never heard Tyre refer to any female, be she mother, grandmother, sister, or aunt.

Having begun this lesson in the hopes of building Tyre's confidence in his new tutor, Belwyn was loath to leave the subject so quickly. In a split-second, he measured the balance between loss and gain. Putting his trust in an intuition that rarely failed him, he decided to continue. It was a decision he regretted to this day. After twelve years of intimate knowledge of his charge, it was the only time that Belwyn's inability to condition Tyre had seemed an impossible demand. It was also the only time he wept.

"You spoke of your lack of brothers. Do you have a sister?"

Blank-faced, the boy shook his head.

"That's unfortunate. I dearly loved a sister only a few years older than me who died of a sickness not even our best healers could cure."

Belwyn kept his delivery conversational, unrushed. He would let the boy respond as he chose. If Tyre changed the subject, Belwyn would not deter him.

"I had a sister once," said Tyre. "She was given to Sturm."

Despite his years of experience in the outside world, a knot formed in Belwyn's gut. Refusing to believe, he searched for further clarification.

"I thought Sturm had no use for a mate."

Even from a twelve-year-old, the contempt stung.

"I told you Sturm has no use for women. They can't take part in the rituals and they live apart from the followers of Sturm. We are a warrior people. Women can't ride, hunt, or fight. They're good for nothing but breeding strong sons for Sturm. A girl-child has no value, so Stheno called for her death. He said my mother should not waste her time tending a worthless girl-child, but should try again to give birth to a son."

Closing his eyes against the immensity of this discovery, Belwyn felt himself suddenly old and defeated. In all the lands through which he'd traveled, a healthy child was so devoutly desired — indeed, when an infant was carried a full nine moons and born without complications, it was an event for fervent rejoicing — that the idea of infanticide because a child was born female horrified him. So distraught was he that, for the bitterest moment of his life, he spoke without thinking.

"Are you telling me your people routinely murder children to serve the whims of a god?"

The boy rose to his feet and walked stiffly to the tent opening. At the threshold of the raining world outside the tent, he paused, firing a retort emblazoned on Belwyn's soul forever.

"You play pupil to my teacher. You tell me I should never be ashamed of my people. Then, when I do as you ask, you see only your ways. I-will-be-the-leader-of-my-people-and-I-follow-the-ways-of-Sturm! Never speak to me again of mating or murder."

Turning abruptly, Tyre strode out into the rain.

Ignoring the pain of the confrontation for the moment, Belwyn concentrated on the enormity of Tyre's revelation. Born and bred in the mild, fertile southern lands, Belwyn assumed that more rugged climes made for hardier, tougher people. He also believed (instinctively, it seemed to him) that despite the differences that divided the patchwork of peoples scattered across this vast, empty world, there was a wholeness to humanity, a shared well of beliefs from which everyone drank. Today it was as if a veil lifted from his eyes. These people of the far north, set apart from a wider world for thirty generations, had succeeded in generating a collection of taboos and prejudices capable of killing their daughters and terrifying their sons. Tyre was a child of this darkness. And worst of all, he had just forbidden Belwyn's entry into those parts of him that were somehow connected to everything that threatened the continuance of life and hope. Belwyn's instructions came back to haunt him:

"Though he lifts his hand to strike you, you will not stop the blow."

And Belwyn wept.

The sound of raised voices startled Belwyn out of the past and into the present moment. Tyre must have heard them as well since he slammed the gate of the horse paddock shut and broke into a run, heading directly for the lodge. Belwyn knew all too well the reason for his haste. Hourn's woman had given birth to a second daughter and Hourn was Tyre's only friend-of-blood. As the childhood friend of Hourn and a fellow member of the warrior clan, Tyre would, of necessity, be a prime participant in the events unfolding within the lodge.

Two years earlier, Belwyn had observed Hourn's mate from a distance at the simple mating ceremony following her capture by Hourn from a rival clan during the Harvest ceremony. Such abductions were part of Lapithian tradition, instituted, Belwyn supposed, to keep the widely scattered tribes from interbreeding. Even so, he knew from a brief comment Tyre made last year that Hourn cared for his mate, a fact Tyre presented to him as a novelty demanding serious disapproval. Hourn's firstborn was a girl-child. Given the youth of Hourn and his mate, Stheno demanded the child's death in the hope that their second child might be male. Hourn begged Tyre, as the chieftain's son, to intercede. Belwyn listened to Tyre's report of what had obviously been a heated conversation, but since it was a forbidden subject between them, he held his tongue. In the face of Belwyn's silence, Tyre squared his shoulders and left the tent. Several days later, a cattle herder informed Belwyn that the infant had been killed. Tyre never revealed to Belwyn what action, if any, he had taken.

Twelve years having passed since their original confrontation, Belwyn knew Tyre had come to value his opinions on every aspect of his life, with the exception of those two unspoken subjects. And in small ways, he had seen Tyre fight the darkness. The fact that he selected the chestnut filly as his mount of choice remained a sore point with many of his fellow clansmen, who by tradition rode stallions and geldings into battle. At the Harvest celebration last year, Tyre's announcement that he, as the designated champion of his tribe, would ride a girl-horse in the cross-country race was greeted with shouts of derision. Mares were rarely, if ever, raced since their value lay in breeding.

The primary event of a seven-day festival in which all the tribes competed in archery and riding events, the cross-country race was a ten-mile course over windswept plains. Not just a race of speed, each rider was required to pick up from the ground a series of small markers carved with his tribe's sign. The perils of leaning down from a horse moving at a run over unfamiliar ground to pluck a marker from the sun-baked earth made injuries not the exception, but the rule.

Belwyn dreaded the race, for even though he trusted Tyre's mastery of everything to do with horses, he feared it would not be Tyre's error, but that of another horse and rider that might bring him to harm. Selecting a spot somewhat removed from the milling crowd on a high ridge, from the resounding blare of the ram's horn signaling the beginning of the race, Belwyn traveled with Tyre. The filly's nimble grace carried her over sand, riverbanks, and grasslands without a misstep, Tyre's lean form hugging her back as their manes mingled in the breeze. Effortlessly, he leaned down to swoop up each marker, gripping her muscled flanks with powerful thighs as she thundered by groups of screaming onlookers. The joyful rhythm of horse and rider soothed his worries, and with a rueful sigh at his misplaced concern, Belwyn let Tyre run free.

Belwyn knew the identity of the front rider long before the restless crowd. He was also the sole witness to Tyre's triumphant look over his shoulder as he neared the final stretch. Arms upraised in Lapithian style, hooves pounding drum-like on the dusty plain, man and mare crossed the finish line to the screams and trilling of Ariod's tribe. For the remainder of the day Tyre tasted the sweetness of victory. That evening, he was cheered and toasted, lifted to the shoulders of friends and strangers and asked to recount the race countless times.

Despite his long tenure with the people of Lapith, Belwyn was still very much an outsider at Harvest gatherings and sensed the distrust his presence created in those not of Ariod's tribe. He also admitted to himself that after more than a decade in this land, he still found the rowdy all-male gatherings bothersome. There were women somewhere, he knew, for he had seen dark-robed shapes standing on the fringes of the race grounds, but they were shadows without substance. He hoped that somewhere in their isolated campsites they, too, were celebrating, although he could not imagine any cause for joy.

The day before the cross-country race, Belwyn witnessed a Lapithian ritual not meant for his eyes. Bored with what promised to be yet another day spent among drunkards, gamblers, and braggarts, he wandered toward the far edge of the enormous plain that had been the site of Harvest gatherings for time out of mind. Belwyn remained a healer at heart, although there had been little need for his skills by this healthy people besides bone-settings and the occasional stitching of a knife wound. (What would the Lapithians think if he told them of the hundreds of children he had brought into the world?) He had been searching for plants unknown to him or his teachers, hoping to find an herb or a root to be added to the lore of which he was a master. Walking with his head down, he was unaware of how far he had strayed until he heard hoof beats on the baked clay earth. Warned by some sixth sense that he would not be a welcome witness to whatever transpired in this isolated spot, Belwyn dropped to his knees, the tall grasses closing like a curtain around him, shielding him from view.

A Lapithian warrior in full battle regalia led a shaggy-maned pony along a dusty path, his destination a tent partially hidden among the prairie grasses, its leather flaps, usually left open to cool the interior during the daylight hours, shut tight, lending it a particularly inhospitable appearance. Stopping some ten feet from the tent, the warrior planted his feet wide apart, crossed his arms over his chest, and broke the silence of that isolated spot.

"My son, your father stands before you."

A tent flap was unlaced, revealing a robed and veiled woman holding the hand of a boy dressed identically to his father, his size announcing him to be no more than five years of age. The boy regarded his father with frank curiosity. At a warning glance from the father, the mother removed the boy's clutching fingers from her hand and pushed the child forward to cover the distance between them. The man knelt in the fine dust, placing his large hands on either side of the small face regarding him with round-eyed wonder.

"Come, my son. It's time to leave your mother and learn to ride."

Grasping the child firmly around the waist, he swung the light body easily into the saddle. Patiently, he adjusted the stirrups to the dangling legs, gentling the pony with a pat on its rump.

"You must give your pony a name."

After placing the small hands on the pommel, he turned the pony around, heading back toward his point of origin. As the figures receded, the boy looked back once toward his mother, who stood motionless long after they passed out of sight.

By the time she slipped into the tent, her head lowered in what Belwyn could only interpret as a posture of hopeless resignation, a vision rose to take her place. Another tent took shape before Belwyn's eyes, complete with an even more imposing warrior swinging a small fair-haired boy onto a beautifully wrought, hand-tooled saddle. An ornately tasseled pony, black with a crooked white stripe running down his nose, pranced nervously in the dust, his ears flat against his head, sensing, perhaps, the boy's terror of the man, the man's guilt concerning the boy . . . and then nothing, the vision fading, leaving only wind and grass and rolling clouds of dust.

Later that afternoon, Belwyn met Tyre at the horse fair, watching as he examined several animals with a discerning eye and firm, gentle hands. As they walked toward yet another booth, Belwyn gave in to curiosity.

"What was the name of your first horse?"

Tyre regarded him quizzically for a moment, one eyebrow arched over a clear blue eye.

"Well, in truth, my first horse was a pony."

Undeterred, Belwyn demanded: "And its name?"

Tyre's answer, when it came, was crisply unemotional.

"He was black with a white blaze. I named him Cinyras."

Tyre was off across the fairgrounds before Belwyn could recall the derivation of the word. Then it came to him. Rendered in the Lapithian tongue, the pony's name meant "a woeful cry."

On the evening following Tyre's victory, Belwyn left the festivities and moved to an outlying fire, eager to ponder the events of the day and meditate in isolation, an activity that was often sorely absent from his busy days with Tyre. The windswept sky was littered with stars and the fire crackled companionably. Belwyn was almost lost in a dream of what-once-was when he noticed a tall, well-formed figure with a mane of flaxen hair leave the sprawling banquet tent and stumble toward the outlying bushes to relieve himself. Chuckling at the prospect of his usually over-disciplined pupil nursing a sore head on the morrow, Belwyn drew himself deeper into his earth-colored sleeping robe.

At that moment, a shadowy shape wearing a facial veil emerged from the line of bushes to Tyre's left, moving toward him hesitantly, almost shyly, it seemed to Belwyn. Tyre was busily retying his breeches when his head rose in apparent alarm. As the shadow approached him, the faint starlight revealed Tyre's facial muscles tightening into a frown. A rounded arm emerged from the veils, a pale hand reaching out to stroke the tightly clenched jaw. Tyre froze at the touch before leaping backward with a feral snarl, his hand reaching behind his back for his skinning knife. A soft, startled cry from the veiled creature accompanied a like move backward. Stumbling on the rough ground, she regained her balance and ran back the way she had come.

Without hesitation, Belwyn jumped into Tyre's thoughts, finding his coolly rational pupil caught in a torrent of conflicting emotions. Shock, arousal, fear, disgust; for every feeling within him there was an equally strong counterpart. Held by his vow, Belwyn could touch nothing in that maelstrom of confusion, but as a healer, he could bring the youth closer to the fire since shock had begun to lower his body temperature. At the simple suggestion of warmth, Tyre staggered toward the nearest campfire.

Closing his eyes and regulating his breathing, Belwyn forced his body rhythms to those of sleep. Upon hearing the slap of leather-covered buttocks hitting the earth, he allowed himself to stir, snort, and wake. Taking in an ashen face, a rapidly rising chest, and glazed eyes, Belwyn ached for his pupil. Even so, pity was inappropriate and, given the wall Tyre had built between them, unthinkable. Cocking open a sleepy eye, Belwyn focused on the knife still grasped in Tyre's right hand.

"Trouble, Tyre?"

Tyre blinked several times, seeming to clear his head, then examined his tutor warily, noting his wrinkled sleeping robe, rumpled hair, and sleep-filled eyes. Beginning to relax, he slipped his knife back into its leather sheath.

"I must remember not to drink so much. I thought a night-hag was after me."

Belwyn grunted and settled back into sleep. Using his inner sight, he felt Tyre's relief that his encounter with the woman had not been observed. Added to this was his body's weariness from the race and the emotional exhaustion triggered by the woman's invitation. Drawing a sleeping robe around his shoulders, Tyre moved closer to the fire and gazed silently into the flames, his face lit by the reflections of his bronze circlet and throat-ring. Soon he was nodding. In the next moment, he slept.

Belwyn studied the victor of this year's Harvest race, shook his head sadly, and sent Tyre pleasant dreams.

Belwyn entered the main lodge minutes after Tyre. As an outsider, he remained close to the timbered doorway while Tyre fought his way through the confusion of men and youths who were on their feet and almost at each other's throats.

Stheno, the Mouth of Sturm, stood in the center of the great earthen room, an imposing figure of age and authority, his waist-length hair pure silver now, his bronze throat-amulet beaten into the shape of an eight-pointed sun. His ritual staff held in his left hand, he raised his right for silence.

Ariod, chieftain of the tribe for nineteen years and the highest-ranking member of the warrior clan, stood slightly behind Stheno and to his right. The tallest person in the room despite his age, Ariod was, in Belwyn's estimation, a hard, but just man. His leather tunic and breeches were ornately embroidered, his amulet of office the silhouette of a running horse. His weather-beaten face, never expressive, was a blank board of judgment.

To the left of Stheno, and the person who had just spoken, was Hourn. Considered small for a Lapithian, although he towered over Belwyn, his hair had a slight reddish cast common to many of his kinsmen. A good match to Tyre, his friend-in-blood, Hourn was quiet, pensive, and rarely spoke. To see his eyes flashing in anger, his hands outstretched to the crowd in a pleading gesture, was to see someone near the breaking point.

As Tyre slipped between Hourn and Stheno, Belwyn noted the measuring glance the father directed toward his son.

As silence finally settled, Stheno began.

"We have listened to the words of Hourn, who contests the death of the girl-child. Hourn is a strong warrior and Sturm has blessed him with strong seed with which to breed many sons. Hourn's woman gives him nothing but girl-children. Hourn must put aside this woman and choose another mate. The choice is clear—none may question the ways of Sturm!"

Belwyn noticed the narrowing of Ariod's eyes at Stheno's rising fervor. Stheno's next words confirmed that he, too, sensed the tribal chieftain's disapproval.

"But I am only Sturm's mouthpiece. The clan must decide the rightness of my words."

Tyre's head rose in alarm as Stheno spoke. The situation was even worse than Belwyn had imagined. It was not enough that the child be killed; the woman, too, must be put away. Ariod opened his mouth to speak, when, incredibly, Hourn interrupted his chieftain with a choked cry.

"Hear me, clansmen! I will not sacrifice a second child nor put aside my woman! If you rule that I must do so . . ." his voice grew hoarse, ". . . I will break the brotherhood of the clan and leave the tribe. I will become nomad."

In this tightly woven association of small clans and larger tribes, to become a nomad meant a life of endless hardship. There would be no communal grazing for flocks and herds, no helpers during lambing and calving, no shearers, no tanners, and, most importantly, no warriors to insure protection from raiding tribes. Beyond the practical matters of survival, it also meant that no child of Hourn's would be welcome into tribal rituals or marriages, and no descendants of Hourn would follow him into the halls of Sturm. To become nomad was to become dead.

In the muttered aftermath of Hourn's declaration, Ariod stepped forward. In the ensuing hush, Belwyn sensed the uneasiness of the assembly. As Tyre had explained to him so long ago, the sacrifice of a first-born daughter was a decision in line with former tradition; to sacrifice a second girl-child was less common. Also, Hourn had raised the stakes for the entire clan. To rule that Hourn set aside his mate meant the loss of a valuable young warrior with close ties to the chieftain's only son. Belwyn sympathized with Hourn's previous attempt to gain Tyre's support, for although he had no real power until his father's death, Tyre carried with him the promise of the next generation of the tribe. His status was based not on what he was now, but what he would eventually become. Yet Tyre stood mute, Belwyn noted with a sinking heart, his eyes hooded, refusing to acknowledge the appeal in Hourn's eyes.

Ariod's voice boomed against the hard-packed walls of earth.

"Choose, my people! You are the clan of the Running Horse, of the tribe of Ariod, of the people of Lapith. Do you rule for the child?"

In one masculine voice came the answer: "Nay!"

"Do you rule for the woman of Hourn?"

This time the response was broken, the disparate bursts of "Nay" less confident. Then, from the center of the room, Belwyn heard two strong voices say "Aye." Their cause was a lost one, for their twin-voiced response was followed by a growl of the negative majority. But in this, the crowning moment of his life, Belwyn stood humbled and relieved. Tyre's answer was entirely his own. His pupil stood firm against tradition and against his god, and for that Belwyn breathed a quiet thanks and slipped out the door of the lodge.

Moments later, Belwyn of Lapith, Beal of Pelion, Searcher of Souls, High Healer and Master of Mysteries, stood on the crest of the rise looking south over the rolling plains, his arms lifted to embrace the morning sky.

"Vena, Vena, even now we come to you!"

Her thoughts came streaming out of the south, her message measured and majestic, issuing the welcome he longed for:

"Bring him to us, Searcher! The Maze stands ready!"

Chapter 2

The Ravine

SITTING CROSS-LEGGED on the ground, Tyre braided multiple strands of supple leather into a new hackamore for Freena. His tent stood in shambles. The low cot he slept on was covered with various items of clothing and footwear examined and summarily discarded. A cedar chest imported from the eastern shore, an incredible luxury in this land without trees, stood with its lid propped open by a short spear, overflowing with weaponry and riding gear—throwing knives, a long-handled axe, sheaves of arrows with differently shaped heads, striped wool blankets, food bags, hobbles, and the fringed, brightly-colored tassels that adorn Lapithian saddles and bridles. A long spear leaned precariously against the tent flap. Next to it lay Tyre's saddle and the oily rag that had recently rendered it into a lustrous heap of well-worn calf-skin.

The autumn nights grew steadily colder. Today the chill pervaded the afternoon. A fleecy vest of lamb's wool supplemented Tyre's regular long tunic and breeches. He worked steadily at the leather, falling into a natural rhythm as he worked, pausing from time to time to pull the braid tight while humming a hunting song under his breath. From the moment Ariod announced that his son would lead the raiding party leaving tomorrow at dawn, Tyre's day became a whirlwind of activity. In the face of this unexpected honor (for Ariod prided himself on his tactical abilities and led every raiding expedition during his tenure as chieftain) Tyre was publicly contained and privately exultant. This unexpected mark of trust from his unemotional and pragmatic father stirred him deeply.

"I'll not fail him. Help me, Sturm. Help me not to shame my father."

Since the day the clan voted against Hourn, the name of Sturm had not crossed Tyre's lips. Wincing, for the wound was still raw, he recalled the misery of that day. In a matter of hours, Hourn folded his tent, packed his belongings, and, refusing all offers of assistance, cut out his sheep and cattle from the herds. Lifting his mate and his blanket-wrapped daughter onto a wooden cart pulled by a team of oxen, he mounted his best stallion and headed east, driving his herds in front of him.

After the clan meeting, inside the empty hall, their farewell was mercifully brief.

"Thanks for your vote, Tyre. I know what it cost you to oppose Stheno and your father." Hourn paused, seeming to compose his thoughts. "In memory of our friendship," he continued quietly, "let these be the last words we speak. Once we leave this hall, all is finished between us. A swift cut hurts least and heals best."

"Let me help you for the first few days," Tyre insisted. "I could keep the herd moving while you scout ahead for water or drive the wagon with the household goods."

"My woman and child ride in the wagon." When Tyre looked away, unable to meet his friend's gaze, Hourn shook his head. "You still don't understand, do you? You stood by me, but you have no understanding of what a woman is, of the joy of holding your child in your arms, even if it is a girl-child. Someday these things will be proven to you."

Clasping Tyre's shoulders in his hands, Hourn released him quickly.

"I wish you and your woman good journey," said Tyre.

Hourn stiffened.

"Her name is Nephele."

With that, Hourn strode out of the lodge and out of Tyre's life.

The sound of a cleared throat brought Tyre's head up from his task. At his quick reply of "Come," Belwyn passed through the tent flap, subsequently knocking over the spear, tripping over the saddle, and landed on the pile of discarded clothing. Tyre smothered a laugh as his disgruntled tutor attempted to restore his dignity. Upon viewing a horse tassel hanging askew over Belwyn's left ear, Tyre collapsed in helpless merriment, hugging his sides as he rolled about on the carpeted ground. Belwyn removed the offending tassel and regarded Tyre with a familiar wry smile.

"Young lord, it gives me pleasure to entertain you so richly. I'm surprised; however, that someone who leads a raiding party at dawn has time to play at setting traps for his tutor."

"You heard?"

Tyre sat up quickly, a broad grin on his face, his pride evident in the gleaming eyes and up-lifted brows.

"Indeed." Belwyn's smile was briefer than usual, a shadow crossing his face. As if something pains him, Tyre thought. "That's the reason I came. I need a favor."

"What favor?"

Belwyn never asked favors of anyone. Come to think of it, Belwyn had been strangely quiet, even aloof, since the day of Hourn's departure. Tyre marked Belwyn's presence in the lodge, but with his attention on Hourn's troubles, didn't check the doorway until after the vote, by which time Belwyn had disappeared. Tyre wondered if his tutor knew he'd voted for Hourn to keep his woman. He shrugged away the thought, irritated at the idea of needing Belwyn's approval. A clear conscience was its own reward. Or so Belwyn had taught him.

"Ariod says you'll raid to the south. He couldn't grant my request since he won't lead the party. So," Belwyn said with quiet deliberation, as though explaining something to a child, "it seems you're the one who must help me."

Growing more exasperated by the moment, Tyre kept a firm grip on his temper.

"If I can do something for you, know that I will. But you must tell me what it is."

"I want to ride with you."

Tyre's eyes widened. A smile followed quickly after. Belwyn had always been protective of him. Tyre remembered his tutor's dismay the first time he discovered his pupil riding underneath Freena's belly, holding onto her girth strap, making himself as small as possible to avoid her flying hooves. Or the scolding he received after breaking his collarbone in a race with Hourn, both boys standing upright on the backs of their horses, trying to maintain their balance with their bare feet. In the aftermath of the accident, Ariod shrugged. Belwyn waited until the bone healed and Tyre could move without pain. Then, and only then, did he administer a severe tongue-lashing, cancel Tyre's riding privileges for a week, and sentence him to hard labor shoveling dung in the animal pens. Tyre smiled at the man who cared enough about him to teach him the difference between bravery and stupidity.

"Don't fret old man. I'll be safe enough. Besides, you know you hate to ride, and I promise you, we'll ride hard."

Belwyn got up stiffly from the floor and moved aimlessly around the tent, glancing unseeingly at the disorder surrounding them. Heaving a sigh, he turned to face Tyre.

"You misunderstand. I'm not asking to be a member of the raiding party. I'm asking to ride with you as far south as you travel. When you turn north again, I'll continue on alone."

During this speech, Tyre became very still. When Belwyn finished, Tyre spoke, his eyes hidden, cast down into his lap where he grasped the forgotten braid in tightly clenched fists.

"Where will you go?"

"I journey back from whence I came."

"And where is that? You never told me or my father."

"A place far to the south. The name is unimportant."

"What will you do when you get there?"

"I . . . I will rest."

"Have your duties exhausted you so much?"

"Not at all. It's just that I grow old."

Tyre vaulted to his feet, eyes ablaze, his deeply tanned face flushed with fury. His voice came out in tight, hoarse bursts of sound, as though he pushed the words out of a hole dug deep inside him.

"Stop playing with me, old man! I'm not a child! Tell me why you want to leave!"

Belwyn regarded him calmly. For the first time, he was the Belwyn of old, his voice warm, his look compassionate.

"You've answered your own question. You're not a child anymore. You'll be four and twenty at the winter solstice. Tomorrow you'll lead your first raid and I have no doubt but that you and Freena will win the race at the next Harvest. You've been a diligent student and you'll be a fine leader of your people. Can't you see it's time for me to go? You no longer have need of a tutor. Your father sees the truth of it. Today he announces to the tribe that you are ready to lead your people. What need have you of an old man, as you name me so often?

"I need you, Belwyn."

The voice shook, but the eyes were unwavering in their desperation. A long silence stretched between them. Belwyn broke it first, his voice soft, his look unfathomable.

"In twelve years I've never asked a favor of you. I ask now. May I ride with you?"

Tyre straightened slowly, consciously willing his pulse to slow, relaxing his muscles, counting his breaths as Belwyn had taught him. How ironic that he should use Belwyn's technique for controlling pain against Belwyn himself! Why had he let this outsider become so important to him? It was obvious Belwyn cared nothing for him. Tyre had confessed his need, yet Belwyn stood dumb. First Hourn; now Belwyn. Soon, Tyre thought bitterly, soon I will truly be alone.

"Aye," whispered Tyre.

Shaken, Beal hurried to the lakeshore, hugging his chest, the region of his anatomy that seemed to ache so often these days, whether from age or a breaking heart, Beal was not quite sure. It went badly, he thought, much worse than he imagined.

His plan seemed reasonable this morning. Beal heard Ariod's announcement with a burst of relief. Having planted that thought in Ariod's mind a year ago, since Hourn's departure Beal worked steadily at the chieftain, almost despairing of gentle persuasion. He'd begun to consider outright control, a tactic that sickened him, until he remembered his own pride as Tyre crossed the finish line at last year's Harvest. Last night, Beal sent Ariod dreams packed with vivid imagery—Tyre riding triumphantly up to the lodge, his sun-colored hair blazing, his spear uplifted as he threw rich booty at his father's feet and knelt to receive his blessing. Ariod woke and announced Tyre's new position as leader of the war party that morning. Now there was little time.

Lowering himself onto the sandy bank, Beal pulled his sheepskin robe tighter about his shoulders and began the steps of internal tranquility necessary for linking thoughts with another adept. Finding Luxor first, Beal felt the nearness of the Legion Commander with surprise—it was too long since he had come into contact with others of his kind.

Luxor's mind was as hale and hearty as his barrel-chested, bear-like body. Beal flinched at the energy and vigor reflected in Luxor's thoughts: the Legion Commander was eager to begin, unable to understand Beal's hesitancy.

"Come now, Beal, we've gone over this often enough! My scouts have been over every hectare. The decoys are good, damned good! Stanis bought them in Agave and I trained them myself. I've promised them they can keep their gear and ride away if they'll hold the party until I get there."

"You, Luxor, and your men, how is your disguise?"

His inner ears heard the laugh that revealed Luxor's huge enjoyment at being able to drop his responsibilities for a few months and go campaigning. That he got to act a role as well was an unexpected reward. Beal was reminded that this was the same Luxor who had accompanied Vena on the first Search for ernani. That he chose, eighteen years later, to participate in this particular mission spoke of his courage and unending spirit of adventure.

"Let's just say I'm nine parts nasty and one part pure demon."

"And the slaves from Agave?"

Beal's mind radiated distress. This had been a point of contention with the Council from the time Luxor first devised the capture. Fearful that Tyre might be injured on the long march from Agave to Pelion, the Fifteenth Mother pushed for using disguised Legionnaires. Luxor remained doubtful, worried that Tyre might detect the fraud. After agonizing over the physical threat to his pupil's life, Beal supported Luxor. Slaves necessary to their mission would be purchased by Stanis in Agave on the caravan's way south.

"Stanis will choose them carefully."

Adept minds could not hide the truth as words did. Luxor was protecting him from envisioning the dangers of Tyre's future.

Having offered what comfort he could, Luxor changed the subject lest Beal brood.

"Well, she's out-maneuvered me again."

Beal sensed the underlying admiration in Luxor's complaint.

"It seems there's a soldier in the Legion who went through Preparation. He's called Phylas, an ernani from Agave. She spoke to him privately, and I don't know what she said, but he left Pelion soon after. The next time I heard anything about him was yesterday, when Stanis told me he bought a slave named Phylas at an open auction and was holding him for our return trip south. Can you imagine it, Beal; to have been a slave in Agave and then returning to it by choice?"

Luxor's story took an unwilling Beal into the past, remembering his last spoken conversation with the Fifteenth Mother twelve years ago. He knew how Phylas had been persuaded and at the thought, his throat clenched and his mind recoiled. Immediately he felt the gruff reassurance of Luxor's thoughts.

"Don't worry, Beal. Your duties are almost over. I'll keep him safe and sound until we reach Agave. Mind you take care of yourself during the ruckus—Lapithians can be dangerous when they're stung."

Alone now, Beal remembered Tyre's face tight with strain, eyes pleading for him not to leave, lips forming the words "I need you." It would have been so simple to ease the hurt, to soften the blow of abandonment. But he had vowed to conduct their separation without inner sight. He'd convinced himself it would be more honest. Now he realized that he sought to avoid his own hurt at touching Tyre's bruised soul.

Stanis' voice came to Beal on the western breeze, its cadences still the rich deep bass that had been silenced by a tongue-cutting in the slave market of Agave. Mute though Stanis might be, his inner voice retained a power and luster few adepts could match. Like Beal, Stanis was a Master of the Voice. He was also a friend of long-standing.

"Don't grieve for your charge, my friend. You've taught him as no one else could. Now it's time to free him from the last few ties preventing him from Preparation."

"Is all well with you, Stanis?"

"All is in readiness for the Golden One to enter Agave."

Strangely touched by Stanis' formality, Beal asked the real question, the one he longed to hear answered one last time.

"Are we sure, Stanis? Sure we offer more than we take?"

Stanis answered with a wordless vision of the world as it might be.

Beal bowed his head, comforted at last.

Man and mare moved as one over the plains, the miles eaten up by the quick trot Freena could sustain for hours. Behind them streamed a wedge of two dozen warriors accompanying Tyre on this, the last raid before winter. The previous evening, a forward scout brought back word of a scavenging party off to the southwest. Tyre grilled him for what little information he could provide. They were of no recognizable clan, but were close enough to Ariod's borders to be considered a threat. The scout counted fourteen riders and three extra mounts. Tyre was satisfied. The odds weren't entirely honorable, but a string of new horses would be a welcome addition to the tribal herds. Lapithian warfare, while wild and noisy, rarely included bloodbaths. Since individual fighting skills were the source of honor, combatants paired off until a victor emerged. Courage from an opponent was highly prized, with the result that combat often ended with the loser receiving no more punishment than the indignity of losing his horse.

Tyre looked back over his shoulder to mark his troop. It was a cool, dry day and the men behind him looked as invigorated as Tyre felt. It's a good day to go into battle, he thought; a good day to bring honor to the tribe.

Far behind him, a lone rider rode slightly off the track, trying to escape the dust kicked up by so many horses traveling across dry ground. Belwyn kept up better than Tyre would have thought. Riding a slight brown gelding that more closely matched his small size, Belwyn made trouble for no one, sleeping away from the others and avoiding Tyre at every opportunity. Last night, Tyre awoke from a restless sleep convinced that something, or someone, was watching him. He opened his eyes cautiously to find Belwyn's unblinking gaze fixed upon him, a deep frown marring his usually placid expression. Still angry at Belwyn's abandonment, Tyre turned over without acknowledging his gaze and went back to sleep.

Tyre turned his thoughts forward to the coming battle, although a nagging voice reminded him that if they fought today they would turn north tonight, a lone rider continuing south.

As Freena mounted a short rise above a ravine, Tyre glimpsed a dust cloud off to the west and immediately reined her in, his arm upraised as a signal to slow and quiet. Freena tugged at the bit, for she wanted to run and showed her impatience by prancing and blowing. As his companions gathered around him, Tyre marked the lay of the land, thanking Sturm that the omens were good. The other party had not seen them. Turning to his second-in-command, an experienced friend of his father who volunteered to ride with the chieftain's son, Tyre's orders were firm and assured.

"Llyr, take half the men and swing around to the east. They'll see you and give chase. When they reach the ravine," Tyre pointed directly in front of him, "we'll spring the trap."

Llyr grunted his approval. It was a classic tactic, having worked hundreds of times in Ariod's raids. Reining his horse around, Llyr pointed out a dozen warriors and motioned for them to follow him.

"Good hunting, young lord," grunted Llyr. With that, he kicked his stallion into a trot and led his party off toward the east.

Tyre reached down to his long spear, releasing the rawhide ties attaching it to the saddle. At his signal, the other warriors readied their weapon of choice, either spear or bow and arrow, checked their knives, and readied themselves for battle. Out of the corner of his eye, Tyre glimpsed Belwyn moving his mount up to take his place on Tyre's right. Frowning, Tyre turned toward him.

"Stay here until the fighting ends. We don't need you disgracing us, even though our prey is small. We'll return for you when we are victorious."

A cruel chuckle traveled through the assembly. Belwyn bent his head in wordless obedience.

Waiting was always difficult when the blood surged before a battle, thought Tyre, trying to calm Freena, who did a delicate dance of frenzy in anticipation of the gallop she knew would follow. Suddenly, Tyre heard the cries and trilling of his people. The rival band was giving chase. Shouting his clan's war cry, Tyre gave Freena her head, sensing, rather than seeing, the surge of his warriors moving down the slope behind him and into the ravine. Hearing Tyre's signal, Llyr was turning his party, closing in on the enemy's left flank.

As they scrambled down into the ravine, Tyre was surprised to find the strange tribe bunched into a group. They had not spread out to make individual encounters as was traditional in Lapithian warfare, but clustered in a circle, spears and bows upraised for protection. As Freena brought him close enough to distinguish mounts and riders, he realized they did not wear any throat rings or tribal tokens.

His practiced eye drawn to one rider on a tremendous white stallion, he chose his man. A fire in the rider's eyes answered his own. Tyre aimed his spear, knowing he had a single throw with which to dismount his opponent. As he let fly the spear, he cursed, for the stallion shifted off to the left, a maneuver that made his spear go wide. As the white's rider lifted his own spear, Tyre made ready to kick Freena forward and lean off the saddle to the right, a move he'd practiced a thousand times before, although he'd never used it in battle. To his amazement, the rider didn't throw, but rode directly toward Freena, his stallion rearing forward, his great hooves aimed at her breast. Trumpeting her fear, Freena turned too late, screaming as the rider buried his spear in her throat. The spear hanging from her neck at a crazy angle, she rose in a death leap, her blood streaming down her withers, and fell over backward.

Tyre jumped off without thinking, kicking his legs free of the stirrups, untangling himself from the reins and removing his knife from its sheath in one economical motion. Landing on his feet, crouched for action, he found himself face to face with the rider's knife. He waited a split second for the man to withdraw and begin the careful ritual of hand-to-hand combat, but the eyes that gripped his offered no quarter. Flat and hard, these eyes signaled that his opponent would play by no rules. In that split second, and for the first time in his life, Tyre knew fear. Leaping backward, he felt a rush of air as a knife slash missed his throat, and tripped over Freena's carcass.

As Tyre fell, knowing his attacker would be on him in the next moment, he heard a wordless cry. Opening his eyes, he beheld Belwyn at his side, holding a short spear in a steady grip, ready to drive it through the body of the warrior who, even now, had his knife poised for the deathblow. The warrior heard Belwyn's cry even as Tyre did, and swiveled to face his attacker. For a fraction of an instant he hesitated leaving a sure kill, a miscalculation that proved his undoing, for with a face unmarked by rage or hate, Belwyn pounded the spear through his chest even as the momentum of the man already in motion allowed him to plunge his knife blade up to the hilt in Belwyn's abdomen. Screaming out his life, his hands pulling at the wooden shaft imbedded in his body, the warrior crumpled to the ground.

With a gasped intake of breath, Belwyn sank to his knees, his shoulders rounded in an agonized shudder. Tyre was instantly beside him, lowering him on his side to rest his head against Freena's dusty flank. Uncaring of the battle raging around him, oblivious to the shouts and screams of dying men and terrified horses, Tyre knelt beside the fallen one. Struggling for composure, he smiled down at his tutor with lips that trembled.

"I told you to stay on the rise."

Belwyn's eyes cleared. His wry tone was as of old, although his lips were clenched.

"You . . . had . . . need . . . of . . . me."

"And as always, you taught me whether I wanted to be taught or not. No, don't move," Tyre added as Belwyn attempted to turn onto his back.

"He's . . . dead?"

The pain in Belwyn's expression had nothing to do with his wound.

"Aye."

The lines of pain relaxed and Tyre caught the shadow of Belwyn's smile.

"But . . . you . . . live."

Bitterness flooded Tyre. He managed to nod his head, willing himself not to cry.

"Draw . . . the . . . knife . . . and . . . set . . . me . . . free." When Tyre hesitated, Belwyn's wan face lit with a teasing smile. "My . . . last . . . favor."

Tyre leaned into the body that death's approach made as frail and unsubstantial as that of a child. Holding one hand over Belwyn's eyes, Tyre freed the knife with a single pull. Belwyn gasped once, then, with Tyre's help, turned over onto his back, his eyes staring up at a cold sun. His gaze was dim now; he focused on Tyre with difficulty. His last words were barely a whisper.

"You . . . are . . . my . . . gift . . . to . . . her."

The discipline that had driven Tyre threatened to depart. Busying himself with the bloodied clothes, mindlessly intent on smoothing out the crumpled garments, Tyre held onto the necessity of order in all things. Shutting his eyes to begin the tribal chant for the dead, his throat closed at the realization that as much as he loved the man who lay so peacefully before him, he knew neither Belwyn's gods nor how his people went to their deaths. Troubled at the thought that this stranger to his tribe might be an outsider even in death, he unclasped the bronze and gold amulet that had not left his throat since the day of his initiation, and fastened it around Belwyn's neck.

"Go to your gods, Belwyn."

Rising to his feet, he surveyed the ravine. It looked like no battlefield Tyre had ever seen. Dead men and horses were strewn everywhere. Some of his men limped from body to body, checking for friends and using their knives to finish the enemies who had turned a simple skirmish into a senseless slaughter. From the few men left standing, it was clear that his clan had emerged victorious, although the sole reason for this outcome was their greater numbers. If the sides had been equal, no one would have returned to the tribe. Of the twenty-five men who rode out, ten survived.

Tyre leaned down to retrieve his knife. Before he could locate it, Llyr appeared at his side.

"Do we bury the bodies or fire them?"

Inwardly, Tyre blessed the older man for his presence today. Restored to leadership, he considered Llyr's question and decided their course.

"We'll fire the bodies of our clansmen and their horses." Tyre's voice hardened. "Leave the others for the dishonorable carrion they were in life."

As Llyr glanced down at Belwyn's bloodied remains, a look of grudging admiration appeared on the face of his father's friend.

"It seems your tutor learned the way of Sturm."

The cost of Belwyn's sacrifice was such that Tyre could offer no reply. Instead, he began sifting through the bodies surrounding Freena's carcass. Llyr's shout made him lift his head.

Following the direction of Llyr's outstretched hand, Tyre saw a cloud of dust pushing down from the west side of the ravine. A troop of men rode their mounts down the eroded incline at full speed, their sweating horses tripping and sliding down the gravel, seemingly heedless of the danger of such an approach. In the next moment it became clear that these riders were not men of Lapith. Swarthy of complexion, heavily armed with short swords and battle-axes, they wore body armor any self-respecting Lapithian would have scorned. His stomach clenched in a knot, Tyre looked around wildly for a weapon. Finding nothing but the broken shaft of a spear, he grabbed it, by which time he was surrounded by a group of hard-faced men.

"Drop the stick, stripling. You haven't a chance."

The man who addressed him rode to the front, the other riders reining their mounts aside at his approach. Tyre looked over his shoulder to find that his men shared his situation. Between them they had a few knives against a troop of forty fully armed men.

Tyre pulled back his hair from his shoulders and settled it onto his back. He was the leader of the raiding party. Whatever the consequences, he must protect his people. Straightening his shoulders, still grasping the wooden shaft, he spoke with the cold authority he had learned from his father.

"I am Tyre, of the clan of the Running Horse, of the tribe of Ariod, of the people of Lapith. What do you want?"

A glimmer of interest showed on the leader's face. The man was burly, thick through the chest with bulging forearms that looked as though they could break bones. His unshaven cheeks were covered with a fuzz of graying brown; one eye sported a black patch hung from a leather thong over his forehead. He regarded Tyre with vast amusement, sending a look of one-eyed delight over his shoulder to his chortling men.

"Why, Tyre-of-Lapith, I don't want anything," he drawled, all traces of humor vanishing as he added, ". . . except you." Tyre frowned, confused until he realized, with sudden despair, that these men were not raiders, but slavers. Grasping the shaft in both hands, he was immediately on the defensive. It was the leader's turn to frown as Tyre spoke through clenched teeth.

"I will die rather than become a slave."

"Then, young cub, I suspect you'll be very unhappy by the end of this day, because you won't be dead, and you will be a slave."

With that, the leader motioned sharply and several men dismounted, their swords sliding out of scabbards as they moved toward Tyre. The leader dismounted, and scorning a sword, started toward the lean figure moving deftly backward, the shaft still a sturdy threat given the desperate glow in Tyre's eyes.

As Tyre retreated, the one-eyed leader looked down at his feet and froze. Crouching down, he examined something on the ground, reaching out to touch a small man with short brown curls shot with grey. Fearful that the slaver was about to loot Belwyn's body, Tyre lost the control he had been fighting to maintain since watching Belwyn die. With a cry of rage and heart-felt sorrow, he swung the shaft up, intending to kill the slaver who dared to defile Belwyn's corpse. At the height of his swing, he felt a smashing blow on the back of his head and fell forward into darkness.

Tyre awoke in the night, trussed with his hands behind his back, his bound ankles attached to the ropes around his wrists. He recognized Llyr's sleeping form beside him and could make out the bodies of the rest of his clan around him. All were similarly bound. Desperate to relieve the cramp in his legs and the ache in his head, he was adjusting his position when a dispassionate voice startled him.

"I wouldn't move if I were you. Lycus gave orders for us to kill anyone who does. Since he isn't called 'The Wolf' for nothing, I, for one, would obey."

Sinking back into his original position, Tyre wondered briefly why he didn't struggle against his bonds and receive a quick death far more honorable than slavery. The sight and feel of his clansmen's bodies around him answered his question. He was still their leader and they were his responsibility. He would stay with them until they were freed, separated, or dead. Only then would he allow himself the welcome release of nothingness. His head throbbing, he began the ritual against pain Belwyn taught him when he broke his collarbone. Deepening his breathing, he concentrated on relaxing his muscles, beginning with his toes. Before he reached his chest, he was asleep.

"What happened?"

"He woke up and saw his men around him. He tried to move. I threatened him, told him you weren't called The Wolf for nothing, and he obeyed my orders."

"He sleeps?"

"Aye. He put himself into a trance the way Beal taught him."

There was a long silence.

"Anything else?"

"He considered goading me into killing him, but decided his duty to his men demanded that he stay alive."

"Who's with him now?"

"Cronon."

"Maenon, did you check the wound? How is it?"

"You've asked me three times already. The flesh isn't broken, but he'll have a bad headache for the next few days. He should be warm enough tonight with all those bodies piled around him. I recommend at least one day of rest before we begin, and a few easy days before you push them. I'll put something for his head in his gruel tomorrow morning."

"I'm sorry I hit him, Luxor, but I couldn't let him kill you. He moved too fast for me to grab him. I tried not to damage him."

"Relax, Rhacius. You followed orders and did your best. That's all that counts."

The fire popped, causing all three men to jump. Uneasily, they settled down again to regard the flames. Luxor broke the silence with an uncharacteristic tone of reflection.

"We got there too late. It's my fault, promising those slaves their freedom if they'd lure them into a fight and hold them 'til we arrived. I would have given them their freedom in any case. All those deaths, when there needn't have been any."

The listeners were silent. Luxor continued speaking, his gruff voice soft with wonder.

"When I touched Beal's tunic I saw it all. The big fellow on the white stallion went after Tyre with a vengeance. He almost had him, but Beal killed him with a spear. Imagine that," his shaggy head shook slowly from side to side, "gentle Beal, the greatest healer of his generation, who, to my knowledge, never touched a weapon in his life, drove a spear through the chest of a man twice his size."

Luxor shook his head again, lost in wonder. When he looked back at his companions, the Commander of the Legion was himself again.

"Turn in, both of you. We'll have a rough day tomorrow. Even if we don't move them, we'll have to attend to the shackling, and that's a rotten business. Tell Cronon to call me if he wakes. And spread the word to go easy on him."

As the pair moved away, Luxor heard Rhacius mutter his orders to the guards on watch.

Alone with the fire, Luxor stretched, sighed, and readied himself to contact the others. Sitting silently, he moved toward tranquility, his thoughts streaming out into the cool night air.

"Beal has offered his last gift."

Chapter 3

Redux

A KICK IN his backside and a curse in his ear woke Tyre from a troubled sleep. Disoriented, he couldn't understand why Belwyn was kicking him; opening his eyes, he remembered everything. Wincing at the bright morning light, he closed them again. The ache in his head pounded at the slightest movement; the simple act of lifting his head was painful beyond measure. As he tried to struggle upright, his whole body revolted. Cramped by the bonds and enforced motionless for so many hours, his arms and legs were dead weights. His clansmen were in a like situation; some of them gave way to the groans Tyre bit back.

"I said move your miserable arse and I meant it! Lycus wants you up on your feet before breakfast. It's going to be a busy day, but you've had a good night's rest, haven't you?"

Tyre recognized the voice of the guard who had threatened him last night and gave him a cold glare as he pushed himself up onto his knees and tried to stand.

"What's the matter, long-hair? Don't you appreciate the love pat I gave you yesterday?" The guard's voice lowered to a menacing whisper. "You're lucky I didn't break your skull for trying to kill Lycus. I don't hold with slaves who don't act like slaves. Try it again and I'll give you more than a bump on the head."

With that, the guard grabbed his bound arms and jerked him upright. It took all Tyre's strength not to moan or lean against the guard's sturdy form for a moment as the blood rushed into his legs. All around him, guards were pulling their prisoners upright. As he waited for the others to be rounded up, he saw flames out of the corner of his eye. Sometime yesterday evening he had been dragged or carried up the slopes of the ravine to the small rise where he had ordered Belwyn to wait. Below, a huge fire was being kindled; men pulling the bodies of horses and men, weapons, and saddles into a huge pile. Tyre noted woodenly that several of the slavers were stripping the dead of their bronze ornaments. His own circlet and bracelets were gone, as well as his knife sheath and belt. A familiar voice behind him brought him up short. It was the one-eyed man.

"Since you were going to burn the dead, I decided to honor your wish. Maybe you've noticed your trinkets are missing. A few of them will make it into the fire, a worthwhile investment to keep your people from trailing us out of this god-forsaken country. They'll think you died in battle, and they won't be too far wrong, will they?"

Any hope for rescue was slight, especially when he considered the slaver's numbers. His father would send scouts if they weren't back in three days. He looked down at the roaring blaze. By the time they arrived there would be nothing left but charred bones and a few bits of metal. His father would be son-less. For a moment this new pain made the one in his head recede.

He turned to regard his tormentor. The rugged face of the one-eyed leader was set with a sneering smile, waiting for a reaction. At that moment, Tyre decided his course. They might hold him prisoner, but he would never give in to despair or self-pity. He was trained to lead, and he would continue to do so, enduring hardship stoically, expressionless in the face of cruelty. Locking away the things that mattered, he would become his father's son: unmoved and unmovable, relentlessly controlled, indifferent to insult. Staring through the leader as if he was not there, Tyre experienced a moment of grim satisfaction as the other man was finally forced to look away.

"Rhacius, you know the drill. Untie them two at a time, let them piss, and get them fed."

Tyre and a warrior named Nerod were the first two untied. The relief of constriction on hands and feet dead from lack of circulation set Tyre's teeth on edge. Barely giving them time to react, the guards shoved them forward to a line of bushes.

"Untie and get on with it. This will be your only chance until midday, unless you want to piss your breeches."

The guards watched them expectantly. Tyre understood this was one more humiliation to be endured. The eyes of one of the guards were alight with anticipation as Tyre and Nerod slowly untied their breeches. In eighteen years, since his father led him away from his mother's tent on the pony, no one had looked on Tyre's nakedness. No one, he corrected himself, except Belwyn on the day of his initiation. Somehow that thought freed him and he urinated into the bushes and re-tied his breeches. He gathered from the guard's harsh laugh that Nerod had not been so lucky. Refusing to witness his companion's humiliation, he stood quietly until they were shoved in another direction.

They were moved to a campfire where a large cauldron held an unappetizing white paste of something resembling porridge. As it bubbled, Tyre recalled he had eaten nothing yesterday in preparation for the battle.

All at once, he was ravenous. A small man ladled out the paste, handing a bowl and spoon to each guard. The guard in front of him stopped the line to complain about the miserly amount in his bowl. Tyre was almost drooling by the time he was handed a bowl. Hiding his impatience, he looked around for a spoon. Annoyed by his slowness, the guard in line behind him growled a curse and shoved him forward. Not expecting the move or understanding the reason for it, Tyre lost his balance and fell on his face, the wooden bowl bouncing on the hard ground, spewing porridge in a wide radius. Jeers and catcalls greeted this display.

"Why, you stupid, clumsy, snot-nosed slave! I ought to make you lick up every drop!"

A fist closed on the back of his head, lifting him by his hair. Tyre bit back a scream at the agony of being lifted by hair that was directly attached to his bruised and swollen skull.

Plunked down on the ground, he gasped for breath, his eyes filled with tears of pain that threatened to disgrace him. When he could open his eyes again, he found a stranger kneeling in front of him. Tyre recognized the cook. Surprised by the concern written clearly in the cook's face, Tyre looked down to find a full bowl of porridge shoved into his lap.

"Eat it all; there won't be anymore until tonight. Use your fingers; and wipe your face before you eat."

Lifting the hem of his tunic to his face, Tyre discovered he'd bloodied his nose in the fall. Lifting a heavy mass of cooked grain into his mouth with three fingers, he almost spat it out, so permeated was it by the taste of bitter herbs. Hunger won out over taste and he cleaned the bowl. A boy in filthy garments lugging a huge bucket filled his bowl with water. Tyre drank deeply, felt the ache in his head lessen, and decided it must have been hunger that made him so weak. The moment he finished, his hands were bound behind his back.

Forcing himself to focus on the activity around him rather than the throbbing of his skull, Tyre noticed that at least fifteen feet separated him from his nearest companion. All of his men were similarly isolated, bound, and accompanied by a guard armed with a thick cudgel and short sword. Although his training as a warrior didn't include the study of capture and restraint (since Lapithians never took prisoners), he recognized the professional efficiency of these men. There's no chance of planning an escape, he thought, until I can get closer to my men.

The man called Rhacius jerked him up, pushing him toward a make-shift forge set up near a supply wagon. A blacksmith was working a bellows. Naked to the waist, his immense body covered with sweat running in dirty rivulets down his sooty, hair-matted chest, he wiped his hands on his leather apron as the band of prisoners approached.

"Who's first?"

Rhacius pushed Tyre to the front of the line.

"This one brags about being the leader. Start with him. The rest of you, move off your prisoners and wait. There's to be no talking amongst the slaves. One word and we'll cut tongues and cauterize stumps. You there, help hold him."

The attack came immediately. Knocked to his knees, Tyre was held tightly by four men, his upper body stretched up toward the forge. His arms were forced out in front, the right one lifted up onto the anvil, and held in a punishing grip. There was a rattle of chains as his wrist was encircled in a wide band formed by two pieces of metal held by hinges, the open ends fashioned with a large hole. As the hinge closed over his wrist, the blacksmith examined the alignment of the two holes, made a minor adjustment, and turning back to the forge, used his calipers to select a glowing piece of iron from the coals. Turning back to the anvil, his advice increased Tyre's sense of despair.

"If you move, I'll miss my aim and you'll lose your hand. One-handed slaves don't have much value."

Frozen by the blacksmith's advice and the weight of the four guards holding him, Tyre watched as the glowing iron was positioned over the hole. With a mighty swing, the blacksmith slammed the hammer onto the shackle. His entire body vibrating from the strength of the blow, the guards dipped his arm in a barrel of water. A three-foot length of chain was attached through the ring and his left arm was lifted to the anvil.

As they turned him over on his back and began the process on his ankles, he began to realize the magnitude of this ordeal—it was not just the fact that he was chained at ankle and wrist, but that there was no key. The shackles were forged solid, as was the chain attaching them. Even if he escaped, he'd be hampered by chains and easily recaptured. As they lifted him to his feet, he was tiredly grateful it was over. Then the imprisoning hands lifted his arms above his head and he felt the inflexible weight of iron circling his waist. This shackle was closed as well, a long length of chain inserted through a loop mounted on the right side of the band. Almost senseless now, Tyre barely felt the hands release him. A rough pull on the chain at his waist drew him away from the forge. He moved awkwardly, the unaccustomed weight and length of the chains hindering his naturally long-striding gait. The throbbing in his head returned, its pounding, combined with the heat of the forge, rendering him almost blind.

Behind him he heard a cut-off cry of dread and the answering ring of the hammer. Shoved down onto the ground, Rhacius' sneer completed Tyre's sense of doom.

"Wait here. The others will join you soon enough."

Shutting his eyes against the light and his ears against the cries that continued to rise from the forge, Tyre escaped into the welcome mist of memory.

The boy crouched on the shore of the broad, shallow lake, the only source of water for as far as the eye could see. He was throwing stones, skipping them three or four times across the motionless surface before they sank. Growing bored with the repetition, he hunkered down to examine some insects swarming near the bank. He was lonely as well as bored. His and Hourn's latest prank of putting a nettle under Hourn's father's saddle was received with a shouted curse and a stiff beating for Hourn, whose father was a strict disciplinarian. Ariod, too, was informed as to his son's mischievous adventures, but the expected punishment never arrived. Sometimes Tyre wished his father beat him; at least it would prove he was aware of Tyre's existence.

"That sigh was heartfelt. Would you care to enlighten me as to its meaning?"

Belwyn lowered himself onto the graveled shore, regarding his startled pupil with a twinkle in his eye. He loved sneaking up on Tyre and did it regularly. Tyre, on the other hand, hated it, since it meant he had not been as attentive as his warrior training demanded.

"Why do you do that?"

"Do what?" Belwyn replied with wide-eyed innocence.

"Sneak up on me."

"Perhaps to teach you that help always comes when you least expect it," Belwyn answered smoothly.

When the boy laughed, an easy silence fell between them.

"What was the sigh for, Tyre?"

The boy looked away with a frown. He might have doubts as to his father's affection but it would be unmanly to confess them to anyone else. Besides, he'd learned early on that a chieftain's son needed to be careful of people. They thought if they paid attention to you, you would do something for them in return. In the year since Belwyn's arrival, he'd never asked for anything. Even so, Tyre didn't want to be in his debt. He decided to lie.

"I was just wishing I could have gone on the raiding party my father took out this morning. It's not fair that I have to wait. I ride better than Rhymer and he's been a warrior for two years."

Tyre knew he was sulking, but one thing about Belwyn, you could tell him how you really felt.

"I know you ride well. So does your father. But a raiding party consists of more than riding horses; it means danger and fighting and the possibility of being injured. Are you prepared to kill a man with a knife?"

The question was a fair one. Tyre considered it for a moment.

"My teacher says I'm fast and flexible. If I had the advantage of surprise, I think I could do it."

"That's not what I meant. Let me put it another way. Are you prepared to thrust your knife into another person's living flesh? To know that you take from him every joy life offers us—family, friends, a cool drink on a warm day, a fast ride on a good horse?"

"I don't know." Tyre's voice was unsteady, and it embarrassed him. Then it made him mad. "My father kills people. He kills them because they try to steal our herds and without them we would starve."

Belwyn got that funny look in his eyes.

"You're right, of course. There are times when killing may be the only course available. But the taking of a life should never be easy or a source of pride."

Something in his tutor's response gave Tyre the courage to ask something he'd thought about for a whole year.

"Have you ever killed anyone?" As soon as it was said, Tyre wished he could unsay it. The look of pained remembrance twisting Belwyn's face made Tyre feel so guilty he blurted out an immediate apology. "You don't have to answer that. It's none of my business and you must pardon my rudeness."

"I want you to feel that you can ask me anything. That's what a teacher is, someone against whom you can test your thoughts and opinions. Truly, I cannot teach you anything; you must learn it for yourself." Belwyn paused, reaching down to wet his hand and then his mouth. "But to answer your question, yes, I have taken people's lives, although it was not in battle."

Tyre was wide-eyed and all attention.

"How did you kill them?"

"You know I'm a healer. Sometimes, when a wound is too deep, or a disease too painful and the outcome certain, I've taken a life. Even though I made sure the death was an easy one, it was always the most difficult part of being a healer."

The next question was slow and guarded.

"Are you afraid of death, Belwyn?"

The answer was slow in coming, marked by painful honesty.

"A little bit, I think, although there are far worse things to fear."

Tyre was incredulous.

"What's worse than dying?"

"Cruelty, pain, loneliness, the loss of a loved one; once these things occur, only courage and endurance can defeat their power to destroy us from within. Death should not be feared because it holds the possibility of escape within it. Sometimes it takes much more courage to live than to die."

The soft lap of the water against the bank was strangely soothing. Belwyn spoke no more, but looked out over the water. Tyre regretted his lie. If Belwyn could talk about things that gave him pain, Tyre should be honest enough to tell him the truth about what he felt.

"I lied before . . . about why I sighed."

Belwyn's gift to him was a warm smile of affection. Tyre lowered his head, suddenly shy. An arm came around his shoulders. For once, Tyre didn't mind the thought of being touched.

"I know, Tyre. I know."

Tyre woke slowly and shifted his position, trying to ease his head into the pillow of his arms. Unable to find a comfortable position, he sat up, keeping his eyes closed against the light. He felt a little better. Experimentally, he lifted his eyelids to find Rhacius staring at him. Ignoring his scrutiny, Tyre turned away, feeling an unaccustomed tension as he moved. Alert now, he noted that four of his clansmen were chained on either side of him, the chain at his waist running through their waist shackles. In various states of shock, most of them were staring sightlessly at their hands and feet. A voice to his left spoke softly, as if through lips that did not move.

"You've slept a long while, young lord."

Tyre turned his head carefully, both to avoid Rhacius' notice and to keep the pain to a minimum. Llyr's expression was grim.

"I thought there were ten of us. What happened?"

"Karn, nephew to Stheno, was burned at the forge. They took him away, they say, to heal him."

Llyr's disbelieving tone made it clear that Karn was dead.

"My head has kept me from listening and learning. Do you know what they plan to do with us?"

Llyr hesitated, looking into the eyes of the only son of his friend-in-blood, a son he wished many times was his own. Outwardly calm, inwardly Llyr was seething—furious that he had not died in battle, furious at being enslaved. All this could have been borne if this boy had not been captured as well. Tyre bore the golden hair of Sturm's favorites and Llyr was livid that he'd been handled so roughly. If this was an example of how Tyre was to be treated, how would he survive in the place whose name alone chilled Llyr's soul? Giving himself an inward shake, Llyr stripped his words of all emotion.

"They are taking us west. To Agave."

Nine figures stood silhouetted on the plain, each one connected to a drooping line of chain curving upward to link to the next one's waist. They shuffled forward toward the setting sun, their heads bent in concentration. Occasionally, one would reach down a hand to the earth then reach up to deposit what he found in the cloth bags hanging from their shoulders. The figure in the center of the line swayed from time to time, his shoulders slumped, stumbling sometimes as he righted himself after bending down.

They had been clearing the site of the slaver's camp for almost four hours, their orders viciously specific.

"Lycus wants the entire area cleared of anything that isn't dust, grass, or gravel. He doesn't want your long-haired friends to track us. He'll be by later to inspect. If he finds anything you missed or anything you dropped, we'll beat the blonde one to death in front of you."

Llyr knew the boy to his right was close to exhaustion. Sheer willpower had kept him on his feet for the past hour, his eyes slitted against the orange ball of fire sinking directly in front of them. Noticing the approach of the one called Lycus, Llyr guessed they would soon be marched to another campsite farther off, a necessary precaution against the possibility of scouts sent to discover the reason for their delay. He cursed himself again for being so vocal in his approval of Ariod's decision to let Tyre lead the raid. During the past few hours he'd made a decision. Now all he needed was opportunity.

Without warning, Tyre collapsed. Face down in the grass, he lay unmoving. In motion almost before Tyre's body touched the earth, Llyr was upon him, holding a stone he had been grasping so tightly that his hand was numb. This deed would erase the blood-debt he owed his chieftain and the son of his friend-in-blood. He would send Tyre to Sturm, where he would live forever in the hall of warriors. Laughing into the ball of fire that was Sturm's home, Llyr raised the hand that would free Tyre from a life without honor.

A knife twisted in his mind. A voice inside his head screamed *"No!"*

Reeling, his eyes clenched shut against the pain reverberating in his mind, Llyr felt himself being thrown violently to the ground by hard hands that wrenched the stone from his grasp. One hand grabbed the front of his tunic; another backhanded him with a blow that nearly broke his jaw. As the world exploded around him, he heard the voice of the one called The Wolf.

"Pull out the chain. Rhacius, take him to Maenon's wagon. Use my horse."

Llyr opened his eyes. The Wolf loomed over him, a single bloodshot eye bulging from its socket, neck cords straining in an effort to control an all-consuming urge to kill.

"I give you my oath, old man: you're going to regret this. Regret it with every breath you take."

For the next few minutes, Llyr heard nothing save the beating of his heart. The heaving chest above him gradually slowed. This time The Wolf spoke quietly, but with savage intensity.

"Cronon, saddle two horses. Gag him, tie his hands to the pommel and bind his legs to the stirrups. Tell Rhacius he's in charge."

The guard he addressed opened his mouth. Upon receiving a single malevolent stare, he shut it with a snap.

As the reins of the horse he was strapped to were jerked forward by the one-eyed slaver, Llyr was certain no part of his punishment would be as cruel as the fact that he would never see Tyre, the son he should have had, again.

Tyre floated on a mist of pain. Hands moved over him. For once he was incapable of minding and his thoughts drifted.

The fall had been long, the landing hard. He remembered seeing Hourn pulling ahead of him, his slender form balanced on the back of his grey colt. The horses were moving at a slow canter, rolling and rhythmic over the smooth piece of ground he and Hourn had chosen with care. Having never lost a race to Hourn, Tyre didn't plan to do it now, even though Hourn's wide-backed grey was more suited to the task than his own rangy roan.

Tyre clicked his tongue to ask for more speed and the roan picked up the pace. Tyre crowed with delight as he began to take the lead, when, with no warning, the roan stumbled. Tyre flew through empty air in a dizzying whirl of colors, dust, and a half-heard cry of alarm. Landing on his left shoulder, he felt something give inside him; his head hit the ground, and he knew no more.

As he drifted on waves of pain emanating from his shoulder and head, a voice nagged at him, never stopping its gentle pleading, repeating a series of words that had no meaning except as sounds. He tried to ignore them, rejecting the effort it would take to understand them, but the voice was insistent, demanding that he turn toward it. Gradually, the words became distinct.

"Come back to me; come back out of the mist. You must wake now, boy, wake and open your eyes. You must not sleep now, boy. Come back to me, Tyre. You can sleep later when it's safe."

Hazily, Tyre tried to identify the speaker. It was someone he could trust, he decided, someone who wouldn't mislead him. Of course, he thought, it's Belwyn! Belwyn wanted him to do something, wanted it badly. Yes, he would do what Belwyn wanted, he asked for so little.

Tyre opened his eyes on Belwyn's anxious face. Dimly, he saw his father peering over Belwyn's shoulder. Groggily, he tried to understand where he was, what had happened, and why Belwyn looked so worried.

"You fell from your horse in the race with Hourn. You landed on your shoulder and broke your collarbone. I set the bone while you were unconscious. You also hit your head on a rock, and we were afraid you might not come back to us. Everything is fine now, and soon you can rest. Now, do you see my hand in front of your face? No, don't speak; just blink your eyes once if you can see my fingers."

He did everything Belwyn wanted, although it was hard to keep his eyes open. Finally satisfied, Belwyn turned to his father.

"He'll live, my lord, I promise you. I won't let him go to sleep for awhile, and I'll keep waking him through the night so he does not enter the sleep that never ends."

"My thanks, tutor," came Ariod's quiet reply. Tyre thought his father might speak again, but in the next moment his face changed, anxiety replaced by impassivity, and he disappeared from view.

Tyre focused on Belwyn, trying to smile at him. His shoulder throbbed against the bandages keeping him immobile. Belwyn must have seen the attempt at a smile, for he smiled back, his eyes bright and, like his father's, strangely liquid.

"Now, my brave warrior of Lapith, who can ride standing barefoot on a horse's back, I'll teach you something to lessen the pain. Listen closely . . ."

A wonderfully cool compress pressed against the back of his head. It dripped cold water down the back of his neck, numbing the dull throbbing that had become so much a part of his being he could not imagine a time it had not been there. A cool, dry hand brushed over his temple and his right cheek. From time to time it stroked his back and shoulders, brushing some of the tension away. He thought he must be lying on a pallet of lamb's wool, so soft was the surface beneath him. So much softer than the ground, he thought. The compress lifted for a moment and he sighed, hoping its comforting coolness would return. A mild voice he recognized from somewhere spoke above him.

"I must renew the cloth for a moment. There now, it's back. Don't think, just rest. That's right—breathe slowly, evenly."

Drifting into sleep, Tyre remembered the voice. It was the cook, the one who gave him the porridge that morning. How strange, he thought (and it was his last thought for awhile), how strange that among slavers there is kindness.

"Damn you, Rhacius, what was that mess-up in the gruel line this morning? Here we are, trying to get the medicine down him, Aldus stalling the line so Maenon can mix it into the gruel, and that . . . that idiot . . .! not only makes him spill it all over the ground, but lifts him up by his hair in the very place you hit him! Can't anybody execute a simple command of 'Go easy'?"

Luxor returned near midnight, his mood dark and his language foul. His men knew him well enough to know that most of his anger was directed at himself. They also knew he expected all questions to be answered quickly and accurately.

"You know what the problem is! Too many men and not enough communication. Half are adept but only two can send—namely you and me. Of the rest, six know Stanis-speech. That leaves nine dependent on the spoken word. Stax is a good man, one of the most respected guards in the fortress. He just didn't get the message. You know you would have thought it was a nice touch at breakfast if the lad hadn't been injured."

Luxor considered the emotions around him. Everyone was tense and full of guilt. Many of the men who were not adept had worn chains not so long ago. The thought of putting them on others sickened them. This mission was volunteers only, and the Council was pleased that nine of them were former slaves purchased in Agave. Not only would they know how slaves were treated, and could thus act accordingly, the Fifteenth Mother believed they would bear up better under the strain of Agave. Few adepts could manage the debilitating pain of walking through those sandstone gates. Luxor was not looking forward to it himself. He returned to the issue at hand.

"How about you, Melos? How did they take the chaining?"

Clean and groomed now, the burly man considered his answer. Ten years ago, he forged shackles for a living. These days, he was an expert at getting them off quickly and with little injury. Today brought back memories he'd rather forget, but when the Fifteenth Mother asked, Melos, for one, wasn't going to disappoint her. At least his part was over, he thought with relief, and soon he'd be back home making wheel rims and shoeing horses. His answer was slow and deliberate, Melos being a man of few words.

"The usual. A few moved. I burned one but the healer says it's not too bad. A few fainted, which makes it easier. The first one, he didn't move a muscle. A tough one, I reckon."

Luxor grunted and moved on.

"Maenon?"

"Melos is correct; the burn is painful, but will heal in time. As a whole, they're a hardy lot. They're stiff and sore, but exercise will loosen them up. We need to make sure they keep drinking. We may have to increase their salt intake if the weather continues hot and dry. I'll wait and see."

"And him?"

Maenon smiled into the darkness. Luxor didn't have to use a name, everyone knew who he meant.

"Tyre will be fine."

Luxor recognized a promise when he heard one.

"All right, orders for tomorrow. Those of you escorting Melos home—and Karn, the one who was burned—should get the wagon packed tonight and depart before dawn. We'll give the rest of them a few extra hours of sleep, get them up and fed, and head due west at a slow pace, letting them get used to the chains. We'll stop every few hours for water and rest. I want Tyre in the middle of the line with eyes on him at all times. No one talks to him except Rhacius or me. We'll pick up the pace in a day or so. If the weather holds, we'll reach Agave in twelve days. Dismissed."

Grabbing a mug for one last swallow of cold tea, Luxor rose to stretch out his back and shoulders. A throat was cleared. Rhacius was regarding him with a decidedly worried frown.

"What is it?"

"I just thought you should know that . . . well . . ."

When Luxor swore softly under his breath, Rhacius tried again.

"Hell, Luxor, I'm no expert! I'm just a horse soldier who's lucky enough to send a little."

Luxor perked up his ears, interested in anything Rhacius considered to be out of the ordinary.

"So?"

"I've been reading him occasionally, just like you said, very carefully and heavily screened. Right after the chaining he was quiet, too quiet, if you know what I mean, all pale and stiff."

Rhacius was not a worrier, and having worked with him for fifteen years, Luxor trusted his instincts. He also respected him enough not to push him, no matter how much he yearned for a few hours of sleep before a quickly approaching dawn.

"Go on."

"He, uh, he was talking with Beal."

"You mean he went into a memory of a moment he'd shared with Beal?"

"It was more than that. He went looking for Beal and suddenly, Beal was there. When I sensed his presence, Beal let me know in no uncertain terms I shouldn't be there. In fact, he slapped up a wall blocking his thoughts from me so hard it made my head ache."

Luxor looked away for a long moment of reflection before making his decision.

"Rhacius, I'm speaking as a member of the Council now. No one, I repeat, no one is to read Tyre again without my specific orders. I want you to send that out now, and again tomorrow morning. That includes you . . ." he paused, ". . . and me."

Luxor was silent so long Rhacius decided he'd been dismissed.

"And Rhacius . . ."

"Commander?"

"Thanks."

A log collapsed into grey ash. Luxor heard a faint chuckle as a figure emerged from the shadows and crouched near the fire.

"So, Maenon, have you taken to spying in your spare time?"

"It's just that I was waiting to tell you something and now it seems unnecessary."

"You sensed Beal's presence?"

Maenon's voice was dreamy, his eyes hooded.

"They brought him to me in bad shape. He shouldn't have stood in the sun for so long. I blame myself for underestimating the force of Rhacius' blow. Anyway, he was leaving us, fading into the sleep that never ends. I was deep inside his mind, trying to get a hold on him, but he wouldn't respond. Gradually, I became aware of another presence drawing him back. It was active, concentrated—stronger than any mind I've ever felt with the exception of the Fifteenth Mother herself. It kept at him far longer than I would have been able to sustain such a call. Beal saved him twice, Luxor; once in life and once after death. If there is such a thing as death."

When Luxor made no response, Maenon's tone changed to one of mild remonstrance.

"Where did you take the old one?"

Luxor blinked and shrugged.

"To a caravan I knew was in the area. The head trader is an old acquaintance and a fair man. He was happy to have a good horseman since he's headed out toward the eastern shore. I indentured him for a year. The trader promised he can return with him when he journeys west next summer."

Chewing on a piece of grass he'd pulled from the ground, Luxor continued.

"I almost killed him; wanted to snap his neck like a twig. I've not been moved to that degree of violence in thirty years. But I stopped and looked deeper, as she always urges me, and all I could see was a pathetic old man crazy with guilt and religious fanaticism. He thought he was sending Tyre to some kind of deity that delights in killing children."

"You felt his love for the boy," Maenon observed, "and it saved you."

"Aye."

Maenon disappeared into the shadows.

Kicking out the remains of the fire, Luxor looked up to the star-bright autumnal sky, deciding tomorrow would be clear and dry. Suddenly, he broke into a jig. Not stopping until he was puffing for breath, he addressed the starry sky.

"I should have known, old friend, you'd never leave us!"

Chapter 4

The Road to Agave

"IS THAT IT, young lord? Is that Agave?"

Tyre squinted along Nerod's outstretched arm. A grimy forefinger pointed toward an earth-colored mound just visible on the western horizon, glimmering wetly as the harsh sunlight struck the desert sands.

"Certainly it lies directly in our path. Your eyes are keen, son of Alwyr."

Proud at hearing this unexpected praise from the chieftain's son, Nerod lifted his chin. He'd always considered Tyre reserved, even distant. In the past few days, he'd revised his opinion. Once the sickness in his head passed, Ariod's son reestablished his role as leader, lifting their spirits by recalling legends of Lapithian heroes around the campfire before they slept, stepping in several times to stop altercations about food and sleeping places. Always, he urged them to honorable behavior, refusing to let them think of themselves as degraded. Nerod tried to follow his lead, maintaining a stony demeanor around the guards, refusing to let their presence daunt him.

Nerod glanced behind him as they resumed the march. Tyre was adjusting the leather headband he'd fashioned out of the hem of his tunic to keep his wildly tangled hair from his face as well as stopping the sweat from burning his eyes. We are all much changed, Nerod thought, comparing their ragged leather clothing to the gaudy decorations that had bedecked them as they departed the tribe. Tyre seemed most changed. He was more deeply tanned than ever, his hair bleached almost white by the sun, his face gaunt, cheekbones and jaw jutting out sharply under tightly drawn skin. Even the guards had changed, Nerod admitted grudgingly. They began as brutes, but after the first few days of horror, settled into a set routine of barking orders that rarely ended in blows if met with instant obedience.

Nerod never considered, as Tyre did daily, that it was not the guards who had changed, but the prisoners. Tyre knew that he, who had never willingly obeyed an order in his life, was falling into the habit of slavery with a speed that frightened him. As his body learned to manage the chains, not fighting them, but adapting his movement to their length and unaccustomed weight, he no longer questioned orders, but strove to obey.

More than the insidious power of the chains, he tried to fight the relentless feelings of despair that often threatened to overwhelm him, refusing to think past the next hour or the next day—afraid to dwell on the horror of the tales told of Agave.

In Lapith, it was a place out of legend, a tale told on long winter evenings guaranteed to widen the eyes of children and bring looks of frank disbelief to the faces of adults. Such a place could only be fantasy, for what did Lapithians know of slaves? Their free, nomadic life precluded the feasibility of slavery. Of what use was a slave if he could not ride, and what Lapithian would accept the curtailment of his own freedom in order to prevent someone from escaping? Beyond those drawbacks, Lapithians held an inbred distrust of strangers. It took Belwyn six years to achieve enough status to serve as Tyre's attendant in his initiation ceremony; another six years and death in battle to have worth in the eyes of an old-timer like Llyr. The thought that a stranger might even catch a glimmer of one of their women sent a shiver of distaste down any honorable man's back. Tyre could remember only one slave who had ever had any contact with his tribe. It was a story passed down from his father in one of the infrequent times he talked to his son about the past.

The story began with Ariod granting passage to a caravan trader who sought to cross their lands. In gratitude, Ariod was gifted with a young male slave. Uncomfortable as a slave owner, Ariod ordered that the boy be taught to ride, hunt, and be trained in the use of weaponry. Not long after arranging his apprenticeship with a clan of tanners, Ariod freed the boy, who left the tribe soon after, telling Ariod he wanted to join one which held no memory of his former status. As far as Ariod knew, he remained one with the Lapithian people.

Too young to remember the slave, Tyre dimly recalled Ariod's relief as he described his departure. As reserved and unemotional as his father was, he made no secret of his hatred for the slavers who sometimes attacked his people. It was no wonder that Ariod was grateful for the slave's departure. Tyre wondered if his fate would be as merciful, but arrested the thought. He had sworn not to consider the future, sensing inwardly that if he did, it would lead to even greater disappointment and despair.

A tightening in his gut warned him that Nerod's guess was a certainty, although he had no intention of alarming the others. He'd guessed the nearness of their arrival by the behavior of the slavers. During the past few days, Lycus tightened security, sending out twice as many scouts as usual, slowing the pace, and increasing food rations. Tyre wondered, with an inward shudder, if they were being fattened for market. He, himself, was rail thin. Even though the bouts of nausea lessened over the course of the march, he had no appetite. The cook, whose name he had never been able to learn, sneaked him pieces of dried fruit and a wedge of cheese that Tyre firmly refused. He would accept nothing his people could not have as well. The cook nodded and withdrew, although he continued to regard Tyre with a faintly worried air.

A bellow from Lycus added to Tyre's steadily growing sense of apprehension. It was still several hours until sunset. To stop now was an unsettling break in the well-established routine of the past twelve days.

"Halt, slaves, and listen. We'll camp off the trail to the right. There's a stream running through there where you can wash. You'll be heavily guarded, and those chains will drown you fast, so don't even think about escaping. Rhacius, move them out."

The line of prisoners moved rapidly down the hill. Even Tyre quickened his pace when he beheld the hilly landscape of scrub-trees, sand-colored earth, and the rippling stream, so different from the grassy plains and shallow lakes of Lapith. The guards released the first prisoner from the waist chain, letting him wade in up to his knees before stopping his progress with an uplifted cudgel. As the prisoner lifted each wrist and ankle shackle away from chafed flesh and bathed it in cool water, his expression of relief caused Tyre to feel an answering response in his own extremities.

Settling himself on a convenient rock, Tyre waited his turn. He'd overcome his usual impatience with waiting long ago. Chained as he was in the middle of the line, he was always the last to be set free. The sound of the running stream soothed the ear as well as the mind, and soon the entire group of prisoners relaxed, most of them stretched out on the sun-warmed sand. Rhacius and another guard leaned against the wizened trunk of a dead tree, dropping their ever-vigilant postures as they indulged in a rare moment of inactivity. Always alert to the possible exchange of information, Tyre eavesdropped on their conversation.

"If Lycus would let us strip them down, we could clean them up right. Even if they wash a bit, the stink will put off any buyer who stands downwind of them. Is The Wolf going soft in his old age?"

Rhacius looked over his shoulder with momentary fear.

"Watch your mouth, Stax!"

Content that Lycus was out of earshot, Rhacius' confidence returned.

"He's afraid to strip them lest the chilly nights make them sicken. There's nothing Lycus likes more than money. He'll get a good price and we'll get a hefty share of the profits."

The other guard was clearly unconvinced.

"What makes you think he'll get a good price? There isn't a muscled one among them and they don't speak the southern tongue. You remember how hard it was for him to find people who spoke their language or were desperate enough to learn it."

Rhacius favored his companion with a well-chosen expletive. Drawing his knife to clean his fingernails, he shook his head at his companion's ignorance.

"Anyone who owns horses wants a slave from Lapith. Since there are so few of them, they're worth their weight in hard coin. When they're up on the platform tomorrow, you'll see."

Busy storing away this valuable information, trying not to dwell on the horror of it all, Tyre froze as a hairy forearm wrapped itself around his throat, a knifepoint pricking at his ribs. Rhacius' lips were so close to his ear he could smell the onions on his breath and feel his spittle spray against his cheek. His threats were delivered in short gasps of venomous spite.

"I swear on my father's murder by a piss-drunk whore, I hate a snoop worse than anything that breathes! I'd slice you open like a rotten sausage, except for The Wolf's threats if you're damaged."

Tyre sat impassive.

"Let's not be hasty, shall we? If I can't cut your throat, I can certainly cut your hair."

As Rhacius spoke he loosened his grip. Immediately, Tyre jerked his left elbow back, feeling a satisfying jolt as he hit bone followed by Rhacius' sharp intake of breath. His instinct racing ahead of his intellect, Tyre wheeled to run. Then, in a moment of scalding self-ridicule, he remembered the chains. Trapped, he turned to face a fully recovered Rhacius. Both of them dropped to the crouched stance of knife-fighting, Rhacius circling him, trying to entangle him in the chains; Tyre moving deftly over and around them, his eyes never leaving his tormentor's face.

"What's the matter, you offal-bred mare's get? Afraid I'll cut your pretty locks? You should thank me, long-hair, for offering to rid you of it. It'll be bad enough on the block without women running their hands through your hair."

As they circled, Rhacius continued to taunt him, playing him with words that put Tyre's heart in an ever-tightening vise. Only his training kept him alert and moving, because with every word, Rhacius confirmed his deepest fears, writing the dreaded scenario of slavery Tyre had composed in the long miles of the march.

"Are you so stupid you haven't figured out why The Wolf thinks you're special? Huh, stallion? We've all seen the proof of it when you piss. What will the gentry pay for your body in rut?"

Rhacius slashed twice. Each time, his blade met empty air.

"Why do you think none of us can touch you, huh, horse-boy? Why Lycus docked my pay for hitting you? Do you think he likes you, slave? He just doesn't want any bruises, so when they strip you tomorrow, you'll be as unmarked as a baby's arse."

Unable to listen anymore, Tyre yearned to still that hateful voice. Grabbing up the chain between his wrists, he envisioned Rhacius' throat wrapped in iron, his tongue hanging out of a mouth filled with blood. But Rhacius wasn't finished.

"Maybe it won't be a woman who buys you, long-hair. Maybe some sodomite will want virgin ass, virgin that is, if you didn't play with the other horse-boys when daddy wasn't looking."

Panting now, Tyre felt hysteria rise. "Unclean!" his mind screamed. Forgetting his fear of the knife, he moved directly toward Rhacius.

But Rhacius had seen something over Tyre's shoulder that made his face go pale. He stood upright quickly, sheathing the knife, and shoved Tyre toward the water. A gruff voice spoke with unusual, and terrifying, sweetness.

"Need some help with the bathing, Rhacius?"

Rhacius pushed Tyre forward again, stammering in his panic to distract Lycus.

"He, uh, he just didn't want to get wet. I, uh, I was, uh, just wishing I had some soap so I could really clean him up."

"Good thinking, Rhacius. You really are a most thoughtful host. Catch."

Something landed in Rhacius' palm. The Wolf's orders confirmed everything.

"Give him a good wash and pay special attention to the hair. I want it to shine tomorrow."

With a cruel bark of laughter, his steps faded away. Tyre stood immobile, knee-deep in the water, his face blank. When Rhacius reached out to grasp Tyre's arm, Tyre started, his eyes showing white.

Rhacius was as tired as Tyre had ever seen him. His face twisted as he straightened with an exasperated sigh. In the next moment, he regained his customary steely control.

"Better get used to it, long-hair. If you don't let me, I'll call some friends and we'll do it the hard way. It'll be the same way tomorrow. They won't beat you to save your looks, but they'll find a way to touch you, never fear. And they'll want to touch more than your hair."

Tyre closed his eyes, concentrating on the coolness of the water. When Rhacius reached for him again, Tyre flinched, but suffered himself to be touched.

Around the Lapithian fire that night, the mood was grim and fearful. The food was especially good since some scouts were able to hunt and the cooks had a few extra hours in which to prepare. Venison stew, well-spiced with sage and wild garlic, onions floating on golden globules of fat, was accompanied by wheels of unleavened bread. The prisoners ate mechanically, making no mention of the change of fare. Tyre ate nothing, his thin frame wrapped in a blanket to prevent his damp leather garments from chilling him to the bone. He returned long after the other men ate, his hair plastered to his head, his face haggard with exhaustion. When Nerod offered him a bowl of stew, Tyre didn't even look at it, merely shook his head from side to side and continued his rapt gaze into the fire.

His silence added to the gloom as each man settled into private contemplations of what tomorrow held. Harad, the youngest of the group, barely eighteen and on his first raiding party, broke the uncomfortable stillness.

"If we knew what to expect, we could face it with honor."

His voice, strained and frightened, awakened in Tyre what had been forgotten in his own private misery. If he could alleviate their fear, it was his duty to do so. Reluctantly, he stepped back into the role of leader.

"The slaver said people will buy us for our skills with horses. We might be slaves, but we'll be able to groom them, smell their scent, and tender them what care we can. Perhaps," his voice grew unsteady, the longing in his words palpable, "if we can gain a master's trust, we can even ride again."

The tension abated in the prisoners. Tyre's information offered hope where there had been nothing but dread, and they wrapped themselves in blankets, settling themselves around the fire for their last night before Agave. The boy who served as water carrier brought around hot, bitter tea, and each man drank a mug full of the steaming brew. As the boy offered the last mug to Tyre, his eyes round with wonder at this tall man who sat so still and quiet by the dying fire, his hand trembled. Tyre moved to accept the boy's offering. When his chained wrist clinked against the battered metal cup, the boy jerked back. Tyre lifted one eyebrow over a tired blue eye.

"My thanks, small one. Perhaps this will warm me."

The boy smiled tremulously, turned, and fled.

Tyre sipped the tea, feeling its warm comfort spread through his veins. The heat of the fire had dried his hair and he moved his hands upward to move it from his shoulders to his back. Bone-tired, he moved down onto the ground, the steady breathing of his people a rhythmic tonic to his troubled spirit. As he placed his head in the pillow of his arm, his last thought was that perhaps Belwyn would visit his dreams.

Tyre's sleep was quiet and untroubled, but Belwyn never came.

The moon was nearly full, hanging huge and heavy-bottomed in the night sky as Luxor presided over the last meeting of the mission. All the adepts were on guard and linked to the proceedings. Luxor tested the myriad of emotions surrounding him, discovering they were all facets of fear. The adepts were terrified that Agave would overcome the barricades the Fifteenth Mother had taught them to erect in their extended period of training, when each of them took instruction in Lapithian language, culture, and riding. The former slaves of Agave had different concerns, mainly, that they would have to face a period in their lives they had striven to forget; a few were frightened of somehow being recaptured and sold. Rhacius and Maenon didn't fear for themselves; they were afraid for Tyre. Luxor accepted it all, calling on the great reserves of strength that had made him Commander of the Legion at thirty and a member of the Council since the ascension of the Fifteenth Mother.

Luxor spoke slowly and distinctly, both with his mind and his mouth. He knew his mens' fears would not be lessened by anything he said, but he could give them activities that might combat them. Using the voice of command at which he was a master, he began to outline duties and procedures. His closing words were searing in their intensity:

"Thirty men entering Agave to guard eight slaves will doubtless draw undue attention. We're helped by the fact that they're Lapithians, and thus rare and valuable stock. The greatest danger will be from the time we pass the gates to our arrival at the stall reserved for us. You must keep them moving. Be watchful for anything that might trip or tangle their chains. If they stumble, help them along as best you can. If they fall, pick them up and carry them. Beware of distractions. Keep your eyes sharp and your mouths shut. Any questions?"

There were none.

"Rhacius and Maenon, stay for a moment."

Contact broken, the group dissolved into the night.

"Did I give them enough to think about?"

Rhacius, having never visited Agave, was curious about Luxor's tactical comments.

"Why the emphasis on entry? Who in their right mind would attack thirty armed men?"

When Luxor's lips tightened, Rhacius knew he had touched a nerve.

"When I was making regular trips to Agave in the early years, I once saw a mob attack a group of female slaves. They were young, beautiful, obviously virginal, and just as obviously intended for harems or pleasure houses. The slaver had a large troop, but they were careless, letting the mob handle the women. The frenzy grew to the point that the slaver got worried, afraid his wares might be spoiled, and started to whip some of the lewdest ones away. The mob ignited, lifting the women and their chains away from the guards. A riot developed. By the end of it, almost two hundred were dead, including every one of the women."

"And you think someone might go after them tomorrow."

"I think it is a possibility and I am responsible for preparing for every possibility." Luxor closed the subject, opening one of his own. "How are you, Rhacius?"

Rhacius' eyes glittered in the firelight.

"He cracked my rib. Maenon bound it and gave me something for the pain. I've had worse."

Luxor's expression softened as he considered his second-in-command. Sensing Rhacius' feelings of self-disgust, he guessed its source was not his wounded dignity at being injured.

"How did the bathing go?"

"A pox on you, Luxor, you know how it went! He fought me until I told him what tomorrow would be like. Then he went cold and still. He flinched every time I touched him. Once we got out of the water, I handed him a comb and he threw it on the ground. When I called Stax over to help, he went berserk. It took four of us to hold him while I tried to get out the worst of the tangles. He simply will not be touched."

Rhacius paused.

"Luxor, what if he goes mad tomorrow?"

Luxor remembered his last conversation with the Fifteenth Mother as if it had been yesterday. Her wise old voice drifted across his thoughts.

"The day in Agave will be the worst, for you and for him. In a single day we will touch his deepest fears, take away his companions, and destroy his identity as

a leader. He is strong, Luxor, and Beal prepared him for this moment. Keep him safe and he'll meet our challenge."

"He won't go mad," Luxor said aloud. "The Fifteenth Mother promised."

The mention of her name gave his statement instant credibility. Rhacius regained his composure and threw another stick of wood on the fire. Closing his eyes, Luxor felt the waves of tension and guilt shimmering around his second-in-command. A proud, ambitious man, Rhacius was one of the first to volunteer for this special duty. Although he and Maenon suspected the importance of what they attempted, they knew no details. The Fifteenth Mother herself had trained Rhacius for his performance at the stream. Not even her careful guidance could absolve him from his guilt. Luxor was a man of war, hardened by years of contact with the world outside Pelion, yet his humanity had never been compromised. Now he turned the full force of that humanity on Rhacius.

"What you feel is natural and right. I would be concerned if you showed no signs of remorse, for that would mean you didn't realize the full extent of his misery. No one promised you it would be easy or that you could avoid feeling dirtied by what . . ."

Rhacius interrupted, asking the one question Luxor was forbidden to answer: "But why? If only I knew why!"

Luxor stood firm against his subordinate's challenge.

"We ready him for the Maze. I can say no more." Luxor felt his advantage and pushed it. "You know her, have studied closely with her. Do you think she takes delight in what you did today?"

Rhacius' reply was muted.

"That's not her way."

"Then it must be enough for you, and for all of us."

Silence reigned until Luxor remembered Maenon's quiet presence.

"And you, healer, what do you have to report?"

"Simply that he ate nothing, drank tea, and fell asleep."

"I know you too well. What did you put in the tea?"

"A simple mixture with no lasting effects. He'll be rested tomorrow after a dream-free sleep."

"One last question. Have you sensed Beal?"

Maenon's response was dreamy, as it had been the night he nursed Tyre. Luxor always suspected that Maenon tended toward mysticism; his response confirmed it.

"He isn't here. He loves him too much to shield him from the necessities of Preparation. Beal will keep his vow."

Luxor nodded. There was nothing left to say.

As his friends made their way to their sleeping places, Luxor turned toward the west. Relaxing into tranquility, he felt an immediate presence.

"We arrive at midday."

The mind he touched matched his in weariness, yet the anticipation and joy of Stanis' reply was unmistakable.

"All is prepared. We await him in Agave."

Chapter 5

Agave

HUNDREDS OF BODIES, unwashed and foul-smelling, moved in the same direction as the line of prisoners pushing their way through the crowded, narrow street. Hands reached out as the chains pulled Tyre forward, grabbing at his shackles, tugging at his leather clothes, ripping and pulling at his hair. The stench and the din resembled nothing he had ever experienced. He tried to keep his head down, both to concentrate on not tripping over his leg chains and to keep the grasping hands away from him. Other prisoners were having an equally rough time and the guards were fully occupied. Rhacius marched stolidly at Tyre's side, bellowing instructions to the other guards, his cudgel raised, hitting anyone foolish enough to cross his path with indiscriminate violence. Lycus could be heard several yards in front, shouting obscenities at the crowd, at his men, urging his merchandise forward, ever forward toward the slave market of Agave.

The line crept slowly along the cobbled, filth-lined street. Beyond the rancid smells, the babble of numerous dialects, and the unremitting pressure of bodies packed against him, Tyre's inability to see the sky was making him claustrophobic. He tried closing his eyes, which only intensified his sense of panic. The chain pulled him violently forward as the crowd thinned. Gasping as cleaner air hit his lungs, he shook his head to clear it from the noise, which continued unabated. Lifting his head, he realized they had entered a huge market place, open to the sky. The chain jerked again as Lycus appeared directly in front of him, his single eye glaring at the world around him, boosting each Lapithian up onto a raised surface by the scruff of their necks, the back of their breeches, anywhere he could get a grip. Hands circled Tyre's waist, and with a heave and a grunt, he was lifted up. More hands grabbed his tunic, pulling him over rough boards until he was thrown in a heap with the others.

His head clearing a bit, Tyre looked around him. The platform, constructed with rough-hewn timbers, stood as high as a man's head above street level. Two massive posts, taller than Tyre and about two shoulder-widths apart, were sunk into the platform, their tops hung with thick-linked chains. A small stand stood in front of the platform on ground level where Lycus could be seen, rifling papers drawn out of a leather pouch, arguing loudly with an obese man whose head was wrapped in a gaudy turban.

The slaver was speaking another language to the fat man, gesturing repeatedly toward the pile of slaves on the platform floor and shaking his scruffy head each time he was interrupted. His patience gone, he shoved the papers into the flabby, gesticulating hands of his adversary and cursed his way up the narrow steps rising from the booth to the platform. Hands on hips, he surveyed the scene which met his single roving eye with pure disgust.

"By all the gods, get up! Stax, get them up! You there, untangle those chains! Look sharp, now! They must be sold today! Rhacius, take over!"

Turning on his heel, he hurried back down the stairs where a group of onlookers already gathered. Jerking the prisoners to their feet, the guards pulled the line down toward the front of the platform. Rhacius paced in front of them, daring them to make a sound, his cudgel slapping the palm of his hand with every step. Once they settled, standing nervously side-by-side, his instructions were brief.

"Stand without moving. Say a word and you'll wish you hadn't. If Lycus lets someone up here, keep still and silent no matter what they do. They're free to examine you if their money's good. And Lycus will make certain of that."

With that, he hurried down the stairs to join Lycus. The remaining guards moved quickly into place, one behind each prisoner, twelve more stationed around the edges of the platform. Cudgels were out and ready and their faces were tight with hostility. Tyre shifted his weight, bringing a curse from the guard behind him and a cudgel pressed in the small of his back.

"Move again, long-hair, and I'll forget Lycus' order not to bruise you."

Unable to move his body, Tyre moved his eyes around the square, noting the myriad of platforms filling the square with human wares. Lycus' platform enjoyed a prime location in the middle of the square near one of the many arched entry passages feeding a continual stream of bodies into the central marketplace. Every color of skin and hair caught his eye. Men, women, children; the aged, the infirm, the crippled; buyers, sellers, spectators; all of humanity seemed to be gathered into a tumultuous riot of madness.

Shifting his attention to the booth below him, Tyre found himself staring at a man whose skin color resembled that of ripe plums, a velvety blue-black save for his palms and lips. A giant compared to those who milled about him in the marketplace, he was as tall as Tyre's father but considerably more massive in frame, his close-cropped black curls shot with silver, his broad-featured face unlined despite his age, some fifty years or more, Tyre guessed. Skirts, or something like skirts, a loose-fitting robe of some kind, swung loosely around his ankles. He wore earrings as well, tiny bits of gold implanted in his earlobes. Tyre might have laughed, so odd did this creature appear to him, a black-skinned giant attired in woman's garb, if he had not spied the curved sheath hanging from his belt. About this time, the black man looked up, running his gaze along the line of prisoners, his eyes heavy-lidded, his expression brooding as he surveyed each man in turn. Upon reaching the end of the line, his attention swung back to Tyre, pinning him with a gaze that seemed to devour him. And then, as quickly as it had begun, the inspection was over. Turning back to face Lycus, his fingers flew in the air in front of him. At first Tyre was confused, wondering what the man was doing. Not until a small boy, as dark-skinned as the man, began speaking in a high treble voice did Tyre realize that the black man could not, or would not, speak for himself. With this understanding came another surprise: Tyre understood the language spoken by the boy. The words were slurred, yes, the vowels soft and the consonants liquid, but they undoubtedly belonged to one of the languages he'd studied with Belwyn. Slowly, Tyre began to translate, adjusting his ear to the boy's strangely sibilant accent.

". . . interest in the blonde one."

Glancing up at Tyre, Lycus frowned, then turned back to address his client, his manner servile again, bowing and scraping, greedy beyond measure.

"You honor me, lord, with your interest, but my thought was to sell them as a group."

Fingers flew and the boy spoke again.

"My master has no interest in a group. He will have the blonde one or nothing. He says he will pay you well, but he will not discuss price until he has examined the merchandise.""

Lycus seemed to hesitate before answering the black man.

"The blonde one is newly taken and not biddable. Until his wildness is tamed, he will not accept such an examination easily."

The black man responded with a single forceful gesture.

"My master says he must be chained."

Lycus' response was immediate.

"Rhacius, chain the blonde one to the poles."

In a blur, Tyre felt the chain being pulled from his waist shackle, separating him from the others. Hard hands dragged him to the poles. When he shouted a curse a leather gag was forced into his mouth. He struggled silently now, but the shackles made the guards' task an easy one. His arms were forced up, the chain between his wrists swinging in a great arc above his head. His arms secured, they chained his ankles to the poles as well, leaving him hanging from his double-shackled, bleeding wrists. He accepted the pain gratefully, focusing on it with all his might, grabbing desperately at anything that might lessen the terror pounding in his chest.

His eyes flew open as a dark-skinned hand reached out to brush his hair away from his face. The eyes that met his were no longer brooding, but curiously intent, a flicker of fire seeming to dance in their depths. Tyre struggled violently. Frowning, the man turned to signal to his interpreter. After a short silence, the boy spoke quietly to Tyre.

"My master says no harm will come to you if you submit. If you struggle, he will order the guards to hold you."

Looking into those dark, mesmerizing eyes, Tyre realized he was trapped. The choice was clear: submit to the one or the many. Nodding to indicate his decision, Tyre closed his eyes.

The examination began. At the first touch, he flinched. Tyre waited for the guards to seize him, but nothing happened. After a short pause, he was touched again. This time he was able to control his response. Hands moved over his shoulders and down his flanks, their pressure firm through his tunic. They moved to his spine, tracing it down to his hips. His muscles trembled as he fought not to react to hands that seemed to sear his skin beneath the thin layer of leather with their firm, steady motion. Down his thighs to his calves, they outlined each muscle, each bone, never hurrying, never slowing, examining him like a piece of livestock.

Tyre, having examined hundreds of horses in exactly this way, understood finally, and with a growing sense of shame, that he was little more than an animal to this prospective buyer, an animal purchased to improve the herd in whatever way it needed improvement.

"My master asks if the slave's sex has been examined."

Tyre's stomach turned over.

"Not by me. I leave that to the pimps and breeders. "

"So my master may continue?"

"He put down a deposit; he can do any damn thing he likes."

Tyre shut his eyes. If only he could faint or go mad. But the hands were moving inexorably down his chest, feeling his ribs as they were spread and lifted by the task of his arms supporting his weight. They moved to his stomach, flat and hard with tension, and then to his belly. As they moved lower, a shudder ran through him. Fingers worked at the knot of his laces, loosening his breeches. Senseless now, Tyre remembered little of what followed.

The next thing he knew, the black man was removing a silken square from his flowing robe and wiping his hands on the delicate fabric. The boy spoke again, his treble piping resulting in the release of the shackles that held Tyre upright.

The chains rattled as he landed in a sprawling heap and lay where he fell, stomach down on the rough surface of the platform, his breath coming in gasps. They dragged him back to his place, reattached him to the chain, and mercifully, didn't order him to stand.

For a long time he lay there, the noise and stink of the market place a distant part of his awareness. Gradually, he came back to the world around him; his first action was to lace up his breeches. The clatter of tin brought his head up, and he looked into the cook's eyes, which were devoid of their usual calm.

"Drink some water. The sun is hot."

After helping him up into a sitting position, the cook untied the gag. Experimentally, Tyre moved his jaw, stiff from the tightness of the leather. Noticing that the gag in the cook's hand was spotted with blood, Tyre tasted the salty sweetness of the gouges he had bitten on the inside of his mouth. As he reached for the ladle, his hand trembled, spilling half the water down his tunic before he could reach his mouth. Rhacius appeared at his side, nudging him toward the back of the platform as Lycus ascended the stairs with another prospective buyer, this one attired in a long leather vest worn over wide-legged trousers stuffed into well-worn riding boots. Lycus, oily and insinuating as usual, leaned into the man, who cast a well-practiced eye over the slaves arranged before him.

". . . excellent horsemen, as you know, my lord. Born and bred with them, they say. Perhaps a trifle thin from the march, but they'll soon fill out."

"I'll be the judge of that," the buyer replied, and motioned for Lycus to step away. Cool and supremely confident, the buyer moved down the line, expertly examining the warriors of Lapith. The first man's mouth was opened and his teeth examined. The second was ordered to spread his fingers and make a fist. Each prisoner moved dully to obey, the cudgels raised to enforce obedience. Tyre understood, with an ever-growing sense of shame, that his treatment at the poles ensured his companions' compliance. His inspection finished, the buyer walked down the steps with Lycus close behind, already beginning to haggle over price. The buyer walked away at one point, turning back when Lycus named another figure. Too exhausted to concentrate, Tyre dropped his head. Soon, Lycus was back up the steps, a smile on his face and an order on his lips.

"Rhacius, we're finished here. While I copy out the bill of sale, move them down the steps. He owns a racing stable in the east and bought the whole group as groomsmen, trainers, and if they prove trustworthy, riders."

When Rhacius lifted an eyebrow, Lycus patted the pouch tied to his belt and grinned.

Turning to go, Lycus hesitated with an afterthought: "Keep the blonde one here until they come for him."

Shackled to the base of a pole, Tyre watched as his friends were herded down the steps. No words of farewell were spoken, although Nerod glanced once in his direction. In another heartbeat, they were swallowed up by the madness of Agave.

Tyre was alone.

They came to collect him in late afternoon. He dozed fitfully at the pole, finally falling asleep despite the constant insults and obscene comments thrown up to him from passing spectators. Lycus greeted each offer with a shrug of his shoulders and uplifted hands. He and Rhacius counted out the profits and paid each guard his share. A few guards stayed on duty around Tyre. He supposed, without much interest, they planned to accompany Lycus on his next raid.

A troop of guards marching up the stairs were cut from the same cloth as those of Lycus. Hard-faced and unsmiling, they unlocked Tyre's chains from the pole and jerked him to his feet. Wordlessly, they escorted him down the steps into the whirling tumult of the market.

Rhacius called to him as they moved away:

"Good journey, long-hair. I hear the black one only buys men."

The journey was quickly over, the guards leading him to another platform set toward the edge of one of the market walls. Tyre wondered if he was going to be sold again, but refused to admit curiosity. Shoved up the stairs, he found a group of chained men resting in a variety of postures in the afternoon heat. He was placed at the end of the line this time, next to a man who was snoring loudly. While Tyre was being attached to the line, the snoring man's chains were disturbed, causing him to grunt, curse, and lift himself on his elbow to regard the newcomer. His beard was a straggly brown mixed with grey and his shaggy hair hung over his ears. He inspected Tyre with something like amusement, lingering over the long hair, ragged leather clothing and shredded riding boots. He spoke the same language as the boy.

"When's the last time they fed you?"

Tyre glanced down at his angular, too-thin frame, a rueful smile tugging at his lips. He replied awkwardly in the same language.

"I have no hunger."

The man's look was appraising this time.

"Slaves are always hungry. You're lucky this time. The cook's not bad and the portions are large. They'll feed us soon. We'll march tomorrow, so force it down. You'll need it."

The man rolled over, ending the conversation. As he did so, Tyre noticed a pattern of old scars crisscrossing his broad back. Hesitantly, he formed a question, practicing it several times before speaking it aloud.

"What are you called?"

The man started, grunted, and replied without turning his head.

"Phylas."

In a few minutes, the snores resumed.

Tyre was sitting with his arms hugging his knees when a shrill scream pierced the din. Startled, he searched for its source, locating it on a platform off to his left. A young girl dressed in a simple gown, her hair unbound, was being chained between the twin poles that seemed to exist on every platform. Having never seen a girl without veiling, he was struck by her slightness; she was small-boned and graceful, with tiny feet and hands. The platform was too far away to make out her features, but he could see she was trying to fight the guards who were lifting her hands to the poles. As a robed figure approached her, she turned her head away. A hand struck her sharply across the face and her body, held upright by the chains, slumped as her gown was ripped off. As the fabric fell to the ground, Tyre looked away. That she should be treated so roughly, more roughly than himself, troubled him.

Hourn was right; he knew nothing of women. He had never known a woman other than his mother, and memories of her were quickly dismissed with vague feelings of sadness and guilt. His feelings for women were those of any Lapithian warrior, to shield them from outsider's eyes and defend them as was necessary to retain his honor. Yet this slight figure of a girl hanging from chains etched itself into his mind, causing tears to rise unbidden. He wasn't sure if the tears were for him or the girl, but still they burned his eyes. Blinking them back, a nagging worry clutched him—he had forgotten the name of Hourn's woman. He could see her clearly as she was lifted into the wagon, her dimpled hands resting on Hourn's shoulders; her veiled head bent down to survey Hourn's upheld smiling face . . . .

In the next moment he found himself with Belwyn.

It was a freezing winter day and the wind blasted across the frozen lake. Tyre burst into Belwyn's tent without waiting for permission to enter, laced the leather flap shut against the cold, and shook off the snow covering the skin he used to wrap his head and shoulders. He was dressed in his usual leather tunic and breeches, although a lamb's wool undershirt could be seen at his neck, and his soft-skinned riding boots were replaced with sturdy boots sewn to water-tight leggings that reached his thighs.

Belwyn glanced up from a particularly pungent solution he was mixing with a tin spoon. Upon seeing Tyre's frowning face and tightly drawn brows, he turned back to his work. Finally finished brushing and stamping off most of the snow from his clothes and leggings, Tyre regarded the mess surrounding Belwyn. On a day when most Lapithians were huddled around a fire telling tales and swapping lies, Belwyn had decided to catalogue his dried herbs and roots, and was experimenting with some new potion whose smell, Tyre decided, would kill the patient long before it could be swallowed.

"Need you mix that vile brew here? I may not share a tent with you anymore, but I study here. Why must you choose today to turn everything upside down?"

A raised eyebrow was the sole response to his fit of bad temper. Belwyn never fought with Tyre; in fact, Tyre realized, he had never heard Belwyn so much as raise his voice. As a child it enraged him, making him goad Belwyn in a vain attempt to pick a fight. But Belwyn, it seemed, could not be goaded and would not fight. When Tyre turned nasty, Belwyn left his vicinity, sometimes for days at a time.

"Stop pacing and settle yourself near the brazier. You're dripping on my specimens."

With a disapproving grunt, Tyre dropped to the floor, crossed his long legs with a scowl, and stared fixedly at Belwyn's back.

Belwyn endured this scrutiny for several minutes before putting aside his work.

"Something has upset you if you've spent your morning walking along the lake. What is it?"

Tyre's eyes narrowed. He'd never been comfortable with the fact that Belwyn seemed to know things before being told; his accuracy was uncanny and it made Tyre nervous.

"How did you know I've been walking along the lake?"

Belwyn's eyes rolled skyward in exasperation.

"Because you missed your language study with me, something you rarely do, and the icicles hanging from your clothing suggest you've been outside for some time. In fact, your lips have gone blue with cold. As to the lake, you always go there to think. Come, warm yourself; there's tea in the pot."

As Tyre rolled the earthenware cup in his palms to warm them, he wondered, as he had wondered countless times before, how Belwyn worked his magic. He'd entered this tent in a black temper begun last night and worsening over the last few hours. Now, in a few short minutes, he was drinking tea, relaxed, warm, and content.

No, not content, he reminded himself, remembering Hourn. Putting down the cup, he stretched full length on the soft carpets, his head propped up by his left elbow, his right hand running his fingers unconsciously through his damp hair. This was going to be difficult, but he had nowhere else to go. He'd walked for hours along the lakeshore and could find no solution. His father was detached; his sole concern the welfare of the tribe. He couldn't go to Hourn again; they'd quarreled until dawn and parted in great bitterness. Belwyn had to listen; Tyre would make him listen. Planting his eyes on the pattern in the woven rug, he began.

"Hourn visited my tent last night. I've never seen him so angry. He ranted against Stheno, criticized my father, and accused me of not being a true friend-in-blood. And all because of that . . . that . . . woman!" The last word was delivered as a curse. In the pause that followed, Tyre turned over onto his stomach and pulled a pillow under his chest.

"Hourn told me last night that he . . . he has . . . feelings for her." This was accompanied by a grimace of distaste. "Not only does he feel strongly about her, he says it has been this way between them since the beginning! Her abduction was a sham; Hourn planned it to the last detail, fooling everyone, even me." Tyre's voice grew bitter with betrayal. "He feared I wouldn't understand. And I don't."

Belwyn interrupted. When Tyre's eyes flicked to his face, what he saw there brought a lump to his throat. Belwyn's profile, lit by the brazier, was strangely beautiful, as if graven out of stone touched by the rays of the setting sun.

"Which bothers you more? That Hourn loves a woman, or that he cares for someone as much, or perhaps more, than he cares for you?"

Tyre was stung.

"Are you mad, old man? I'm not jealous of a woman. She has nothing to do with our friendship. She knows nothing of Hourn if she can't know him as I do, as a warrior of skill and cunning."

"Yet she knows him as you cannot, for she knows him as a woman knows a man."

"I've told you I will not discuss mating, old man."

"You've also told me we may not discuss murder. But that's why you're here, isn't it? Stheno calls for the death of the babe and Hourn asks your help."

A grudging silence hung between them. Tyre broke it with a shake of his head.

"He says she'll grieve for the girl-child. He says he can't bear to watch her grieve."

"Is it so difficult for you to imagine another's grief?"

"But she's a woman! She's nothing like me!"

Belwyn stood up, his eyes boring into Tyre's. When he spoke, Tyre heard something new, something he had never heard before from his soft-spoken tutor. It was a voice of grandeur; a voice heavy with prophesy.

"Son of Ariod, I cannot help you if you refuse to be helped. I speak of a woman's mysteries; you speak of the simple act of mating. I speak of grief and heartbreak; you dismiss her feelings as somehow different from your own. A day will come, Tyre of Lapith, when you will share grief with a woman. Until that day, we'll speak no more of this."

His expression changed and he was the old Belwyn again, regarding his pupil with sad, affectionate eyes.

"My only wish is that when that day comes I'll be by your side."

Tyre looked back to the platform. The girl had vanished. This time he couldn't stop the tears.

Belwyn was dead and Tyre was lost in the chaos that was Agave.

"It wasn't part of the plan to stay here," Luxor fumed. *"We should be outside the city gates by now. Damn it, man, why do you delay?"*

"Softly, Luxor, softly. You've worried long enough. Now you must pass those worries on to me," came Stanis' reply. *"I waited because he needs time, old friend. He did well today, but we must not push his body so hard that his spirit cannot follow."*

They were gathered in a tiny room on the second story of an inn overlooking the marketplace. Out of deference to Stanis, and for purposes of security, they used inner speech. Carmanor, who was replacing Rhacius, kept watch out the window, his attention fixed on a figure sleeping on the platform below.

Luxor's tension abated in the face of Stanis' calm.

"It's my fault we're still here, and I apologize. The crowds were rotten and everyone was jangled. Then that idiot, Olipah, gave me trouble with the papers. He wanted some kind of extra fee for reserving a large platform for only eight slaves."

Stanis replied: *"You need not apologize, my friend. You've brought him safely to Agave, when the chances of that were small. Now, what says Nazur Kwanlonhon of the gift we give him?"*

Luxor was too finely trained an adept not to know he had just been soothed and redirected. Clearly, it was time for him to relinquish his authority to Stanis. Wistful at the thought of giving up Lycus the slaver, a role he had played in earlier campaigns and one that satisfied him even now as the old soldier he had become, he removed his eye-patch, straightened in his chair, and gave a good soldier's report.

"Nazur will take the Lapithians east as promised. He's grateful for the opportunity to learn their skills firsthand. Once they arrive at his racing stables in Endlin, they'll serve as bondsmen, each of them earning a fine horse as payment. With luck, they'll be back in Lapith in time for next year's Harvest."

Stanis nodded, well satisfied.

"Nazur Kwanlonhon is a man of his word."

Each of them felt a strong rush of memory overcome Stanis, who had found few such men in his travels. Blocking that part of his mind from them, Stanis addressed the watcher by the window.

"We must consider other matters. Carmanor, what of Phylas?"

"We spoke briefly while they were being fitted with boots. It's dangerous for anyone to see the signed speech so his report was brief. It seems he shed tears and slept."

Stanis turned to the honey-haired woman sitting beside him, her serenity a powerful presence in this tension-filled room.

"Chloe?"

"I can report that he ate a little, a few spoonfuls of stew, some bread, and a wedge of hard cheese. It's not much, mind you, but his stomach is shrunken. The drugs in his tea will help him sleep. His wrists are cut, but bleed no more. I'll clean and bind them tomorrow night." She shifted the direction of her thoughts. *"It's you who touched him, Stanis. Share with us what you learned."*

The shift in inner speech was subtle as Stanis began. As he proceeded to describe his first meeting with Tyre of Lapith, the intensity of his thoughts was felt by all. This was a Master of the Voice. Only the Fifteenth Mother herself could fill the mind with greater clarity and beauty.

"He is unblemished in body, troubled in mind. As Beal warned us, there are places of terror within him. Today he faced one of his greatest fears with a reservoir of strength that kept him conscious, even though he longed to leave his body. He has shut the gate against madness, finding the courage to endure."

"There's something else, Stanis."

Maenon stood directly behind Chloe, his healing partner and lifetime mate.

"I've obeyed the Council's ruling that no one may read him. Even so, this afternoon, soon after he spoke with Phylas, I'm certain Beal was with him. I can't explain my certainty of Beal's presence, although I think it may be because I trained under him when he was High Healer. I didn't read Tyre, but something important happened, something that brought Beal to him."

Maenon's announcement sent a ripple through the linked minds.

"I will inform the Fifteenth Mother. Now, we must say our farewells and go to our rest. The journey is long. We must maintain our strength of body and purpose."

Maenon and Chloe departed first, arm in arm. Rhacius touched his palm to his breast in the Legion salute; Carmanor returned it. The Commanders of the Cavalry and Infantry battalions of the Legion of Pelion moved down the passageway together to check on their charge. Luxor and Stanis remained seated in the ancient wooden chairs, staring into the fire burning in the decrepit fireplace. Opening their minds, they sent their thoughts racing toward the south. Contact with her came quickly, her mind keen with anticipation.

"He has passed safely through Agave."

Her sigh passed over them, a cooling breeze drifting across the rooftops of the desert city.

"Maenon believes Beal is with him still."

They felt her sudden surge of hope, naked and wild in its intensity.

The connection broken, they kept their thoughts to themselves as the city around them writhed and mumbled, for the beast that was Agave never slept.

Chapter 6

The Road to Pelion

ON THE PRETENSE of tightening the laces of the boots they'd been issued last night, Phylas dropped to his knees. Glancing back, he checked on his charge, who was moving along steadily, seeming to limp a bit, although the new boots explained that. The pause over the laces was not brief enough, however, and the chain dragged him forward, forcing him to pick up his pace until he could get back in step. That his body was one big ache disgusted him. Too much soft living in Pelion, he decided, a smile softening his craggy features.

Nomia was her name, and even as he spoke it in his mind, he felt her tugging at his heart. She would be nearing her time at the next full moon. Although she never spoke of it, he knew she was anxious, for this child would be her first. When he told her about his meeting with the Fifteenth Mother, she frowned, bit her bottom lip in a gesture that never failed to enchant him, and insisted he go. That was one of the things that drew them together in the Maze; not just her beauty (although he cherished her beauty) but her courage.

He remembered the first time they met, the night she was shoved roughly into his cell. He knew they were bringing him a woman, but was unprepared for the tigress who invaded his cell, livid that the guard had been rough with her and cursing until she ran out of breath. He'd been glad she was tough, glad she could stand up for herself. He'd been without a woman for so long and was weary of the constant loneliness of the cell. She brought energy and fire into his life; after Nomia, the cell was never the same. Then, too, Phylas would always bear a scar from the fruit knife she pulled on him. But, as he teased her now, what were a few more scars?

The moons spent with her during Preparation were a balm on his bruised soul. And since the Fifteenth Mother was responsible for sending Nomia to his cell, he would do anything she asked, even if it meant going back to Agave, a place that had almost killed him.

"Don't do this thing if the pain of returning is too much to bear."

Phylas hadn't seen her up close in three years. She's aging badly, he thought, until he looked into her fathomless grey eyes.

"I'd like to help, Mother. It's just that I, uh, I still wake up screaming sometimes, and Nomia, she, she . . ."

The prospect of waking up alone filled him with dread.

"Fear no nightmares. There will be none on your journey. As to Nomia, I'll look after her myself. She'll be waiting at the gate the day you return, her body rich with your first son."

It took a moment to sink in.

"Son?" he repeated blankly, certain the old woman was teasing him, probably paying him back for all the trouble he and Nomia caused in the Maze. Her lips tugged at the corners, her eyes danced, but she did not smile.

"Your eldest boy. The one you will call Prax."

It was then that he made up his mind to go. Damn the woman, she always had this effect on him. It was the sheer gall of her he admired, asking him to submit to slavery again when she knew very well what it would cost him to pass through those sandstone gates again. He'd asked one more question, knowing before he asked it he probably wasn't going to get an answer. Still, if he was going to return to that hellhole, it better be for a good cause.

"This man I'm to protect on the line, is he truly so important?"

As he expected, she didn't answer him directly.

"He may be the reason for the Maze, for Preparation, indeed, for Pelion itself."

And that had been good enough for Phylas.

It was later in the afternoon and Phylas felt better. Maybe five and thirty wasn't so old after all. The midday ration was cold, but filling, and his body was finally warming up to the exercise. He was even enjoying the countryside, he decided with a grin; him, a city rat who'd never smelled a flower that hadn't been cut two days before. His last journey over this road hadn't been one for sight-seeing. His back laid open in more places than he liked to remember, he'd traveled in a wagon, a healer working over him, keeping him blessedly drugged. He was in such bad shape that he stayed in the House of Healing for a full moon before they took him to the Maze. Maybe that's the reason he wasn't as frightened as the others. Somehow he'd known from their treatment of him that he had a chance for life here. He wondered, idly, what his charge thought of their destination. As an afterthought, he wondered if the long-hair even knew where they were heading. Swearing under his breath, he kicked aside a rock. They wanted him to play a part, but they'd told him damn little about it.

His stride was broken when the chain jerked him suddenly backward. Fighting the momentum of the chain, Phylas planted his feet, gritting his teeth as the iron shackles hit his ankles. When the line finally stopped moving, he turned to find the long-hair down on one knee. Phylas was puzzled. He could see no blood or bruise from a fall. Why had he stopped?

"You hurt?"

The long-hair looked up quickly and shook his head. About the time he got to his feet, Carmanor came charging up in a cloud of dirt, gravel, and bad temper.

"What's the problem, slave? Why did you stop?"

The long-hair's response to Phylas was shy gratitude; as Carmanor spoke, his features transformed into hard-edged granite. As he shook his head again the incredible hair shimmered in the sunlight. Phylas had never seen such hair on a man before, neither the color nor the length. His people, and the people of Pelion, tended toward swarthiness and close-cropped curls.

When the long-hair made no response, Phylas heard Carmanor suck in his breath. If Phylas knew anything about his commander of the past two years, he knew Carmanor had no patience with insubordination of any kind. Phylas waited for the explosion.

Grabbing the slave by the hair at the nape of his neck and jerking his head back, his mouth inches from his ear, Carmanor snarled, "Hear me, slave. We've got a twenty-day march over hostile territory and I have better things to do than play nursemaid to your worthless hide. Keep moving, and the next time I ask a question, I better get an answer. Now, move!"

Phylas had to admire the long-hair's spirit. He'd seen seasoned veterans pale in the face of Carmanor's wrath. The long-hair didn't even flinch, just kept looking in front of him as if Carmanor didn't exist. As the line started forward at Carmanor's shouted command, Phylas read the commander's frowned question in his eyes. All Phylas could do was lift his shoulders to convey his ignorance.

Phylas figured out the mystery that evening. The slaves from Agave were allowed their own campfire and jostled for position to be as close as possible to the warming blaze. The long-hair didn't join in the fight for position and seemed to hang back from the fire. Seating himself as far away from the group as his chains would allow, he unlaced the ties of his boots. Phylas watched him from under half-closed eyelids as the other boot was unlaced. As he pulled it away, working it carefully off his foot, his heels and toes, covered with raw blisters oozing blood, were revealed.

"Footsore are you?"

Looking up quickly, the long-hair recognized Phylas and relaxed. He spoke slowly, as if he wasn't quite sure of the words, but his accent was as pure as any native of Pelion.

"I am unused to such hard—no—stiff boots."

His quick correction of his mistake made his eyes brighten. All at once, Phylas decided he liked him. He wasn't a coward, he wasn't a complainer, and he could laugh at himself. Phylas would take the first step.

"What are you called, long-hair?"

He got a strange look on his face before he replied: "Tyre."

"Well, Tyre, they've got a healer traveling with us and she'll soon take care of those feet. We're valuable property, you know."

He'd added that last comment as a joke. Tyre didn't smile.

"Please, Phylas, say nothing."

Phylas faced his first difficult decision. He could either earn Tyre's trust by keeping his mouth shut, or betray him so they could take care of him. If they'd given him more information, he wouldn't be in such a fix. Well, the Fifteenth Mother told him to follow his instincts, so he would. He'd say nothing.

Phylas grunted, seemingly indifferent, and lay back to catch some sleep before the evening meal. He was dozing when he heard the distinctive cadences of Chloe's voice. He had only to hear it and he was back in the wagon with her bending over him, singing to him, talking endlessly about nonsensical things, giving him something to hold on to. She had saved him with that voice.

She was working her way down the line, pushing away shackles to examine wrists and ankles, asking about cuts or bruises that might have occurred in Agave, soothing the men without seeming to try. Carmanor was her silent escort, present to ensure order. Despite his presence, the men responded to her as Phylas did three years ago. Their voices lost their aggressive edge, their features softened, and soon they were purring. Phylas thought of Nomia, deciding she shared this talent with Chloe—the gift of offering comfort. He recalled the times he'd awakened from the old dreams, and how Nomia held him against her breasts as if he was a child, murmuring to him in words that made no sense other than the fact that they expressed her pity and her love. He'd always hated the thought of someone pitying him, but Nomia's pity was a blessing.

Soon Chloe was bending down at Phylas' feet. As she lifted her eyes to his he spied her silent greeting deep within them.

"And you, slave, have you any hurts?"

"Well, lady," he drawled, "none that show."

He saw the laughter bubbling inside her as the other slaves hooted their enjoyment, but nothing showed on the outside. She turned toward

Tyre, who had removed himself even further from the fire, his legs hidden in the shadows. As she approached him, he refused to meet her gaze, concentrating instead on the ground.

"And you, slave, have you a cut or bruise I may tend for you?"

Her voice was like liquid silver. Phylas shivered at its beauty. Tyre would respond to her. No one could deny that voice; Phylas was sure of it.

Tyre shook his head, the firelight dancing over his long mane.

Chloe hesitated and tried again.

"You must let me care for you. Our master holds me responsible for your well-being. Should you sicken during the march, I will be blamed. Many have told me my hands are gentle."

Her approach was not so studied this time and the begging note was clear. Tyre seemed to hesitate for a moment before repeating his silent gesture of refusal.

Chloe sighed. She had tried and failed. Now they would have to do it the hard way, the way she dreaded. Carmanor took over.

"Maybe the lady didn't make herself clear. You will be examined tonight and every night!"

With that, four guards stepped out of the darkness. Tyre looked up, weighing the consequences. His shoulders drooping in defeat, he swung his upper body around and held out his shackled arms. The guards retreated at Carmanor's signal and Chloe knelt.

She worked quietly and quickly on his injuries, pushing the manacles up on his forearms so she could get at the cuts and bruises circling his wrists. She hummed as she worked, cleaning the wounds, applying a thick white paste and wrapping linen around them. Tyre didn't move, didn't seem to breathe. When she finished, she waited expectantly for him to present his ankles.

When he swung them around toward the fire, Phylas heard her sharp intake of breath before she began to scold Tyre, speaking as she would to an erring child.

"You should have come to me with such a hurt! Come, I'll clean away the blood so we can see . . . there . . . yes . . . that's better. Let me smooth on the unguent. It feels good doesn't it? Cool and moist. Stay still while I wrap it. Now, the other one and it will soon be over."

Phylas listened as she cooed her gentle murmurings, never stopping her descriptions of everything she was doing, wrapping her patient in a soft blanket of healing.

"I'll find some sandals for you to wear. I'll change the bandages tomorrow morning and again in the evening."

With that, she was gone in a ripple of the leaf-green she always wore. Phylas watched her departure with regret.

He looked back at Tyre, who was staring down at his bandaged wrists and feet, a bewildered look on his face; as if, Phylas decided, he had experienced something he could not, would not, understand.

The woman brought Tyre his food. It surprised him to think someone cared whether he ate or not. It also surprised him that for the first time in a long while, he was hungry. He ate every bite—some kind of fowl he'd never tasted before, rice cooked with spongy wild mushrooms, and pieces of dried fruit. Strong, bitter tea was served last, and finally he could wrap himself in the cloak they'd issued him and close his eyes.

As he waited for sleep to come, he counted off the days of his captivity. Fourteen days, he thought, fourteen days and I've come to the point that I'm grateful I wasn't hit or shamed. Today has been a good day because one person called me by my name and another touched me with hands that did not hurt.

He fought against it, but the memory of those hands came back against his will. When he first become aware of the blisters, he thought of saying something but decided against it. He didn't want to call attention to himself and become the butt of every jibe, as it had been with Rhacius. When he'd finally stumbled, he'd been ready to give in and tell a guard. Unfortunately, Phylas got there first. How could he complain about blisters in front of a man who had, from the look of his back, been flogged almost to death? Biting his lips, he walked on. By the time they made camp, he could feel the blood and raw flesh sticking against the inflexible leather and rubbing with each step. Then Phylas mentioned that the healer was a woman.

She was a mystery, Tyre thought. Her voice when she begged to help him had been of such beauty it almost overcame his dislike of being touched. He prepared himself for that first moment of contact, steeling himself as he had yesterday when he hung from the poles. All too soon, the wall against feeling crumbled, and in the gentleness of her ministrations, he found peace and comfort.

He examined her again when she came to take away his bowl, trying to see her clearly, putting aside the memory of her touch. Her green gown was simple and a trifle shabby, her honey hair dimmed by strands of gray, the skin around her eyes and mouth starting to show the lines of age. She was not old or young, fat or thin, beautiful or homely; her appearance had nothing to do with her essence, for she was at the same time strange, yet familiar. Abruptly, Tyre knew what he recognized. She was as Belwyn was—the quiet, soothing voice, the skillful hands, the sense of acceptance and peace surrounding her.

Belwyn would be pleased, Tyre thought as he drifted further into sleep. In two days, two women had touched him; one with her grief at being sold, another with her inward sense of peace.

The small black boy hobbled the horses efficiently, standing on tiptoe in order to put their nosebags in place. Initially, he'd been afraid of the black stallion his master rode. In time, he became accustomed to its great size. His thin face smiled at the stallion's contented nicker before he began munching the oats. The boy made a quick inventory of the campsite—the food was stored, the dishes washed clean in a nearby spring, and the horses fed. Now it was time to attend to his master. He moved briskly toward the campfire and began to bank the logs so the morning fire could be made more easily. A gesture from his master stopped him.

"I'll tend the fire tonight, Lukash. You've done enough. Rest, small one, and dream of all that you desire."

The man's fingers flew, not so swiftly that the boy couldn't understand him. His parents were deaf and mute, and until their death and his enslavement, he spoke as easily with his fingers as with his lips. His new master's language was somewhat different, but in the moons since Lukash was purchased from his last owner, he adapted easily to the new signs. In those days and nights of reasonable orders and plentiful food, he and his master existed in silent harmony—the boy grateful for the peace denied him for four of his nine years; the man grateful for his devotion.

Encouraged by his master's praise, Lukash posed the question that had bothered him since they'd left the city of slaves.

"Master, where do we journey?"

A flash of white teeth signaled his master's pleasure. His fingers signed quickly:

"We journey south to the city of Pelion."

The boy spoke more slowly, his toe tracing circles in the dust.

"Master, what will become of me in Pelion?"

A large pink-skinned palm lifted the boy's chin. A compassionate smile lit the dark eyes that were usually so distant.

"Once we enter Pelion, we'll choose a place for you to live—a place where you'll have friends, and food, and study."

Each sign made the boy's face brighter. Satisfied, he moved to his blankets. As his eyes closed, he glimpsed the glitter of gold in his master's palm. Gold, he thought, like the hair of the last slave my master bought.

How strange it must be, he thought, resting his cheek on his dusky arm, to have hair the color of gold . . . .

Stanis helped the boy move toward sleep, adjusting his dreams away from the nightmares that had plagued him since the death of his parents. He was unsurprised by the boy's connection between the throat amulet and Tyre. Lukash was not adept, but had been made sensitive since birth to the unspoken things of life. It was this sensitivity that brought him to Stanis' attention. Shaking his head, Stanis amended his thoughts. It was not just Lukash's sensitivity and his easy acceptance of having a mute master, but the bird-like frailty of his half-starved body that reminded Stanis of another black child sold into slavery after the death of parents. No one shielded that child from his nightmares; even so, they passed, as Lukash's would pass, upon entering Pelion.

Stanis pushed away his melancholy, returning his attention to the throat-ring that shone a deep bronze in the dying fire. He remembered Luxor's guilt and grief as he handed over Tyre's final gift to his tutor.

"I don't know if I did the right thing or not. Perhaps I should have left it on him when I put his body into the flames that first night. But it's a warrior's token, and Beal hated war with the fierceness of any healer. Also, I knew that with Beal's death we'd lost an important part of the plan. We always thought he'd return and help with Preparation. I hoped this might unlock something . . ."

His excuses dwindled into silence.

"Luxor, both of us know there is no easy pathway, only a series of difficult choices to lead us through the labyrinth. You made your decision. Having done so, it is woven into the fabric of the future."

Now, in the solitude of the night, Stanis admired the smooth heaviness of the metal. Two round metal strands, one of gold and one of bronze, entwined one another. At the center of the ring, two horse heads lifted toward a many-pointed sun. As the metal warmed in his hands, he sent his thoughts toward it. The breeze shifted to the southeast.

Stanis found himself seated on a broad plain . . .

The boy's long legs ate up the distance as he ran toward the huddled figure seated on a low rise. That morning, the wind shifted from northwest to southeast and the snow ended. The seated figure's brown hair blended into the fur-lined cloak wrapped around his slight shoulders. His head turned at the sound of the boy's feet crunching through the crust of light snow.

"Belwyn, where have you been? I've searched everywhere for you—the lodge, the tent, the shore—I even looked in the stables! But . . . what troubles you, Belwyn?"

Tyre's expression changed from indignation to concern as he noticed the harried look on Belwyn's usually placid face.

"The clear sky called to me. I was weary of the confines of my tent."

Belwyn's light tone belied his troubled thoughts. How could he tell the boy he was lonely? That Tyre's rapid approach to manhood saddened him? In a few weeks the winter solstice would mark his eighteenth year. As that day approached, Tyre was caught up in the preparations for his indoctrination into the warrior clan. The pain of this impending separation caught Belwyn unprepared, for this was a part of Tyre's life he could never share. Soon Tyre would take his rightful place by his father's side, riding out to fight in raids geared to hone his skills as a future chieftain of the tribe. Choosing to ignore Tyre's concern, Belwyn turned his attention to a glint of metal held in a tightly clenched fist.

"What do you have there?"

Belwyn watched with interest as the blue eyes suddenly shifted their focus to the western horizon. The tall body folded itself awkwardly onto the ground; lean legs crossed themselves as the long-fingered left hand unconsciously adjusted his hair to his back. Tyre had always been taller than his boyhood friends. In the last year he'd grown into a young giant, towering over everyone except Ariod. Gone were the days when Belwyn could see his face without looking up. Now, he regarded the profile beside him and saw the man Tyre would become, with a strongly defined brow marked by straight golden brows over deep-set, sandy-lashed eyes. His cheekbones were those of a true Lapith, high and prominent; his nose high-bridged with flaring nostrils. The mouth was wide and well shaped, able to relax into quick laughter or tighten in stubborn fury. That he was his father's son was evident nowhere in his coloring, but was unmistakable in the carriage of his chin and the set of his jaw. His voice, deeply resonant, was Ariod's as well.

"I came to bring you this."

Belwyn was handed a throat ring with the horse heads of Tyre's clan and the golden sun of Sturm. The craftsmanship was superb and bespoke the loving care of a goldsmith commissioned by Ariod at the last Harvest.

"It's beautiful. Thank you for showing it to me."

He held the amulet out, waiting for it to be reclaimed. Tyre's hands remained clasped in his lap. The tawny head moved away from him, the boy's expression masked behind a curtain of hair.

"I want you to keep it for me."

As bewildered as Belwyn might be, impatience never yielded fruit with Tyre. Content to wait, he fingered the cold metal and felt it warm to his touch.

"It's for my initiation. I need someone to help me in the rite. I wanted . . . I mean, I wondered . . . if you'd assist me."

Belwyn, too, considered the horizon.

"What would my responsibilities be?"

"The ritual is an ancient one. The first day I will purge myself. After that, only water may pass my lips until the ceremony is concluded. I may not speak or signal to anyone. I'll live in a small tent built especially for me. No one may enter except to bring me water, tend the fire, and dispose of my waste. The second day I'll be escorted to the lodge by the older men and taught the secret words and signs. On the third day, you'll help me with the difficult part."

Tyre cleared his throat, looking askance at his tutor before continuing.

"I'll use an axe to break the ice of the lake at the deepest part. The elders will tell me where to make the hole. Once I'm finished, they'll turn their backs while I disrobe. Then, with my skinning knife, you'll cut me . . ."

Belwyn drew in his breath.

"I'm a healer, Tyre. I can't . . ."

"Listen to me first before you refuse."

The boy's voice quavered and broke. Belwyn had no need of inner sight to sense his distress. Grudgingly, he nodded his head.

"They're small cuts, made with a skinning knife. An elder will show you the shape and you can practice on leather. Every warrior in the clan wears Sturm's sunburst on his chest. As soon as you're finished, I'll chant a prayer and jump into the ice pond. When I come out, you'll wrap a heavy fleece around me and the elders will approach. Once you place the amulet around my neck, it's over."

The boy's voice thickened during this recital. The last few sentences were barely louder than a whisper.

"You understand, the others will see nothing of the ritual: only you will . . . will see me and . . . touch me."

Knowing what this admission cost his pupil, Belwyn gave him time to recover.

"I understand the honor of being asked to assist you. I have two questions before I make my decision. Will you hear them?"

The mane of wind-blown hair nodded twice.

"I would think that such an important occasion in your life should be shared between you and your father. Wouldn't Ariod be a better, more proper choice?"

Tyre's reply revealed his trouble.

"Most youths are assisted by their father or their uncle. But I . . . my father and I are not . . . are not . . ."

For once, Belwyn didn't help him.

"No one has seen me unclothed since I was a child. I know you think us overly modest, but it is our way. I've considered this for several years, and the thought of . . . of my father . . ."

Tyre's mouth twisted and a wild look came into his eyes. As quickly as it arrived, it departed. Tyre was in control again.

"It's an old wound from my boyhood, but I cannot cure myself of it.

As Tyre spoke of his father, Belwyn sensed a door being opened, only to have Tyre slam it shut. What was the wound and how had Ariod inflicted it? Tyre's relations with his father were unfailingly respectful and polite, yet absent of warmth. This was the first indication that it resulted from an incident during childhood. Belwyn experienced a wave of discouragement. Would the boy never open himself to the light? Putting aside private frustrations, he concentrated instead on the down-turned face beside him.

"You lead me to my second question. I know of your modesty, and I ask for your honest answer. Will seeing and touching you affect our friendship?"

The boy's face, drawn with worry, relaxed into a smile.

"Of course not. Nothing can mar our friendship."

Belwyn's smile matched the glow on his pupil's face.

"Then I accept. I'll keep this for you until I clasp it around your neck."

They stood together for a moment without words. With anyone else, Belwyn would have felt the need to seal this promise with a touch to communicate what words cannot express. With Tyre, silence would have to suffice.

Images of the frozen lake whirled and faded as Stanis sensed the approach of Carmanor and Chloe on horseback. The slave camp lay nearby, yet far enough away for Stanis' presence to go unnoticed.

The reason for his isolation from the others was his unwillingness to share with them the degree of Tyre's spiritual damage. The Fifteenth Mother's plan to bring Tyre to Pelion hinged on Tyre's abandonment by his tutor Belwyn, the removal of his fellow warriors, and with their loss, an end to his identity as privileged son and sole heir of a powerful tribal chieftain. Rhacius, Phylas, and Chloe were links in a chain forged to prepare Tyre for the regimen of the Maze. Unfortunately, the death of his tutor wounded Tyre far more deeply than Belwyn's planned departure for other lands. Touching Tyre's mind in the market place was like probing a fresh wound. From his own experiences in the Agavean slave market, Stanis knew Tyre would be terrified. Even so, he was unprepared for Tyre's raw, inconsolable grief as he mourned the death of Belwyn with every breath. As Stanis wiped his hands at the termination of the examination, he resolved to grant Tyre a much-needed respite. Stanis would allow him breathing space during the course of this twenty-day journey, putting his trust in Chloe's songs and Phylas' friendship.

Carmanor's thoughts, centered on Lukash's sleeping form, formed a silent question.

"He sleeps deeply, Commander, and will sense nothing."

Chloe arranged a blanket on the ground beside him and nestled close, seeking warmth after the cold ride.

"So, you've touched him at last, Chloe. Your impressions?"

Chloe's inner voice retained the luster of her spoken word.

"He's so strong, that one! And so unforgiving! He blames himself for Beal's death and the enslavement of his people. To punish himself, he chooses not to eat. I sang him a healing song as I dressed his wounds."

"But you are not content?"

"He needs more than my simple gifts."

Stanis nodded slowly, his fingers continuing their quiet contemplation of the bronze and gold necklace.

"And so we take him to the source of his healing."

Carmanor crouched near the fire, the flat planes of his face contracted into a crooked frown.

"Rhacius did his duty with the lad. I have merely to glance at him and he turns to stone. I admit I questioned the necessity of Phylas' presence at first. I thought the Fifteenth Mother was being over careful. Now, I'm not so sure."

"What do you sense, Commander?"

The adepts in the Legion were not trained in the Greater Mysteries, yet Carmanor's career had been marked by a series of shrewd, some would say uncanny, guesses.

"I know you chose this group of ernani yourself, but I sense danger in the group. I'm glad Phylas is there . . ."

A contortion racked Stanis' mind, his giant body vibrating with the force of unbidden thoughts. His tongueless mouth opened, his lips framed soundless words, while Carmanor and Chloe listened to an inner voice springing from a distant place within him.

"Danger, discord, deep fears, old hatreds, strife, and pain—pain that begs for destruction."

The images faded, the reverberations echoing hollowly in their linked minds. Carmanor recovered first.

"And Phylas will somehow prevent this?"

Stanis' perceptions were blurred now, incomplete.

"Cause, prevent, delay, or somehow restore balance, I cannot say. I sense only that he is necessary."

Feeling Chloe shiver against his robes, Stanis guessed it was not the result of the cold.

". . . city called Pelion. Three or four more days at the most. Anything will be better than this foul rain. I'm wet to the skin."

An answering growl was the sole reaction Dino received from his fellow slaves and he was understandably angry. These guards were the most closed-mouthed he'd ever known. He'd taken his life in his hands to eavesdrop on Carmanor's briefing. The least this ungrateful rabble could do was thank him for handing them the information everyone had worried over since leaving Agave. Muttering curses under his breath, Dino settled down under his soggy blanket, trying to avoid a muddy place. Receiving a jab in his ribs from his neighbor, he sighed, resigned himself to sitting in the puddle and concentrated on remembering the last time he was dry.

Five days of steady rainfall made for short tempers. This afternoon's downpour found them sinking to their ankles in mud so deep that Carmanor, whom they'd come to detest for his unfailingly bad disposition, grudgingly called a halt in mid-afternoon. After a brief conference with his men, he'd ordered them into a close huddle under a stand of leafless birch that offered precious little protection from the damp chill that set their teeth chattering and their joints aching. The only one who failed to complain was the long-hair in the strange leather clothes. In truth, Dino had never heard him utter a word. Still, he'd been a slave long enough to know some things were best left alone.

The reaction he'd been longing for finally arrived.

"Pelion, you say? I've heard of Pelion."

Lowered heads lifted as interest stirred. The speaker was a wiry fellow, his looks indistinguishable from the others since they were all filthy, shaggy-headed and, with the exception of the long-hair, bearded. Eris was his name, Dino remembered.

"Pelion. It's far to the south, I've heard, a huge fortress built on an outcropping of rock. A rich city with a black banner." Eris frowned, scratching his beard as if trying to remember something, although to be fair, thought Dino, it might have had nothing to do with remembering and everything to do with lice. "So, Pelion, you say? Well, friends, now I understand why the black one was so careful in his selection."

A chorus of rueful sighs and filthy oaths affirmed his statement. Examination and selection by the black one was not a pleasant memory.

"Why do you say that, slave?"

Dino knew this speaker as well. Phylas, by name, and a hard man to kill if you considered the whip-scars marking his back. Dino avoided him at every chance. He'd stayed alive this long only because he was a careful man.

"Because, slave," Eris' sneer was purposefully insulting, "they need men in order to breed. Their women are insatiable and their men are eunuchs."

"If that's so, why would anyone choose you?"

The men chuckled as Phylas' retort drew blood. Eris' eyes narrowed into glittering slits, leering at the long-haired youth by Phylas' side.

"Better ask why they want you and your horse boy. Don't you think I've guessed why he doesn't have a beard? No doubt he lacks the equipment those women want so badly."

Phylas' face lost its humorous gleam. He'd tried not to be obvious about keeping an eye on Tyre. Given the forced intimacy of their living conditions, it was easy to see why others might share Eris' opinion. Even so, this had to be dealt with or there'd be hell to pay for the next few nights. Deciding his course, he addressed Eris with unadulterated malice. Not for nothing had he misspent his youth as a thief and a murderer.

"Watch your tongue," Phylas hissed, "or I'll rip it out by the root!"

"Why so testy?" Eris purred. "Does the truth hurt?"

Eris' hand reached out to grab his shoulder. Phylas shook it off, intent on making Eris back down, edging toward him in the mud, the others giving way before him, clearing a path between the feuding pair who swore and spat at one another under their breaths, careful that the guards not hear them over the steady patter of the rain.

What happened next defied explanation. One moment Phylas was face to face with Eris, the next he was flat on his back, the slaves' chain wrapped around his throat. Taken off-guard, Phylas' usually quick reflexes failed him to the point that he couldn't get his hand between the chain and his neck. Pandemonium erupted around him as he struggled for breath, until, as a fog of nothingness threatened to engulf him, he heard a direful voice:

"Release him!"

The chain's pressure on Phylas' throat eased and he took a much-needed gasp of air. His eyes flew open to see Tyre towering over Eris, his long-fingered hands wrapped around the shorter man's throat in a grip promising strangulation. As Phylas began to breathe regularly again, he realized that Eris, eyes bulging from their sockets, had dropped the chain. Even so, Tyre gave no indication of loosening his grip. Phylas had seen men kill before, and Tyre's face promised death. A voice ripped across his consciousness.

"This accomplishes nothing. Let him go!"

Carmanor stood beside Tyre, no weapon in sight, his attention fastened on Tyre's hands as if, Phylas thought, he could break that iron grip with his eyes alone. Gradually, the killing frenzy left Tyre's face. Long after his hands relaxed their grip they lingered, trembling in the air as Eris crumpled silently to the ground. For a moment there were but two sounds in the universe, Eris' labored breathing and rain dripping from the branches of the birch trees.

"Remus, fetch the healer," Carmanor ordered crisply, increasing his volume as he turned his attention to the prisoners huddled at his feet. "Spread out the full length of your chains! No talking, not a sound, or I'll know the reason why!"

As Carmanor turned to go, Eris' hoarse complaint stopped him in his tracks.

"He nearly killed me and you do nothing! Are you after the horse boy too?"

"My job is to deliver the merchandise intact," Carmanor replied frostily. "Punishment will be meted out in Pelion. Another word from you and you'll be lost due to an unfortunate accident, even if it means a dock in my pay."

Eris held his tongue, his features contorted in hatred. The slaves spread out, grumbling at the loss of the protecting shelter of the trees. Phylas rubbed his bruised neck. Searching for Tyre, he spotted him sitting with his back to the others, his head bowed, not bothering to cover himself from the downpour.

I am the greatest fool who ever walked the earth, thought Phylas to himself. Take care of the long-hair? What had the Fifteenth Mother been thinking?

With a grunt of pure self-loathing, Phylas squatted in the mud.

A blanket dropped over Tyre's head and shoulders. A silvery voice began its song. Tyre stopped its melody.

"I'm unhurt, woman. Spend your time tending those who are."

He listened to the moist squelch of her retreating footsteps.

Try as he might, Tyre couldn't stop trembling. The man who attacked Phylas brought back all the dread, all the fears that had retreated during the long march. He'd wanted to kill him for bringing back everything that hurt. Drawing a shaky breath, he tried to calm himself. Belwyn taught him to face his fear and put a name to it. Today Tyre learned its name.

Pelion.

Chapter 7

The Mother of All

SHE-WHO-WAS-VENA climbed the hundred steps to emerge from the covered staircase onto the open ramparts of the northernmost tower. Lifting her eyes to survey the sky, she greeted the dawn as she did every day. "For today," she reminded herself, "is no different from any other day," although, in her heart of hearts, she knew that to be a lie.

Harbingers of dawn appeared in the east, streaks of amethyst splashed against the black vault of night. Stars blinked and dimmed, retreating to western skies where the moon, a pale crescent, grew paler still. In that breathless moment when the domination of the heavens hangs in the balance, the moon not yet vanquished and the sun not yet victorious; She-Who-Was-Vena heard the tremulous notes of a waking skylark. As the last trill faded, the bird took flight, winging north, its black body silhouetted against lavender skies.

She-Who-Was-Vena shrugged deeper into her cloak, feeling in this first morning breeze the end of summer. From the hem of her cloak to the hood covering her hair, all of her clothing was made of silk imported from the eastern shore, dyed and re-dyed to take on the hues of midnight, a deep true black like the luster of obsidian or the petals of a rare black tulip.

This particular morning the cheerlessness of her garb struck her hard, for she had worn gayer raiment in her time. Tall and slender, light of foot and quick with a word or a jest, she had played many roles, each with its own rewards, until an unseen hand beckoned, demanding that she change her way of life and even her name. In a previous life she had been Vena—student, apprentice in the House of Healing, mate to Beal—until, over the course of their lives together they rose in rank to become High Healers and Masters of their guild. Now she was known simply as Mother, the fifteenth of that line since the founding of the city some five hundred years ago. There is irony here, she thought, imagining herself standing penniless and alone in front of the northern gates, a thin, bedraggled girl-child emerging from the wilderness to beg admittance to a city the likes of which she had never known. Now she ruled that same city, leading it toward enlightenment or oblivion.

Shivering into the cloak, she turned her back on the dawn to contemplate the fortress that functioned as her prison and her home. Prison was perhaps unfair, yet since her original entry through the northern gates, she could count the times she had left the city on the fingers of one hand. Even this salutation to the dawn was only a brief respite from duties pressing on her.

"Calm yourself, Vena," she thought, using the old name, the one that must remain unspoken.

A rooster's crow broke Vena's reverie. The city below her stretched, yawned, and began to wake. Smoke from newly kindled fires rose from thick-set stone buildings housing the bakery and the forge. The northern gate swung wide as the flocks and herds were led out to graze on pastures beckoning with grass retaining the green of an especially fertile summer.

It was not always so. Years of deprivation and sickness, when the south wind brought with it a bone-eating disease no healer could cure, threatened all who lived within city walls. Those who survived opened their eyes to find a depleted population surviving on starvation rations. A slow healing followed. With crops replanted and herds restocked, the city clung closer to life, building deeper cisterns, larger granaries, and thicker walls.

Even if the coming winter was especially hard, the orchards and fields had yielded unheard of measures of fruits and grains, all of them dried and stored against threat of disease or hunger. Safe for this winter and the next, she thought. Yet for how much longer can our existence be assured? Since the founding of the city, its citizens protected their fortress, keeping out the plague-ridden, the slavers and marauders; striving always to discover the knowledge of how and why they came to be here, for still, at the core of their rituals, their rites, and most, especially, their books (for they were people of the book, now and always) lived the knowledge that their ancestors were not native to this world.

This single strand of memory, hoarded by those who came before, handed down to those who came after, fueled a constant search for meaning, for some better way of life, a higher plane of existence, the essence of which had been lost in the dark ages, long before they found this rocky redoubt in a verdant valley and began to build. A yearning like an itch that cannot be scratched lived on in Vena as it had in her fourteen forbearers. No answers existed; only questions, and, from time to time, an all-too-brief moment of clarity that struck with the force of prophecy.

The lines in her careworn face deepened as she considered the tiny gains they had made since founding the city. Lifespan had increased to the point that many (she among them) lived past their fiftieth year, yet she read in the volumes housed in the Greater Library tales of women and men doubling that count and more. The birthrate remained low, the result of a nagging infertility not even the most gifted healers could explain. Yet these problems paled in the presence of what she saw as the greatest danger to her adopted people and the world as she wished it to be.

Troubled, she turned toward the north again, seeking out the Maze, the Place of Preparation. If she squinted (for her eyesight was not what it used to be) she could make out its familiar outlines near the farthest extremities of the northern walls. Set off from the rest of the city, surrounded by stone walls of triple-deep layers, decked with turrets housing guards and watchers, the Maze beckoned to her with the promise of something remarkable beyond belief.

This is my child, she thought, comforted by its homely forthrightness, for it was aptly named, the twisting labyrinths within its tile-roofed buildings designed as a self-sufficient world within the vastness of the city. Although her failing eyesight could not reveal the details of its plan, her inner eyes swept over the arena, the training grounds, the kitchens, baths, and living quarters. Towering above the Maze's low-slung buildings, the high-roofed Sanctum rose like the spray of a fountain that falls limply, elegantly, into a placid pool.

Begun in the reign of the Thirteenth Mother, the construction of the Maze made physical and financial demands on every citizen of the city. Vena's immediate predecessor, the Fourteenth Mother, lived to see the completion of the structure and began plans for the introduction of life into its twisted corridors and serpentine passageways. As High Healer and so a member of the Council at the time of the plan's inception, Vena remembered her predecessor's keen regard as they worked late into the night.

Vena felt a strong bond to the Fourteenth Mother, perhaps because like herself, She-Who-Was-Ilena rose from the ranks of the healers; perhaps because Ilena was the closest thing to a real mother Vena had ever known. High above the city streets, in the Fourteenth Mother's private apartments, they developed a plan for their shared dream, a plan entailing dangers and risks they could only imagine, yet must somehow prepare for, lest their tiny hold on civilization eventually wither like the desolate landscapes evident from the watchtowers on the gateless southern wall.

Piles of papers and scrolls littered the table where they worked, Vena revising the Legislation for Preparation from notes taken in the last Council meeting.

"Vena . . .?"

The sound of her mentor's voice, hoarse and low, her raspy breath a harsh reminder of her advanced age and growing infirmity, caused Vena to lower her quill.

Moving closer to the old woman, Vena ventured a light touch on her arm. The voice she so often heard raised in laughter and banter was often silent now, as if the elder woman rationed her strength, harboring her reserves for the work that remained.

"Those who enter Preparation must be strong in body and mind. To be successful, they must be changed, yet retain their strength. That is the crux, the double-edge to this whole notion. We must woo the strong with strength, yet neither of us must break. To bend, Vena, to bend without breaking, will be your greatest trial."

Content though she was in her work as High Healer, Vena heard in the Fourteenth Mother's advice an intensity of purpose that brought her up short. There was no greater mystery than the selection of the Mother of Pelion. Yet, She-Who-Was-Ilena's implication was clear. Putting embarrassment aside, Vena replied, "My trial, Mother? What are you saying?"

She-Who-Was-Ilena regarded her closely, her pale face in marked contrast to the black garments that seemed to absorb the dim light of the tallow candles surrounding them. With a rueful smile, she continued speaking in the silent voice heard only by their linked minds.

"I would not hurt your feelings, for no one has embraced our way of life with more diligence or duty than you. Yet you are not native born, as all wearers of the black robes have been since the founding of the city. For many, such a choice might be unthinkable, but I, I see the fitness of it. As we turn to the outside world, as we seek to bring others into our fold, you will be invaluable since you have lived life beyond these walls."

"Long ago, Mother."

"Even so, Vena, even so. To be an outsider is to see with different eyes."

Vena curbed her impatience, for no one argues with a woman wearing black. She-Who-Was-Ilena continued, speaking aloud this time, as if what she said deserved the testimony of the spoken word.

"It is not an easy life. You will be doubly alone, for I sense the strength of your bond with Beal. When the time comes, you must go forward, always forward, no matter the price you must pay."

Another onslaught of the chilling wind sank into Vena's bones. Her transition to Fifteenth Mother was as agonizing as She-Who-Was-Ilena predicted. Yet she left her post at the House of Healing, accepting a lonely existence over a community of friends and colleagues, and worst of all, put aside Beal, the mate of her heart, to live forever on memories of love. Alone, but undaunted, from the first day of her reign she began her efforts to legislate the Maze's organization and develop its population of two hundred souls. Eighteen years later, she wondered if the Maze would spell the destruction or the continuation of her city.

The sun, having risen above the horizon, began its gradual ascent, the battlements ablaze with light reflected off bits of quartz buried in its stones. Out of the corner of her eye Vena noticed a moving shadow, started, and then relaxed as she recognized Stanis.

He must have returned to the city last night, passing through the northern gate as the evening trumpet sounded. He went to my rooms at first light, she thought, then tracked me here. He gestured rapidly, a blaze of concern on his face as he noted her tiredness.

She smiled briefly as she formed a response in her mind.

"I'm not cold, just lost in thought. Please, Stanis, a few minutes more?"

Nodding, then turning away so as to allow Vena the peaceful isolation she craved, Stanis' profile caught the bright rays of morning light. His dark skin lit by golden sunlight, he became a bronze statue of untold strength and dignity. Marking his transformation, she remembered her first journey out of the keep, the first Journey of Preparation.

So many years ago it was, yet the memories living inside her mind remained vivid, intractable. Without effort, she called them to the forefront of her consciousness, finding herself eighteen years younger, a mature woman of forty who was more frightened than she thought possible. Having lived in a hermetically sealed world based on law and discipline, it was time to venture back into a world of chaos and ruin. To people the Maze was her goal—to bring within its thrice-thick walls and empty rooms the first group to walk the Path of Preparation.

Their destination was the western city of Agave, a twenty-day journey over scrublands and desert. When the Council decided that secrecy was to be given the highest priority, the party of fifteen studied a dialect spoken in one of the eastern provinces. Her entourage consisted of nine members of the Legion along with the commandant, Luxor; several attendants skilled in cooking and foraging; and a pair of attuned healing partners, Chloe and Maenon. Disguised as a group of merchants, they trained hard before their departure, checking and re-checking supplies and security measures, as well as preparing themselves to endure severe physical hardship. Sadly, it was not physical discomforts that nearly overcame them, but the pain of emotional encounters.

Once the group was assembled and trained, the Council proceeded to challenge the idea of so precious a personage as the Fifteenth Mother being physically present during the search, suggesting politely that she use her formidable mental powers to monitor the progress of the mission from afar. For the first time since taking office, Vena used her veto to overrule her advisors.

What they did not know, and what Vena could barely admit to herself, was that she was not exactly sure how selection should be made. She knew the requisites by heart, having drafted them with She-Who-Was-Ilena in that tower room so many years ago: men between twenty and forty, physically healthy, emotionally unconnected with others, and thus, in the world beyond city walls, most likely slaves, orphans, or soldiers-of-fortune. Men without families, men without direction or prospects; in other words, as she had remarked to She-Who-Was-Ilena, those who were lost. In that instant, their name was born: "ernani," or, "the lost ones."

But how to find them? Their search stretched over three moons, nearly a hundred days of grinding effort as they journeyed in broken patterns through ancient forests, over scrublands bordering the desert, visiting every outcropping of human life, searching in villages, slave camps, and peasant yards. By the time they reached Agave, Vena had collected exactly eight ernani; eight, when she needed double or even triple that number.

They were a motley crew, from a gangly redhead whose bond they purchased from a surly sword-maker, to a charming thirty-year-old drunkard who, while inebriated, sold himself for a cask of homemade brew. Her dedication to the mission effectively stanched any qualms about the ethics of purchasing human beings. The physical improvement of those eight derelicts as they received good food and medical care over the course of the march convinced her they were being offered the chance of a far better existence than anything they would ever experience in the world outside city walls.

But nothing, not the dirt, the hunger, or the rampant disease and hopelessness of the world beyond city walls, prepared Vena for Agave. She faced the prospect of visiting that city with dread, a place whose very name was a curse, and for that reason exhausted every possibility before actually entering its sandstone walls. Agave was a word whispered to young children to threaten the consequences of misbehavior. Other towns and village fairs might occasionally host a traveling slave trader and his merchandise, but Agave's markets offered neither produce, cloth, pottery, livestock, nor any other ware. The markets of Agave sold human flesh.

Leaving the ernani they had already assembled outside the gates with a small guard and plentiful supplies, she made the first journey into the city of slaves accompanied by the healers and her strongest guards. Once inside the sandstone walls, they were quickly lost in a warren of rude shacks and hovels lining crooked streets littered with human and animal excrement. In the course of a single hour, Vena witnessed more disease and disfigurement than she would have believed possible—amputees, cleft palates, crippled survivors of the dread bone-eating sickness, the blind, the branded, the starving, all crowded into a raging stink of sheer hopelessness. And all of them begged to be bought.

The healers paled as they passed so many in need; the guards, already grim men, became grimmer. The entire party, including Vena, grew increasingly disoriented and emotionally unbalanced as they moved toward a rising drone of noise and confusion. The cobbled street led to a large square open to the sky, the din and stench of that awful marketplace causing Vena's gorge to rise in her throat. There, heralded by the screams of a populous gone mad, the noonday sun forming a nimbus around a black, close-cropped head, Vena caught her first glimpse of Stanis.

His wrists shackled and hung high above his head, he stood chained between two rough-cut timbers rising from a large wooden platform located in the center of the marketplace. As she lifted her eyes to his, his huge naked body tensed, the cords of his thick neck standing out in relief against sweat-drenched skin, his mouth open in an incoherent scream. The sound of the lash laying open his back was a briefly-recalled memory as she realized the blood covering his mouth and chin was the result of the raw stump at the back of his throat.

As his eyes flew open, glazed with tormented tears, Vena found herself imprisoned by his gaze, his agony reaching out to her until, unaware and unprepared, Vena found herself writhing under the lash, feeling the fire of open wounds, gagging on the taste of her own blood. In that instant, Vena felt everything the slave felt, his anguish passed from his senses to hers. Bludgeoned by his attack, still she heard his silent appeal for help:

"Someone, anyone, make this stop!"

Her years of training prevailed, and in a moment of slowed time, she slapped up a barricade to protect her mind from his, furious with herself for being so easily overwhelmed. Yet it was not her anger, but her curiosity, which spurred her to action. Never, in all the years of using her gifts, had she experienced such a mental assault. Not one to hesitate when faced with the extraordinary, Vena went to work, opening herself to the thoughts and emotions of the slave's tormentors.

Methodically, she noted the hysterical cry of the crowd, the gleam of enjoyment in the eyes of the man raising the whip for the next blow; the bored slouch of the auctioneer, lounging indolently against the booth directly below the platform. Coming out of her trance, she stepped forward to address the slave-dealer, who picked idly at his cuticles.

"What must I bid for the giant mute before you make him so sore he'll be of no use to me tonight?"

Eyes alight with greed, the auctioneer straightened, examining her as the second blow bit into the slave's flesh. Cutting off the distraction of the beating, Vena leveled her concentration on a leering face regarding her with unconcealed dislike. Laughing in her face, his mouth a hole of rotting teeth, he replied, "Well, old woman, what did you have in mind?"

Vena met his challenge with hands on hips; her bosom thrust forward, her mind sending him images of her mating with men in a myriad of erotic postures.

"Old? Why, my mother birthed me at five and thirty while my father died in her bed at twenty-three. The way I see it, there's nothing I'd like better than a man who can't answer back."

The sensual images she was sending him were replaced with those of wealth; fat cattle, ripe cheeses, barrels of beer. Just as suddenly, she supplied him with a vivid picture of the dark-skinned slave lying face-down on the wooden platform, his back scored so deeply that the white ribs showed through, a cloud of green flies gorging themselves on his lifeless flesh.

Frowning, eyes flickering with doubt and greed, he turned and shouted a curse to the wielder of the whip, ignoring the disappointed groans of the crowd. Out of her control in that moment of action, he turned back to her with a suspicious glare.

"Have you no interest in why he's being whipped?"

Five seasoned guards materialized at her side. *"Bless you, Luxor,"* she thought, and became even bolder, leaning closer to flirt with her inquisitor.

"As you see, I've little worry over bodily harm, but, yes, tell me, what did he do?"

Hesitating at the sight of five well-armed and cold-faced mercenaries, the auctioneer replied, "He nearly killed one of the men who held him down for the tongue-cutting."

"Ah, but since it's out, he won't be tempted to try again, will he? Besides, I'll keep him too busy to think about murder."

Sensing at that moment his capitulation, she drove a hard bargain anyway, despising him even as her mask rendered her as beguiling and as lusty a matron as he had ever met. The deal set and the coins exchanged, she turned to Chloe and Maenon.

"Why all this effort for someone who is mute?" Maenon asked.

Vena sent him a drilling thought.

"He called me! Called me without a tongue! Tend him, heal him, and don't question my judgment again!"

Maenon stood white-faced. Chloe retreated with her hand raised to ward off the mental blow. Turning on her heel, Vena felt their minds snap to attention, freed from the emotional jangle worrying at them (and at her) since entering Agave. Glancing up to the platform, she watched as Luxor's men retrieved the key to the shackles from the dealer and unchained the slave from the post. His size prevented them from carrying him, but two of the tallest men grasped him around his waist, supporting him down the stairs of the platform.

As he came nearer, she was surprised to find that he was conscious. Quickly, she entered his mind, shielding him from her own consciousness. Although pain blanketed his thoughts, other emotions emerged: shame at his nakedness, especially in front of the woman who had bought him, wonder at the gentle touch of the guards, and strongest of all, grief at the loss of his tongue.

Vena moved toward him, removing an apron she had tied around her waist that morning in the hope of adding the appearance of bulk to her tall, thin frame. Without uttering a word, she leaned forward and reached behind him to tie the apron around his hips, careful to avoid the welts on his back. He flinched, then subsided, and she communicated with him for the first time.

"How are you called?"

Blinking with shock, his mind provided her with the sound of a rich bass voice that would never again be heard by human ears.

"Stanis."

Agave remained a nightmare, but they weathered the first storm and buckled down with renewed vigor to the quest for ernani. Stanis' wounds healed, although he continued to mourn the loss of his tongue. Vena could communicate easily with him using inner speech, and in fact, found his ability equal to that of the most gifted adepts, but her experience as a healer told her he needed another way to communicate. The finger speech that was second nature to her now evolved on the long journey home, Luxor, Chloe, and Maenon becoming proficient as well. Luxor, a strategist to his boot soles, recognized the advantage of a silent language that did not demand psychic adeptness, and soon all the Legion officers could communicate in Stanis-speech.

Stanis proved the worth of his calling in ways Vena still regarded with wonder. With no knowledge of their world or their mission, he intuitively understood the type of men they sought, and after thirty years of experience as an ernani (Vena remembered the bitterness of his smile when she explained the meaning of the word) could lead them unfailingly to the places such men might be found. Their return to the fortress brought a novice class of twenty-four ernani. Upon reaching the northern gates and delivering their charges to the Maze, Stanis dedicated his gifts to the city, and from that day, became a Searcher of Souls, committing himself to the task of bringing ernani to the city.

Freed by Stanis as surely as she had freed him, Vena put aside her traveling clothes and began her work within the Maze.

For seventeen years Stanis wandered the inhabited areas of the known world, sometimes gone for days stretching into years, bringing Vena the ernani he selected from the flotsam and jetsam of a defeated populous. Recently she had recalled him, sending out her thoughts to the lonesome stretches of northern plains, western mountains, and eastern shores, sending him this simple message:

"Stanis, it is finished. Return."

He arrived a year ago. Silver hairs laced his tightly woven curls as he knelt before her. Sensitive to the formal nature of his greeting, she said quietly, "Your slave price is repaid a hundredfold. You need travel no longer."

Brilliant eyes regarded her solemnly as he reached into a pocket hidden in his voluminous, travel-stained cloak. Slowly, he stood; his immense frame unfolding to reveal a form unbent by time and hardship, his palm outstretched to her in offering. As she reached out to accept his gift, his mind leapt out at her, returning her to the slave market, complete with the sound of the lash and the smell of blood and filth. In her hands she clutched the remains of a linen apron, its ties ragged with age, its waistband dyed with the rust-colored stains of his blood.

Turning to face the stone hearth of the never-dying flame, she placed Stanis' offering on the grate. Side by side, they watched as the cloth burned itself into sacred ash . . . .

The banner snapped in the morning breeze, bringing Vena out of reverie, reminding her that this day brought her one more step toward a future imagined by the Ones-Who-Came-Before. Her message to Stanis was only partially complete: One part was finished; another part would begin today when a group of ernani purchased in Agave passed the northern gate.

The slender figure of a woman in black lifted her arms to embrace the fully lit sky.

Morning had risen on Pelion.

After the heat of the forge, the hallway in the Sanctum was cool, the stone benches a welcome change after days spent squatting in mud, the early morning sunlight blinding as it flooded in through the arches. Tiny flecks of trapped quartz, summoned to duty by the sun, sparkled gamely from their stone prison, turning the austerely regimented rows of arches into a cavern of alternating white light and mauve shadow.

Those same arches, an imposing line of them stretching the full length of this, the largest edifice in Pelion, gazed indifferently down on those who waited. Like so many things built of stone, they cared little for things composed of flesh and blood, judging them unsuitable to the task of maintaining the structural integrity of something that had stood for five hundred years and would stand for another millennium or two. Removed though they might be, they were not entirely without sympathy, having found, over the passage of centuries, a commonality with the mortals who sat on the benches lining the inner wall. Like the arches, the mortals waited; not so patiently, perhaps, for nothing is quite so patient as stone; nor so gracefully, since human beings possess a tendency to fidget. Even so, the men waited, as the stones had waited from time immemorial, in the genial hush of morning.

That hush was broken on occasion when pairs of booted feet strode, or dragged, or stomped, from the benches to the immense bronze doors. Through those doors each slave from Agave passed in order of the chains that once bound them. The chains were gone now, as were the iron shackles, replaced by manacles fashioned out of silvery, lightweight steel.

Tyre was examining his now, remembering the heady feeling of freedom the removal of the shackles gave him only hours before. The forge was enormous; people busily casting bronze and other metals, an entire section devoted to fashioning farm implements, a group of young apprentices polishing bowls and goblets to a smooth, pewter finish. A hearty, well-fed smith removed their shackles, sneering at their poor craftsmanship, beaming as the slaves expressed astonishment at the lightness of their new manacles. Tyre's astonishment extended to everything connected to this city called Pelion.

Changes in the countryside began two days before they reached their destination. The hilly scrub country through which they passed became more rolling until the entire landscape was dotted with fields and orchards. Even in this season of changing leaves and cooler nights, the richness of the land was obvious. Fallow fields had been plowed under to prepare them for spring planting, hay mounds dried lazily in the afternoon sun, and as they moved farther south, herds of sheep, goats, and cattle were evident off to the west.

Yesterday, in a moment arresting enough to rouse Tyre out of the monotony of the march, he spied a group of horses grazing in a field whose grass retained the green tinge of summer. They were a smaller, stockier breed than the long-limbed steeds of Lapith, better suited to hills and rough terrain than the broad, flat plains of the north. As the troop passed by, the lead stallion, a thick-maned roan with a small, delicate head, lifted his nose to catch their scent. Deciding there was ample cause for alarm, he called the others to him with an ear-piercing whinny. Wheeling in a large arc, they moved off toward the south, the stallion nipping stragglers as they disappeared over a hill.

Late in the afternoon, an hour or so before dusk, Tyre caught his first glimpse of Pelion, an enormous walled fortress rising skyward, dominating the countryside around it. Situated on a high escarpment of what looked to be solid rock, its turret-lined walls rose several hundred feet from the floor of the valley, its gray stone battlements gleaming pale orange in the rays of the setting sun. A massive wooden gate stood directly in their path. Even at this distance he could see a steady stream of people and carts entering the city through its northernmost portal. Just as Carmanor halted the troop to make camp, the clear, echoing call of a trumpet was answered by the boom of the heavy gates swinging shut.

They arrived at the gate the next day just after dawn. Carmanor, at the head of the line and mounted on his dun gelding, rode up to a guard post surrounded by a troop of men dressed identically in leather jerkins, baggy-legged breeches, and long woolen cloaks dyed a rich earthy brown. Their sole ornament was a bronze clasp at the neck of their cloaks; their weapons, short swords in scarred leather scabbards, hung from wide belts. The exchange between them began with a rapid exchange of salutes, each man's open palm resting briefly on his breast. A man stepped forward and held the reins as Carmanor dismounted.

"Greetings, Commander."

"I seek entry into the city with ernani bound for Preparation. We'll need escort to the Forge, then on to the Sanctum."

"You are expected, Commander. All has been prepared."

The rank split in the middle and the gate creaked open, pushed from within by men dressed in identical garb. At Carmanor's command, the chain moved forward and Tyre passed into Pelion.

Surprisingly, even at this early hour, the street revealed by the opening of the immense gates was crowded with people, many of whom stood in a cluster behind parallel rows of armed men. When the forward movement of the chain faltered, Tyre wondered if the other slaves were as awed as he was at the enormity of the city. On either side of him, as far as the eye could see, lay wide streets covered in square paving stones lined with timber and masonry buildings of two or more stories. Beyond the crowd hovering near the gates, more people moved along the streets in a busy rush of morning activity. At Carmanor's brusque command, the chain moved forward again.

Tyre began to notice faces in the crowd. Among them was a woman with hair like flames who studied each slave as he passed by, her cloak thrown back to reveal the contours of the child she carried inside her body. As the line of slaves approached, she backed away, a shadow seeming to pass over her face. Catching her bottom lip between her teeth, her attention moved quickly to Tyre, her frown deepening. Her reaction troubled Tyre, until, with a flash of insight, he determined why she was there. His initial assumption that she, and all the others, gathered at the gate before departing for their work in the fields was incorrect. The men on the chain were not just an object of curiosity, but the reason for their presence. The rows of solemn faces regarding the line of shuffling prisoners reflected a wealth of emotions: horror, pity, disgust, curiosity, and wide-eyed wonder, as if the slaves' arrival in their city promised something dangerous, something strangely threatening, yet, at the same time, something of value.

Now Tyre sat with the others in the hall of arches, waiting for he knew not what.

The great bronze doors of the hall swung open. A woman dressed in dove-grey robes, her hair braided in a coronet on the top of her head and covered in a sheer veil of the same silvery color, walked silently toward them, stopping several paces away from the bench and reaching out her hand to accept the key Carmanor offered her. The key held lightly in her hand, she turned a grave face toward the man sitting next to Tyre.

"How are you called, stranger to the city?"

In the softest voice Tyre had ever heard emerge from this loud, bawdy man, he answered: "Phylas."

"Come then, Phylas."

Without waiting to see if he followed her, she moved back down the corridor toward the open doors.

Phylas stood and cleared his throat.

"I never thanked you for my life, Tyre. I thank you now."

Phylas made as if to go, stopping at the last moment to speak without looking back, his attention focused on a point beyond the bronze doors.

"If I don't see you again, long-hair, I wish you well."

Phylas marched stolidly along the arched hallway, the bronze doors shut with a metallic ring, and Tyre sat alone.

Since the day of his madness, Tyre rebuffed Phylas' efforts to revive their former friendship. Stubbornly, he forced his concentration inward, only allowing himself to notice his surroundings when it was necessary to eat, relieve himself and suffer the ministrations of the healer, who continued her nightly inspections. The man he almost killed continued to regard him with glares and swallowed curses; the other slaves left him strictly alone. Try as he might, he couldn't protect himself from the terror mounting with each swing of the chain and each step south. The passage through the northern gate broke through his self-induced trance, his first look at the Maze finally moving him beyond fear, beyond terror, into a state of dulled acceptance. Stone walls built three-layers deep, manned watch-towers thirty paces apart, armed guards at every gate, every door, and every hallway they passed—there was no possibility of escape. Whatever lay behind those bronze doors could no longer be avoided.

The grey-garbed woman appeared in front of him.

"How are you called, stranger to the city?"

Straightening himself in one fluid movement, Tyre gave the answer of his heritage, the only thing he possessed besides the clothes on his back.

"Tyre, of the clan of the Running Horse, of the tribe of Ariod, of the people of Lapith."

"Come then, Tyre."

The woman glided over the threshold. Attendants swung the doors shut behind them. The room they entered was vast, an occasional column serving as a reminder that this was, indeed, an interior space. High windows near the vaulted ceiling let in shafts of dust-filled light. The stone floor echoed with the sound of Tyre's sandals as the woman led him toward a stone pedestal rising in cylindrical perfection several feet above the floor. Curved steps led up its sides, the railings polished to a high sheen of burnished bronze. Facing the platform rose a series of steps leading up to a rectangular block of the same white stone. No decorations or carvings marred the simple lines of the stonework. In the middle of all that whiteness burned a scarlet flame. Several objects stood on a simple stone table on the same level as the altar. A goblet of gold, one of silver, a marble bowl, and a pearl-handled knife were arranged in a square, each one equidistant from the other.

The woman led him up the circular stairs and onto the platform. Now he stood directly on the level of the table and the altar, a few feet separating him from the quietly burning fire.

The woman turned to address him.

"You will disrobe."

Tyre regarded her steadily.

"I will not."

Her eyes never wavered in their regard.

"This is a sacred place. No harm will come to you here."

"It is not the way of my people."

"You must learn our ways. If you will not do this of your own free will, it will be done for you."

Their eyes locked.

Without any apparent signal, attendants appeared on the platform beside him. Tyre offered no resistance as they raised his arms above his head, attaching the manacles to two hooks mounted into the stone pillars on either side of him. He saw the gleam of metal and heard the rip of leather as they efficiently cut away his garments. His feet were lifted and the sandals removed. As quickly as they had come, the attendants vanished, taking with them every fragment of his clothing. The woman's voice came from behind him as she moved down the stairs.

"You will be alone for awhile."

Tyre closed his eyes. The air was cool on his naked flesh; the silence of the place enveloped him. His heartbeat slowed as he willed himself to relax. In time, he passed into a kind of trance and his thoughts drifted into dreams of the past . . . .

He stood naked and vulnerable on the ice of the frozen lake. Belwyn's eyes never left his face, their warmth helping him forget his nervousness and the bitter cold. With the dexterity that marked his work with herbs and potions, Belwyn made four interlocking cuts, carving Sturm's eight-pointed sun into Tyre's chest, his touch so deft the pain didn't begin until after the knife completed its work. He experienced again the icy shock of the water and the comforting folds of the sheepskin being wrapped around him. The rest of the ritual was a blur—the clasp of the amulet around his throat, the congratulations of the elders, and a brief nod from his father. Belwyn hurried him into his tent, refusing to leave him alone. The stubborn set of his jaw announced his determination to minister to his pupil, and Tyre was finally grateful for the steady rubdown of soft cloths that left his shivering flesh warm and rosy. Not until he was completely dry and dressed in his new warrior finery did Belwyn leave him . . . .

A muted bell sounded from somewhere behind the stone altar, jarring Tyre back to the present. A dark figure moved into view. As it approached the altar, it seemed to Tyre that the flames leapt higher. Raising its hands, the figure rubbed its palms together over the flames as if to cleanse them. As it moved toward the table, the extreme contrast of black fabric moving across a field of white made it seem to float.

Dismissing superstition, Tyre concentrated on the triangular shape of the being's face, a face lined with age, the cheeks a hollow indentation underneath jutting cheekbones, the skin beneath the jaw sagging into folds paler than parchment. His wonder at the age of this face, far older than anyone Tyre had ever known, vanished the moment he chanced to look into the being's eyes. Grey as the winter skies above Lapith, clearer than a mirrored lake, luminous and liquid, they seemed not to blink.

Only when the figure began to speak did Tyre realize a woman was addressing him. He lost the sense of her first few words in the shock of that discovery—expecting to meet the black man, he was unprepared to meet a woman. The husky rasp of her words continued without pause.

"The Maze is the Place of Preparation, and for that Preparation you have been chosen. Today all things begin anew. Naked you came into the world; naked you begin your life with us. By what name do you wish to be known in this, your new existence?"

Even without grasping the underlying meaning of everything being said, Tyre sensed that a ritual was being acted out. The woman spoke formally, her words muted but compelling. A response was called for.

"I remain Tyre."

Ignoring his hostility, she continued: "All who enter the Maze must be free of blemish. You have been examined by a Searcher of Souls. I must confirm your acceptance."

With that, the old woman moved down the steps of the altar and mounted the circular stair. As her head appeared over the railing, Tyre realized, with a blush that began at his toes and rose to his hairline, that she was examining his naked body with intense scrutiny. She moved up the curved staircase unhurriedly, taking in his lower body on all sides. Soon she reached the height of his waist, and finally stepping onto the platform, stood directly in front of him, her eyes fixed on the sunburst carved into his flesh. Her eyes flickered for a moment, like a ripple over his father's lake, and she was moving again, this time behind him to continue her inspection. Refusing to give in to panic, he gritted his teeth in an attempt to maintain what dignity he could. If this woman could look on him without embarrassment, he could meet her glance without shame. She ended her journey with her eyes lifted to his face. Surprisingly tall for a woman, she seemed to drink in his features, memorizing them for some future reference. He blinked and she was gone.

She spoke from the altar now, her veined hands with their ridged nails caressing each of the objects arrayed on the table's surface.

"These gifts are given to all who would live in the city of Pelion. First, the water of life."

Raising the silver chalice over the flame, she walked to the edge of the steps, standing mere inches from Tyre. After dipping her fingers into the goblet, she sprinkled his head and shoulders, the drops sparkling on his bare skin like sun-struck dew.

Returning to the table, she chose next the golden chalice and repeated the ritual of passing it over the flame.

"Second, wine of the grape, the source of ecstasy and inspiration."

She raised the goblet to his lips, and, unthinkingly, he drank.

The marble bowl was lifted to the flames. Tyre caught the fragrance of a spice unknown to him, a heady scent, richly aromatic in the thick, dust-filled air.

"Third, the sacred oil. To the head it brings depth of thought. To the heart it brings strength of purpose. To the sex it brings hope of creation rekindled."

An oily substance anointed his forehead, his chest, and his loins. So involved was he in listening to the marked cadences of her speech, in watching the graceful surety of each gesture, he didn't balk at being touched. Afraid that he was being placed under some kind of spell, fighting against its power to transform him into something he was not, he shut his eyes, shaking his head to clear away foreign sights and smells.

"These gifts are given to those born in the city and all who pass through the northern gate. For those who enter the Maze, we ask that your gifts be returned in honor of the Makers. That accomplished, you may leave Preparation."

At the mention of departure, his mind began functioning again, putting together the pieces of the puzzle.

"So these Makers are some kind of . . ." he hesitated, searching for the correct term in the southern tongue, realizing that Belwyn had never taught him this particular word.

"You search in vain," the old woman said, "for a word that does not exist in our vocabulary. We know the meaning of 'god'," she pronounced the word in Lapithian, "having learned it from other peoples, but we resist its use. Here, we celebrate the Makers, who brought us to a world of their choosing. Some call them Sowers; some the Old Ones."

Having fancied himself something of an expert in the southern language, it came as a shock to Tyre to discover how poorly he grasped its subtleties. Backtracking over the previous information the old woman offered, he wondered if he had heard aright.

"These Makers are female?"

The old woman frowned again, her knitted brows revealing the depth of her concentration.

"Female in the sense that they create, yes. Female in the sense of being women, no. Certainly no more than the soil from which seedlings sprout is considered female."

If he hadn't been stark naked, or in chains, or plagued by a growing sense of confusion, Tyre might have laughed aloud. It wasn't enough that he'd been captured, enslaved, and purchased by a lascivious black man. Now he had to endure the ravings of a madwoman.

"I'll serve no Maker, Un-Maker, or what you will."

"Who speaks of serving?" she asked with a puzzled air. "I spoke of gifts. Service is for those who wish to be of service. Your task is this: to complete the circle of giving. By doing so, you enter the Realm of the Gift."

Here he stood, a slave with no possessions and little hope of procuring them, and this woman demanded a gift.

"I possess nothing of value."

A faint smile appeared on the old woman's lips.

"Of what use are riches to the Makers? A man's gifts are three: his beauty given with the hair of his head; his strength given with the blood of his veins; his fertility given with the seed of his sex."

Tyre's gaze fixed on the pearl-handled knife left untouched on the table. This was the truth of Preparation. He was to be shorn, bled, and emasculated. A deep surge of anger displaced all other feelings, a sudden wave of protest at the cruelty of this god caused his backbone to stiffen. If this was the price of freedom, he would begin now. His voice rang out in the hushed chamber, a warrior's cry, the Lapithian call to battle.

"I have a gift for these Makers of yours. I give them my hair."

Half-hoping to astonish the old woman, he was disappointed. Nodding her assent, she picked up the knife, passed the blade through the flames, and ascended the staircase once more. Halting in front of him, she looked deep into his eyes.

"You give this gift of your own free will?"

Without bothering to reply, Tyre inclined his head to the knife. The razor-sharp blade cut smoothly through the tangled locks, cutting steadily from shoulders to back, the loosened hanks falling in whispers on the stone floor. After the last length was cut, she knelt, sweeping the burnished pile into a great mound, and lifted it into the cradle of her arms.

Raising the golden mass above the flames, she cried out in a loud voice:

"Tyre gives his first gift!"

As the smell of burning hair replaced the heady scent of the oil, Tyre remembered frowning up at a stranger's head of short, dark curls.

"Only slaves and tutors have short hair."

Bitterness brought a burning wetness to the back of his eyes. At last, he and Belwyn were equals.

Tyre paced frantically inside the cell. They lengthened his chains before shoving him inside, the guard called Grasos unlocking his right wrist to attach the manacle to the frame of a bed drawn to the middle of the room and bolted to the floor. With a few words, this dull-eyed monster of a man (the only person other than his father Tyre had ever been forced to look up to) indicated a tin bucket for waste, a fireplace with kindling, a tinder box, and a sliding grate under the door through which food and water could be passed. When Grasos left, the sound of a bolt slamming shut punctuated the claustrophobia that had Tyre teetering on the edge of panic.

The chain allowed exactly four paces before he was forced to reverse direction. The ceiling was low, with iron-barred windows running the length of the cell on the wall opposite the door. He could see neither moon nor stars, nor catch the slightest whiff of a breeze from his position near the fireplace. He was caged, buried in a tiny room inside a labyrinth of passageways that seemed to have no end, only more locked doors.

He had been shoved and pushed from room to room since he left the Sanctum. In one room he was weighed and measured, the hated hands turning him this way and that, oblivious to his shame and discomfort. Another room contained a healer who examined him thoroughly, paying special attention to the back of his skull, his wrists and ankles, and the skin peeling from the blisters caused by the long march. Shown to a tiled room with a row of buckets filled with warm water and a grate in the floor, he washed himself thoroughly, too grateful to be clean to mind the fact that the guard's eyes never stopped their observation of his every move. Yet another room held a barber who doused him for head-lice and evened the ends of his shorn locks. Since there was no mirror, Tyre could only speculate at to what his reflection might reveal. The barber offered to shave him, but like all Lapithians, Tyre had no facial hair and refused the offer.

The next room was larger and full of weapons and strange-looking equipment whose purpose eluded him. A burly man, stripped to the waist, examined him like a prospective horse-buyer before putting him through a series of exercises, asking him to jump over a barricade, run a short distance, pull a bow, throw a spear, climb a rope—an endless list of commands he obeyed to the best of his ability, although many of the things he was asked to do were awkward and confusing. When he did not hold the sword properly, the man swore at him, shaking his head in disgust. Several other weapons Tyre had no knowledge of, or even any name familiar to him.

Through all of this, he was naked. At first he was conscious of little else. Gradually the endless parade of rooms, guards, and the endless poking and prodding of his flesh, transformed his embarrassment to resentful resignation. He despaired of ever being able to cover himself again until the last door opened and he was issued a loincloth (and shown how to wrap its unfamiliar folds around him) and a pair of leather sandals.

Throughout this exhausting day of orders and reprimands, explanations and corrections, he never saw a single familiar face. Nor did he see the sky. But it was the cell that brought him to the brink of despair. In the thirty-four days since Lycus enslaved him, he had walked and slept in open places, his eyes free to roam the world around him. Tonight, his body and his vision in chains, he could find no comfort, no release from the frightening experience of total imprisonment.

At last his body revolted against the tumult in his mind. Hunger pains racked him as he shivered in the cold, dank room. The tinderbox provided a spark and soon a small fire blazed in the fireplace. He reached for the food shoved under the door several hours earlier, and ignoring the unfamiliar stool, sank to his haunches to wolf down the meat and vegetables, cold now and covered in solidified fat. The mug of tea was cold as well, the same bitter brew he drank so often on the march. Grabbing up a blanket from the bed, he wrapped it around his shoulders, huddling near the fire. As his flesh warmed, his eyes grew heavy, and lying down on the floor with his manacled wrist under his cheek, he escaped the cell in the only way left him.

Tyre slept.

In a high tower room lit by torches and tallow candles, the Fifteenth Mother of Pelion leaned back into her high-backed chair. Resting her head against its pillows, she passed a veined hand over her eyes and brow. Her adult life had been lived in anticipation of this day. Now that it was finished, she was weary unto death. She performed the ritual of Blessing for each ernani that morning, a task demanding total concentration. Searching out flaws and weaknesses, judging how and if they might be overcome, calming some men, challenging others, she was cursed by most and spat on by one who had to be held by attendants for the entire interview. Only her long years of experience ensured her outward placidity. There had been so many ernani since the Novice class, yet each was unique, proof of the endless variety of human beings. Smiling briefly, she remembered Phylas' blessing three years ago.

Recently released from the House of Healing, he was weak and thin as he stood before her. He listened carefully to everything, accepting the gifts without hesitation and with a growing sense of relief. When she told him of the gifts he must offer in turn, a grin split his face. After glancing down at his limp member, he announced:

"I'm not sure I'm up to it, but if you'd like to help me with that third one . . ."

Charmed by his bawdy confidence, she thought instantly of Nomia, a woman who came to her for a private counseling session.

Nomia appeared in her tower room one morning clad in the silks of an apprentice hetaera and therefore a member of one of the most selective guilds in Pelion. Made up of men and women who studied the art of joining, they served as practitioners and teachers of the craft of sexual union. As the counseling session began, the red-haired beauty's eyes filled with tears. Troubled by this lovely face so full of woe, Vena probed for details.

"Nomia, what brings such sadness to your heart?"

Blinking back her tears, Nomia confessed her trouble.

"I came early to my profession, the youngest apprentice ever selected for admission. I've excelled at my studies; my teachers predict a long and glorious career, one in which I might achieve the highest rank offered by our Guild. Even so, I've grown unhappy of late. I thought, perhaps, if you thought me worthy, I might enter Preparation."

Vena's interest quickened.

"What do you hope to find in Preparation that eludes you now?"

Nomia leaned forward in her chair.

"I've heard that the women who undergo Preparation experience a special sort of joining, one that goes beyond the body. This is what I yearn for. Still . . ." catching her lower lip between her teeth, she bit down hard, ". . . most women chosen are virgins or widows. Maybe an ernani would not want a hetaera."

"No false modesty, if you please," Vena replied sternly. "There remains one requirement of Preparation you haven't mentioned. Look deep within yourself and tell me if you are prepared to offer the third gift."

A vibrant smile was Nomia's answer.

The Fifteenth Mother was satisfied.

"You are accepted. I will call for you when I find someone worthy of your talents. Be restored to brightness."

Vena chuckled to herself as she remembered the first few weeks of Phylas' and Nomia's acquaintance. Forbidden entry into the cell from the evening trumpet to the morning bell, the guards reported nightly altercations with sounds of crockery and furniture crashing against walls, the din of raised shouts and curses echoing continually down the passageways.

Summoned one evening by a panting guard who informed her that she must open the cell—they had heard a blood-curdling scream, then silence. She hurried as quickly as her swollen joints would allow and unbolted the door, swinging it open to find Phylas lying in Nomia's arms, his eyes fixed with adoration on her lovely face while she kissed a shallow cut above his third rib. Looking up as Vena entered, he grinned, and said good-naturedly:

"You sent me a hell-cat, didn't you, Mother? It took me until tonight to learn that instead of trying to tame her, I should let her wield the whip."

As his horny hand reached up to stroke her flaming curls, Nomia inclined her head to cover his lips with hers.

The Fifteenth Mother closed the door.

A candle sputtered. Vena reached for a goblet of wine to wet her lips. Her hand shook with a small palsy she refused to acknowledge. Hearing a soft scratch at her door, she sensed Stanis waiting patiently, bearing a tray of bread, cheese, and fruit. When she greeted him mentally, he entered, set down the tray, and lowered himself into the leather chair that had long ago been molded to the shape of his body. Vena selected a ripe red plum.

"I'm too tired for finger speech, Stanis. Let me speak aloud, my friend, for tonight I feel every one of my years."

Startled by her rare admission of age and fatigue, Stanis felt the weariness and trouble hovering over her spirit. Respectfully, he waited for her to begin.

"He sleeps at last, only because Ladon drugged his tea. He paced for hours. I should have predicted the difficulty of adjustment from his life outside to the confines of the walls. Beal would have foreseen such a problem."

"You've sensed Beal's presence?"

She pondered his question as the sweet juice of the plum refreshed her.

"If you mean his active presence, as Maenon and Rhacius described it, then, no, I have not. But he's everywhere in Tyre. As soon as Nerissa left him alone after the disrobing, he went immediately to Beal. Even as I placed his offering on the sacred flame, he ached with the loss of his tutor. It is difficult, Stanis, to find the one I love . . . loved . . . in every corridor and passage of Tyre's mind. But I must bear it, and bear it I will."

Her thoughts stiffened her resolve and Stanis felt the immense strength of her will as she put aside her private grief. Gently, he placed the bronze and gold amulet on the wooden table before her. Its highly polished surface reflected the light of the candles.

"Beal placed it around Tyre's neck on his eighteenth birthday. There it stayed until Beal's passing. I read it a single time so that you might find its power untouched. As Luxor hoped, it reveals things that were hidden."

Stanis departed into the shadows, the door closing silently behind him.

Reclining into the soft comfort of the cushions, Vena cast her thoughts adrift.

A golden figure stood alone. Diagonal streaks of morning light split the darkness of the Sanctum interior, causing the bits of dust in the air to surround his naked body with a hazy glow of radiance. He stood with his tutor on a frozen lake, Beal's love, like the sheepskin robe, protecting him from the cold. When he registered her arrival, she sensed the subtle shifts of his inner concentration—his confusion as to her identity, his unbroken pride in his name, his revulsion at the idea of foreign gods.

As she moved up the stairs, she saw him as a man. The deep tan of his face, throat, and forearms contrasted with pale skin never touched by the sun. Clean-limbed, wide-shouldered, he was thin, yet not so thin that she could not see the promise of power in shoulders, arms, and chest. His sex nestled in golden curls like those under his uplifted arms, the smooth surface of his chest unmarked save for a scar located above his heart. His back revealed every bone of his ribs and spine, the curved buttocks tightening as he felt her gaze.

Wide-spaced blue eyes under straight brows appeared beneath a tangled mass of hair streaked white from the sun. Unlike the others, who dropped their eyes to escape the intensity of her gaze, he withstood her searching glance with quiet defiance.

The ritual of blessing went smoothly, the beauty of the words and gestures evoking his wonder, curiosity, and unquestioning acceptance of the three gifts. His forehead wrinkled as she answered his questions, his innocence palpable as he considered the poverty of slavery.

Not until she explained the gifts necessary for Preparation did she feel the tremendous resistance within him. With dismay, she saw his eyes find the knife, felt his fury, and finally, his contempt. His gift was an insult, a promise of future rebellion. She considered refusing it, but the rite demanded that a gift given freely be accepted, and so she cut the glorious hair and dropped it onto the flames. Tyre's first gift was one of hatred.

As she tasted Tyre's bitterness, the vision began to swirl with a chorus of voices chanting, the words indistinct and unfamiliar to her ears. The power of the half-sung, half-spoken music swelled and became clear. Individual voices emerged, some unknown to her, others as familiar to her as her own reflection in a glass. Ilena's hoarse croak whispered to her in the tower room, *"To bend without breaking."* Nomia took up the echoing murmur: *"A special sort of joining,"* as Beal's beloved voice continued the chant, *"I speak of a woman's mysteries."* In and around those voices wove

Chloe's wordless song of healing, connecting the melodies in a shifting pattern of chords, urging them on in a glorious crescendo.

From the height of that crescendo rose a single voice of such poignant beauty that it dwarfed the sound from which it was born. Soaring above the chant, its sweet tremolo broke free and continued alone, the vision shimmering with the vibrations of that single, glorious voice. As it reached the final note of its obbligato, the vision evaporated and the music ended.

Vena turned her gaze toward the tiny window of her chamber. A new moon hung high in the autumn sky. She had been reminded of the way, reminded that she was merely a helpmate in a plan forged by the labor of her predecessors and fifteen generations of sacrifice. She might be lonely, but she was never alone.

Closing her eyes, she recalled the glory of that single voice.

Tomorrow she would visit the singer.

Chapter 8

In the Garden

"WE'VE ALWAYS KNOWN she would leave us, but to enter Preparation! I—we've—heard of the dangers. Not that we question your judgment. If you say she must go, then go she must. It's just that we love her, you see . . ."

Inwardly, Vena winced at the worry in Megara's eyes. Outwardly, she maintained the calm exterior created to ease the difficulty of this visit.

Megara and her mate, Evander, had come to the House of Healing in the years before Vena assumed her present duties. As High Healers of Pelion, she and Beal honored the couple's request for a consultation. Though they knew the couple by sight, they had never worked with them as patients. Megara and Evander were native born; neither was adept. Megara was an administrator in one of Pelion's nurseries; Evander was a journeyman in the Guild of Weavers, a skilled artisan who had recently held his first exhibition in a well-known gallery. They were childless, having undergone every treatment known with no results.

It didn't take long to discover the purpose of this private session. Megara's administrative duties made her privy to many Council decisions affecting city government. Lately, she'd heard rumors that the Council was considering bringing outsiders into the city. It was Megara, her round face eager, her plump hand held by Evander, who pleaded with Vena and Beal.

". . . so I—we—thought that if you're going to bring strangers into the city, why not bring some children?"

Her voice caught and Evander's hand tightened around hers.

"It's not just for us, although we would dearly love a child, but for all those who are childless."

She faltered again before rushing on.

"We would love any child, no matter the age or gender, and would undertake the raising of such a child as a sacred trust."

She looked beseechingly at them, first at Beal, then at Vena.

Beal's mind recoiled at the reminder of the grief of childlessness. Vena, having carried their child for nine moons, lost it in a difficult delivery. Almost mad with grief, she lay like one dead, Beal holding her in his arms, his tears mixed with hers, ravaged by the thought that not only the babe, but Vena might be taken from him. Vena recovered, but there would be no child of their bodies.

Vena put aside her own grief so as to form a reply.

"The plan you speak of is still in its early stages. As members of the Council, we may not speak freely of it, although I can inform you that there has been no talk of children in regard to the plan. We will, however, bring your request before the Council."

Beal interrupted.

"Consider this: If a child was delivered into your care, would you be willing to dedicate your son or daughter to service within the Maze? Consider your answer carefully, for it might mean surrendering that child at adulthood."

Probing their minds as they regarded each other, Vena sensed the closeness of their mating. Megara was the aggressive one, who would face anything, even the certitude of eventual separation, to obtain the child she yearned for. Yet any hesitancy on Evander's part would cause Megara to reconsider her position. Her love for him would not allow her to cause him pain, even if that pain lay twenty years in the future. Evander caressed her plump cheek with a square-tipped finger before answering:

"To lose a child at adulthood would be a heavy blow, but if we are given a child, we have the strength to return our gift when the time comes."

The interview over, the couple left, hand-in-hand.

Their hands are still entwined, mused Vena. Evander was now a Master of his guild, his work-worn palm etched with deep lines while Megara's plump hand appeared unchanged. Twenty years may have passed, but their love admitted no passage of time.

"She knows well enough how deeply we care for Kara," Evander reminded his mate, before turning to address Vena. "Kara is our life, but we are ready to return our gift. Tell us what we must do."

Vena took a deep breath.

"I've come to tell you of Kara's selection for Preparation and to deliver her to the Maze."

Unprepared for the rapidity of their loss, Evander blanched and Megara gasped. Nothing Vena could do or say could possibly ease their distress.

"I'll leave you alone so you may prepare to bid her farewell. Try not to let your sorrow attach itself to Kara. She'll be comforted if she senses your sadness. She'll be troubled if she senses your fear for her well-being."

Vena headed toward the garden, then, as an afterthought, turned back to address Megara, whose tears ran freely down her cheeks.

"She'll need a cloak, for the evening air is chilly. Anything she brings will be taken from her at entry. Offer her only your love at parting."

Evander folded his mate in his arms, his lips pressed against her hair, murmuring to her in the private words that mean nothing, but say much. Vena moved toward the garden.

The girl was working among the roses, her gloved hands cutting back the thorny stems and setting mulch around the roots to protect them from the coming of winter. Heedless of the dirt and muck staining her robes, she knelt in the rich earth, a knitted shawl tied around her head and shoulders for warmth in the gathering dusk. Vena noted with a healer's eye that Kara's form had widened at the breast and hips, the slimness of her girlhood changed to the curves of maturity. Still unaware of Vena's presence, the girl rose to contemplate some chrysanthemums in woeful need of trimming. Bending to retrieve a pair of shears, she knelt again. Then she began to sing.

At the sound of her clear soprano, Vena felt a sudden onslaught of memory. The song was one of childhood, a lullaby sung by every mother to every child of Pelion. But Kara had not learned it from Megara. Someone else had taught it to her in an earlier time.

"I've returned!"

Vena looked up from her table in astonishment, her pen splashing ink on the document she labored over in the dim twilight.

Beal's eyebrow cocked as he took in the darkening chamber and the unlit candles.

"One would think you were wise enough to light some candles. Here, I'll do it for you."

Vena leaned back in the cushioned chair, deducing from the travel-stained cloak and muddy boots that he had rushed up the stairs to see her. Touched by his eagerness, she noted that he was thinner and new lines were etched in his darkly tanned skin. He'd been gone for almost nine moons, their longest separation since their mating, and she had missed him. Their parting was bitter, almost as bitter as the day she told him about the black robes. But he was back and she was glad of it. She would let no memories of the past disturb their reunion.

After lighting the tallow candles on the brass candelabra, he pulled up a comfortable chair by her side. Sighing with contentment, he put his booted feet on another chair, placed his hands behind his head, and regarded her with unconcealed delight.

"You've no idea how good it is to be home!"

"And you, Searcher of Souls, have no idea how much you have been missed."

A stray thread on his woolen vest claimed Beal's attention.

"Have I been missed, Vena?"

His tension passed to her as he addressed her by the name that must not be spoken. It was the old battle, begun when Vena heeded the call to duty. In time, he accepted the loss of his mate in his house, his bed, and as a workmate in the House of Healing. But it was the loss of her presence in his mind that gradually became intolerable. As a member of the Council he retained the right to connect with her in shared planning sessions, but the true intimacy of adept mates was gone forever. Nine moons ago it became unendurable. Resigning his position as High Healer, Beal became a Searcher of Souls. Vena fought against it with every argument at her disposal; her judgment was overruled by the rest of the Council and Beal left for the east.

Capitulating for a moment to his sudden rush of feeling, Vena let him see the emptiness of her days without him. Her eyes filled with tears that must remain unshed, she spoke from her heart.

"Now and always, I miss you every moment of every day."

Brown eyes caught gray ones in a fast embrace, the candles flickering at the quiet intensity of their joining. Beal recovered first, a shy smile on his lips.

"I've something to show you. I want you to meet the newest ernani to enter Pelion."

He was out the door of her chamber in an instant, returning just as quickly with a large bundle held carefully in his arms. Vena was mystified. All ernani were escorted directly to the Maze and certainly no ernani could be lifted by Beal's slight frame. A small arm emerged from the bundle and reached up to touch Beal's face. Placing the bundle on his knees, Beal pulled away the coarse fabric. Seated on his lap, smiling up at the face regarding her with paternal pride, a girl-child of no more than two years of age gurgled words in an unfamiliar language.

"Beal, what have you done!"

Beal considered her a moment, his hands never stopping their gentle stroking of the dark head nestled close to his chest. Vena sensed his disappointment in her, although his explanation remained neutral and carefully respectful.

"I've brought a lost soul home to Pelion. This particular soul comes to us from the eastern shore where her mother was a patient of mine."

Beal's lips tightened, always a signal of his displeasure.

"She was not truly ill, unless you consider starvation a disease. She gave everything to the child, who, as you see, blooms with health. I eased her dying as best I could and took the child, thinking I would find her a home on the journey back."

The child's head was drooping now. Beal shifted her weight into his arms, pulling up the blanket around her shoulders. When he looked up at Vena, he chose his words with care.

"You will understand, Vena, you who know me so well. I've delivered countless children into the world and nursed as many through childhood illnesses. Yet never have I felt for a child what I felt for her since the first moment I lifted her in my arms."

At Vena's questioning glance, Beal qualified his response.

"No, she's not adept; at least she shows none of the signs. And no, what I feel for her is not parental love. For want of better words, I can only say that she carries joy within her."

Vena held out her arms for the child. She came without protest, her dark eyes glowing in the candlelight, her mouth open to reveal perfect white teeth. Fascinated by Vena's black veil, she tugged at it. When it didn't budge, she held it in front of her eyes and looked through its delicate folds, laughing when she discovered she could see through it. When Vena untangled her fingers from the veil, she let go, transferring her attention to Vena's hand, her chubby fingers tracing the path of the lines in Vena's palm. Satisfied in some childish way, she looked up into the gray eyes regarding her so seriously, and laughed again, her sweet warble echoing in the stone chamber.

Settling herself into training mode, Vena entered the child's mind, finding it awash in the multiple sensations of childhood—the color and texture of Vena's robes, the light from the candles, curiosity about the strange room and the many papers with squiggly lines, the woman who held her so tightly. In the complexity of all these thoughts and feelings, Vena could find no hint of fear or distrust. The child's mind was unsophisticated, equally open to everything that touched her senses, unable to pursue a single line of inquiry, yet independent and alert. And Vena knew, as Beal knew, that this child was somehow important to the future.

This knowledge frightened her, for nowhere in the prophecy was a child mentioned. Disturbed, she regarded Beal, who, sensing her question, provided a solution.

"I want to give her to Megara and Evander if they'll renew their promise to relinquish her at the specified time. You can oversee her schooling and prepare her for entrance into the Maze. We don't know how she'll figure in the plan, but it will be revealed."

Vena nodded slowly in agreement and the child squirmed. Beal relieved her of the unaccustomed weight, settling the child in the cradle of his arms. Then, humming an old lullaby, Beal rocked the littlest ernani to sleep.

As the girl reached the end of her song she began to hum the melody without words. The chrysanthemum trimmed, she reached around for a pail of water and in doing so, discovered the silent figure standing behind her. Startled, she gasped aloud before bursting into tinkling laughter.

"You frightened me! How long have you been listening to my silly song? I'm glad you came. The nights grow cold and you know it grieves me to watch the flowers fade."

The girl ran lightly up to her, extending both hands toward the old woman. Grasping those outstretched hands, Vena marveled at the warmth of the girl's skin through cloth gloves. Like the plants she tended, Kara held the promise of spring within her.

Vena led the girl to a small bench under a bare trellis that made the place a bower of blooming vines in the summertime. Taking her face in both hands and pushing away her shawl so that it rested on her shoulders, Vena examined this child of music and laughter. Masses of dark waves parted in the center to form a frame around a heart-shaped face. Her hair usually hung free, but today, in deference to her work, she'd pinned it in a knot at the back of her neck. Her brows slanted upward over dark almond-shaped eyes ringed with black lashes. It would have been a pretty, but ordinary face if not for two features: a firm jaw that accentuated a long, slender neck and pearly, iridescent skin that glowed as if lit from the inside.

Satisfied with the signs of outward maturation, Vena resolved to examine the growth of the spirit within.

"Tell me, child, does your training progress? Does your teacher offer hope that you'll ever be able to carry a tune?"

The girl laughed again, charmed by Vena's tender mockery.

"She despairs of my counting and pulls her hair at my clumsy attempts at composition."

Vena's smile deepened.

"Is the music training everything you yearned for?"

The girl's eyes grew dreamy with recollection. She knew from childhood that her father wanted her to apprentice in his guild, for her fingers possessed a natural dexterity that would have meshed perfectly with the weaver's art. She knew just as surely that the Fifteenth Mother would welcome her entry into the House of Healing. But from the time she could stand she sang. When her parents took her to the Sanctum for her dedication, the beauty of the chants transported her to a different world, a world she was determined to join. The announcement of her intention to apprentice with the Musician's Guild was her first step toward independence. Thankfully, the three people closest to her accepted her decision and urged her to excel. Kara answered the Fifteenth Mother's question with a full heart.

"Everything and more."

The gray eyes that always seemed to look into her soul narrowed for a moment as they posed a question that took her unaware.

"Could you bear it if you could not study any longer?"

"Is something wrong with my music? Did my teachers give you a poor report?"

A raised hand silenced her and the question was rephrased.

"Slowly, child, slowly. My question is a simple one. If you were asked to give up your training for awhile, perhaps for a long while, could you leave it behind with good grace and walk another path?"

Trepidation filled Kara. She knew, had always known, the facts surrounding her birth and adoption. Five years old at the dedication ceremony, she remembered it still. Rededicated at ten, she offered her first gift. Frightened and alone on the marble pedestal, she looked up into the gray eyes that waited now so patiently for her answer, and had been comforted. The small silver-bladed knife cut off a lock of her hair and the Fifteenth Mother let her place it on the sacred fire. Even now she remembered the tears of happiness in her parents' eyes.

Then, five years ago, she awoke in the night, her body racked with chills, her feet frozen and her belly aching with cramps that came from deep inside. When she found traces of blood on her nightshift, she flew to her parents' chamber, crying with pain and fear. Her mother received the news with joy, assuring her that she was a woman now. The next morning she and her mother gathered the bloodied shift and walked to the Sanctum (for a woman's second gift was either the dark blood of her menses or the bright blood that signifies the end of virginity). Again, she stood on the pedestal and made her offering, awed by the beauty of the ceremony.

She had been given so much—her talents for music and gardening and a loving relationship with parents and the woman sitting beside her. In that moment, she recognized the rightness of her decision.

"Of course I could put my studies aside! There's only one thing I need to know. Does this mean I can never sing again?"

The innocent grief behind this question wrung Vena's heart. It was time to tell Kara everything and stop her imagination from making the decision more difficult to bear. Vena stroked her hand and spoke calmly, trying to ease the girl into a state of acceptance.

"You may sing whenever you wish. It's just that I've come to take you to the Maze. No, don't pull away from me, child. I know you've heard rumors, although I've no idea what has been said. Trust that I love you and would never knowingly do you harm."

The hand relaxed and the throb of the heartbeat that showed so clearly in the hollow of her white throat slowed.

"You, and many women like you, will enter the Maze and live in the women's quarters for one moon. There you will study many things—the healing arts, crafts of a practical nature, and other things connected to the Path of Preparation."

The girl was listening intently to every word. Vena continued as quietly as she began.

"Then, after this time of training, an ernani will be selected for you." The girl started. "You will live with this ernani for a period of time. During that time, it's possible that you and he will join together."

"What if there's a child from this joining?"

"There will be no child during Preparation. The healers have medicines to prevent conception and will monitor your menses carefully, never fear."

The girl sat silent, pondering everything that had been told her. Vena decided it was time for Kara to explore her fears.

"Now, my child, tell me what you've heard that made you pull away from me when I mentioned the Maze. I'll answer you truthfully, as I always have."

The long-lashed eyes were remote; the answer tentative.

"I've heard that the ernani are cruel and uncivilized men. That they're trained to kill within the Maze. I've also heard that they treat women badly."

Vena sighed. Although bits of truth existed among these rumors, it was distressing to learn that her people had so little understanding of the plan that might enrich their lives.

"Some of what you've heard is true; just as much is false. Do you remember when I asked your father to take you to the north gate last year?"

The dark head nodded.

"Tell me what you saw."

"A group of men in chains entered the gate at dawn and were taken to the Great Forge. They were pitiable, beaten and bruised, covered in filth. One of them could hardly walk. I could see their bones, they were so thin."

"Now I ask you, are these men cruel or has the world outside Pelion been cruel to them? How can they give kindness to others when they've never experienced kindness themselves? As to being trained to kill, they are taught to defend themselves and others. Many of them join the Legion and defend our frontiers against invaders."

Vena heard the penitent tones of one who could admit her faults freely.

"I'm sorry for doubting you."

"You must question what you do not understand. That is the way to knowledge and truth."

Vena had two more questions for the girl.

"What of your monthly flow? When was your last one and was it as painful as the others?"

The girl responded without blush or hesitation. Her body was no mystery to her. She also understood the reason behind the question since she'd sought the Fifteenth Mother's advice about something none of her friends seemed to experience.

"My last flow ended two days ago. It was a little less painful, so perhaps the herbs you prescribed made a difference. Mother says a woman who has trouble with her monthly flow often finds that it disappears once she's no longer a virgin . . ." her face brightened, ". . . so perhaps the Maze will cure me!"

In that moment, Vena's admiration of this gallant songbird who could laugh at the upheavals of life soared into the dying garden.

Her next question confirmed her love of the girl.

"What of your riding lessons?"

Dark eyes brimmed with merriment, all sadness forgotten. A mystifying message arrived at their home three years ago: "Kara must learn to ride a horse." Her parents were dumbfounded. Native-born citizens of Pelion never rode; in fact, horses were barred from the city streets. Only the Legion used horses, plus merchants who took caravans to far-away markets to obtain certain rare goods that the self-sufficient city didn't produce on its own. But whatever the Fifteenth Mother wished must be performed, so Evander took her once a week to the Calvary headquarters where she took riding lessons from a man whose scarred face soon revealed a soft heart and a warm regard for Kara.

"Grudius let me take a few low jumps this week and couldn't believe his eyes when I didn't fall off. My bottom was sore the next day, but I didn't mind. He started me on that pony," her nose wrinkled in distaste, "but now I have a bay mare with one white foot he saves just for me. I asked him her name, and when he said she didn't have one, I named her Henna." Her enthusiasm evaporated. "I suppose I should tell him I won't be riding again for awhile."

"He'll be told. Now, you must say goodbye to your parents. This will be hard for them, my child, so kiss them quickly."

Kara rose at the Fifteenth Mother's command, still eager to ask the sole question for which Vena had no answer.

"How long will I be in the Maze? When is Preparation over?"

The Mother of All stood, her tall figure suddenly forbidding.

"There are many questions I will not be able to answer for you within the Maze. That is one of them. Understand that you are always free to ask, but I must be free as well not to answer. I'll meet you outside. Don't forget your cloak."

The girl ran toward the house.

Vena stood for a while in the garden, admiring the moon through the branches of a gnarled cherry tree. By the time it waxed again, Kara would move toward womanhood.

Vena hoped she would still be singing.

The stars Kara could see through the high window over her bed were unfamiliar. The loss of familiar constellations was puzzling, until she remembered that this chamber faced due north while her window at home faced south. The faithful moon shone down on her, a silver crescent reclining on its back, lounging on its starry bed, its twin tips curved in a welcoming smile. Kara smiled back, glad that at least one thing remained constant in her life.

From the time of her earliest memories, nothing was quite as pleasurable as watching the moon rise above the treetops to float on the dusky seas of the night sky. She was never a rebellious child, being more interested in pleasing others than pleasing herself, but on more than one occasion the moon caused her to disobey. On clear nights, long after the lights were put out and her parents were safely asleep, she would cast aside the blankets and stand upright on the mattress to gaze through her bedroom window, her arms crossed on the window ledge, her chin resting on her forearms, content to watch until it rose so far above her window that it passed out of sight. Once, when her mother caught her at it, she waited for a reprimand, for the hour was late and the night air outside her window frigid. Instead, her mother joined her at the window, kneeling beside her with her face upraised, content to watch with her as the stately moon progressed upward toward the vault of the heavens. "Moonchild" her mother called her that night, a name that lingered fondly on Megara's lips as she tucked in the bedclothes, kissed her daughter's forehead, and bid her good-night.

As a child, Kara admired the moon's freedom. Compared to the fixity of the stars, it seemed a footloose wanderer, free to move however it willed. As she grew older she came to appreciate its mutability, its nightly changes of shape and coloration. Compared to the sameness of the sun, it seemed mysterious and even magical in its ability to alter its appearance. When her menses began, she learned that she was, indeed, a moonchild, as all women are, the fluids in their bodies in continual flux, ebbing and flowing like the tides of the great oceans, waxing and waning like the phases of the moon.

This moon, too, gradually passed from view, rising high above the Maze to hang suspended in a cloudless night sky. Calmer now, her eyelids growing heavy, Kara's fingers moved quickly over her hair, removing the pins that held it at the nape of her neck. Shaking her head to free the weight of it, she picked up the new comb and began her nightly ritual. After running the comb through the heavy waves to clear away the tangles, she applied the brush in long, firm strokes that soon had her hair crackling. Her new nightshift was made of cream-colored cotton, as was her shift for daytime wear. Three woolen dresses were issued to her, each one cut to hug her form at the waist and drop in folds to the floor. A simply draped, but beautifully woven hooded cloak completed her wardrobe. There were no mirrors in this chamber, or anywhere in the women's quarters, yet her quick eye for beauty told her that the soft pastels of the three dresses—azure, sea-mist, and rose—were perfectly suited to her coloring.

It was strange sharing a sleeping chamber with so many women. As an only child, she always had a room to herself. She slid under the coverlet, enjoying the sensation of a clean body, a new nightshift and the freshly laundered bedding. Tired, but not yet ready to sleep, she remembered the baths she was led to after the Fifteenth Mother left her in the care of a woman named Nerissa. Kara didn't consider herself modest and often visited the public baths with her friends, but in this large tiled room filled with strangers, she felt unusually shy. Noticing her hesitancy in disrobing, Nerissa placed a hand on her shoulder.

"It can be a trifle overwhelming living in a community like this one. You'll soon find that everyone here is eager to make friends. There's only one thing I need to warn you of tonight. It's forbidden to discuss your life before the Maze with anyone here. You're not to discuss your family or any details about your former life. The reason for this will become clear in time. After you bathe, you'll be shown to the sleeping chamber. We rise early here, so sleep well."

After placing a light kiss on Kara's cheek, Nerissa left her side. Stripping off her clothes, Kara waded into the pool. Several women greeted her, and one, a petite brown-skinned girl with black eyes, introduced herself as Thalia. She was a chattering and somewhat nervous girl, Kara decided, but she was warm-hearted and instantly shared everything she knew about the Maze.

They sat on the tiles surrounding the bathing pool while Kara worked patiently at drying her hair.

"I arrived last night, but before I came I heard that some of these ernani were bought in Agave. My sister's mate said they marched through the north gate yesterday morning."

"Nerissa says we aren't to talk of life in the city. Perhaps it would be better if you don't tell anyone about the ernani. After all, we can't be sure they're meant for us."

Thalia's face burned with the implied criticism. Embarrassed, she couldn't help retaliating.

"Don't tell me you aren't interested in knowing who your ernani will be!"

Kara's reply was kindly, yet firm.

"I trust the Fifteenth Mother to choose for me."

Sipping the tea an attendant brought them, they spoke of other things. Alone in her bed, Kara remembered the men on the chain. She told the Fifteenth Mother they were to be pitied, but she didn't admit how they much they frightened her. She'd never been struck or even scolded by anyone. How would such a man treat her if they disagreed, or, worse, if she displeased him? Remembering the Fifteenth Mother's promise that she would not be harmed, she buried her doubts.

Adjusting the pillow beneath her head, she listened to the breathing of twenty other women, who, like her, were gathered together to walk the Path. As she relaxed into sleep, she recalled Thalia's question.

Interested? Yes, she thought, I'm interested . . . .

The man who entered her dreams was soft of voice and full of laughter. He had no face, no form, but he beckoned to her with a shadowy arm and flung her upon Henna's back. Her hair flew behind her as she rode. He was near her although she could not see him. Henna ran with the breeze and Kara had never felt so light, so beloved. She burst into song.

"Nerissa, how did you leave her?"

"She seemed slightly nervous at the bath, so I asked Ladon to add a sleeping potion to her tea. She took awhile to settle, but when I looked in on her, she was singing in her dreams."

"Ah."

They sat quietly for a while, enjoying their own thoughts. Nerissa cleared her throat, a habit the Fifteenth Mother recognized as a prelude to unwelcome news.

"Do you remember a woman called Thalia? Her sister told us during an interview that she was desperate for a man. I was inclined not to believe the sister since there seemed to be some jealousy between them over the sister's mate. Now, I'm not so sure."

"Tell me what happened."

Nerissa's voice went flat and unemotional as she readied herself for the Fifteenth Mother's displeasure.

"She told Kara that ernani bound for the Maze arrived yesterday from Agave."

"What was Kara's reaction?"

Nerissa smiled, her usually sedate face full of enjoyment.

"I must be more formidable than I realize. She informed Thalia that I told her not to speak of such things and suggested she not repeat her story to anyone."

The Fifteenth Mother nodded, unsurprised by Kara's compliance to the rules.

"Thalia must be removed before the others rise tomorrow morning. You gave her a single rule today and she broke it. We have no time to waste on those who cannot pass one simple test of obedience. We give them rules that may save their lives. This is a dangerous place and we must protect them as best we can."

Nerissa nodded her agreement.

The Fifteenth Mother was as yet unsatisfied.

"Come, old friend. Tell me what's in your heart. What do you think of this joining? You've seen both of them now. Tell me, Nerissa, have I prepared her correctly?"

This plea for confirmation revealed a need that Vena was unable to share with anyone but Nerissa, for this was Nerissa's area of expertise—the joining of ernani and the women of Pelion. The Fifteenth Mother might consult with her from time to time, but Nerissa was Mistress of Joining, and came to her position after a lifetime spent in the Hetaera Guild. The Instructor of the Maze organized her thoughts as her training demanded and began. With every word she spoke, Nerissa sensed the relief of her oldest and dearest friend.

"I see a balance possible between them. Her joy, innocence, and trust should mediate his hatred, guilt, and suspicion. Yet the exchange should work equally the other way. She lacks his independence and courage. His are the skills of leadership, hers the ones of judgment."

"She dreamed tonight that she rode galloping over the earth. Yet Grudius reports she is over-careful on horseback and reluctant to spur her horse into anything quicker than a trot. Unlike him, she's aware of some of her deficiencies, and should be easier to mold."

"Of him, I can be less sure. There is danger in him, but in some ways that danger is the source of his strength. I'll be able to judge more clearly after I begin the sessions with the men."

Nerissa finished her report, looked over to the woman in black, and drew a blanket over her sleeping form. Today was a difficult day, Nerissa thought, and our difficulties have only just begun.

Remembering Kara's dream song, Nerissa hummed it to herself as she closed the tower door quietly behind her, careful not to disturb the Mother of All's repose.

Chapter 9

Molding

THE WIND AGAINST his face brought water to his eyes. Legs and arms working in unison, he flew across the plain, measuring the distance with long, even strides. The finish line stretched in front of him. Summoning his reserves, he took four more running strides and passed over the line scratched across the dirt. Dropping over at the waist, his breath came in short, deep pants, his mouth open to bring the air more quickly into his lungs. All too soon, the image of the empty plain disintegrated.

Tyre opened sweat-filled eyes on the training ground, an oblong arena open to the sky, set in the midst of the Maze. Around him, men were collapsing on the dirt, one of them retching, all of them straining for air. The sky above him hung leaden with the promise of rain. Goose-flesh raised on his bare arms and legs as he regained his breath. A blanket was thrown at him. Wrapping it around him, he ducked his head, hoping not to be noticed as the trainer approached the group. Eyeing them impassively, the trainer issued the last order of the day, imperious as always in its assumption of perfect obedience.

"Training is ended. Wait for your guard at the gate."

Tyre joined the herd heading toward the locked gate. With the others, he waited in line to retrieve his sandals. On other days there had been brief conversations between the men as the long day ended and they waited to be escorted to their cells. Today no one spoke, not even Dino, who had fast become their mascot and could usually be counted on for a ribald comment or a good-natured jest. Rama, the man usually paired with Tyre for arms training, stood nearby. He, too, clutched his blanket around him like a shield, avoiding eye contact with everyone.

Once the man in front of Tyre cleared the gate, Grasos lumbered forward. Tyre held out his arms, wrists up, while the manacles were locked on. Grasos moved him down a passageway that, even after a fortnight, remained indistinguishable from any of the others Tyre passed through daily. Tyre followed the enormous figure, walking stolidly toward the cheerless cell. After many twists and turns, Grasos stopped at a door identical to the ones lining every corridor through which they'd passed and pushed it open. Tyre held out his right hand to be unlocked.

This done, he waited for Grasos to lead the way inside so Tyre could be chained to the bed.

"The other one, ernani."

Confused, for Grasos gestured to his left hand, Tyre held it out, not sure what to expect. The key turned in the lock and the manacles were tossed over the guard's massive shoulder where they hung like a child's plaything. Cocking an eye at Tyre, Grasos offered a rare observation.

"You won."

"Won?"

"The race."

The door shut in his face, the bolt slamming into place. Tyre frowned. Was Grasos implying that Tyre was not being chained to the bed because he won the race? It made no sense. He won the archery and javelin sessions regularly and had never been rewarded. The events of the day had so unnerved him that he'd looked forward to the race announced at the morning meal. In the arena, under the sky, free of the manacles and moving through space, he was able to escape this place, if only for a moment. He hadn't known that he'd won, or particularly cared if it was true. In any case, the trainers never announced winners. If you won, they'd move the target back or increase the number of laps. If you lost, they'd assign more exercises or increase the weights he hoisted daily. Either way, your body would be pushed a little more, its aches and pains an eternal condition of existence.

He lowered himself onto the bed with a groan, suddenly glad to be alone. At least no one could hear him. Realizing that if he didn't get warm quickly he'd be stiff tomorrow, he started a fire and wrapped a blanket from the bed around his waist to cover his legs, pulling the other one more tightly around his shoulders. He kept waiting to be issued more clothes as the winter brought colder nights. He waited in vain. It was never as cold here as it was in Lapith and the training rooms were kept so warm that he was usually sweating in the first few minutes of exercise.

The grate opened and a tray of food was pushed inside the cell. When his stomach growled a warning, he put the tray on the stool, pulling it in front of the bed to serve as a table. There were no utensils, but he ate easily without them, scooping up the stew with the flaky bread. He was hungry all the time now. With the constant demands on his body, and his thinness after the march, he ate three meals a day and could have eaten more. He thought he was putting on flesh, but it was difficult to tell. The wrapped loincloth offered no hints as to changes in his size.

The meal finished, there was nothing else to do but sleep. He relieved himself in the tin bucket and replenished the fire. As he lay down on the bed, he recalled that he was not chained and so was not forced to sleep on his left side. Rolling over to the right, he pulled the coverlet over him. Pillowing his face on his right arm he looked up at the sky, trying to ignore the bars covering the window. Even though the night sky was cloudy, the stars and the moon absent from view; it was a relief to see something other than the dull uniformity of walls.

Sleep eluded him despite the fact that the morning bell would wake him at dawn. Abruptly, he remembered what tomorrow would bring. His curses reverberated in the silent cell. Against his will, the changes in routine that began after the morning meal drilled themselves into his mind.

All too quickly, the days assumed a pattern of grueling routine. Roused by a bell, he was given a few minutes to relieve himself before the doors clanged open and he marched with the others toward the dining hall. A breakfast of porridge, dried fruit and nuts, and fresh milk was served on long tables set with benches. There was little conversation as the head trainer announced the events of the day.

Next, they were marched down yet another passageway, where they waited for individual sessions with the healer. Daily, the healer asked Tyre if he slept, if he was eliminating regularly, and if he noticed any unusually stiff or sore muscles. Tyre said as little as possible, enduring the examination with little gratitude and no grace.

On the third day, Tyre pulled a muscle in his back while lifting the weights. Unused to this particular kind of exercise, he assumed his soreness was normal and said nothing to the healer the next morning. Rising too quickly from the examination table, he hadn't been able to prevent a quick intake of breath as the muscle cramped. In a trice, Grasos was lifting him up on the table, the healer working over him, locating the soreness and kneading his back, deaf to Tyre's protests. The rest of the day was spent sitting next to the braziers while he watched the others train, a poultice to draw away the soreness strapped around his ribs.

Training sessions began with group exercises devised, Tyre decided, to loosen them up and avoid injuries. Individual work followed. Tyre's trainer seemed to concentrate on his upper body, demanding repetitions of movements with the weights that left his arms shaking and his chest muscles trembling. The midday meal, the largest meal of the day, followed.

Tyre continued to be amazed at the richness and variety of the food provided for them in a season when most Lapithians were reduced to thin soups and bread. Several kinds of meat, fish, rice, beans, vegetables, fruits and fresh loaves of bread were washed down with steaming mugs of tea. After the meal they were escorted to another room, where arms practice began.

An expert with a bow and a throwing spear, Tyre hit every target the first two days. He considered not cooperating and purposefully missing his aim, but his natural competitiveness born of years of friendly rivalry with Hourn won out, causing him to actually enjoy the practice until he pulled the muscle. That day he watched as a man repeatedly missed his holds in a wrestling match and lagged well behind the pack in a series of foot races. The next day the man disappeared from the group. Dino, who seemed to have a better rapport with his guard than anyone else, reported that evening as they waited to be returned to their cells that he had asked about the missing man. The guard's reply was brevity itself:

"Not good enough."

It was a cruel awakening, a reminder to all of those called "ernani" by the guards (a word no one had ever heard before) that this strange title not withstanding, they were still slaves who could be sold or disposed of at the whim of their owner.

The pulled muscle sore but healing, Tyre's return to arms practice was greatly changed. The bow and spear put aside, he was drilled instead in weaponry he'd never handled before—long and short swords, shields, battle-axes, sword and dagger in combination, each of them demanding strength, accuracy, and timing. In these sessions Tyre was a raw beginner and quickly lost the confidence restored in the first few days of imprisonment. He trained endlessly on proper grips, stances, footwork, thrusts and parries, and was often paired with Rama, who handled a sword as if it was an extension of his arm and regularly beat Tyre down to his knees.

At the conclusion of one particularly discouraging session, Tyre wondered if his left arm would ever recover its feeling after an unexpected blow sent his shield flying, upset his balance, and left him sprawling face-down in the dirt. A strong hand reached down in front of his face. Rama's usually forbidding countenance relaxed into a measuring smile, white teeth gleaming in his dark face.

"At least your timing improves. You landed two blows."

Tyre accepted the proffered hand and was pulled to his feet. Grasos appeared at his side, handed him the shield, and addressed him more sharply than usual.

"Any injury?"

Tyre frowned him away. Turning back to Rama, he demanded: "Teach me how that's done."

Rama's smile extended into a grin and they began again.

Rama hadn't been smiling this evening, nor had anyone. It began with the bath, the first real departure from the monotony of daily routine. Directly after the midday meal, they'd been escorted to a tiled room containing a row of copper tubs full of steaming water. Not having bathed since the day of his arrival, Tyre assumed his captors did not hold cleanliness in much regard. He washed his face and hands in the basin of water that appeared in his cell every evening, but the rest of him was streaked with dried sweat and dust, his hair stiff with caked dirt from the training ground. Each man scrubbed down from some buckets placed near the door, then soaked in the tubs as they used yellow cakes of soap on hair, beards, and bodies. Tyre washed his hair twice, dunking his head into the water and wishing he wasn't so tall since his length made it impossible to fully immerse himself in the warm, soap-scented water.

It might have been the break in the rigidly enforced pattern, or memories of better days, but soon the room was awash with water, naked men splashing each other with well-aimed jets of water and soap flying from tub to tub. The guards watched closely but made no attempt to control the mayhem.

Dried and dressed in clean loincloths, expecting to be taken to the arena, they were herded into a room they'd never seen before. Large windows opened onto a bare garden, letting in the wintry light through bars running horizontally and vertically across panes of thick glass. They were directed into wooden chairs placed behind long tables arranged to face a single small table and chair. Looking around the room, curious in spite of his self, Tyre saw walls lined with drawings and maps and several leather-bound books stacked on the small table in front of them. Rama sat on his right; Dino on his left, the latter jabbing him with an insistent elbow, gesturing with a jerk of his head toward the door. An incredulous Tyre watched the guards file out of the room. The last one, a taciturn fellow called Echetus, turned to address them from the door, waiting to speak until the men settled into an uncomfortable silence. His eyes full of cold menace, slapping his cudgel into his palm, he dictated the rules.

"You will sit here until you are told to do otherwise. At the slightest disturbance we will be in this room and on your arse. You've noticed that others have disappeared in the last few days. One problem from any of you and you'll be back in Agave as fast as you can stumble there."

By the end of his harangue the atmosphere had turned cold and cheerless. As he moved through the doorway, a figure in dove grey slipped past him, heading for the front of the room. The door was pulled shut and no lock was turned.

A flicker of recognition ran through the men as they identified the woman who had led them through the bronze doors on the day they entered the city. She stood gracefully before them, her braided silver hair shining like a crown under a gauzy veil that fell to her knees. She regarded them closely, seeming to refresh her memory of them as she saw them that first day. After perusing each face, she spoke.

"You will address me as Instructor. From this day forward we will meet for two hours in the afternoon before you are taken to the arena. My purpose is to begin your instruction so that you may be joined with a woman. With the woman who is chosen for you, you will proceed toward the giving of your gifts."

She waited, neither encouraging nor discouraging a response. Dino shifted in his chair and cleared his throat.

"What was that part about a woman?"

Fourteen men couldn't suppress a chuckle of enjoyment. The fifteenth sat with lips tightly folded.

The Instructor's eyes brightened at Dino's jest.

"You'll be paired with a woman chosen by myself and others. She'll share your cell from the evening trumpet until the morning bell. During that time, the guards may not open your door. During the day, she, like you, will continue her studies."

"You mean this woman is being trained to handle weapons so we can fight it out every night?"

The woman's husky laughter mingled with the men's.

"Not exactly, Dino. Most of them will continue studies begun in the city. We ask them to renew certain other skills—healing, for instance, and basic herb lore."

Someone behind Tyre spoke up.

"Just tell us when you'll give them to us. I've no use for her studies—we won't need them in the night."

The Instructor considered the speaker.

"They'll come to you when and if you're deemed ready by me. These women are not whores, Suda. If they are raped or mistreated in any way, you'll be punished severely and sold."

Suda spoke again, chastened, but curious.

"Who are these women if they're not whores? What kind of woman would agree to live with brutes and slaves like us?"

The Instructor sighed as she lowered herself into the chair.

"Only you know if you are, indeed, a brute. But, to answer your question, the women selected for Preparation are, like you, unmated. Unlike you, they enter the Maze by choice. Also unlike you, they may choose to stay or go."

In the quiet that followed, Tyre tried to fathom her explanation. That a freeborn woman would willingly choose to live in a cell with a slave made no sense. Others seemed to share his conclusion.

"I don't understand," said Pandar. "What do they hope to gain by mating with a slave?"

"Has slavery given you so little regard for yourself that you believe you've nothing to offer a woman? All of you are strong and well formed; some of you led respectable lives before you were sold into slavery. Have you nothing inside, private and untouched by the ugliness of your lives, that could be found valuable by another?"

When there was no response by Pandar or any of the men, she added, "As to what may be gained by such a joining, time will provide you with an answer."

Tyre spoke up, not troubling to hide his disbelief.

"The old woman spoke of gifts necessary to free us from this place. Does this mean that once we give our . . ." his mouth twisted, ". . . gifts to this woman, you'll be satisfied and we may go free?"

She regarded him steadily.

"Not just your gifts, Tyre, but the gifts the woman will give as well.

"What if we don't want the woman chosen for us?" Rama demanded, others in the group nodding their heads and muttering among themselves.

"That's a sensible question, which I'll answer by describing the contract of joining. At the fullness of this moon, you'll meet the woman chosen for you. There will be no warning or formal introduction; she will simply be brought to your cell. For one moon you'll live together as I've described. You may join together or not; that is the choice of you and the woman. At the next full moon, after private counsel, the contract may be ended by either of you. If, however, you both choose to continue, you must honor your contract for another three moons. During that time it's expected that you will join your bodies together."

Rama's next question had already formed in Tyre's mind.

"What happens to us if the woman chooses to leave?"

Tyre read the answer in the sadness of the Instructor's face.

"That's a more difficult question. It's possible you may be joined to another woman. It's equally possible that you'll be removed from the Maze."

Rama nodded slowly, studying his enormous hands. Tyre swallowed hard, closing his eyes for a moment before opening them to stare out the window. All the men were shifting uncomfortably in their chairs as they began to understand the immense change in the rules. For a fortnight, in the training rooms and the arena, they pushed their bodies toward some goal known only by the trainers. In another fortnight, their nights would be spent with a woman whose choice to leave them could send them back to Agave. They might be slaves, but here in the Maze they were well fed, free from punishment as long as they performed as ordered, and had consistency and security in their lives.

The woman in gray opened one of the books on the table in front of her.

"We'll begin your instruction now. You're expected to listen and ask questions appropriate to our study. Nothing you ask will shock or insult me as long as it's to the point. The first subject is anatomy."

And so the first lesson began. As the Instructor continued, fifteen men slowly straightened to attention in the hard wooden chairs. Life and the distant promise of freedom were now dependent on a woman's whim.

Kara's days passed quickly, studying happily with teachers who praised her progress with a needle and assisted her in her fumbling attempts at cookery. Her knowledge of weaving so impressed her teacher that she dismissed Kara from the class, suggesting that she study pattern making. The morning sessions were more difficult, although she observed that several of the women were troubled by these studies and guessed they were probably maidens like herself.

As Nerissa advised, Kara never spoke of her reasons for entering the Maze. She looked for Thalia at the morning meal, but was unable to find her. When she inquired about her, Nerissa responded with information rather than explanation.

"She was dismissed. Not all who come here are happy; not all are worthy. Others may depart as well. Don't dwell on their departure; study and sing for the ones who remain."

Kara sang every night after the evening meal. Another girl was accomplished on the lute and they quickly found each other through their music. She was called Minthe, a delicate creature whose nimble fingers plucked the lute strings, weaving a subtle accompaniment around Kara's vibrant soprano. Last night they brought their concert to an end with the performance of an ancient love song of Pelion. At its conclusion, the women drifted away to their beds, forgoing the lively chatter that usually characterized their preparations for sleep. As Minthe placed her instrument in its case, Kara saw her bite her lips to still their trembling.

"Minthe, tell me of your unhappiness."

Minthe regarded her with woe.

"It's forbidden to talk of our life before the Maze."

"Surely no one will mind if you share sorrow with a friend."

Minthe weighed Kara's words before speaking from her heart.

"I was mated to a friend from my childhood. He was killed when a Legion scouting party attacked a band of slavers who were raiding in the old forest to the northwest. That song was one we sang together. I came here because I despaired of ever knowing anyone as well as I knew him. I thought here, perhaps, I could meet someone who . . . who needed me."

Kara held her tight, stroking the dark braids and thin shoulders. As Minthe quieted, Kara contemplated her complete ignorance of everything to do with mating or sharing her life with a man. She adored her father and played and studied with boys throughout her twenty years. But they were familiar, those boys who grew to manhood, and none of them ever looked on her with anything except friendship. She met many men during her apprenticeship, but her studies were difficult and time-consuming. Any time spent together was for the purpose of reviewing material and sharing their passion for music. Laughing at herself, she admitted that not only her body was virginal, but her emotions as well. Holding Minthe in her arms, she was reminded that love could bring pain. Perhaps she'd kept those men at a distance without realizing it, choosing ignorance over involvement, keeping herself in a safe cocoon woven by family and friends.

"Thank you for trusting me with your grief. Come now, we must hurry to bed before they take away the torches."

The next morning confirmed Kara's feelings of inadequacy. Gathered in a small library whose walls were dotted with drawings and maps, the women studied daily with Nerissa. The iron bars covering the windows overlooking a meager garden bothered Kara. Her feelings of dismay increased when Nerissa explained that the bars were necessary since the ernani sometimes gathered in this room. Shocked for a moment, Kara reminded herself of the chains around the prisoner's ankles and wrists. It never occurred to her that they might wish to leave Pelion—that anyone who lived here would ever wish to go elsewhere. She never left the city walls except for riding lessons. Her father sometimes traveled with the Guild's wares, returning from those trips with a tired slump to his shoulders, his only hint of what lay outside the walls his tight embrace of mother and daughter upon his return.

This morning they entered the library to find one of the large wooden tables drawn to the middle of the room, a space cleared about it, and a smaller table nearby holding a tray of assorted bottles and clean cloths. Nerissa greeted them with her usual warmth and asked them to gather around the table. She waited until the chattering quieted before beginning the lesson for the day.

"We've been studying techniques of healing and you've done very well. Today, we'll change our course somewhat and begin our consideration of the male body."

Nervous giggles wafted through the room. Nerissa smiled, but maintained her air of seriousness.

"Some of you know more than others so we'll start very simply. Soon all of you will be living with a man in great intimacy. The ernani's physical training is rigorous, so rigorous that you'll often find them stiff and sore. If you ease their aches and bruises, you give a caring gift few of them have ever received."

Smiles were replaced by large eyes and the room hushed.

"In a moment a man will join us and we'll begin."

One girl squeaked in alarm. Nerissa shook her head in warning.

"Dias, your modesty rings false. Gelanor is a member of the Hetaera Guild and an accomplished teacher. If you cannot approach this simple task with seriousness, perhaps you're not worthy to walk the Path."

"I ask pardon, Nerissa. It's just that I . . . I've never touched a man before."

"Which is why you'll begin today."

The door swung open and a man of trim build and the typical dark coloring of Pelion entered. He smiled at the girls, his eyes merry and alert, before greeting Nerissa. She gestured to the table.

"Everything is prepared, Gelanor."

Methodically, he removed his jerkin, shirt, and shoes, folding his clothes neatly and laying them across a wooden chair. Unbuttoning his loose breeches, he pulled them off, revealing a simple loincloth, jumped up onto the table, and lay down on his stomach. Nerissa unfolded a cloth and floated it over him, leaving his back and shoulders bare. Pillowing his face on his hands, Gelanor smiled at them again.

Nerissa lifted a small bottle in her hands.

"First cover your hands with this lotion. This will allow your hands to move more easily as well as soothing Gelanor's skin. This is especially healing if the skin is chapped or burned by wind or sun. Now, who would like to begin?"

She held out the bottle. No one claimed it. Searching through the group, she said quietly, "Kara?"

Picking Kara out from the direction of Nerissa's gaze, Gelanor winked at her.

"I promise I won't bite, nor do I stink. I bathed very carefully this morning."

While the others giggled, Kara stepped forward to accept the bottle. The lotion was fragrant and slightly oily in consistency. She moved beside the table and waited for Nerissa's instruction.

"Begin by placing your hands above the shoulder blades. Work in small circles. You must loosen the muscles under the skin first before applying any pressure."

Kara bent over Gelanor's still form. As she followed Nerissa's directions she quickly forgot the women around her, concentrating on the muscles moving under her hands. Gelanor's skin, mahogany in color and finely textured, glowed where the lotion touched it.

"Begin to work more deeply. Put your weight over your hands. That's better. Try to distinguish each muscle under the skin as you work. Good."

The lesson continued until she finished his upper shoulders. Nerissa called a halt and gave Kara a cloth with which to wipe her hands. As she stepped back into the circle, Gelanor turned his head and winked again.

"I'll be asleep before long if you're all so gentle. And to think I was afraid you might bruise me."

Peals of laughter greeted his teasing. Several hands reached for the bottle this time. The lesson continued, Gelanor's body gradually beginning to shimmer with oil. Each woman did a small section: an arm, a hand, the lower back, chest, and stomach. Nerissa removed the sheet and they worked over thighs, calves, and even his feet. By the time they were finished, the air was thick with the odor of spice.

That evening, Kara sat on her bed and gazed up at the half moon peeking shyly through the window. Hugging her pillow, she recalled the play of her fingers over Gelanor's shoulders. She'd never guessed at the pleasure a touch could give her. It was such a simple thing, and as Nerissa said, a gift of caring. How would it feel if a man touched her in return? A quiver of anticipation ran through her as she considered hands stroking her and the scent of the fragrant oil seemed to float on the cool air of the sleeping chamber. If the hands belonged to someone like Gelanor, it would be something to cherish. With that thought, she curled into a ball and slept.

When Nerissa extinguished the torches later that night, she noticed Kara was smiling in her sleep.

They gathered in the official quarters of the Fifteenth Mother, a tower room nestled high in the northwest quadrant of the city's walls. Stacks of papers and writing paraphernalia had been cleared away, the scarred surface of the table reflecting the candlelight, as did the six pairs of eyes intent on the woman who sat at the head of the table. Some of the worry lines etched on that face over the past several moons faded as she beamed at the man who had just finished speaking.

"Gelanor, Gelanor, what should we do without you? You enter a roomful of nervous women and a quarter of an hour later their laughter echoes in the halls. Tell me, how do you work your magic?"

Deep-set eyes twinkling at the woman in black, Gelanor favored her with an impish grin.

"You must not thank me too much, for I'm amply rewarded for my labors. What other man can boast of being handled by fifteen women in a single day?" Making a face, he added, "Then there's the benefit of skin so drenched with oil I'll be forced to bathe for several days to remove it all."

His mournful tone reduced everyone to helpless merriment. Even Stanis' usually unsmiling face was touched by laughter. As the laughter subsided, Vena focused intently on the Master Hetaera.

"Nerissa tells me that one young woman, Kara by name, began the lesson. What were your impressions of her?"

"I remember her," Gelanor responded enthusiastically. "She's the one who made the session a success. When Nerissa called on her, I made a jest and she forgot her nervousness. Her touch was tentative at first, but gained in confidence as she worked."

Vena nodded slowly, offering no response.

Taking her silence as permission to depart, Gelanor rose, and with a quick nod to those assembled, left the room.

The woman in black turned next to the man whose enormous frame was crammed into one of the wooden, high-backed chairs. He met her eyes with a self-conscious nod.

"You've been silent for several days now, Grasos. Are we making any progress?"

Like many men big of body, Grasos spoke slowly, as if he required additional time to move his thoughts from his head to his mouth.

"He seems to be settling into the routine. He still speaks to no one, although I catch him listening to the others at meals and while they wait for the healer. Today was difficult. He was edgy and distressed after the session with the Instructor. Even so, he won the foot race easily."

"Did you leave him unchained as we decided?"

"Yes. He was surprised, I think. Surprised and suspicious."

"Thank you, Grasos. You are the best of keepers for one so important to our plan."

Blushing at the unexpected compliment, Grasos freed himself from the chair and left the room with his head held high.

"And you, Zelor, is there anything we should know about the training sessions?"

Zelor, Luxor's son, had known the Fifteenth Mother since childhood. As burly and as opinionated as his father, he entered the Legion on his eighteenth birthday. It was difficult rising through the ranks as the son of the Legion Commander, but Zelor inherited both his father's adeptness and his tenacity. No one trained harder or was more exacting in his studies than Zelor. Rhacius' second-in-command, he had been granted leave for special duty within the Maze, immediately acquiescing to the Fifteenth Mother's request that he put aside the military operations that were his passion to become the Head Trainer of the ernani. Like his sire, he camouflaged his deep regard for her behind a brusque demeanor.

"It goes better with the sword. The added flesh and work on his upper body helps, although his refusal to be bested is the main reason for improvement. He's stubborn, that one."

"And Rama?"

Zelor's face darkened.

"I know what Grasos thinks about my pairing them together. Rama sent Tyre flying once and Grasos has never forgiven him. But I tell you, Mother, I'd much rather have him fighting a skilled mercenary who's an expert with a sword, than someone of lesser talents who might kill him purely by accident."

Vena made haste to sooth his ruffled feathers.

"Your judgment in this has never been questioned. My question concerning Rama was poorly phrased. My interest was in knowing if you have read Rama and what was revealed."

Confidence restored, Zelor leaned back in his chair.

"At first he couldn't understand why he was matched with a rank amateur and resented the placement. Lately, he's come to understand he's being used as a teacher. As his pupil improves, the discovery of his natural ability to teach surprises him. Eventually I'll have to separate them. For now, their pairing serves them both."

A few more ernani were discussed, with Nerissa asking most of the questions. After Zelor was dismissed, four members of the Council remained.

"Luxor is away to the south and will join us when he can. We have a fortnight until the full moon, my friends. Nerissa, you had your first meeting with the ernani. Has it changed any of the pairings you planned?"

"The session with Gelanor has made me reconsider. Dias is too nervous and flighty to be joined with Suda. He's afraid of the brutality he's been capable of in the past. Chione, the widow, is a better choice. She's older and wiser in the ways of men."

"And so Dias will join with Dino?"

Nerissa threw back her head and laughed. Some silvery hairs freed themselves from her tight braids and floated softly around her lovely face.

"They deserve each other! A virgin will utterly confound him and he'll laugh at her when she's foolish."

"One word about the women, if I may, Fifteenth Mother."

Vena turned to the man on her left.

"You've been remarkably silent all evening, Ladon. And you are not one to ask for permission to speak. What's amiss?"

Ladon was struck anew by the Fifteenth Mother's skills of perception. He'd thought her occupied with the others and thus unaware of his silence. You're a fool, Ladon, he told himself, if you underestimate her again.

"It concerns the menses of some of the women. Many are off-schedule, not a surprising development considering the complete change of life they've experienced. We must remind their healers to keep track of these changes."

"There's something else, Ladon."

It was not a question.

"It's Kara. She began tonight after Nerissa put out the torches. I sensed her pain and went to her. She's in great discomfort, although she rests more easily now that I've given her the drugs."

A shadow drifted over Vena's face.

"I understand your concern, Ladon. You worry for her when the time comes that a healer cannot help her."

Nerissa interrupted before Ladon could form a reply.

"It's my responsibility to alert the ernani to these matters. You've my promise that I'll do so, although I think both of you exaggerate Kara's fragility."

A relieved look spread over Ladon's finely boned face. Vena hadn't practiced her craft for eighteen years. Even so, she would never forget the special agony reserved for healers attuned to a patient who could not be reached. She felt it when a knife was thrust into Beal's body and again when it was removed. She tried to brush away the fog of bereavement, opening her eyes to discover that Ladon and Nerissa had taken their leave. Only Stanis remained.

Opening her thoughts to him, they grieved together over the empty chair Beal occupied as a member of the Council. As her grief ebbed away, Vena became aware that Stanis was troubled as well, and that his thoughts were not full of Beal, but of Tyre.

"What is it, Stanis? What troubles you?"

Without warning, a dark wind blew over her. Above her the stars quaked in the heavens. The sun was in eclipse: floods of water covered the land and raged in turmoil. Over the sound of the wailing wind a voice of prophecy cried a warning:

"Danger . . . danger from within . . . deep fears . . ."

Sometime during the vision, her body moved of its own volition toward Stanis. He held her tightly, willing his strength to pass into her. Slowly, she disengaged herself, placing an open palm against his dusky cheek.

"You fear half, Stanis, and I shall fear the rest."

Chapter 10

Misery

ERIS SCROOPED MOUNDS of rice into a wooden serving bowl, cursing under his breath as the gummy grains stuck to the bottom of the pan. Since dawn, when the fires were lit and he began his new work assignment in the kitchen, the cook had been keeping a close eye on him. Gritting his teeth to contain his annoyance at performing this task unfit for anyone but a kitchen drudge, Eris removed the last stubborn grains and held up the pan for the cook's inspection.

"Good. Now soak it in water so it'll be easier to clean after the meal."

Eris did as he was ordered until the cook recalled him.

"Stay in the kitchen. Refill the platters and bowls as they're brought to you. Keep everything covered so the food doesn't cool too rapidly. The healer keeps a careful watch over everything they eat, so don't be surprised if he walks in."

With that the cook moved out into the dining hall, where he began overseeing the servers who were readying the tables.

This was the best place Eris had worked since meeting the witch on the day they reached Pelion. In the weeks that followed, he worked deep in the belly of the Maze, slaving in the laundry, stacking firewood and shoveling coal for the braziers, disposing of waste down the drainage system connected with the city sewers. Every filthy task demanding heavy labor was his, and Eris much preferred living by his wits than the sweat of his brow. This was the first time he'd seen the upper levels of the Maze and he wanted to stay here. Even women's work was better than being sent down below.

He wondered again if the witch in the black robes was behind the demeaning work assigned him. When she fixed him with those colorless eyes and asked him why he'd attacked the slave with the whip scars, he suspected she held a grudge against him.

Anyway, the kitchen wasn't so bad and he'd always have plenty to eat. He'd already met Baldor, a simpleton he could befriend and manipulate. If Baldor would do the heavy lifting for him, this place would suit his plans. He'd been in worse places than this and found ways to escape. It was just a matter of time and opportunity.

The doors to the eating hall swung open. Eris peered around the kitchen door as a group of men entered, their hair still wet from a bath, he supposed. As soon as they were seated on the long benches they fell on the food, focusing their attention on how rapidly they could get it from the bowls to their mouths. Each man seemed to have a guard who stood directly behind him, their brown-clad figures lining the walls like statues. The men were clad in loincloths, all of them well muscled and, except for a few bruises, in excellent condition. As he looked them over, he felt a faint glimmer of recognition at some of the faces. When he spotted a blonde head, a rush of sudden anger twisted his gut. Just then he was interrupted by the entry of the cook, who bustled in on an errand and shot him a warning look.

"I told you to stay here. Start on those pots. There's plenty to do with three meals a day. You'll have time enough to rest in a few days when we won't have to prepare the evening meal."

Eris was curious, but started scrubbing.

"What happens then?"

Annoyed, the cook spoke without looking at him.

"Why, the women will enter the cells, of course."

With that, the cook was out the door.

Swallowing his curses, Eris put his energy into his task, scraping a knife against the sides of the stewpot, the sound of metal against metal torturing his ears. Here he was, sweating in a kitchen over grimy pots while the men with whom he'd been chained enjoyed a good meal and were provided with women for their needs. Eris hadn't had a woman since he left Agave and she was a common whore, hired by the slaver who'd purchased his contract and delivered him into that hellhole. He'd thought the witch was punishing him for trying to kill the slave with the whip-scars, but the horse boy tried to kill him in return and there he sat, as healthy as could be, flesh and muscles covering a frame Eris remembered as thin to the point of starvation. Hands shaking with fury, he finished the pots before resuming his place at the door.

They'd finished eating and some kind of head guard was talking to them, reading names from a list. The men groaned and rolled their eyes at the news. Eris watched the horse boy glance over to the black man beside him and smile. So, Eris thought, he's already found a companion for protection, just like the slave with the scars. The head guard made another announcement and the men rose from the benches to leave the hall. As the black man rose, he motioned for the horse boy to go first and said something Eris couldn't hear. The horse boy hesitated, but the black man just smiled and pushed him toward the door. Not just protection, Eris thought. No, the horse boy needs more than just protection.

Tyre was in a rebellious mood long before he reached the library. He'd sat through these endless sessions in stony silence for days, trying to hide the fact that they shook him to the core of his being. From the first day it was obvious he was the only one who had never lain with a woman. Even though the idea was distasteful in the extreme, it irked him that his pride made it impossible for him to let the others suspect he was different from them. He decided his only course was to let them think he was still angry about the Instructor's high-handedness and hope no one noticed that he alone could offer no information or insights, or even pose a question about the subjects they discussed daily.

After the Head Trainer announced their departure for the library, Tyre felt Rama's eye on him. Perhaps his expression betrayed his reluctance, but whatever the reason, Rama made it clear he understood Tyre's situation. Stepping aside, he motioned for Tyre to go first. When Tyre hesitated, Rama said:

"If she's a virgin, she'll know no more than you."

Tyre frowned and turned away, realizing with a sinking feeling in his gut that everyone else must have noticed his silence and interpreted it as Rama had. His one hope, which he refused to let himself dwell on, was that this women would be as inexperienced as he was. The thought of a woman laughing at his fumbling efforts to please her tied his stomach in knots.

His nerves wrangled and painfully self-conscious of his inability to speak, he sat through the session without paying attention. He was dimly aware of the Instructor's presence and the fact that some of the men were responding; the subject matter remained a blank. Then, the Instructor held up a page from one of the books. A sharp wave of nausea brought the taste of bile to the back of his throat. Swallowing hard, he stared at the picture, biting the inside of his mouth until he tasted blood. At its taste, the nausea returned again. This time he couldn't control it. Rising unsteadily to his feet, his hand over his mouth, he pushed past the legs of the men between him and the door and rushed out. Running down the corridor, he found a corner, where he vomited until there was nothing left inside him.

Unbidden, the picture came to him again and he was no longer in the Maze.

Tyre was sleeping when something woke him. A woman was crying, a voice like his mother's, but thinner and frightened. Now he could hear other sounds—a kind of low grunting. It was dark where he lay, but he could see light coming from his mother's side of the tent. He climbed off the cot and walked toward the cloth hung between his mother's bed and his sleeping place. Pulling back the cloth, he called out for his mother.

A man was riding his mother like a horse. She was looking at Tyre now and so was the man. Then Tyre saw the blood running down the back of her legs. The man, too, when he moved away from his mother, had blood on a thing sticking out from his belly. The man looked angry. His mother pulled a blanket around her and reached out her arms for Tyre. He ran to her and felt her tears on his cheek.

The man growled at her: "Don't think it ends here. Soon the boy will leave you and the tribe needs more sons for Sturm."

The man left the tent and Tyre was rocked to sleep in his mother's arms. He didn't see the man again until he came to take Tyre away on a black pony with a white stripe running down his nose.

Sick and cold, Tyre wiped away the perspiration from his forehead. Someone was behind him. He knew before he turned it was Grasos. Tyre readied himself to face the guard's reprimand, but the voice hissing at him was strange, yet at the same time, oddly familiar. Still groggy from the affects of the retching, Tyre tried to clear his vision while the voice kept harassing him, cursing him. In time the words became distinct.

"What's the matter, horse boy, too much rich food? Or does the thought of putting it to a woman make you sick? Lapithians don't like women much, do they? Is that why they mount them from behind? So they don't have to see their faces?"

Tyre put a hand out and grasped his tormentor by his shirt, pulling him up to his face. His blurred vision clearing, he recognized the slave who tried to kill Phylas, his mouth open, and each question adding to Tyre's torment. To close that gaping hole, to stop those taunts that only increased his nausea and rage, was his sole desire. Pulling back his right fist, he smashed it into the face. Cartilage crunched under his knuckles. As he drew back his fist, he saw blood. Without thinking, he hit again, not even caring where the blow landed, just wanting to hurt someone as much as he hurt inside. As he pulled his arm back a third time, an iron hand gripped his shoulder. Someone was pulling him away from the man who sank into a heap at his feet. He was swung around, his arms pulled behind his back, and Grasos locked on the manacles. The Instructor stood pale-faced and staring intently at Tyre before turning her back on him and walking away. Grasos half-carried, half-dragged him to a door, threw him onto a bed, and left him alone in an unlit cell.

The Fifteenth Mother was as frantic as Nerissa had ever seen her. She paced up and down the length of the library while Grasos stood watch at the door, his worried eyes following her every move. Ladon waited by the window and, with the calm typical of a healer, gazed out over the empty garden. Stanis arrived, lowered himself into a chair, and sat staring at his hands. Zelor entered, slammed the door behind him, and the meeting began.

"There's nothing to discuss! They're your rules! You wrote them and they've never been changed or set aside. `The punishment for striking any guard, worker, or staff member in the Maze is punishable by instant removal. In exceptional cases, removal may be avoided by the ernani's agreement to undergo punishment which must be publicly witnessed.'"

"Don't quote my words back to me! I'm not in my dotage and I remember them perfectly!"

Vena's words were sharp, bitten off and spit at him. Zelor froze, the color draining from his face. Vena was instantly contrite.

"Zelor, forgive me. I'm just an old woman who feels the earth opening under my feet. Stanis warned me and now it has come to pass. I'd like us to review this together. Come, Zelor, sit by me."

He grasped her outstretched hand and everyone gathered around the table, the Fifteenth Mother flanked by Zelor and Grasos. It was rare, but not unheard of, for guests to link minds with the Council. For this reason, the Council members established their mental connections more carefully than usual, issuing a formal, if unspoken, invitation for Zelor and Grasos to join them before beginning their session.

The Fifteenth Mother indicated that Nerissa should begin, and she did so without hesitation, taking them back to her lesson with the ernani in the library, providing an unedited account of what passed in front of her eyes, every detail precise, clean-cut, a procession of perfectly wrought images flashing on the stages of every mind in the room, allowing each Council member to see an exact duplication of the events that led to Tyre's upset.

There they sat, eye-witnesses to the madness of Tyre, seeing a progression of actions recounted in turn by Nerissa, Grasos and Zelor. Through Nerissa, they saw Tyre's complexion take on a greenish pallor, watch him bring his hand to his mouth and run from the room, and heard through Grasos' ears the sound of Tyre vomiting somewhere along the corridor. Next, they traveled with Grasos as if riding on his shoulder as he pounded down the corridor, hearing Tyre's strangled cry and the unmistakable sound of a fist smashing into someone's face. When Grasos grabbed Tyre's golden-skinned shoulder as it moved back to strike a third blow, the Council saw what Grasos saw—a wild-eyed, staring Tyre. They also felt Tyre's weight as he collapsed on Grasos and was half-carried to the empty cell.

Finally, through Zelor's eyes, the Council saw a crouching man crumpled against a wall, his face bruised and so swollen his features were unrecognizable, his mouth a bloody hole with two teeth missing and another hanging by its root. They heard Zelor question him and winced at the ghastly sounds issuing from his ruined mouth.

"Why did he attack you?"

The man shrugged his shoulders.

"You did nothing to provoke him?"

The man shook his head, grimacing at the pain of movement.

"Why were you in this hallway? It's a long way from the kitchen."

"Wass . . . losss . . ."

The Fifteenth Mother broke the connection.

"Lost? Could this be true, Zelor? What do we know about him?"

"As an ernani deemed unfit for Preparation, he was given the same option everyone gets: a year's work within the Maze in exchange for an apprenticeship in the guild of his choice. Mostly, he's worked down below. No one seems to remember much about him. All the laundry steward could tell me was that he's a loner. He started work today as a cook's assistant in the ernani's dining hall. He could easily have been lost."

The Fifteenth Mother considered for a moment before turning to Ladon, who had resumed his contemplation of the garden.

"Tell me how Tyre might be punished, yet restored to good health by the next full moon."

Zelor interrupted before Ladon could speak.

"But he must agree to be punished, a public punishment witnessed by everyone in the Maze! He's stubborn, that one, and fearsome proud. He'll never agree."

The Fifteenth Mother regarded Zelor for a moment.

"I know a man who's both stubborn and proud. Even so, he's agreed to do many things he did not want to do. Do you think Tyre is so different from you, Zelor? He will agree. Like you, he will agree."

Zelor's mouth hung open then shut with a snap, the tops of his ears red with embarrassment.

The Fifteenth Mother stared expectantly at Ladon, tapping her foot with nervous energy. He scowled as he maintained his gaze out the window. Inside, he was screaming at her.

"I'm a healer!"

And she was reasoning with him.

"You know as well as I do that this is the only way left to us. We cannot break the rules. You can treat him and stay with him afterward. Don't desert me, Ladon. Don't desert him."

Ladon sighed and turned away from the window to make a suggestion that gained Zelor's and Grasos' instant approval. The three of them left together. Nerissa reminded herself she needed to gather the women. Before she reached the door, the Fifteenth Mother called her back.

"What picture were you showing the ernani when Tyre left?"

"It was from a book of pleasure that depicts various ways of joining. The page I held up shows a man entering a woman from behind."

Vena examined her keenly.

"Don't blame yourself for what happened. You could never have predicted this. And you were correct, I think, in advising Grasos to give him a moment alone."

Nerissa sent a thankful smile over her shoulder as she departed. Vena turned to Stanis, a trembling smile on her lips.

"Tyre will agree, will he not, Stanis?"

"If you cannot reach him, he cannot be reached."

The door swung open, a sudden shaft of light sending the shadow of a dark figure across the bed on which Tyre lay. Grasos pulled him to his feet and swung him around to face the source of the shadow. He wasn't surprised to see the woman in black, the one they called the Fifteenth Mother. In the hours he'd lain in the darkness, he'd accepted the fact that he would be punished. There was no reason, no excuse he could give for his actions. Even if there was, he didn't think this old woman would be moved by excuses.

Gray eyes took his measure. She was using the formal voice he remembered from the ceremony at the altar.

"Ernani, you have broken a rule presented to you on the first day of your arrival. Your choice is this: to agree to the punishment selected for you by the Council or to leave the Maze. The punishment will be administered in public. When it is over, all will be as it was. If you refuse the punishment, you must leave the Maze, and so will be returned to Agave and sold."

"Can you tell me what the punishment will be?" Tyre asked.

She knew she blinked her eyes in surprise. Inside she was exultant; he never considered not accepting the punishment. Touching his thoughts, she found, to her astonishment, that he felt he deserved it.

"I can only say that you will not be scarred."

"When will the punishment be given?"

"As soon as you make your decision, Grasos will lead you to the arena and it will begin."

She felt his relief. He would rather have it be done quickly and finished.

"The man I hit. Did I kill him?"

"Why do you ask? Do you long for his death?"

The fierceness of her reply made him take a step backward.

"I . . . I only wondered."

She felt him open a door and then slam it shut. His distress stemmed from the picture Nerissa showed the men. Of that, she was sure. Tempted to explore her theory, she decided it was cruel to delay what he was already preparing himself to face.

"What is your choice, ernani?"

"I choose punishment, Fifteenth Mother."

"Take him, Grasos. When all is ready, I'll speak to the people and make the offering."

Alone in the cell, she shook her head. This one never failed to do the opposite of what she expected. She'd prepared herself for shouting, outraged pride and refusal to submit to the rules he obviously despised. Instead he was quiet, guilt-stricken, and placidly accepted the pain she promised him. What had moved him to such a fit of temper that he could almost kill a complete stranger with his bare hands, and then ask after his health a few hours later? Then she remembered that for the first time, he had called her by her title. *"Ah, Tyre,"* she sighed, *"no wonder my beloved loved you so well."*

The women fluttered like a flock of migrating birds, grabbing cloaks from the wardrobes lining the sleeping chamber, tying and pinning hair so it would not escape from under their hoods. Their voices were high with tension, disturbed by the announcement that upset their afternoon routine.

"I heard from one of the serving girls that he went berserk and killed a kitchen helper in the dining hall!"

"That's not what I heard. It was an ernani he attacked, crippling him for life."

"Well, whatever he did, I heard he did it with his bare hands. Oh, please let him not be the one chosen for me!"

Nerissa's instructions revealed few details.

"Put on your cloaks and be sure your hair and faces are hidden underneath your hood. A rule was broken. You, with all the residents of the Maze, must witness the punishment of an ernani. We'll proceed to the arena. Once we pass out of these chambers, you'll speak to no one."

The journey was a long one, down damp, twisting corridors so different from the cheerful airiness of their rooms. Finally, they passed heavily guarded doors and found themselves in an oval arena. Along its walls ran a dirt track. Nerissa led them over the course and onto the dry grass in the center, where a timber structure supporting thick climbing ropes stood. People gathered around its wooden supports, several hundred or more. Nerissa guided them to the place where the Fifteenth Mother's black robes could be seen surrounded by Legionnaires. Her arms lifted and silence descended.

"People of the Maze, we're gathered to witness the punishment of one who committed a violent act. He accepts, of his own free will, the punishment to be administered. He stands freely to signify his submission to our laws. Watch in silence. Remember: his debt is paid in full today."

From the opposite direction of the gate through which the women entered the arena, Kara watched a tall man with blonde hair approach the center area. As he stepped up to the dangling ropes, the guard who walked beside him unlocked the manacles that held his hands behind his back. The ernani wrapped his arms around the ropes, grasping their thickness with his hands. Kara stood close enough to see the guard reach into his vest pocket and produce something that he held up to the ernani's face. Moving behind the ernani's back, the guard untied the knot of his loincloth and pulled it away. As the cloth was removed, the man's jaw set and he closed his eyes.

He stood with his right profile to Kara, facing the Fifteenth Mother, whose hands remained upraised. Behind him, two officers of the Legion removed their leather belts and, holding the buckle in their fists, wrapped them tightly around their hands, the long ends held away from the ground. They stood at attention, their eyes on the Fifteenth Mother. When she lowered her hands, they began.

The sound and sight of leather striking flesh made Kara look away. The man made no sound, nor did the crowd. The Legionnaires alternated blows, maintaining a steady rhythm. Nerissa's quiet command made Kara look up.

"Watch, Kara. We must honor his offering."

From her position, Kara could see the marks appearing on the man's shoulders and upper back. He didn't move at the first few blows. Now he flinched as the belts hit flesh already turning a deep, angry red. His head lost its proud carriage and hung down over his chest, his eyes shut tight. The ropes supporting him shook slightly as a long shudder coursed through him. At that exact moment, the Fifteenth Mother lifted her arms and the blows ceased. The ernani lifted his head, the ropes swaying as he released his hold, his chest rising and falling as he looked directly into the Fifteenth Mother's face, whether in defiance or gratitude, Kara couldn't be sure.

A whispered sigh ran through the crowd. With bowed heads, they dispersed. Kara looked over her shoulder as she followed Nerissa's receding form. The man had slumped forward onto his knees.

That was her last sight of him, kneeling in the dirt, alone in the vast emptiness of the arena.

A pillow was placed underneath his cheek, offering relief from the scratchy woolen blanket on which he lay. A hand appeared in front of his face. Tyre knew instinctively it was waiting for him to surrender the piece of leather into which he'd ground his teeth. When he opened his mouth, deft fingers removed it. Next, a cup was held to his mouth. Lifting his upper body onto his left elbow to drink, the movement awakened the fire of the welts. He bit back a groan. Recovering, he took a sip of water, feeling its coolness wash down his parched throat.

"Would you like some more?" the healer asked.

Tyre shook his head and lowered himself carefully back down on the bed. An involuntary shiver ran over him and the coverlet was pulled up to his waist and tucked around his hips and legs.

"Grasos, build up the fire. He must be kept warm tonight. Once that's done, you may leave us."

Tyre heard the tinder being lit and the door clanging shut, but kept his eyes closed, concentrating on keeping the pain at bay. Liquid was poured into a basin and a cloth was immersed and then wrung out, the sound of the drops hitting the surface of the water reminding him of raindrops falling on his tent.

"This solution will lessen the pain of the welts. I'll begin at the top of your shoulders and work down. Don't be afraid to moan or curse aloud if you want. I'll tell no one."

Tyre opened his eyes to regard the speaker.

"I never learned your name, healer."

"I'm called Ladon."

"You were in the arena this afternoon?"

"Everyone who lives or works within the Maze attended the ceremony. In this way we pay tribute to you, who make the offering of your own free will."

Tyre was silent for a moment as the cloth was laid over his shoulders. The first impact was painful, but as the healer promised, the fire was soon reduced to a dull throb. As the cloth cooled his flesh, he asked another question.

"Who were the women near the Fifteenth Mother?"

Another cloth was wrung over the basin.

"Which women?"

"The ones near the front in the hooded cloaks of many colors."

The second cloth touched him and he gasped, letting out his breath in a low moan.

"They are the women who will be mated in a few days to the ernani."

Tyre guessed who they were when he saw them huddled around the Instructor. Grasos told him what to expect and explained how he could steady himself with the climbing ropes. The leather for his mouth took him by surprise. Who could have guessed that Grasos would anticipate his fear of crying out, bringing even more shame down on his head, especially in front of so many people, more people than he ever imagined lived in this gray-walled prison. Unprepared for the removal of his loincloth, he forgot his nakedness with the first stroke of the belt. By the tenth blow, he was holding onto the ropes with trembling arms, trying to keep himself upright. In time, he lost count—blind, deaf, and dumb to anything but the crack of leather over bruised skin beginning to swell. His arms aching, he began to shudder uncontrollably, afraid that if the blows continued he'd be forced down to his knees. At that instant, the blows stopped.

Another cloth descended. This time he cursed more loudly, groaning as he released his indrawn breath.

"So the woman who'll enter this cell saw me for the first time today; naked, beaten, hanging from those damnable ropes. I can only imagine the excitement and joy with which she'll greet me."

Ladon understood the reason for the scathing self-ridicule issuing from Tyre's clenched, white lips. As a member of the Council, he must not interfere. As a healer, he owed his patient peace of mind. Ladon applied another cloth, waiting until Tyre's breathing returned to normal after his initial jerk of pain.

"You must understand that for us, and for the women who have chosen to walk the Path, you paid the debt you owed in full. You're not a criminal in our eyes and no one will ever refer to your punishment again."

Tyre heard the Fifteenth Mother's speech to the crowd, but it meant little to him. Ladon's explanation brought a small measure of comfort and suddenly he was reminded of Belwyn, who could always make him see light when there was darkness all around him.

"You remind me of someone I once knew."

Ladon's response was nothing more than conversational.

"And who was that?"

"He was called Belwyn. He was my tutor before . . . before I came here."

Even now, Tyre could not speak of Belwyn's passing.

"How do I remind you of him?"

"You have his ways. Not just with the gentleness of your hands. He would have spoken to me as you just did."

Ladon shut his eyes at the force of his memories of Beal. Beal, who taught him herb lore and diagnosis. Beal, who chose Ladon as his successor and at his departure for the north twelve years ago, pulled him aside to whisper the words of his trust.

"Look after him, Ladon, when I send him to the Maze. I do not know him, but something tells me he will need your care. He will be wild and headstrong, bitter and unyielding, and this place will cause him great suffering. Care for him, Ladon, and remember that a true healer treats the body and mind as one."

Ladon placed a cloth carefully over angry welts that revealed no broken skin. Zelor's men were skillful and Tyre helped them by not moving, making it possible for them to place their blows. Confined to his back and upper shoulders, the welts would begin to fade in a matter of days. *"I've tried to ease the way, Beal,"* Ladon thought, before turning his attention to the man whose hair shone palely in the fire's glow.

"The worst is over. The skin should be growing numb; the next application will help reduce the swelling. It's time for you to sleep now.

I'll stay through the night. Now, let me show you how to control the pain. First, concentrate on your breathing . . ."

A low chuckle from Tyre brought Ladon up short.

"I told you that you reminded me of Belwyn." Tyre's voice had been roughened by pain. Now it was low and full of longing. "Did you know him, Ladon? A small man with short brown curls?"

Ladon smiled. Beal, having foreseen this moment protected him from speaking an untruth.

"No, Tyre. I've never known anyone named Belwyn."

Blue eyes dimmed, then closed. Ladon watched as the bunched muscles on the long, well-formed body gradually relaxed into smoothness. As Tyre's facial muscles slackened, Ladon strained to hear the mumbled words coming from his lips.

"Good . . . to . . . have . . . someone . . . to . . . talk . . . to."

Ladon settled onto the uncomfortable stool and began applying the cloths. Tyre never stirred. Ladon would be gone long before his patient awakened. Even so, he hoped another would soon soothe the ache of Tyre's loneliness.

Kara did not sing that night. The ernani punished in the arena was the source of endless speculation. The gossip whispered from person to person, embroidered with each telling, filled Kara with distaste. She pleaded a headache, and since her monthly flow began the night before, a healer handed her a cup of herb tea without making a fuss. Retreating to a small window seat, she sat alone and momentarily forgotten by the others.

Enjoying her isolation, a rarity in this bevy of women, she thought back to the figure slumped against the ropes. He seemed so alone in the deserted arena. She wondered if he was alone now, with only his pain to keep him company.

Idly, she began to compare him with Gelanor, the only other man she'd seen unclothed. The comparison was not exact, since Gelanor retained his loincloth, but she'd seen the shape of his genitals through the thin fabric. And in any case, the morning sessions with Nerissa had prepared her for a man's differences. The fact of the ernani's nudity was not what intrigued her. It was how he differed from Gelanor's trim, almost delicate form, with its tight curls of black hair running across his chest, narrowing at his stomach, and running down into the white folds of the loincloth. The blonde man was huge in comparison, with long arms and legs and hairless skin. Where Gelanor's body was firm and slender, the other's was heavily muscled, with bulges rising from his arms and chest as he clenched the ropes in his hands. The clarity of her vision made her wince for him. Nerissa's voice scattered the image.

"Are you in much discomfort?"

The Instructor sat beside her, her brow furrowed with concern.

"Not any more. The cramping is worst in the first few hours and then subsides. I . . . I wasn't thinking about myself."

Unsurprised by Kara's admission, Nerissa settled her robes around her and regarded the troubled girl. She must tread carefully, she knew. The Fifteenth Mother's instructions were clear. The unforeseen trouble of this day must be handled.

"What troubles you, child?"

"What did this man do, that he deserved such punishment?"

Nerissa weighed the advantage of truth over misdirection. She could soothe the girl with a veiled answer, or tell her the facts and let her interpret them for herself. *"Truth, Nerissa,"* she decided.

"He beat a man unconscious with his fists. If he hadn't been stopped, the man he attacked might have died."

The girl's eyes widened with alarm.

"Why would he do such a thing?"

"Sadly, I must confess I do not know. Such an action might have meant his removal from the Maze, but the Fifteenth Mother tempered justice with mercy. He's shamed and sore, but alive and still able to walk the Path.

Not long after, Nerissa moved away to join another conversation in progress. Although troubled by the violence of the act described, Kara felt calmer, more at ease. While sipping her tea she decided she was being childish about not sharing her music with the others.

Kara found Minthe and soon the night reverberated with a choir of women's voices raised in lush harmonies of ancient songs.

Chapter 11

Meeting

HER QUESTION LEFT hanging unanswered in the air, Nerissa sighed and closed her book.

To a man, they were looking out the barred windows as if their combined concentration could push the sun toward the western horizon and thus bring on the night. Although they could not see the moon, they knew it climbed steadily upward in the eastern sky. Like her, they watched it nightly, the ernani from their cell windows, she from her private chambers. Tonight it would hang ripe and heavy in the crisp night air.

She knew she must prepare them. Some had a few more hours to wait; some had days. Pouring her good-will out over the room, Nerissa felt a satisfying response of well-being replace their agitation. Open conversation with them revealed ignorance, superstition, and bewilderment, but with a single exception, each man entered the discussions. And even the silent one tried to learn and understand.

"Tonight begins the contract you've prepared for. Don't be disappointed if you're alone upon waking. The moon waxes full with its blessing for three nights. You'll not be alone by the time it begins to wane."

Their tension evaporated. They would be joined; the Instructor said it. Irrepressible Dino couldn't resist a jest to express his relief.

"You can't fool us, Instructor. We know you've aroused us day after day so you can have us all for yourself. Tomorrow you'll tell us it was only a test and we'll line up for your favors."

When the men burst into laughter, Nerissa found herself blushing. It had been many years since a joke about joining broke through her calm demeanor. Still, there was an undercurrent of truth beneath Dino's teasing and the men's response. As a hetaera, she knew the sessions aroused them, although they hid it with lowered eyes and much crossing of legs. As the only woman they'd seen in countless days, she knew they desired her, for she'd retained her beauty even into her fortieth year. Hopefully, her studied remoteness would allow them to transfer their feelings in good time. Her sadness at their rapidly approaching abandonment of her flavored her reply.

"I shall tell you no such thing, for tomorrow another teacher will sit at this table. My time with you ends this afternoon."

A wave of dismay passed over them as she pushed on.

"Tomorrow you'll begin studies in reading, writing, and figures. Those of you who have some knowledge of these things will be tested by your new instructor and go on to study other subjects."

Crusty Suda charmed Nerissa with his wretchedness.

"And we'll never see you more?"

She sent him a grateful smile before continuing.

"It's possible you may need counseling over the course of the winter moons. If you have such a need, any of you," she tried hard to avoid looking directly at Tyre, although she spoke primarily to him, "about any of the subjects we've discussed, you have only to tell your guard and you'll be brought to me."

Her tone became more severe and several of them looked up in alarm. They knew Nerissa well, probably better than they had known their own mothers. If, she reminded herself, they had ever known their mothers.

"Remember this, ernani: you're not to discuss private matters with anyone other than your mate or myself. Your life from dusk to dawn is your own. Once you begin to compare or judge yourself by others, you break our covenant."

She shifted abruptly to a more compassionate mode, confidant they would heed her warning and the thinly veiled threat.

"You are used to the cells; the women are not. All will be unsure and some may be frightened. Go slowly with them and they will repay you in time." She paused, letting them sense her concern for them. "You are not alone in this; I am always here to help you along the Path of Preparation."

After gathering the well-worn books of her calling, Nerissa left the library.

Later that evening, Echetus told her the men sat silent and unmoving until the guards arrived to escort them to the arena.

The next few days were ones of confusion and increased anxiety for Tyre. As Ladon promised, no one treated him any differently after the punishment. Zelor eased up on him for a few days, but soon he was back in the ring with Rama and in the dust as often as he was on his feet. It wasn't the training or the still-vivid memory of the beating that troubled him; it was the fact that the other men were acting strangely.

Rama was one of the first to change. One day he was his usual dour self, the next he was smiling at nothing, letting Tyre land blows he'd tried and failed a hundred times before, easily distracted, and, Tyre thought, simply not there.

Dino's change was the opposite. Once an easy-going irascible jester, he was transformed into a madman. His temper was so short that anyone paired with him for arms practice shot Zelor a piteous glance and girded himself for a battle to near death. Formerly the most loquacious one of the group, he spoke to no one, and shot Tyre a murderous look in response to a simple request that he pass the salt bowl at midday meal.

Not all the changes were ones of behavior. The first day of the full moon, Tyre arrived at the morning meal to find Suda, the brawniest and unquestionably the dirtiest one of the group, groomed to perfection; his hair trimmed, beard and moustache gone, his fingernails cut and free of dirt. At least Suda seemed abashed by his transformation, Tyre thought grudgingly. The others simply went crazy and didn't care who noticed. Pandar worried over something that often had him talking to himself, as if trying out ways to approach some mysterious inquisitor. This evening he rushed past the others at the arena gate, his guard puffing after him, vainly waving the forgotten manacles in the breeze created by Pandar's departure.

Young Brimus, the only man who was Tyre's junior, began the annoying habit of humming to himself. Waiting next to him for the healer the second morning, Tyre was nearly moved to violence when the same melody was repeated endlessly and decidedly off-key. Finally driven to distraction, Tyre asked him sarcastically if he knew another tune. Flushing bright red, Brimus stopped humming. After a few minutes passed he was at it again, oblivious to Tyre's snort of pure disgust.

Tyre's anxiety stemmed from the fact that everyone around him was changing while his life continued as before. He walked behind Grasos the first evening with trepidation mixed with an equal measure of anticipation, but his cell remained empty. Tonight was the worst. Zelor ordered him to remain behind to drill him in a wrestling hold he'd missed once too often. The surly trainer seemed to take delight in slamming Tyre repeatedly on the hard mat. Even more bruised than usual after the bout, he waited impatiently at the gate for Grasos, who lurched down the hall to fetch him long after the evening trumpet sounded. As he followed that giant pair of shoulders down the passageway, he heard the musical sounds of women's voices raised in conversation and laughter. The dimly lit corridors, usually rank with the smell of unwashed bodies and waste buckets in need of emptying, bloomed with the fragrances of perfume, spice, and cooking oil.

His cell door swung open, the dismal dreariness of its four walls hitting him like a blow to the gut. For some unknown reason, and for the first time since his initial release, Grasos chained him to the bed. He paced for hours, ignoring the food when it appeared in the grate, finally curling up in front of the fireplace as he had the night of his arrival. He lay there, staring into the crumbling logs, finally admitting to himself how lonely he was. Belwyn was dead, Phylas had vanished, Rama was unreachable, and except for his conversation with Ladon on the night of the beating, he was wretchedly alone.

Perhaps the Instructor lied to him in that final meeting. Perhaps the reason for his beating convinced them he was unworthy of the promised joining. Tomorrow they would remove him from the cell, and like the others who had disappeared, no one would mention his name or ask about his fate. Tears of self-pity filled his eyes and he blinked them back, furious with himself for letting a few voices and smells unman him. He tried reminding himself that women were unimportant to true warriors of Lapith, but shook his head, disgusted with himself. He was no warrior. He was a slave in a prison with no exit. His loneliness was a gaping hole inside him, gnawing away at his pride, his self-esteem, and his manhood.

Fighting the chain linking him to the bed, he turned over on his other side and stared up at the moon hanging low and swollen in the winter sky. With a hunter's practiced eye, he decided it would begin its wane after one more night. He considered climbing into bed, but upon remembering the other men were sharing theirs with soft bodies the like of which he'd never known, he chose to remain where he was. A log on the fire disintegrated into ash. Tired, aching both inside and out, he closed his eyes on the glowing coals, and slept on the cold hard floor.

The Fifteenth Mother raised her eyes from the coals warming her chilly northern tower to find the others regarding her with fascination. She was unaware of the fact that her eyes were full of tears and had been for the past hour. She entered Tyre's thoughts from the moment he lay down by the fire and hadn't left him in all that time. Straightening herself, stiff from sitting for so long in one position, she blinked rapidly and went to work, her tones crisp and business-like, clicking off orders that soon had everyone's mind bustling, her tears forgotten by them in their flurry to do her will.

"Zelor, I want him tired tomorrow night. So tired he'll be asleep on his feet when Grasos comes to get him. For once, forget Ladon's cautious reminders and run him into the ground."

She paused for a moment, and then made an addendum to her command.

"I also want him dirty; filthy, in fact. Grasos, offer him a bath in the morning and allow him to have it if he chooses. When you pick him up in the evening, turn cross if he suggests it and nasty if he insists."

"Ladon, remind the cook they're to be fed tomorrow night. Delay the delivery of the food until two hours past the evening trumpet. Also, make sure the portions are smaller than usual."

"Nerissa, encourage Kara to eat good meals at both breakfast and midday. Give her some food for her pockets before you leave her in the cell. Imply that you're not sure if the evening meal will be served and you don't want her to go hungry." Gray eyes danced with mischief. "A piece of bread or fruit, perhaps, or a rind of cheese."

The faces gathered around her were becoming increasingly bewildered.

"Stanis, it's time for you to reappear. Arrive at the arena with Lukash in the afternoon at which time you'll inspect them like the owner of a fine herd of cattle. Look them over carefully and speak only to Zelor. Most of them are too involved with joining to worry about you, but Tyre will."

Nerissa interrupted.

"Aren't you being unnecessarily cruel? He's worried and anxious enough over the fact that he's not been joined."

Vena stared at her old friend. A sudden peal of laughter startled them even more than her rapid-fire instructions.

"Does no one understand what I plan here? This will be the first time he's ever been near a woman of his own age, the first time he'll ever converse or share a meal, the first time he'll ever do anything at all with a woman! Do you think him a fool? He knows tomorrow is the last night. I'm trying to ease his fears by making his body and mind so tired that her presence will glow like a beckoning star to a hunter lost on a cloudy night."

She grew suddenly serious.

"I'm also trying to protect her. She knows as well as he does it will be tomorrow night. Try as best you can to cushion the blow of the cell. She knows she'll be allowed to furnish it with anything she desires, but it will be a shock to her. Let her take some extra candles. And stay with her until Grasos warns you of their approach."

The candles flickered as if blown by an unseen presence.

"Well, my friends, there's nothing left to say. Tomorrow night is the fruition of eighteen years of my life and fifteen generations of planning. We've done all we can to prepare them and now we must wait. Here begins the hardest task of all, for we can meddle no longer. Their door does not open until dawn."

Brimus pulled away from him in the straightaway. Tyre dug his toes deeper into the mud to get some traction. He saw the smaller man splash through a pool of water, almost losing his footing when he misjudged its depth. Tyre jumped the pool with his longer legs and suddenly was out in front. Almost at the end of his breath, he flew across the finish line, dropping to his haunches in the oozing muck. The other men appeared almost immediately around him, all of them in latter stages of exhaustion. In time they all breathed easier and rose up to try to scrape the worst of the mud off their bodies. They'd arrived at the arena this afternoon to find the track had been sprayed with water during the night.

Zelor turned a deaf ear their complaints, growling, "It keeps down the dust."

Tyre bathed that morning but as he looked down at himself he knew he'd never been so filthy in his life. Perhaps Grasos would let him rinse off if he promised to hurry. With that thought in mind, he rushed off after the others to be called back by Zelor. Dragging his feet, dismayed at being singled out two nights in a row, he found himself the target of a nasty grimace.

"Where do you think you're going?"

Frowning, Tyre kept his temper.

"Back to my cell."

"I think not. I think you're going to run three more laps."

Tyre must have misunderstood him.

"Three more laps?"

"You heard me the first time. The quicker you begin, the quicker you'll be finished."

There was no reasoning with Zelor even when he was in a good mood. Today he'd been as surly as a half-broken colt. Tyre slouched toward the starting pole, shaking out his arms and legs, trying to stretch out his hamstrings. Zelor's hand dropped and, bone-weary, Tyre took off over the dusky track, dodging as many mud puddles as he could.

As he ran, he decided why Zelor's temper was so foul. Tyre looked up at one point this afternoon to see the black man from Agave signaling to Zelor, the small boy interpreting as usual. Tyre immediately saw visions of himself walking back to Agave in chains. Not long after, the black one moved toward him and Rama to observe their sword practice. Feeling his eyes upon him, Tyre missed an easy parry and heard Zelor's curse of pure frustration. The embroidered robes moved on to observe another pair as Tyre forced his mind back to Rama's attack.

Nearing the final stretch, he asked his tired body for one last burst of speed. Somewhere he found the energy and crossed the finish line to Zelor's grudging, "Not bad."

Grasos was waiting for him with an impatient frown.

"Could I scrub down somewhere? Just to get the worst of this off?"

Grasos locked the manacles and walked away as if he had not heard. Tyre tried again.

"I promise I'll be quick."

Grasos came to an abrupt halt, so abrupt that Tyre almost ran into him.

"You had a bath this morning. One bath a day."

Grasos lumbered forward again and they were at the cell door. Grasos unlocked his manacles and shoved him roughly inside. The bolt slammed shut behind him. The cell was empty. He'd been so busy today he'd forgotten to worry about it. Now, his spirit as downtrodden as his body, he leaned back against the door with a sigh—a sigh that was answered by a soft sound from over near the window. Tyre looked up in astonishment. It was long past sundown and without a fire the cell was dungeon dark. As his eyes adjusted to the gloom he could make out a shadowy figure standing behind the bed.

Straightening to his full height, he took a tentative step forward, the shadowy figure backing away from him as he did so. From the rapidity of her breathing he guessed she was badly frightened. His mind raced through the sessions with the Instructor but nothing helpful came to mind. Then he remembered Freena. Moving very slowly, he turned away from her and walked over to the fireplace. Never stopping his slow, careful movements, he dropped to his haunches and reached for the tinderbox. He laid the fire, struck a spark, and heard another soft gasp. He stayed where he was, feeding the fire, feeling her eyes on his back. He knew he was filthy but there was nothing he could do about it. His loincloth was fairly clean except where it touched his skin. Perhaps it wasn't the dirt, but his state of undress that frightened her. He reached for the foot of the bed and pulled off the blanket folded there. Puzzling for a moment over what to cover, he decided his upper body was probably more upsetting than his legs, and wrapped himself up in the scratchy cloth. All too soon his legs began to ache. Wondering what to do next, he'd almost given up hope she would make the first move when he heard her speak.

"I . . . I'm called Kara."

He wanted to look at her, but decided to wait a bit longer. When Freena was cut from the free-running herd as a two-year-old, it took her three days to accept a handful of grain from his outstretched palm. He modulated his voice so it would reach the corner and no further.

"I'm Tyre."

He heard her footsteps on the stones, moving away from him toward the other end of the cell. There was a rustle of fabric and then she was moving toward him.

"The Instructor let me bring these. They'll help dispel the gloom. Is there a bit of tinder you can use to light them?"

A cloaked figure, hood drawn, held two fat candles in pottery bowls. Wordlessly, he picked up a slender twig and reached out to light the wicks. As he lit the second one he heard a gasp signaling more than her previous nervousness, and looked up into heavily-lashed eyes staring back at him in horrified recognition.

"You're the one . . .!"

Stung, he pulled the blanket close and retreated toward the door. He'd held on to Ladon's promises with such hope. It was clear they'd been false, at least where this woman was concerned. He couldn't hide his bitterness.

"The one you saw beaten in the arena."

Nothing prepared him for her response.

"I wondered . . . did someone care for you . . . afterwards?"

He spoke without thinking, touched that someone thought of him that wretched night.

"A healer stayed with me until dawn. He helped my back and talked to me."

Hearing the longing in his voice, he was furious with himself. No woman must suspect his frailty. He hadn't even seen her face and already he was making confessions.

As if she read his mind, or perhaps because the fire was blazing directly in front of her, she placed the candles on the narrow mantle and reached up to unfasten the clasp at her throat. He watched with growing wonder as she pulled back the hood and a mass of dark waves tumbled over her shoulders. An unfamiliar scent wafted past him, something akin to windflowers blooming on the plains. Removing the cloak, she shook her hair out of her face and looked around for a place to hang it. Finding no hooks or pegs, she laid it across the foot of the bed. As she moved, he saw a woman of such unexpected beauty that his knees went weak. Every move was unconsciously graceful, the fire highlighting the curves of her body under the tightly laced rose-colored bodice.

Tyre looked down at his muddy torso, the bare skin revealed where sweat ran in rivulets, knowing he must smell abominably to this immaculately groomed and scented creature. His curse rang long and loud, breaking off as he remembered he was no longer alone in the cell. He waited for her to retreat back into the corner. Instead, her bright laughter soared through the cell.

"Why do you curse so foully? Have you forgotten something you ought to have remembered, or has dinner been delayed and you're merely hungry?"

At her mention of food, his stomach growled. When he looked down at it, shocked by its betrayal, her amusement increased.

"It seems you've given me an answer of sorts. Here, let me see if I can find something to quell your curses and your growls."

She rummaged for a moment in the pockets of the voluminous cloak. Turning to him with a teasing smile, she held both hands behind her back. It was a childish pose, standing on her tiptoes, her eyes shining with fun, trying not to laugh out loud. Was this what he feared?

"Choose one."

Tearing his eyes away from her heart-shaped face, he considered the placement of her shoulders. Noticing the right was lower than the left, he pointed to it with confidence. When her face fell he knew he'd chosen the hand with food. She pouted for a moment, looking up at him curiously.

"How did you guess so easily?"

He could play games as well.

"First let me see what I've won."

She hesitated then held out her hand. In it was clasped a golden pear. Stepping forward to claim it, he froze as she started to back away. Standing stock still, he waited as she took a deep breath, lifted her chin, and placed the fruit gently in his outstretched palm.

He bit deep into its ripeness, the juice running down his chin. Mindless about anything except his hunger, he ate it quickly, licking his fingers to catch the last few drops of sweet juice. When he looked back at her again, she was staring at him. Catching his eyes, she blushed and turned back toward the fire, holding her palms out to its warmth. Looking down, he saw the forgotten blanket on the floor, an answering blush creeping over him as he realized she'd been looking at his body. More embarrassed than he'd ever been in his life, he stood motionless and tongue-tied.

Like an answer to his prayers, the food grate slid open and a tray with two bowls of stew, two pieces of bread, and two mugs of tea was pushed under the door. Tyre reached down to pick it up. The woman's voice was calm and matter-of-fact.

"There's no table. Where do you eat?"

Matching her tone, he jerked his head toward the small stool near the fireplace.

"I sit on the bed and put the food on the stool."

As she bent to move the stool the curve of her hips showed clearly through the folds of the dress. His groin ached, and with a jolt he realized he had to reclaim the blanket and sit down. Praying she wouldn't look at him, he placed the tray on the stool, keeping his back to her as he retrieved the blanket from the floor. After wrapping it securely around his waist, he took up a defendable position on the bed, leaning up against the headboard. She seated herself near the foot of the bed and was examining the tray of food. He breathed easier.

Soon they were both concentrating on the meal. Tyre was ravenous and would have licked the bowl if he'd been alone. She picked at hers, eating a few mouthfuls, and finally put down the bowl and picked up the mug, rolling its warmth between her palms. He tried not to stare at her uneaten food but she caught him looking and laughed.

"Yes, you may have it."

All of a sudden he was guilty. Maybe his presence had made her lose her appetite.

"No, you must save it. Perhaps you'll be hungry later."

Her smile deepened as she considered him for a moment. Then she surprised him again.

"Tyre, what did you do today?"

He suspected she might be teasing him. Her steady gaze made him take her question seriously.

"I rose at dawn and ate with the other men. Then I bathed and saw the healer. We worked with weights in the morning session and I did curls and presses after the group exercises. I ate the midday meal and studied in the library. Then I competed in two wrestling sessions; practiced short swords with Rama; ran five laps of the track with the others and three more by myself."

Her eyes widened during his recital. When he finished, she pushed the bowl toward him.

"Please take it."

He nodded his thanks and finished it, finally feeling his hunger ease. She waited until he swallowed the last morsel of bread and reached for his tea.

"That track you ran, is that where you . . ."

He guessed the direction of her thoughts.

". . . got so dirty? We run regardless of the weather," he replied grimly, "although they wet the track on purpose today."

"Did you ask for a bath?"

"Of course I asked for a bath! Do you think I enjoy smelling myself or scratching away at this filth? The rule for slaves is one bath a day. They offered it to me this morning, not this evening."

She must have heard the self-loathing in his voice, for, to his astonishment, she reached over to place a consoling hand on his forearm. For an instant he saw the paleness of her skin against his mud-stained flesh. Then a lifetime of ingrained habit made him jerk violently away from her, pulling his arm back and up to elude her touch. She shied like a yearling, shrinking away from his upraised hand and uttering a sharp cry of distress, disappeared into the shadows at the far end of the room.

As he listened to her panting in the dark corner, the unexpected delight he'd felt in her company crumbled into ruins. What a fool, he thought, what a sad and miserable fool! You long for her trust and then, when she reaches out to you of her own accord, you frighten her out of her wits and make her hide in a corner. He was beyond disgust. And he was exhausted.

He got to his feet with a groan he didn't even try to stifle, pushed the tray under the grate, moved the stool back to the fireplace, and turned toward the tin bucket. Too tired to imagine a subtle way of relieving himself, he placed his back to her and freed himself from the loincloth. It took a moment for him to accomplish it, but he urinated and washed his face and hands in the basin. He knew without looking she hadn't moved although her breathing slowed. Grabbing up the blanket, he wrapped it around his shoulders and curled up on his left side facing the door, his back to her, pulling the coverlet up to his waist. At least I'm covered, he thought, and won't stink too much. He spoke quietly, expecting no response, knowing he deserved none.

"Sleep well, Kara. Blow out the candles. And . . . thank you for the pear."

She made no answer. He willed himself to sleep but it eluded him. He was listening too hard for any hint of movement. It occurred to him that she was probably listening for his breathing as well, so he slowed it to the steady tempos of sleep. Soon he heard her moving in the corner and from the rustle of fabric, guessed she was undressing. His body's immediate response surprised him. He'd only felt arousal in dreams. Tonight it had happened twice because of a woman who was certainly not a figment of his imagination. He became conscious of an unfamiliar sound directly behind his back. Unable to contain his curiosity, he turned his head as slowly as he could, and saw her outlined against the window.

The moon was too high now to be seen but its light shone down on her pale shift and glowing hair. She was brushing it in long, powerful strokes from her hairline to the tip of each curl.

His fear at her reaction if she discovered his observation was stronger than the hold of her beauty. He pressed his left cheek into the hard mattress. The fabric of her gown rustled as she crossed to the mantle and blew out the candles. Then, ever so slowly, she approached the far side of the bed. Feeling her eyes upon him, he breathed slowly and steadily, her fragrant scent transporting him to another woman's arms, someone who held him long ago, surrounding him with unstinting love and care.

The mattress yielded to the weight of her body. He could tell she was lying with her back to him and guessed she was looking out the window and up into the regions of the stars.

The still-tender skin on his upper back complained at the scratchiness of the rough blanket. His right thigh cramped, begging him to change his tightly curled pose. Trying to move imperceptibly into a more comfortable position, he let out his breath.

A quiet voice replied: "You're welcome, Tyre."

The morning bell woke him. His first sensation was the fact that his face and exposed hands were almost numb in the frigid air of early dawn. The second was more mysterious and took him a moment to identify. As cold as his face and hands were, it made no sense that his lower back and legs were warm and relaxed. Not until then did he remember he was not alone in the bed.

Sometime in the night, she had moved. She was nestled close to him, her hips snug against his lower back, her legs draped around the curve of his buttocks, her feet between his thighs. It crossed his mind that she might be trying to arouse him and he tensed for a moment. But her breathing revealed nothing more than a deep dreamless sleep. As he turned his head over his shoulder, one look at her provided a clear explanation of her closeness. She lay on her side, her hair awash over both of them, the blue cloak the same shade as the tip of her nose, which was the only part of her face he could see. She must be freezing with only the thin gown and the cloak for protection from the cold. Puzzled, he couldn't remember ever being this cold in the morning, then cursed himself for a fool. Since his first night in the cell, he habitually placed all the remaining wood on the fire before collapsing into bed. Last night he'd failed to do so and the fire had been out for hours.

Disentangling himself from her hair, he moved away from her. He thought she awoke, but, instead, she rolled over into the warm indentation left by his body. He placed the coverlet over her and considered tucking it around her before discarding the idea. She was sleeping too contentedly to risk the frightening reminder of his presence. Yawning and stretching out his back and shoulders, noticing hardly any stiffness, he felt better than he had in many mornings. Inadvertently, he remembered the heat of her body pressed against him. Turning toward the fireplace, he brushed away the ash and started a fire, patiently adding tinder until it was ready for the larger pieces of kindling. I can repay part of my debt for a good night's rest, he decided, and she can sleep a few more hours in comfort.

He heard the jingle of the manacles in Grasos' belt from down the passageway. The bolt slid back, the door opened, and he slipped out.

Kara waited until the bolt slid back into place and the sound of Tyre's footsteps disappeared down the corridor. Then she stretched out in the bed and pulled her hair over her shoulder. Running her fingers through its mass of tangles, she could smell Tyre's strong scent rising from the bedclothes. Under the layers of dirt and sweat she could distinguish the scent that was his alone. It permeated the cell when she entered last night with Nerissa, making the bare cell seem inhabited, not quite so shabby and depressing.

She chose her place behind the bed with care, since it would allow her to see this stranger before he could see her. His bulk seemed immense, lit only by the torches behind him in the hallway. After the door closed and the bolt slid into place, she watched him look guardedly around the room before leaning against the closed door with a sigh that had seemed ineffably sad.

When he moved toward her, it took all her courage not to cry out. She'd been told countless times she would not be harmed, but alone in the dark room with an enormous stranger, all her instincts told her to scream, run, hide, anything to escape the cell whose door would not open until dawn. Perhaps sensing her terror, he turned away. As the growing flames revealed his crouching form, she gasped at the thought of facing all that bare flesh. Covered in the blanket he was not nearly so intimidating—until he lit the candles for her.

She'd never gotten a clear view of the ernani's face when he stood for the beating. The hair, however, was unforgettable. When she saw the blonde roots of the muddy clumps of his hair, all her fears were realized.

Yet he surprised her repeatedly with his gentleness, although she knew instinctively that gentleness did not come naturally to him. She cringed when she remembered his upraised hand. She'd always been a quick student; she would not touch him again without his permission.

The air warmed due to the roaring fire he built. She felt drowsy and lazy. Dreamily, she remembered her feelings upon awakening. His back was solid against her and her hips fit perfectly against him. Her feet got so cold during the night. She dimly remembered his thighs closing around them, even rubbing them together as if to reassure her that he would keep them warm. If he had not been so dirty, perhaps . . . .

Startled at the completion of that thought, she snapped out of her daydream and was suddenly invigorated. Today she would begin turning this cell into a home of sorts. It would take every minute to ready it before the evening trumpet.

She bounced off the mattress and dressed quickly. Banging on the door to alert a guard, she was surprised at how quickly it opened. Nerissa appeared in the doorway, her eyes passing swiftly over Kara, her worried frown transformed into a look of profound relief.

For the first time, Kara felt irritation toward the woman who had been as a mother to her since her arrival at the Maze. Lifting her chin and straightening her spine, Kara sailed through the door without a backward glance, feeling, rather than seeing, Nerissa's consternation and surprise. She might still be a virgin, but she had spent her first night with a man.

She was no longer a child.

Chapter 12

Moon Child

CONSTRUCTION BEGAN ON the Maze in the recent past, a mere seventy years ago, although its appearance harkened back to the early days of Pelion, when a quarry on the southern face of the escarpment provided the granite necessary to build the walls. The Thirteenth Mother, an architect by trade, took obvious delight in designing this multi-leveled stone labyrinth whose purpose was to confuse and confound. Corridors turned and twisted back upon themselves, many of them terminating in dead ends. Stairways appeared to go up, then, at the first or second or third landing would angle off in a completely different direction, then descend to yet another level, each passageway lined with identical iron doors. Stories abounded of ernani lost forever within its bowels, of skeletons in corners and ghosts around every bend. The Council never contradicted these rumors, believing, and rightly so, they would strengthen the power of the place to discourage escape attempts. Stewards and servants were taught the passageways necessary for their work, nothing more. Even the guards of long standing remained cautious, rarely diverging from their accustomed routes.

When the designer of the Maze turned her attention to the matter of the women, she was concerned not so much with security (the thought which ruled every decision regarding the men), as with their ability to adjust. After the first night of joining, they were encouraged to make the cells more inviting, bits of furniture, rugs, linens, and kitchen accessories being put at their disposal. The daylight hours were spent in the dayroom, an enormous chamber on the top level of the Maze where they continued their studies in the many areas of interest they pursued before entering Preparation. Scholars and members of the guilds were regular callers, sharing their expertise with anyone interested in their subject.

Throughout the morning, the dayroom hummed with the sounds of looms, potters' wheels, the hammering of precious metals and the whisper of shears through fabric; afternoons were devoted to books, music, drawing, and needlework. With the exception of the two hours following the midday meal (when the ernani studied with their own group of teachers) several women pursued academic research in the Maze library, the volumes necessary for their fields of study transported from the Greater and Lesser Libraries of Pelion. It was expected that each woman excel in a craft or scholarly pursuit of her choice. Those less schooled than the others, many of them from the outlying provinces, could be found in a pleasant corner of the dayroom every afternoon, reviewing spelling words, reciting multiplication tables, their heads bent over tablets and copybooks, their fingers splashed with ink.

It was Vena, in her position as High Healer, who suggested to her superior that the women of the Maze deserved a place of isolation. The first moon was passed in communal living, organized to unite them as sisters as well as drilling them in skills deemed necessary for their well-being in the cells. The moon of joining presented a different set of difficulties to women who, for the most part, were natives to the city and gently bred. Their days passed in the company of women, their evenings spent in the close confines of a cell designed to encourage intimacy with the ernani, Vena argued that they needed a place to be alone. Grudgingly, her more economically-minded predecessor agreed.

The solarium was the result, the latest addition to the Maze. Designed for meditation, it harbored the troubled of spirit. The room was not large, but windows surrounding it on three sides filled it with light regardless of the season. The garden outside its thick-paned windows, an elaborate one filled with fruit trees and flowers of every kind, its walls covered with climbing roses and wisteria, its pathways lined with evergreen hedges pruned to perfection, was meticulously tended by a gardener chosen by the Fifteenth Mother herself. Furnished simply but comfortably, its stone floor was covered in a deep-piled rug, with a fire burning in its brazier throughout the day serving not just as a source of warmth, but as a reminder of the flame burning in the Sanctum.

The rules of the room were explained to the women on the morning after they entered the cells. It was a difficult morning for some, and Nerissa's voice was softer than a caress as she showed them the one place within the Maze where solitude could be found.

"The solarium is a place for reflection and the facing of difficult truths. You may enter at any time during the day. The Fifteenth Mother and I often visit this place and gladly offer our counsel, but you may decline our help without insult taken."

Kara found herself in the solarium that afternoon without remembering clearly any decision to go there, having never sought refuge here since being joined with Tyre. A master from her guild had given her a lesson that morning. She welcomed the discipline demanded as she worked on the scales and variations necessary to the exercise and presented the paper she had prepared on an ancient text. Her teacher complimented her on the flexibility and breath control she had retained during her time away from the guild. Kara did not reveal the fact that up until the last few days, she sang every evening for hours at a time.

The first time she sang for Tyre, he overwhelmed her with his appreciation of her voice. Music became part of their evening ritual from that night on. The meal ended and cleared away, he would recline on the brightly-colored rug in front of the hearth, a pillow beneath his tawny head, and listen to her sing the songs of childhood, planting, harvest, and holidays. Once, after much teasing and cajoling (for he could be stubborn) she persuaded him to sing for her and was charmed by his rough, untrained baritone. His songs were foreign to her knowledge of music. Despite her unfamiliarity with the language, her ear detected the pulsing, slightly chanted rhythms of battle within them. Yet when she asked him to translate, his lips folded into a thin forbidding line. In that moment, it occurred to her she had never sung him a love song.

Kara avoided further thought by looking out the window, finding the garden blanketed in white. Her practiced eyes took in the trees and hedges, noticing their limbs and branches trimmed and shaped by a master gardener. How lovely it was to see a garden after almost two moons passed within this place! Suddenly she longed for her parents and their unquestioning, undemanding love. Then she gave herself a hard mental shake.

"You are lying to yourself in a place dedicated to true feelings. You came here to think about that night, and so you must begin."

Cooking was a profound mystery to Kara. Her heart sank when she discovered she would be responsible for the planning and execution of the evening meal. In some way that completely defeated her, her hands, so deft with a shuttle, grew clumsy when they tried to knead or carve, transferring food from pot to bowl was a terror to her, and making a simple loaf of bread an exercise in sheer frustration. Her first meals were the essence of simplicity: stew or soup, day old breads provided by the kitchen, fruit and tea. Tyre never complained and ate everything she put before him, but she soon tired of the same fare night after night. Three days ago she decided to devote her time to the creation of a memorable meal.

Her menu was simple, but for Kara, it was the boldest of adventures. She requested a plump fowl, rice, greens, and the makings for a jam pudding from the storehouse. Returning to the cell early in the afternoon, she began her preparations. She plucked the bird, seasoning and lacing it before putting it onto the spit, rinsed the rice several times and salted it for cooking, and began the pudding, all in good order. Everything went well until the trumpet sounded, at which time she realized the rice was overdone and sticking to the pot, the fowl was still not cooked through, and worst of all, the gravy was thin, grayish in color, and full of lumps. Faced with the prospect of total disaster, she became a screaming harridan, waving a long-handled fork in the air and shouting profanities she'd learned from Tyre. At that exact moment, he entered the cell.

Turning on him in a rage, she threw the fork at him, mortified at the thought of him witnessing her failure. He caught the fork one-handed and regarded her with open-mouthed dismay. Coming to her senses, she looked down at the grease-covered apron protecting her dress and ran a hand through her flour-streaked hair. Spinning away from him, she tripped over the bowl containing the pudding and sent it flying before landing flat on the hearth. With a cry, she jerked her arm away, only to discover she'd burned the inside of her forearm on a cooking pot. Running for the bed, she buried her head in the pillows.

"Are you hurt?"

She shook her head, refusing to meet his eyes, more embarrassed than when he caught her staring at his body.

"Show me your arm."

He spoke so reasonably that her humiliation eased and she sat up. Tear-filled eyes took in blonde hair clean from his recent bath, wide-spaced blue eyes under golden brows, and firm lips that seemed to be resisting the impulse to smile. She wondered if she would ever become accustomed to his beauty; it struck her anew every time she saw him. He sat beside her patiently, waiting for her to extend her arm. When she lifted it toward him he examined it without touching her, his hair falling between them. The impulse to brush it away from his face, to feel its promise of silk against her palm was strong, but since that first night she was careful never to touch him, fearing a repeat of the explosion that met her first attempt. He looked up at her, a smile dancing around his lips.

"It's not a bad burn. You can bathe it and wrap it in cloth and the healer will give you some ointment tomorrow. Now tell me, Kara: Why did you throw that fork at me?"

He was speaking to her as if she was a child! She was not a mewling infant who must be indulged. She was a woman grown and she had a right to her anger.

"I threw the fork because I was angry—angry at myself for my difficulties with the meal—and angry with you because it's because of you, and this place, that I must do something that I hate, that I have no gift for!"

She controlled her tears, with the result that they welled up in her eyes, half-blinding her. He had a strange look on his face, not laughter or pity (which she half-expected) but a kind of recognition. She was unprepared for his response.

"I, too, am often angry with this place and what it makes me do. Bathe your arm and your face and take off your apron. I'll finish preparing the meal."

With that, he left her and busied himself at the fire. Her first impulse was to stop him and try to salvage the meal as best she could, but she was frazzled and untidy, and besides, she thought rebelliously, if he thinks he can do better, let him try! Calming herself, she went about arranging her garments, brushing out the tangles of her hair and looking after her burned arm. When she finished and he was still bent over the hearth, she sat down on the bed and was soon asleep.

She woke to a familiar voice chiding her into wakefulness.

"You've slept long enough! Any longer and the poor bird will drop its meat into the fire."

Sitting at the small table, Kara looked down in awe. The fowl was falling apart, the white meat tender and the dark meat moist. He must have started the rice from scratch, for it was perfectly cooked, and the gravy had no lumps. Finding the pudding beyond repair, he sliced some apples and arranged them on the greens. She looked up to find bright blue eyes glittering under a cocked eyebrow, waiting expectantly for her reaction. It came in the form of an accusation.

"You know how to cook!"

He let out the first true laugh she ever heard him utter as he filled her plate. In between bites, they talked. For the first time, Kara learned something of his life before the Maze.

"Every man in my tribe knows how to cook. It's not fancy fare, but it fills the stomach. Every boy learns to hunt, so I was taught to cook venison, rabbit, quail and dove at the same time I learned to use a bow and a throwing spear."

She accepted his explanation without comment. Her father was a much better cook than her mother, although he was rarely in the kitchen. Like many people in Pelion, they either bought or traded services for their meals.

"Do the women of your tribe cook as well as you do?"

There was a long pause, which she ascribed to the fact that they were both still eating. When he spoke there was something different about him, as if he was hiding something.

"The women cook," he added cautiously, "although I'm not sure if the manner of their cooking resembles ours."

"Do you mean you don't eat together?"

Nodding, he reached for the kettle to pour the tea. Kara was determined to keep him talking. He never spoke of his life before coming here; in fact, he rarely spoke at all.

"Is there some reason behind this custom?"

With a gesture she had come to recognize, he pulled his hair back from the sides of his face and pushed it toward his back. Gazing into the fire, the mug of tea held in his large, capable hands, he spoke as if he was reciting something he had rehearsed.

"The reason is that the men and women of my tribe live separately from one another. A boy lives with his mother until he can sit astride a pony, at which time he goes with his father and learns the care of herd animals, leather-working, hunting, and war."

Troubled by what she was hearing, she struggled to understand.

"And the girl children?"

He took a sip of tea, refusing to meet her eyes.

"I can't answer that question with any surety, having never lived among girl children. They live with their mothers until they are mated, when they receive a tent of their own."

He was holding something back. Even so, she persisted.

"So when a woman takes a mate, she leaves her mother's tent to live with him. If she has boy children, they are taken away from her, but the girls remain in her care. Is that correct?"

Tyre swallowed hard. Pinning her with an intense gaze, he told her what she didn't want to hear.

"That is not correct. Men and women live separately, as I said. A woman does not choose a mate. Usually she's abducted from another tribe and brought to live in the women's section. Her mate lives with his father, his uncle, male cousins, or by himself."

"And . . . and the woman who is abducted only sees her mate . . ."

Kara couldn't finish the sentence.

". . . only sees her mate when he wants to join with her."

Kara could see nothing, hear nothing. The pulse in her throat pounded. These women were treated like chattel, and worse, their male children were taken from them, never to be seen again. The anguish of their lives filled her with pity and growing anger. How could they be treated with such brutality?

Taking a deep breath, she considered the man who sat across from her, regarding her from under hooded eyes. Abruptly, the enormity of his explanation occurred to her. He was telling her he had never eaten a meal with a woman before entering this cell, although undoubtedly he used their bodies when he felt the need. No wonder he was so secretive, so revolted by her touch. Her presence was unwelcome, unwanted, something to be endured as slavery was endured. How pitiful her attempts at cookery must seem to him! His refusal to tell her the meaning of his songs was not prompted by shyness, but scorn. No doubt a woman lacked the ability to comprehend them. Her anger grew so intense she could no longer control it. Rising from the table, she addressed him in a voice icy with dislike:

"Is it difficult, Tyre, living with someone you despise?"

His eyes flared brilliant blue; his jaw clenched tight. She lifted her chin, waiting for the blow. His face turning to stone, he turned his back on her.

Kara did not sing that night.

The next few evenings were unbearable. The contentment of the cell vanished, and with it, her peace of mind. She returned to her simple cookery with no enthusiasm and their meals were eaten without conversation. She did not sing, nor did he ask her to. The meal cleared away, she changed for bed, hardly caring or wondering if he watched.

Once in bed, the real misery began.

They began each night with their backs to one another, separate and alone. The morning bell found them huddled together, his back pressed close to hers. Those had been the moments she treasured. Through the cloth of her nightshift, she could feel the satiny texture of his bare skin, and if she turned her head she could observe the smooth ripple of the muscles in his back and shoulders as he yawned and stretched in the cool morning air. One morning she woke to find her head nestled against his shoulder. Shy that he might wake and find her turned toward him, she tried to move away. Finding his fingers entangled in her hair, when she tried to remove them he muttered in his sleep and pulled her close. Giving up, she rubbed her cheek against his smooth shoulder, breathed his scent, and went back to sleep. When she woke again, he was gone.

Now she was painfully self-conscious and unable to sleep, fearful she might inadvertently touch him. She understood why he jerked away from her so violently that first night, threatening her with an upraised hand. Women were objects of contempt and derision, not worthy of a man's attention unless he was aroused. She could only explain their former closeness in the bed by the fact that when he slept she was merely a body, although his reticence at touching her when he was awake proved she didn't attract him enough for even that physical need. She lay sleepless for hours after retiring, as did he. There were dark circles under his eyes this morning. Groaning as the bell woke him, he rose stiffly from the bed, grimacing as he tried to loosen muscles forming knots under his skin.

She was worried, more worried than she was the night Nerissa delivered her to the cell. In six more days she must attend a private session with the Fifteenth Mother, at which time she must decide whether to renew her contract with Tyre or leave the Maze. Desperate as she was to escape the misery of the cell, memories of the early days, of brief moments of kindness, of his honest enjoyment of her singing, plagued her with doubts as to the rightness of her actions. At the bottom of all these feelings was the knowledge that if she left him, he would probably be taken from Pelion and sold into a life of such horror she could not wish it on anyone, no matter how much he despised her.

She'd faced her feelings as truthfully as she could. The solarium offered no solution although its peace restored her tranquility. She remembered the Fifteenth Mother asking her how men who had never known kindness could be expected to be kind.

It was necessary for Kara to try again. Her resolve made her square her shoulders, lift her chin and walk slowly back to the cell.

Tyre lifted himself tiredly onto the table and turned over on his stomach, waiting for Ladon to begin the daily ritual he no longer minded. He answered the usual questions upon arrival, hesitating at the last one, asked as Ladon observed his bloodshot eyes.

"Haven't you been sleeping?"

He wanted to tell the healer everything, ask his advice, share his woes; then remembered the Instructor's threat. Resisting the impulse, he shrugged his shoulders.

Actually, he hadn't slept at all since the night she hurt him so badly he couldn't think about it without cringing. He'd tried so hard not to frighten her, to win her trust, even though she never touched him again after that first night. Every evening he raced back to the cell from his bath to bask in the glow of her presence. The night she threw the fork at him, she charmed him even with her rage, her capacity for anger surprising him more than a little. When she admitted her hatred of this place, he was reminded that she, too, was a slave. Not a slave as he was, but a slave in the sense that she couldn't escape. He corrected himself bitterly—she couldn't escape for six more days. Ladon's unerring hands found a sore spot and he flinched.

It was the cooking that trapped him. Why had he been stupid enough to help her by finishing that meal? He tried to avoid the direction of the conversation, but she was insistent, and finally he told her everything he didn't want her to know. The expression on her face devastated him, for it was a twin to the one Belwyn turned on him so long ago. The difference was that he no longer possessed his former confidence in the rightness of his traditions. Twenty nights with Kara made him understand what Hourn tried to tell him. To see her dark eyes erupt into laughter, to hear her voice raised in song, to wake with her head on his shoulder, her body warm and pliant, her hair covering them both in a silken web; these things transformed his former contempt to wonder. Yet he could not trust himself to express these things, he, who was ignorant of how to please such a mysterious creature.

As Ladon ran a practiced hand firmly down his back, Tyre groaned aloud. Beyond his sleeplessness, his body missed the nightly warmth that helped relieve the aches and pains of training. Ladon broke through his misery.

"You've lost weight, you obviously aren't sleeping, and your tendons are pulled so tight I fear you'll injure yourself in training. I advise you to do whatever's necessary to make peace between you and your mate."

Tyre decided his course of action as Ladon spoke. He would put away his pride and tell Kara what she meant to him. If she still couldn't forgive him for how he'd been raised, there was nothing to be done. But he would try.

By the time Tyre reached the cell door, he'd rehearsed his speech a hundred times. Grasos swung open the door. In a moment of panic, Tyre realized he was alone. No evening meal simmered in the pots. Neither candles nor fire were lit. He'd waited too long and Kara was gone.

Barely knowing what he was doing, he sat on the bed and buried his head in his hands. Now he would be taken from the Maze and sold again in Agave. Even that horrible thought paled in comparison with the idea of never seeing Kara again. Suddenly, he was furious with her. How could she have so little regard for him, fleeing the cell without telling him she was going? He'd been honest with her, painfully honest, even though that same honesty had broken every bond they'd created between them.

The door swung open and Kara stood before him. He saw at a glance she was exhausted, with smudges of weariness underneath each eye. She smiled down at him, her lips quivering a bit. It was the first smile he'd seen in three days. Noticing her arms were full of bags and bundles, he rose to help.

"I know I've kept you waiting, but I was delayed this afternoon. I stopped by the storehouse and the kitchen and they helped me put together a meal of sorts. It will be cold, but if you light a fire, we can have tea."

They ate the broken meats and cheeses with bread and fruit. Neither spoke, but the silence was no longer awkward, merely the companionable silence of two very tired people. Tyre kept trying to find a way to begin his speech, but she looked so weary he couldn't bring himself to disturb her. He was reclining as usual by the hearth; Kara had curled up in a wooden chair where she was nodding in the warmth of the fire. He got to his feet, stood by her chair for a moment, steadying his resolve, and lifted her into his arms. She was surprisingly light, and he held her easily, resisting the urge to press his face into her fragrant hair. He expected a protest, but she only smiled sleepily at him, seemingly content to be in his arms.

"Oh, Tyre," she yawned, "I'm sorry I fell asleep. I thought of many things today and wanted to tell you . . ."

He stopped her before she could finish.

"Not now. We can talk tomorrow. We'll sleep tonight and all will be well."

She yawned again and nodded, rubbing her cheek against his chest like a contented cat. He lowered her to the bed, lifted her skirts and removed her leather slippers. He considered undressing her, but decided they were both too fragile for that. Drawing the covers over her, he built up the fire, relieved himself, and crawled into bed. For once, he lay flat on his back. He was almost asleep when he felt her turn toward him. Hardly daring to breathe, he turned to regard her. She was edging toward him slowly, watching him with fearful, hopeful eyes. Smiling his encouragement, he lifted his arm so she could reach him. After she'd nestled into position, her head pillowed on his shoulder, he pulled her close. She let go a sound that was almost a sob, and then lay quietly. Tyre's last thought before sleep overtook him was to wonder at the fact that words hadn't been necessary. The simple exchange of touches had healed the breach between them.

It was the sounds that woke him. They invaded his dreams, pulling him insistently toward consciousness. Groggy, still unsure of what woke him, he heard the soft cries again, turning toward them to discover they emanated from Kara's throat. She'd moved away from him and was thrashing in her sleep, rolling her head back and forth as if denying some horrible truth. All at once she curled into a ball, her knees drawn up to her chest, and moaned. She was panting now, holding her hands over her stomach and fighting against the bodice of her dress, as if its tightness pained her.

Still not fully awake, Tyre thought she must be having a nightmare. When she moaned again, he realized she was ill, and dreadfully ill. When he called her name, she didn't wake. Panic rising inside him, he got out of bed and knelt beside her on the stone floor. Taking hold of her shoulders, he began to shake her, calling to her repeatedly. Finally, she opened her eyes, cloudy with pain. When they focused on him he spoke quietly yet with urgency.

"You've been crying in your sleep. What's wrong, Kara? Are you ill? Where do you hurt?"

She didn't answer his question, but stared blankly at him, a deep surge of color rising to her cheeks. Pulling herself away from his grasp, she moved sluggishly to the edge of the bed, still holding her stomach. She stood, swaying a moment before stumbling toward the corner where she kept her clothing. Puzzled, he followed her, afraid she might faint. Her fingers worked at the laces of her dress. When he approached her, she frowned and shook her head.

"Go back to bed."

"But I want to help. Tell me what's wrong."

She sighed, her breath catching as she did so, a dull sheen of perspiration visible on her face in the dim light from the window.

"I'm not truly ill. It's my monthly flow. I often have pain and tonight, probably because I've not been sleeping well, it's worse than ever. There's nothing you can do."

Even as the words crossed her lips, she braced herself, bending over double as another spasm passed through her. Deaf to her protestations, he grabbed her nightshift, picked her up and carried her back to bed. He unlaced the sides of the gown with hands trained to work leather since childhood. She stopped fighting him and sat very still, her eyes closed, panting again. He wrestled the dress and shift off her, drawing the nightshift over her head and arms. Lifting her onto his lap, he pulled the shift down over her legs, cradling her when she moaned and twisted in his arms. When the spasm passed and she opened her eyes, he was still holding her. Frantically, he tried to recall everything he'd been taught.

"What do you use for these days? Is there something I can get for you?"

She blushed again and he lifted her chin with his hand.

"This is a woman's gift, isn't it? The gift of fertility, of life kindled anew? At least that's what the Instructor told us. Why are you embarrassed if I'm not?"

Her pain-filled eyes searched his face.

"Aren't you embarrassed?"

He answered her honestly.

"Perhaps a little, but it will pass."

She considered his sincerity, her face softening, and told him where to find the cloths. Soon he was sitting with his back braced against the headboard, Kara resting with her head against his chest. Her hands and feet were freezing, so he held her hands in his and wrapped her feet in the coverlet. Her hair was sodden with perspiration, her skin cold and clammy to the touch. The pains did not seem to be easing and Tyre was worried. Already tired before the ordeal began, Kara, always pale of complexion, was grey with fatigue. Blue veins showed clearly under her skin. Her body tensed for another wave of pain, and he held her tight. When it left her, she was sobbing.

Tyre had never felt so inadequate in his life. His boyhood hardened him against revealing any indication of pain or suffering, his father's stern bearing his model for how he must face the world. In these moons of slavery, he'd moved even deeper into himself, hiding his feelings from everyone, not even allowing himself the indulgence of thinking of Belwyn, the only person who truly understood him. Now he held a crying woman in his arms whose sobs reminded him of the small boy he once had been, lying cradled in his mother's protective embrace. If he was to help her, he would have to pry open a secret place lying hidden and unused. Calling on everything he'd learned from Belwyn and the Instructor, Tyre began.

Carefully, he lowered her with him until they were lying on their left sides. Then he whispered softly into the ear next to his lips.

"Put my hand where the pain is and I'll try to ease it. Hush, Kara, don't cry. Please don't cry. You were made to sing, not to cry."

His right arm found the hem of the nightshift and he moved his hand up the side of her leg and hip and around to the front of her body. She didn't flinch at his touch as he had feared she would and her sobs subsided. When his hand reached her stomach, she moved it down well past her navel. Just as he touched the cotton padding wrapped around her loins, she stopped. As she pressed her hand against his, beneath his palm he could feel a tremor begin deep in her womb. Slowly, he began to massage her. When he felt her push herself gratefully against his hand, he knew he could press harder. Her skin was smooth and grew pliable under his touch. When the cramping began again, he talked to her, whispering an endless string of endearments and assurances, words he'd never spoken to anyone, words that sprang unbidden to his lips, words that came from a distant memory of long ago.

After a while, she stopped struggling against the pain. The cramping continued, but rather than stiffening as each wave began, he helped her count her breaths, urging her to keep them as even as possible. In time, she fell asleep, her skin whiter than the sheets they lay upon. He massaged her until he was sure she wouldn't wake. Content that she would sleep, he pulled the blankets up around them and resting his chin on the crown of her head, waited impatiently for the coming of dawn.

Tyre stood waiting for Grasos at the first peal of the morning bell. When the door opened, he was out and running down the corridor, following the well-known route that led to Ladon's examination room. Grasos called after him, heavy footsteps pounding behind him, but Tyre was beating on the door long before the guard caught up with him. Grasos was furious.

"What do you think you're doing, ernani? You don't move in the corridors without chains! Give me your hands."

Tyre held out his wrists, begging as the manacles locked around them, "Kara's ill. She's been ill though the night. I tried to help, but she's so weak, so white . . ."

The door opened behind him. Ladon stood bleary-eyed, running his hands through his hair. Tyre never stopped explaining, and Ladon was pulling on breeches, throwing packets and small glass vials into his pockets, and running out the door. Tyre turned to follow only to find himself facing Grasos' barrel chest.

"The healer will help her. You must go to the morning meal."

"Grasos, please, I need to know if she's alright!"

"She will be cared for. You cannot go."

The full weight of slavery descended. Everything he desired was a futile wish; any expression of his needs was deemed inconsequential and subsequently overruled. Squaring his shoulders, Tyre took the only course left him.

"If I cannot see Kara, I demand to see the Instructor."

Grasos nodded his head.

"We'll proceed to the dining hall. Once I arrange a meeting, I'll take you to her."

It wasn't what Tyre wanted, but it was something.

Nerissa watched the snow fall in the tiny garden outside the library and tried to prepare for the coming interview. Roused from sleep by Grasos' mental call of alarm, she was instantly alert, hearing Tyre beg for help, sensing his panic. Ladon's mind joined hers almost immediately. To her quick inquiry as to Tyre's presence during treatment, Ladon responded with a command delivered in full Voice.

"If her condition is as serious as he believes it to be, I'll need all my powers of concentration. Keep him away!"

Grasos stalled Tyre while Nerissa reviewed her options. Her request that Grasos supply Tyre's mind with her image was met with speed and rewarded with success.

She contacted Zelor immediately, instructing him to ignore Tyre throughout the day and to prevent him from using weapons. With his customary military efficiency under stress, Zelor suggested Tyre be assigned to clean and polish equipment. Nerissa rewarded his cleverness with a mental kiss. Next she turned her thoughts to the Fifteenth Mother, to find that she had been with them from the beginning. Her explanation for her presence was simple.

"Tyre woke me."

Stunned, Nerissa realized for the first time how deeply the Fifteenth Mother was attuned to Tyre of Lapith. Nerissa's knowledge, although not her experience, had accustomed her to the connections forged between healers and their patients. Now she was reminded that the Fifteenth Mother possessed not only that gift, but the power of her fourteen forbearers. Nerissa had barely formulated a question when an answer was supplied.

"You must continue to handle everything as you see fit. I am attuned to Tyre, but may not interfere in any part of his mind. This is why no one else may read him, for the urge to control is strong. Beal resisted for twelve years and I continue the struggle. They must remain untouched."

The door swung open and Tyre stood before her, his shoulders slumped with weariness. Nerissa assumed her Instructor demeanor; much as she pitied him, her role was not that of confidant. That role was Ladon's, just as Zelor was tormentor and Grasos was jailor. The consistency of performance was demanding, yet necessary.

"You asked to see me, ernani?"

He was wary of her. She was connected to the roots of his fears: women, sexuality, and his imprisonment.

"I wondered if you could give me news of Kara."

"What news do you require?"

His reply was gruff.

"Is she recovered?"

"She was given medicine and slept until noon. She rose, bathed, and is working at the loom. She intends to prepare the evening meal although she was informed a meal could be provided by the kitchen."

He absorbed everything, his face impassive. Annoyed by his refusal to admit his feelings, she decided to goad him.

"Is there anything else?"

"I . . . I have a question for you."

"Yes?"

"Is it . . ." he paused, frowned, and began again. "Is it normal for a woman to experience pain during her . . . her . . . monthly flow?"

Tyre had asked his first question. Nerissa rewarded him with the truth.

"Few women suffer as Kara does, but it happens that way for some. It's most prevalent among virgins."

Seeing his eyes flicker, she realized he had not known. She took another chance, keeping her focus undirected, giving him information rather than suggestion.

"With women who suffer such pain, the condition is helped and sometimes eradicated by joining. The muscles used during sexual union are exercised, and at the moment of release, the tension in the womb lessens. In a way we do not entirely understand, this can affect monthly pain."

A dull flush rose over his golden skin. The hetaera that was always part of Nerissa responded momentarily to his beauty.

"Is that all, ernani?"

"Yes, Instructor. Thank you for your help."

It was the first civil response she had ever heard him utter.

"You're welcome, Tyre. I'm always here."

His shoulders were straighter when he left the room.

Chapter 13

Songspell

COOL OF HEAD and calm of mind, Ladon epitomized the essence of what it was to be a healer of Pelion, for they were a special kind of adept and much respected among the inhabitants of the city. Not only his character, but his background promised him success in his profession, for he was the child and grandchild of healers, as was his sibling, Cydon. That Ladon was a student of Beal as well as Beal's successor as High Healer guaranteed Ladon's ascension to the Council, although there were some who questioned his ability to work successfully with and for the ernani. How could this quiet, well-bred man become an advocate for wild and oftentimes rash ernani with their tempers and their tendency to solve problems with their fists? Could Ladon stand his ground as their champion when it came time to disagree with the Legionnaires and, to their minds, their all-important training regimens?

Those who harbored such doubts about Ladon put them to rest this day, for cool and collected he was not. Striding into the Council Room, he threw off his cloak, took his place, and without a word or a glance to his colleagues, addressed the Fifteenth Mother with force and fervor:

"We must talk of Tyre. He's lost flesh, has great circles under his eyes, and every muscle is either strained or sore. I can only imagine his condition after the night he just passed. I remind you that his body is adjusting to foreign physical activity. He spent four and twenty years on horseback. Now we ask him to develop an entirely different musculature."

"What can be done?"

Ladon recognized the Fifteenth Mother's most soothing voice but he was in no mood to be soothed.

"He needs to soak in a hot bath every night. He also needs regular massage. All the men do, yet no time is allowed for it in their schedules. Slow reflexes and muscle fatigue cause injuries."

"If these things were implemented, would your fears be put to rest?"

As upset as Ladon was, he considered her question, reviewed his patient's condition, and reaffirmed his diagnosis with a single nod.

Zelor sent a strong mental vote of approval toward the healer. Ladon's head came up in surprise. He and Zelor were rarely, if ever, in agreement when it came to issues of training.

The Fifteenth Mother seemed surprised as well, and following Zelor's lead, continued the conversation using inner speech.

"You've not told us of this worry, Zelor, yet now you support Ladon. What's happened?"

Zelor was not his father in terms of adeptness, but the images he reconstructed of Tyre over the last few days were troubling. His usual grace was gone and he stumbled several times for no apparent reason in a sword session with Rama. They watched as Zelor upbraided him, trying to rouse his temper. Tyre nodded numbly, leaning wearily on his sword throughout the harangue, rubbing his right shoulder as if it pained him.

"Today, as we agreed, I gave him light detail. He polished, waxed, and rubbed all day. But he can't do that forever. The healer is right."

The Fifteenth Mother broke their connection and sat for a moment, her eyes shut in concentration. When she opened them, she spoke without inner voice, proof she was concealing something.

"We'll give them a few days to settle. Zelor will reduce Tyre's training somewhat but do nothing to make him suspicious. We're about to change the rules. No longer will we offer private bathing facilities to men or women. Nerissa, schedule a session with Gelanor for the women."

Her grey eyes flickered briefly to Stanis. As if acceding to a privately offered suggestion, she confided to them her concern.

"Given the proximity of the next full moon, we must proceed carefully with this. We cannot risk pushing them too far before they renew their contract. Ladon worries over the condition of Tyre's body; I worry that this same body is the source of much of the trouble in his mind. If he frightens her again, the damage may be irreparable. Somehow, we must help them strike a balance."

The mood was somber as the Council concluded.

Rubbing a back protesting her work bent over the fire, Kara heard the blast of the evening trumpet. She eyed the new copper tub beside the door with longing, sorry she didn't have enough time to use it before Tyre arrived. Instead, she washed her hands and face in the basin, took off her apron, and taking out the pins from her hair, started brushing. As she began the familiar routine, her heart took its familiar leap at the thought of Tyre's form filling the threshold of the cell.

In the past few nights, they came to an unspoken understanding. Their evenings reverted to the familiar patterns begun before the disruption. Kara resumed her litany of songs, Tyre was as silent as ever, and both of them avoided physical intimacy. Neither spoke of the days remaining before the fullness of the moon. Yet once the fire was built up and the candles blown out, they retained their new companionship in the bed. Tyre welcomed her nightly, eyes gleaming under sandy lashes as he held her against him and they drifted into sleep. He still had no words for her, but for now, it was enough to feel the comfort of his solid presence, and her sleep was deep and restful. She struggled for patience, understanding instinctively that the walls surrounding him were nearly as impenetrable as those encircling the Maze.

Kara's days were long and oftentimes lonely. The cell became the focus of her life and the days were merely hours to be passed until it was time to prepare for Tyre's arrival. Kara continued her daytime studies, as did all the women, but between them, there was a distance. The close friendships made in the first moon remained intact, but the rule of privacy made certain confidences impossible. Before their morning sessions with Nerissa began, she reminded them they might share discoveries, admit difficulties, or ask questions as they approached the subject for the day, but the rule of privacy was sacred. Not even the name of their ernani was to be shared with anyone.

In the days before joining, none of the women understood the necessity of such a rule, and several argued with Nerissa, insisting they needed the solace and advice of their new friends. Adamant, Nerissa informed them that at the first word, they would be dismissed and their ernani sold. Kara thought Nerissa harsh, but since her joining, she was grateful for her foresight. She didn't want to know which of her friends had joined with their partner and which had not, and she felt fiercely protective of everything she and Tyre shared. After almost thirty days of difficult adjustments, secrets and privacy were necessary to protect her self-esteem and the still-fragile nature of their relationship.

Yet despite the strictness of the rule, one could speak without words. This morning Minthe's eyes danced as she told Kara she was making music every night. Queenly, elegant Varuna, her close-cropped hair revealing ears formed like perfect shells, had wrapped herself in a brilliant vermillion shawl that set off her chocolate skin and flashing eyes and teeth. She disliked displays of affection, yet today she threw her arms around Kara and favored her with a smooth cheek pressed against Kara's own. Chione, the widow, looked placidly content, knitting away at a shapeless garment far too large for her compact form. Others revealed nothing by appearance or action. These were the women who filled Kara with compassion, for she knew that they, like her, were thankful for the protection of a rule that guaranteed freedom from comparison.

It was Dias who shocked Kara the most when she saw her standing off to herself as the women gathered in the dayroom. Normally plump and full of face, in the past few weeks Dias' cheeks had lost their bloom. Running her eyes over the solitary figure standing with downcast face, Kara noticed that her dress appeared to have been slept in. Her concern must have shown in her face, for when Dias looked up, instead of greeting Kara, as was her custom, she retreated to the window, standing apart from the others who were gathering around a large table.

Nerissa's arrival in a muted whisper of grey silk brought the room to its customary hush in her presence. As usual, she prefaced her lesson with a slow, careful perusal of the fifteen faces surrounding her, and, as always, Kara felt those eyes penetrate her soul. Nerissa's contemplation of Dias was more extended than the others, her brows lifted to ask a silent question answered by a quick shake of Dias' head. Crossing quickly to Dias, whose eyes widened with alarm, Nerissa drew her insistently toward the circle, Dias hanging back, head lowered, shoulders hunched, unable or unwilling to break Nerissa's hold on her arm. Despite this obvious show of reluctance, Kara thought she detected something like success gleaming in Dias' eyes when she entered the circle at last, her hand gripped tightly in Nerissa's own, almost as though, Kara mused to herself, Dias enjoyed playing the martyr's role.

A hum of pleasure greeted Nerissa's opening words.

"Gelanor returns to us today . . ."

Before she could finish, a ripple of excitement ran through those assembled. Gelanor was a topic much discussed in the sleeping chamber before they entered the cells. His return was a welcome one.

". . . although this visit will be slightly different from the last. I realize you may have questions best answered by a man. We'll begin the session as we did before, with the simple gift of a caring touch. You may practice or renew your skills as you choose."

Gelanor stepped lightly over the threshold to be met by a smattering of applause. Showman that he was, he gave a quick bow before beginning to disrobe. Stripped to his loincloth, he sat down on the table, took the cloth Nerissa handed him, and in the blink of an eye, holding the cloth to his waist with his left hand he removed the loincloth with his right. The women laughed as he tossed the loincloth on top of his clothing, yet in some way, his gesture was reassuring rather than ridiculous or bold. He was telling them without necessity of words that he trusted them, that they had grown, and that he was happy to be a part of that growth. The exercise began, several women rushing forward to the claim the bottle of oil from Nerissa.

Kara listened and watched, but eventually removed herself from the group. She found herself wondering if Tyre would ever invite her touch as gracefully as Gelanor, or smile at her with such easy charm. Contained, serious, troubled, Tyre rarely smiled, and she'd only heard him laugh once, on a night that transformed their harmony into discord. Nerissa's voice brought her back to the lesson, which was drawing to a close.

"Kara, would you like to greet Gelanor again?"

If Nerissa had volunteered Kara's participation without her permission, or phrased her request in any other manner, Kara would have refused. She felt far too vulnerable to venture touching Gelanor when she could not touch Tyre; she was afraid the comparison would sadden her. Gelanor caught her eye and winked, and knowing a refusal would hurt his feelings, she stepped forward to accept the proffered bottle. Nerissa placed a light hand on her shoulder.

"I'm moving the others to another table where a guest from the House of Healing begins a session on herb lore. Join us when you finish."

Nerissa glided away. Suddenly, Kara felt foolish and afraid. If Tyre did not want her to touch him, surely no one else did. She made to put down the bottle but was interrupted by an outstretched hand.

"Those women have mauled me without mercy. One of them hasn't trimmed her fingernails and nearly skinned me alive. Please make up for your graceless friends with your gentle touch."

He was lying on his back, and as she looked down at him, the wisdom in those dark eyes belied his childish complaints. In reply, she spread the lotion over her hands and began to massage the arm he'd held out to her, starting at the shoulder and working down to the fingertips. He closed his eyes and it seemed that both of them relaxed. Her question rose unbidden from her throat.

"Gelanor?"

He didn't open his eyes.

"Hmm?"

"I . . . I . . ."

His eyes flew open and the hand she was holding grasped hers firmly.

"Take a breath and ask the question."

He let go her hand. Unthinkingly, she continued to massage his arm as she struggled to put her question into finished form.

"Is it possible for a man to hold me with great tenderness yet feel no arousal?"

There was no laughter in his eyes, only attentiveness to her question. In that moment he was no longer Gelanor the guileless clown, but a Master of his guild.

"Why are you convinced he's not aroused? There's more than one sign of obvious physical need that reveals a man's affection. Does his face light up at your arrival? Do his eyes follow you as you move about the room?"

Kara cast about in her memories, finding Tyre's face filled with a radiance signifying more than simple relief when she arrived so late from the solarium to find him seated on the bed, his posture sad and defeated. She knew as well that his eyes always followed her as she moved about the cell, as if continually reassuring himself of her presence. And, too, she once caught him looking at her when she changed into her nightshift. He averted his eyes without apology or explanation, but they burned an intense blue before they left her. Perhaps she misjudged him.

"I've seen those things."

"Some men are slow to begin. He, like you, may be inexperienced."

"Do you mean he might be a virgin?"

Kara had never considered such a thing! Gelanor seemed amused by her astonishment but chided her all the same.

"Men are born virgins just as women are. Don't worry what he is or is not. Your task is to cherish whatever he is able to offer you, and to offer him in return what gifts he will accept."

Heartened by his words, Kara waited impatiently for the night.

Tyre ducked a slashing blow to his head, not noticing the outstretched foot of his opponent until he tripped and a sword hilt smashed down between his shoulders, sending him facedown in the mud. The weather had turned warmer of late, the snow melting, and the puddles of yesterday had dried to the consistency of thick paste. Scraping the sludge out of his eyes, Tyre's mounting frustration erupted into full-blown rage. He bathed carefully this morning, risking Zelor's wrath countless times by refusing to exert himself in any activity that might produce more than a light coat of perspiration. He was determined not to bathe tonight. Zelor announced the new rule at the morning meal and Tyre heard it with a sinking heart. The other men greeted it with amused chuckles and Pandar actually clapped his hands. Only Dino seemed to share his apprehension, although Tyre thought he detected a twinkle in the jester's eyes. Remembering

Kara's distaste of his filth and odor the first evening they met, Tyre refused to let anything ruin their new-found tranquility.

And now Dino had ruined everything. Tyre leapt out of the mire with a Lapithian battle cry and a raging desire to kill. Something in Dino leapt to the challenge. Suddenly the two of them were not exchanging the logical blows of arms training, but cutting and slashing in a dirty fight with no rules. Dino was more experienced with a sword, but Tyre had a longer reach, so the match was nearly even. After a swift exchange left them both blown and weary, they crouched warily and started to circle. In that instant, Tyre was jumped from behind and held above the ground, his arms pinioned and his legs flailing helplessly in the air. When the iron pincers around his chest tightened with his struggles, he gave up. He looked across at Dino, who was being held by Zelor, whose eyes almost popped out of their sockets with the effort to contain the still-wriggling Dino. Giving up, Zelor dropped Dino to the ground, pulled a cudgel from his belt, and tapped him on his head. To Tyre's delight, Dino slumped facedown in the mud. His delight was short-lived.

"Drop him, Grasos."

Tyre fell flat on his buttocks in the cold slime. Zelor crossed his arms over his chest, circling Tyre with a look that boded nothing good for his future. Tyre could hear Zelor's teeth grind.

"Ernani, you make me so angry I'm tempted to beat you senseless with my bare hands. However, you're so filthy I've decided to let someone else do it for me."

Zelor's hiss became a roar.

"We've one hour until the trumpet. In that time you will wrestle, in the mud, with Samos, who seems to be in as foul a temper as you are. Since he outweighs you by half your body weight, and is currently undefeated, I'll watch with enthusiasm as he tears you limb from limb."

By the sound of the trumpet, Tyre was a groaning mass of mud. Limping gingerly on a leg that had almost been twisted out of its socket, he tried, without much success, to scrape some of the muck off with his loincloth. Giving up, he tied on the sodden rag and waited at the gate.

Rama stood nearby. He had been unapproachable since joining and Tyre no longer tried to engage him in conversation. He was surprised when Rama spoke.

"What's her name, Tyre?"

Surprise gave way to shyness.

"Kara."

"Ah," Rama ruminated for a moment. "Mine is Varuna."

There didn't seem to be anything else to say, so they stood silently until the guards came.

Tyre swallowed the lump in his throat, readying himself for the door to open. The brightness blinded him for a moment after the semi-darkness of the corridor. He blinked, and saw Kara. She stood in front of the mantle, her sage-green dress shining in the firelight, the flames casting a halo of light around her gleaming hair. And he stood encased in hardening mud.

"Tyre, is that you?

He growled a wordless reply.

"It is you! I recognize your voice!" Her head tilted to one side. "Are you hungry?"

Tense and nervous, Tyre was in no mood for teasing. His retort was sharp.

"I am not hungry. I'm dirty, limping, sore in every muscle, and all I want is a little peace!"

The laughter died on her face. Immediately he was sorry he was the cause of its loss. An awkward silence stretched between them. She broke it first.

"I regret that my presence takes away your peace," she cleared her throat, "but at least I can offer you something to clean away the dirt and help the soreness. The tub behind you was delivered today. Use it and I'll not disturb your peace again."

As she turned back to the hearth, she unclenched her fists and spread her fingers in front of the fire. Tyre inspected the tub, noticing several kettles of water warming by the fire. She'd prepared everything for him and he'd cursed her like the ungrateful lout he was. With a discouraged slump in his shoulders, he pulled the tub away from the wall and closer to the fire. Then he remembered he was going to have to strip in front of her. She'd seen him naked in the arena, and the loincloth left little to the imagination, but that was nothing like the intimacy which began tonight. Something in him balked at the idea. Stopping what he was doing, he dropped onto the stool.

"Have you bathed today?"

She turned to regard him and shook her head, her dark brows swept upward in surprise.

"If I take a bath, you'll have to do the same."

"What! Why?"

Hearing her distress calmed his.

"This is something we both have to face. If we decide together how it will work, neither of us need be uncomfortable."

The minute he'd said it he felt better; he could stand his own embarrassment if he knew he wasn't alone.

She walked to the end of the bed and sat on the chest. As she gazed into the fire, the long lines of her throat melded into her upheld chin and the hollow in her throat began to pulse. She turned to him at last, her gaze serious, her brow furrowed.

"I feel shy about bathing in front of you. Still, I think you're right. Since it must be faced, we'll face it together tonight."

Color rose to her cheeks as she spoke. It relieved him to think she shared his dilemma. Perhaps they could make sense of this together. He worked it out slowly, choosing his words carefully, trying to be worthy of her trust.

"I'll always be dirtier than you so it makes sense for you to go first. Every evening when I return, I'll move the tub near the fire and fill it with the water you've heated. You can disrobe while I work. While you bathe, I'll keep my back to you and try to scrape off as much dirt as I can with a sponge and a basin. Once you're finished, I'll begin. After I finish, I'll clean up the floor and move the tub back to the door. Is that all right?"

He looked up to find her smiling at him. This time there was no teasing in her gaze. He was unprepared for her frankness.

"You said you would keep your back to me, but you made no mention of me looking at you. Do you want me to turn my back?"

He was glad his coat of mud prevented her from seeing him blush. The thought of her eyes on him was not nearly as frightening as it had been a few minutes ago.

"Kara, I leave that up to you."

She rose, moved to the other side of the bed, and began to unlace her gown.

Tyre was washing his hair for the second time. The mud had dried by the time Kara was finished and he'd been able to peel most of it off without too much trouble. She bathed quickly. He soaked for a long time. The hot water eased his aches and pains, his spirits rising as each layer of dirt was scrubbed away. He was aware of her, and could see her out of the corner of his eye where she sat combing her hair. He ducked his head forward and came up blinking away the water to find her standing directly in front of him. To his dismay, she held a cloth in one hand and soap in the other.

"Would you like me to wash your back?"

He almost choked. She was offering him a chance to redeem himself for his earlier hostility, so he measured that against his private fears. She'd been honest, so he'd answer in kind.

"That's thoughtful of you. It's just that I'm not used to . . ." he tried again, ". . . I'm not sure if . . ."

Her gaze grew curious. Exasperated with himself, he decided any attempt at an explanation would only make things worse. He'd been able to hide his arousal in her presence for almost a moon. Perhaps he could do it now. Wordlessly, he leaned forward, leaning his forearms on the rim of the tub for support. She moved behind him, pushing aside his wet hair, and began to run the cloth over his shoulders, her touch light and efficient. Humming to herself as she worked, she seemed unaware of the tension that was beginning to claim him. The cloth moved gradually down his back. As it grazed his lower ribs, he felt the first twinge. Breathing slowly, he tried to think of other things, but nothing seemed to help. Soon he was fully erect and the cloth had moved to just above his buttocks. Unable to prevent a tremor from coursing down his spine he heard her cry of concern.

"Here I am, taking my time, while you're catching a chill! There, I've finished!"

Now he had to stand up. Gritting his teeth, he rose to his feet, reaching a shaking hand for the cloth she'd placed on the stool. Passing it quickly over his skin, he wrapped it securely around his waist. Shivering from the combined effects of air on his wet skin and his present condition, he moved closer to the fire. Almost immediately, she appeared beside him, looking up at him with those huge, dark-lashed eyes.

"You're aroused."

It was such an unavoidable statement of fact he almost laughed aloud. Her next question was even more ludicrous.

"Did I do that to you?"

"So it would seem."

Thankfully, he sounded cool and collected, even though his skin burned. Perhaps she would believe he was standing too close to the fire.

"What will happen now?"

"If you're afraid I'll ravish you, you needn't worry."

"No, I meant will your . . . your arousal go away now?"

"Not if we don't stop talking about it."

The whole situation struck Tyre as remarkably silly. He stood there, shivering and dripping by a fireplace, a towel wrapped around a protuberance nothing could hide, while she revealed innocence even greater than his own. There was nothing to be done but try to maintain his dignity. Pulling the cloth off, he started to dry his hair with it. She moved back a step, although he felt her eyes on him, the mere thought of her watching him making him blush again. After drying himself thoroughly, he looked around for his loincloth. It was damp and grey with mud, but he had to wear something. He was reaching for it when she pressed something into his hand.

"I made this for you. The other one can be laundered so you'll always have something clean to wear."

He accepted her gift with a grateful look.

The first bath over, they sat down to eat.

Kara watched as Tyre methodically cleared the table, scraped away the remains of their meal, and began washing the dishes and pots. Even though he'd proven himself the superior cook, it remained Kara's task to plan and prepare meals. He offered to perform these chores every evening and she was happy to accept. It became her quiet time, usually spent with needlework or mending. She'd hemmed the loincloth with careful stitches for the past several nights, but unused to seeing women's crafts, or perhaps simply uncaring of what she did, he never asked about her work. She sensed his gratitude for her gift, although, as usual, it was not expressed in words.

Tonight she sat in the high-backed chair with empty hands. She needed time to adjust to the feelings that overwhelmed her when she saw the proof of his body's reaction to her touch. After almost thirty nights with him, she'd come to accept the fact that they would not join their bodies together during this moon. A certain part of her was relieved, another part was confused and even, if she was honest with herself, a little hurt. That he was aroused he could not deny. But he was more withdrawn than ever during their meal, his mood grim and his face expressionless.

She found herself hesitating to suggest what she'd planned for the evening, inspired as she was by this morning's session with Gelanor. Remembering the sight of Tyre's back beneath the dissolving cover of mud stiffened her resolve to begin tonight. The soapy water revealed a multitude of bruises and scrapes. An angry red mark between his shoulder blades looked as if it had been inflicted that day, his elbows were rubbed raw, and his skin was chafed and cracked from repeated exposure to wind, water, and dust. Nerissa revealed nothing to the women as to the daytime activities of the ernani, saying only that it was physically demanding. Tyre never spoke of it after his brief description during their first meal. But tonight, for the first time, her teasing caused him to reveal the effects of his daily sessions. That admission, combined with Gelanor's reminder, made her course seem clear.

The dishes were clean and Tyre placed the towel on the drying rack. He bent to light a twig and reaching up, began to light the small candles lining the mantle and the ledge of the window which gave them additional light in the rapidly darkening winter nights. His limp was less pronounced than it had been when he entered, but his lips tightened as he stretched to reach the candles on the window ledge. Kara smoothed the folds of her gown. She would not let his aloofness prevent her from trying to help him.

"You move so stiffly. I wonder, are you in pain?"

His hand hesitated for an instant before he lit the next candle.

"A trifle sore, but not too bad. Soaking in the bath helped my leg. Why do you ask?"

"If I could ease your soreness, would you let me?"

His eyes sparkled with unaccustomed humor.

"I doubt the trainer would listen to your request. In fact, he despises me so thoroughly he'd probably make my life worse if you spoke to him."

"I'd never be allowed to speak with your trainer, Tyre. I meant if there was something I could do myself, something that would help, would you let me try?"

She had his full attention now. Resting his back against the stone wall, he crossed his arms over his chest. The candles he had just lit illuminated his hair and face; the rest of his body stood in shadow.

"And how would you accomplish that?"

Holding up her hands, she smiled at him.

"With these."

He must have felt the light of the candles and resented what they might reveal, for he moved completely into shadow. His voice conveyed doubt verging on suspicion.

"What do you propose?"

The idea that this powerful man was hiding in a corner, threatened by the sight of her two slender hands tickled her. As she began to laugh, all doubts fled. All she could do was offer. The choice was his.

"You act as if I'm threatening to torture you! These hands may not be skillful at cookery, but they are quick at needlework and weaving, and are trained in other ways. With a little time and patience from you, I can ease away some of the soreness and help your poor skin."

He was silent for so long she took pity on him.

"If you don't want this simple gift of caring, Tyre, you've only to say so. The gift is mine to offer, yours to refuse."

"How would you give me this gift?"

His question caught her off-guard. For a moment she didn't understand him, until she realized he might have no experience with what she proposed.

"First we'll drape a cloth over the bed to protect it from the oil. You'll lie down and I'll either stand or kneel next to you. I cover my hands in a lotion rich in oils and massage your skin, kneading the muscles as I go. All you must do is lie still and concentrate on breathing slowly and evenly. If I'm skilled, you'll be asleep before I finish."

She could tell he was weighing it in his mind. Then, all at once, he was in motion, pulling out a sheet from the linen chest and spreading it over the bed. Taking the lotion and some hairpins from the small tray that held her brush and comb, she went over to the bed where he stood staring down at the spotless white sheet. Sensing his reluctance, she kept her voice mild and unthreatening.

"I must pin up my hair to keep it out of the oil. While you're waiting for me, lie on your stomach on the edge of the bed nearest the fire.

Twisting her hair into a knot at the back of her neck, she quickly inserted the pins. Finishing her hair, she considered his prostrate form. Taking another cloth from the chest, she floated it over his lower body, drawing it up to his waist. That seemed to reassure him, and turning his head away from her, he cradled it in his arms, his blonde mane masking his face from her view. As she rubbed the lotion over her hands, the fragrance filled the room, and she could hear his breathing start to even. She knelt beside him, hoping her hands might bring him rest and succor.

Tyre bathed in a sea of unimaginable sensation. His skin seemed alive as her hands glided over him. She began near his shoulders, spreading the oil over his gradually warming skin before beginning a journey that began at the back of his neck, moved down his spine, and ended at his waist. Once he knew what to expect, he'd let the tension leave him, enjoying the novelty of the experience and feeling a calmness begin to radiate outward from some place deep inside him.

Her hands grew firmer as she worked, the pressure increasing as he stopped trying to control his reactions, trusting her not to take him by surprise. Standing by the wall, watching her uplifted hands, he'd been fearful of what she proposed. Then her laughter trilled out, and in that instant, he knew he could trust her. Like the woman healer on the long march, Kara's hands brought only rest and healing.

She was lingering over certain places now, not leaving his shoulders for a long time, avoiding the place where the bruise was forming from

Dino's blow. When she finally reached his lower back, he was sorry she was nearly done. Never lifting her hands from his skin, she slid her hands back up to his neck, telling him without a word being spoken that she wanted him to remove his arms from under his head and let her begin on them.

Throughout this voyage of hands over flesh, she hummed a melody with a refrain so haunting, so beckoning, that it soon became a part of him. Her song entered him and wrapped itself around his heart, just as his body was wrapped in the fragrant oils she spread so lavishly over his skin.

He basked in the dying glow of the fire, rejoicing as muscles grew heavy and flaccid. She told him he would sleep, yet he wasn't weary anymore. Her ministrations transported him from one existence to another, a place he had never been before and one he hoped never to leave.

She began his other arm now, the one toward which his face was turned, and he opened his eyes to find her dark ones glowing over him. Her white hands gleamed against his more golden tones, and he delighted in the sensation of both seeing and feeling the movement of her hands down his arm, never stopping until she reached each finger. At last, with a lingering caress down the length of his arm, she left him.

"Stay still. I'll feed the fire," she whispered, completing the power of the spell she wove. He could not have moved had he wanted to.

Candles dimmed and sputtered out, the fire blossomed, and hairpins tinkled on the metal tray. Soon the mattress shifted with her weight. Tyre rolled over in one fluid motion and took her into his arms. She came without reluctance, letting him place her against his side, smoothing her hair over her shoulders and across his chest. Resting his cheek against her head, he felt her heartbeat slow and begin to match his own. Together they watched the heavy-bottomed moon hang low in the clear winter night. His voice was low and full of longing.

"That song. I've never heard you sing it before."

"Sleep, Tyre."

But he was not satisfied.

"Stay with me, Kara."

She knew what he was asking. Renew our contract, walk with me on the Path, help me give my gifts, all this he wanted but could not, or would not, say. She had thought him proud; tonight she learned it was not pride, but ignorance, and as Gelanor hinted, an innocence that matched her own.

Kara spoke no answer, but rubbed her cheek slowly against his chest. She would stay.

Tyre's lips brushed her hair, and they slept.

Chapter 14

Exorcism

SHOVING HIS SWORD back in his scabbard, having easily disarmed Pandar, Zelor hawked and spat in the ernani's general direction.

"I know I missed that feint again, trainer. I was, uh, distracted."

"Distracted? Were you, now? I never would have guessed!"

The trainer's sarcasm shifted to a resounding roar.

"Idiot! You've been distracted for three days! Straighten up or you won't last three more. I've no use for laggards. Learn the skills or be replaced!"

This was Zelor's first stint of duty in the Maze and he was stymied. Confidence being one of his most valuable traits (or one of his most annoying, depending on one's point of view) he knew his staff to be excellent and his own behavior flawless. Admittedly, his assignment had its difficulties: administer a rigorous course of training designed to change thieves, beggars, assassins, and mercenaries into a disciplined corps who could take (and eventually give) orders without fighting among themselves; turn former slaves into free men able to defend themselves with an assortment of weapons; transform bodies weak from starvation and ill-treatment into stream-lined instruments of power and grace. Three moons into their training, the ernani's performances were almost as bad as they were during the first days of joining.

Confident though he might be, Zelor was no fool. Taking his observations to the Council, he let them see with their own eyes what he'd observed over the past week. Ladon's suggestions had been followed to the letter, but nothing seemed to help. Three fist-fights in as many days, missed holds, missed feints, a sudden rash of injuries, none of them serious, but enough to make Zelor increasingly uneasy. Appalled at the mercurial changes which ran through the ernani with frightening regularity, he demanded explanations, and more importantly, suggestions at the next meeting of the Council.

When Nerissa responded first, rushing to the defense of her motley crew, Luxor interrupted her with a raucous laugh, smashing a brawny fist on the table for emphasis.

"Zelor's right and you know it! Nothing's crazier than an ernani in rut!"

Nerissa winced at Luxor's vulgarity, but the waves of humor rippling around the table proved his opinions were shared by everyone. Luxor hadn't served in the Maze for years, not since he served as Head Trainer for the Novice class. Stories of his nasty tenure were still circulated with admiration by old-time guards like Grasos and Echetus. Even though he and his father were often at each other's throats in quarrels that caused Zelor's mother to make regular retreats to her sister's house, Zelor had copied his father's methods as Head Trainer down to his swaggering gait. When Luxor spoke again, Zelor was all attention.

"They twist with the wind. One day they're working well, focused, aggressive but controlled; the next they attack their own shadows." Luxor paused, continuing in a tone not of laughter, but of admonition. "The only thing that keeps them safe is discipline. I'd rather you administer a beating than have one of them lose an eye or a limb due to laxity."

Nerissa tried again to offer an explanation.

"I know they try your patience, but the second moon period changes almost every condition of Preparation. During the first moon the men are desperate to please; now, deeper levels of communication are required. For the first time, the women feel as trapped as the men and there's often resentment among them. Add to this the fact that the newness of joining is lessening. They're forced to begin to share their lives, and for the most part, these men have never shared anything with anyone. Luxor is correct when he says they fight shadows—they fight the phantoms of the past."

The following day, with low-scudding clouds promising a winter storm, Zelor cancelled work in the arena and divided the men into teams. Sessions were conducted in pairs, each ernani competing for his team, the winning team allowed to leave practice one hour before the trumpet. The series of events Zelor marked out in the practice room were wrestling, sword and dagger, and long sword. He watched closely, as did his men, for speed, dexterity, aggression, and control. So far, the ernani had responded well to the challenge. The session Zelor was watching ended and he announced the winner. Throwing his eyes to one of his men, he indicated he would take over the match in which Tyre was currently engaged.

Rama was fighting as beautifully as ever. Zelor observed his perfect form with the admiration of a connoisseur. Sometime in the black man's past a master swordsman had taught him well, and Rama's life as a sword for hire allowed him ample time to practice. Watching as he skillfully avoided an overhand blow with a leg glide, Zelor could barely resist the impulse to applaud. If Rama finished Preparation, and was so inclined, he would become Master of the Sword in Carmanor's command, passing on to future generations his graceful, deadly, mastery.

Zelor's attention moved to Rama's opponent. Tyre has improved, thought Zelor. What he lacks in experience he makes up for in temerity and sheer grit. Rama had become more alert during their sessions of late, his respect for his opponent growing. One thing Zelor was sure of: if Tyre ever suspected a weakness, that lapse would be attacked with ferocity. He expected no quarter and gave none, making him the most dangerous man in the group. The others were inured to slavery and its unremitting sameness. Tyre fought against it with every blow he struck, whether it landed or not.

After Tyre's ill-fated session with Dino (a moment Zelor hoped someday to forget) he had trained strictly with Rama. When Zelor heard the Lapithian call to battle reverberate through the arena, he'd summoned Grasos with a mental scream, sending up a grateful prayer when he realized Tyre and Dino were both unharmed.

Now, watching Tyre's eyes smoldering in ruthless intensity, Zelor wondered what phantom he was fighting today.

Kara looked around the cell, finding, to her relief that all was in readiness and still an hour remained until the evening trumpet. She'd been looking forward to a bath all day. Now she'd have time to have one and warm more water before Tyre returned. She was no longer so shy of undressing in front of him, but yesterday her monthly flow ended and she wanted to bathe in privacy for once and clean away all reminders of her show of blood. In a repeat of her former difficulties, she was awakened by Tyre in the middle of the night, his strong hands lessening the cramping and allowing her to sleep. Still, it was not easy to share a cell during these times and she sank down into the scented water with a happy sigh.

Picking up the cloth, she soaped herself lavishly, enjoying the feel of the bath oils that made her skin slick and shiny. Tyre was not the only one whose skin was chapped and reddened. This winter was more severe than usual and Kara had no one to cover her with oil every night. She dismissed such an uncharitable thought, refusing to let anything disturb her sense of well-being. After all, this second moon had brought with it much cause for thanksgiving. Tyre was talking to her, and it filled her with delight.

Kara stumbled onto the means of his communication by sheer chance. Suffering from a sore throat threatening to become a full-fledged fever, she was ordered to rest and forbidden to sing by Ladon, who reminded her that serious illness would force him to transfer her to the House of Healing. His threat succeeded; Kara was determined nothing should disturb their new-found peace. Tyre allowed and seemed to welcome her touch. Lately, he had even reciprocated with a few clumsy caresses of her face or hair, always when she least expected them. He was trying hard to overcome whatever it was that kept him away from her. It charmed her to see his awkwardness and the flush on his golden skin which always followed her silent acknowledgement of his touch.

Casting about for something to fill their hours in the face of her enforced silence, Kara was sitting in the dayroom when Nerissa approached her.

"Kara, child, why do you frown?"

"Since Ladon's forbidden me to sing, I was trying to think of something we could do together after the evening meal."

Nerissa frowned in turn. Her days were full of counseling and teaching, yet she would drop everything to help with a simple problem of little merit.

"Have you ever tried reading to Tyre? I've just borrowed this book from the Lesser Library to read for myself, but you may use it until you have time to find one more to your liking."

She proffered a palm-sized, leather-bound book of obvious antiquity. All books were precious in Pelion and this one was worn with many readings. Before Kara could open it to read the title page, Nerissa relieved her curiosity.

"They're tales of exotic lands and the people who inhabit them. Since you've never lived outside the walls, perhaps Tyre can tell you if they're works of truth or imagination."

Nerissa glided off in another direction, leaving Kara exultant. If Tyre enjoyed her singing, surely he'd like to hear tales of far-off lands. She almost skipped out of the dayroom, but controlled her childish impulse and walked with womanly grace to the cell.

The meal over, Tyre reclined in his usual place on the rug, his bright hair gleaming in the light of the cheery blaze. Kara pulled the book out of her cloak pocket and waved it triumphantly in front of his nose.

"Look, I found a book for us! Since I can't sing, I'll read to you!"

Cocking his brow over an eye with a decidedly mischievous glint, a look beginning to replace his former taciturn stares, he asked coolly, "What makes you think I can't read it for myself?"

Truth be told, Kara never considered the possibility that Tyre could read. Of course the ernani were being schooled, but Kara's mother taught basic reading and writing skills to children, and certainly no one could master reading in a few short weeks. Her dismay must have given her thoughts away, because Tyre's face lit with a rare grin.

"Never mind. How could you know I'm not an illiterate lout if I've never told you otherwise? Here, give me the book. I'll read to you and give your throat a rest."

Soon he was lying propped up on a pillow, the book held to the firelight, and reading with surprising animation, stumbling only occasionally over words that even Kara would have had difficulty pronouncing. The tale was pure fantasy, Kara knew, and told of lovers and dangers and mythical beasts, yet somehow the subject seemed fitting for their cozy fire with the wind whistling through the cracks. Tyre finished the story and closed the book, stretched himself cat-like, and rearranged the pillows beneath him.

"Who taught you to read so beautifully?"

A shadow she had seen before darkened his face. This time, instead of retreating from her with a shrug, he looked up.

"I was taught your language and how to read and write it by a man who was my tutor for twelve years. He taught me everything I know and was my closest friend."

"You speak as if he were lost to you. Did he leave you to teach some other boy?"

He clenched his jaw, his eyes awash with memories.

"He teaches no longer. He met his death saving my life."

Every throb of Kara's warm and loving heart urged her to wrap her arms around him and give him permission to shed the tears he was trying to contain. Tyre looked up to her at that moment, his mask of isolation descending. He turned back toward the fire, flipping through the pages of the book. Finding something in the table of contents, he spoke again with studied neutrality.

"This sounds interesting. A tale from the eastern shore."

The evening wore on and the little book was finally closed, but what had begun that night continued to grow. In bits and pieces, Kara learned the general details of his life. Several topics remained forbidden—the story of his enslavement, the religion of his people, and anything to do with his family, but she came to know what questions would be answered and what information would be withheld. His stories of life on the northern plains made her hold up her own life for examination, finding it dull and commonplace in comparison. Tyre's revelations bound her closer to him than any physical gesture could have done. She might be a woman, but she knew he did not despise her. Best of all, he was beginning to trust her.

Tyre took one step over the threshold of the cell and froze. Kara, her hair pinned up to reveal the long length of her neck, was rising from the bath, the water cascading off her pale, translucent skin. She was apparently unaware of his presence, for she stepped out of the tub and walked leisurely toward the stool on which the drying cloth rested. Tyre gulped, and remained frozen, his eyes ranging over her breasts touched with dusky rose and lowering to see her slim legs, pink from the warm water in which they had been immersed and the nest of dark curls that crowned them. Never had he seen such beauty, and his jaw dropped at her perfection. In the days since they began to bathe in the cell, he had caught glimpses of her, and he had touched her only a few nights ago when her time had come upon her again. Yet this was something different, something disturbing and threatening, for all he wanted to do was take her in his arms and feel her bare skin against his; to loosen her hair and feel its fineness against his chest and stomach. Even though his body responded instantly to his desires, his mind whispered to him of danger.

She must have heard Grasos slide the bolt, for she turned with a gasp, holding the cloth instinctively in front of her to shield herself from his eyes. His gaze must have devoured her, for she turned a bright luscious pink as she scolded him.

"You're early! And you frightened me! What happened to your promise to turn your back?"

She was not angry at all. Embarrassed perhaps, but he could tell his reaction pleased her in some mysterious way. He jerked his eyes away from her with an effort, heading for a kettle boiling on the grate.

"It's difficult to keep my promise when I walk in to find you in such a condition. The trainer dismissed my team an hour before the trumpet. How was I to know you decided to take a bath before my arrival?"

His attempt at humor fell flat, revealing too many of his real concerns. Why had she bathed without him? Hadn't they agreed not to hide from one another?

Kara put aside her modesty.

"It's just that I wanted to clean myself after the last few days. It was good to soak forever and feel myself restored."

Her admission was brave and Tyre appreciated bravery. Grunting his understanding, he started to strip. She watched him for a moment before busying herself by the bed, drying herself thoroughly, dressing herself in a loose robe, and working out the tangles from her unpinned hair.

Tyre sank into the hot water with a gasp. Try as he might he couldn't find the accustomed peace of mind that usually accompanied his entry into these four walls. He searched his mind, trying to locate the source of his trouble, finding it in the Fifteenth Mother's parting words to him at the end of the first moon.

He had refused to meet her eyes throughout the interview, replying to her inquiries with nods and shakes of his head. Her closing remarks made him look up, meeting lined, weary eyes which, despite their weariness, fastened on him with hypnotic force.

"I see no reason to keep you any longer. Kara chooses to continue her contract and you seem to agree. I remind you, however, of a requirement of the next three moons—that you and Kara join your bodies together. She has told me she is willing. I must assume you are as well since this is a necessary step toward the giving of your gifts."

Her assurance that Kara wanted to join with him pleased him, although he knew it from the moment she sang him her first love song. It grew increasingly difficult for him to mask his arousal around her. Lately, he'd ceased trying. Daily she saw the evidence of his need; tonight she revealed her own eagerness. Tired of fighting any longer against half-formed fears, he recalled the vision of her rising from her bath. Standing up in a rush of water and suds, he reached for the drying cloth.

At the sound of the splashing water, Kara looked up. As he moved toward her, throwing the cloth to the floor, she stood, her face alive with excitement, opening her arms to welcome him home. Stripping away her loose robe, he closed his eyes at the feel of her warmth against his still-damp skin. Looking down, he saw himself reflected in her eyes. She was so trusting, so sure of him, although her lips trembled. He lowered his mouth onto those lips and stilled their trembling. Tasting her for the first time, his kiss was long and deep, and to his surprise, she returned it, running her tongue over his lips and inside the smoothness of his mouth. A wave of trembling overcame him, and she was smiling up at him, all cares forgotten, her eyes shining under heavy lashes, her cheeks flushed with passion. When she pulled him down to the bed he followed her willingly.

She knew his body from the nightly massages. He was a stranger to hers. His first touch was awkward, fumbling, and he paused, waiting for her laughter. Instead, she took his hand between her palms and stroked it lingeringly.

"There's no rush, no hurry. Study me well, Tyre; I long for your touch."

So he began his exploration of her body. She lay contentedly in his arms, her head thrown back and her hair spread in glorious abandon over the bedclothes. Her eyes were closed and her lips slightly parted, the hollow of her throat pulsing with the beat of her heart. He began at her long, slender neck, kissing and stroking, watching in wonder as a slow flush followed every stroke of his hand, every touch of his lips and tongue. He imprisoned her breasts in his palms, her tender nipples rising at his touch, hardening as he nuzzled them with his mouth. When he suckled her, she gasped her pleasure and rolled her head from side to side, uttering moans he echoed inside himself. He moved his mouth from breast to breast, tasting and smelling her heady scent as her flesh grew ripe and swollen beneath him. His hands moved slowly down her, caressing her stomach and flanks, stroking her lightly at first and then with more strength, feeling her tremble at each touch. His fingers grazed the top of her soft mound of night-dark hair and she lifted herself up, pushing her hips against him, yearning for his touch, begging him to continue his journey.

Pressing his palm against her he felt her dampness. Confident at last, he looked at her full length as she lay beside him. Her mouth was open now, her breasts rising and falling in long deep breaths, her legs slightly parted and the curls above them wet with desire. She was so delicate, so fragile; he might crush her with his weight. Her eyes opened, eyes that told him she wanted him inside her. Unable to disappoint her or deny his need any longer, Tyre moved into position above her.

Smiling through a shining veil of tears, she opened her legs, moving her hips into his waiting hands in a gesture far more ancient than any song she could sing for him. Ready to enter, he looked down at himself.

Unbidden, the punishing images rose to his eyes and he choked back a cry. Great, breaking waves of nausea crashed over him. Suddenly, there was no desire, no passion, only a terrible need to escape her, to save her from his hands which were trembling with emotions so intense he wanted to hurt someone so as not to hurt himself. She was touching him now, climbing up his body, her face raised to his with a troubled frown. He grabbed her shoulders, his fingers digging deep into soft, yielding flesh, and marked her wince of pain. His voice harsh and cruel, fighting the panic inside him, he watched as she withered between his hands.

"Let me be, woman. I've told you not to trouble me, not to show yourself to me. This is what will happen. Do you see now, woman? Let me be!"

He left the bed, but not before she sank into the tousled bedclothes with her fist in her mouth, tears coursing down her cheeks, her eyes so full of fear they mirrored his own. Sick, sweating, his stomach heaving, he curled into a ball on the hard floor, and, welcoming the chill of the stones, held his stomach until the nausea passed. Her sobs filled the cell, each one stabbing him with remorse, guilt, and finally, an agony of hopelessness.

He had hoped Kara's love would deliver him, but it seemed that nothing could lift from him the burden of the past.

Vena found Kara in the solarium. She sat alone by the undraped window, her cheek resting against the panes. The chill from the draft had turned her lips blue and sent spasms of shivers coursing through her slight frame. The face she lifted to the old woman was as colorless and frozen as the snow blanketing the garden. Her eyes were dry, her lips cracked and swollen; her hair had lost its luster overnight. When Vena touched her hand, her skin offered no welcoming warmth but was as cold and dead as her eyes.

"Your misery called me from my tower room. Come, child, rest your head on my breast for a moment."

Healing instincts made her pull the girl toward her and wrap her in one of the bright wool blankets lying scattered about the room. At Vena's touch, Kara crumpled against her and lay shivering in her arms, her eyes staring at the frozen garden. When she began to mumble, Vena bent to listen.

"All dead. Everything's dead. Frozen. Buried in the cold hard ground."

Vena rocked her slowly, rubbing the blanket against her and willing the icy skin to warm. She fought her impulse to enter Kara and heal her from within. This was the fruit of her plan and the taste was bitter. She had hoped, as Beal had hoped, that the littlest ernani would free Tyre, but the price of this Preparation was seeing Kara torn apart. Nothing Vena could offer her was worth this price.

"Tell me, child. Tell me what happened. Let me share your hurt."

As Vena continued rocking her, the girl told her everything, everything Vena had sensed when she was awakened by Tyre's silent scream of rage and disappointment at the betrayal of his body by his mind. The old woman knew as well that Kara had passed through countless emotions in that long night of sobs, and now was blessedly empty. Though it would renew Kara's anguish, Vena must put her on the rack.

"You were ready for him and suddenly he was not there. Where did he go, Kara? Think hard for me, for the old woman who has loved you for so long. What did he say?"

"He . . . he was disgusted . . . He . . . he told me it was my fault, that I . . . lured him. He couldn't even say my name. I was . . . woman. Only . . . woman . . ."

The despair of that last word lacerated Vena. This is what it comes to, then, the old battle fought so many times before. She, Vena, would not allow it, and as she shouted those words in her mind, her spine stiffened with resolve. She would break the rules she had wrought with effort and defended with tenacity. She would do what must not be done. She turned the girl in her arms and willed her to listen, using full Voice on a mind that had never been touched.

"You will put this out of your mind. You will go to the women's dormitory and bathe and refresh yourself. This evening you will go the cell as usual. A meal will be provided for you. Do nothing; say nothing, no matter what happens. Eat and drink everything and prepare yourself for bed. I make you a promise. If you do this for me tonight, you'll never have to enter the cell again. One more night, Kara, only one more night . . ."

The girl's eyes were glazed by the time she finished, for Vena had used not suggestion, but command. Her eyes finally clearing, Kara nodded in silent agreement and stumbled to her feet. As she reached the door of the solarium, Vena watched her straighten her slender shoulders and lift her chin. This gesture convinced Vena of the rightness of her decision. Nothing was worth the destruction of a human soul. Nothing.

The grate slid open and Tyre reached for the tray. Before he could open his mouth to call Kara, she appeared by his side, as white and silent as the columns in the Sanctum. She had not spoken, did not even look up from her book when he entered. The cell was tidy although no fire burned in the hearth. He asked her gently if she wanted him to light one, but she never raised her eyes from her book.

He expected rage, tears, fury, contempt, but found an empty shell. Kara was gone, as surely as everyone he had ever cared for had gone. He could not even blame her, for he had driven her away. Kara's departure brought back the loss of Belwyn and he could feel himself ripped open, bleeding slowly on the inside.

He forced down the food and finished the tea, noticing she ate everything carefully and without relish. Finished, she put down the book, disrobed, and donned her nightshift. Standing by the window, she counted out the hundred strokes of the brush, pulled down the covers and slipped between them. Throughout her ritual, Tyre was aware that he was not even in the room with her.

He cleaned up the dishes without thinking, caught in the discipline of routine and thankful it gave him something to do other than stare hopelessly at her blank face. Now he was dozing by the fire. He pulled a blanket onto the floor and wrapped himself in it. Hearing her regular breathing, he was thankful for the blessed nothingness of sleep.

"Grasos, Ladon, tonight I undertake something I have forbidden others to do. Even so, I'm convinced I must proceed no matter the consequences. Tonight I break my own rule. If you have second thoughts, tell me now. There's no turning back from this. Once begun, it is done."

Her voice harsh, her eyes impenetrable, Vena stood in darkness between the two men. It was midnight and they stood in the passageway next to Tyre's cell. Ladon noted that she didn't use inner speech and guessed she was saving her strength for the struggle that waited within. He had drugged both food and drink, insuring that Kara and Tyre would sleep through the night and awaken late in the morning. He disapproved of the amount the Fifteenth Mother required, but one look at her grim, tightly-drawn face made the protest die in his throat. Grasos was equally tense and held his cudgel loose in his hand. She commanded that no one was to pass, no matter what happened inside the cell. Grasos pledged that no one would cross the threshold he guarded.

Satisfied with Grasos' response, she issued Ladon's instructions. He had never been a soldier, never touched a weapon, but Ladon knew in that moment the fear of those who march headlong into battle.

"I want you with her throughout the night. Touch her, Ladon, and keep yourself attuned to her. Don't leave her for an instant, no matter what you may see or hear. They have joined their hearts, even if his mind and body resists. My greatest fear is that she will wake when she senses his fear. As you love me, Ladon, keep Kara floating far away. I cannot bear it if she is hurt anymore than she has already been hurt. Have I your promise?"

Reading it in his eyes, she turned slowly toward the door. Grasos slid the bolt open, and together, the Fifteenth Mother and the High Healer of Pelion stepped across the threshold.

Vena settled herself on the floor and gathered her strength around her, pulling energy from the flames and the heat of Tyre's body. She ran through the concentration exercises learned in her youth from the Thirteenth Mother. Before she made contact, she remembered her predecessor's dictum, that she must bend, not break, the mind of the man sprawled at her feet. With an inhalation of breath, she gripped his shoulders with both hands and entered.

She knew this part of his mind well, having walked its rooms and corridors before, finding everywhere Tyre's memories of Lapith and

Belwyn. Here the sun shone, the wind blew, and a boy rode a fast horse across an empty plain. Everywhere, too, she sensed the careful work of Beal, not just in the study of languages or mathematics, but Beal's work with a boy who lacked a father as well as a mother, who enjoyed no deeply felt emotional ties with anyone except his friend-in-blood, Hourn, and, in time, his beloved tutor.

But Vena had not come to observe, but to act, and so she pulled Tyre deeper, ever deeper, into the labyrinth of his mind. Here she found rooms with open doors and endless images of Kara, but did not slow her progress, sensing Tyre's reluctance to continue, his wish to stay in the place in his mind where Kara lived. All too soon, they entered corridors whose doors were half-shut, then tightly shut and bolted. No light shone from beneath their sills. Damp air surrounded them, damp because of tears, she guessed, shed and unshed, rooms full of grief and disappointment.

Beal had never been here before, of that Vena was certain. One door with three bolts claimed her attention and, trusting her instincts, Vena commanded it to open. One by one, the iron bolts slid back and the wooden door creaked open, its hinges rusty from disuse, the air inside laced with the scent of fresh blood. Tyre's mind cried out a warning, but Vena took no notice as she forced him inside.

There, inside a leather tent, a man mounted a woman from the rear.

The woman moaned, keening softly so as not to disturb the child sleeping nearby. The man rammed into her, grunting with each stroke, heedless of the pain he caused as he entered flesh still tender from the birth of a girlchild. Blood ran unstaunched down the back of her thighs. With every thrust she ducked her head, gritting her teeth so as not to scream. A frightened voice called for his mother, the curtain parted, and a small boy entered, worried and confused. Vena saw through a five-year-old boy's eyes the blood on his father's quickly shrinking erection.

Her mental vision locked on the rape in front of her, she refused to allow Tyre to shut his eyes. He writhed and grimaced between her hands, unable to look away from the image she forced on him. Undaunted, she demanded he look again, not as a child, but as a man. She showed him the cruelty and savagery of the act, but as she did so she fed him the images she had gleaned from Kara's mind—the welcoming spread of her legs and uplifted hips inviting his presence within her, her eyes glistening with tears of love and desire. After each image, she forced him back into the room, making him see, touch, hear, smell the difference between his mother's tears of anguish and Kara's tears of passion, the fragrant scent of Kara's perfume and the nauseating odor of blood, his mother's whimpers of pain and Kara's moans of delight, the bloodied arousal of his father's body and Kara's vision of Tyre rising over her, his skin golden and shining, his eyes glowing brilliant blue.

As he began to quiet between her hands, she allowed him to rest. His breath came in deep gasps and his clenched fists relaxed. Vena left him for a moment and contacted Ladon. He acknowledged her presence briefly, careful to keep his connection with Kara intact. To her unspoken question, he answered:

"She floats far above the city, although he disturbed her even there. They are more deeply connected than we guessed. I fear for her if you return your attention to him while she remains nearby."

Vena weighed Ladon's advice against her rapidly diminishing strength. She had begun the cure of Tyre's fear of the primal scene he witnessed as a child. Kara and time would open the door wider and dispel the strength of that memory. Having accomplished what she intended, the longing to retreat was strong. But the darkness and what lay beyond it taunted her. Refusing to let its power prevent the possibility of total victory, she accepted the task.

"Take her even farther away, away from Pelion. Return her to the eastern shore, from the place Beal found her. Take her to her mother, Ladon, and keep her safe for me."

Ladon didn't waste words with his promise.

Turning back to the man who now lay quietly by the fire, Vena readied herself for the battle that might be her last, pushing away her cowardice. This was the Golden One, the one revealed by the prophecy of so long ago. She must trust in her mission and free herself from doubt.

The entrance was easier this time. The door she had forced opened stood slightly ajar, a faint light spilling into the passageway. As she moved down the rapidly darkening corridor, Tyre intensified his struggles, resisting every step, fearful of what lay ahead, trying to drag her back from the course yawning in front of them. She fought him down the hallways, refusing to be swayed, pulling him indomitably into the darkness, oblivious to his cries and moans. The last door was made of iron, the bolt frozen solid in the lock. She stared at it, her strength depleted, her will nearly spent. She reached her goal only to find herself empty of the power to open and enter.

As she stood memorizing the moment of her defeat, another presence joined her by the door. The mind which made itself known to her was as gentle as she was strong, as tender as she was courageous, a mind of compassion and understanding, a mind without fear. Beal chided her, as he had always done.

"Must you do everything alone? Come, my beloved. Embrace me."

Effortlessly, she joined the mate of her heart and together they willed the door open. Tyre screamed as the bolt scraped and the hinges ground against one another. His scream seemed endless, an outpouring of grief and shame freed from a lifetime of denial. Holding Tyre between them, Vena and Beal looked within.

A woman hung from the rafters of an earthen lodge, her body swinging slightly as a gust of wind blew open the door. The boy missed her and went looking for her. Scared, lonely, his dirty face smeared with tears, he stumbled over the threshold, afraid of this place his mother had told him he must never enter. He looked up past the long, white-blonde braids, past the swollen tongue hanging from the gaping mouth, to her eyes, bluer than the cloudless summer skies over Lapith, but vacant now and staring. The room was warm and flies had already gathered on her face.

She had been angry with him since the night he saw the man in their tent. At every question he asked, she became quieter and more withdrawn, until at last she forbade him to speak of it. He knew he had displeased her and knew how he had done it. He had seen things he ought not to have seen. If he had stayed in bed, if he had not seen her nakedness, she would not turn away from him as she did so often lately, as if the sight of him sickened her.

Suddenly, the boy began to scream. He had seen dead animals before and knew flies ate them when they died. He screamed and screamed for she was lost to him and he had driven her away.

Vena and Beal began their work.

Beal reminded him of the death of his sister, the tiny babe he resented from the moment his mother explained to him she carried another child within her. His mother had grieved the loss of that daughter, and Beal found the memory of her tears and spread it before the groaning man, demanding that he bear witness to her grief and the growing trouble in her mind. Vena led him back to the night of blood, reminding him of his mother's relief as she held him in her arms, his small hands brushing away the tears running down her cheeks. Vena made him listen again to his mother's careful warning that he should never enter the men's lodge. She wanted to spare him, and so chose the one place she believed he would never go. Her silence had not meant anger, but sorrow at the unavoidable loss of her son. Soon he would be taken from her and she could not bear the thought of life without him. She chose, instead, to leave him, and though the choice was bitter, she did it with every care for him, for Tyre, the child of her heart, who brought her sunshine and gladness for the first and only time in her brief life.

Vena looked down at the sobbing man held tightly in her throbbing, vein-covered hands. Beal's inner voice echoed hollowly in the cell: *"Tyre, you must turn toward the light! Go to her in the morning, young lord, and open your heart. Sleep now, and rest easy in the thought that you are loved."*

Gradually, Tyre quieted and loosed a ragged sigh.

Releasing their charge, they turned to regard one another, Beal's brown eyes glowing into hers of grey. Once again, she experienced the completeness of their union.

"In time, we'll be united once more."

And Beal was gone.

Vena sagged against Tyre's body. Ladon was instantly by her side, helping her stand. As she straightened her robes, she noticed he was staring at her. Refusing to acknowledge his concern or curiosity, she inquired after Kara.

"I did as you commanded. We journeyed east, where she played and sang with her mother. She sensed nothing, not even when both of you were screaming."

Surprised, Vena swallowed, the raw flesh protesting the salty liquid coursing down her throat. So tired she could hardly shuffle toward the door, she rapped once and waited. Grasos appeared with cudgel in hand, worry etched into every seam of his homely face. With one look at the old woman, he lifted her in his arms, and together they left the Maze.

Tyre woke more slowly than usual. Brushing aside the blanket, he noticed purplish bruises on either side of his upper arms. The pattern of the bruises resembled fingerprints. Since he had wrestled yesterday, he ignored them. His head felt foggier than usual and there was a faint hum in his ears, but otherwise he felt better. Blinking away the fog, he wondered why the cell was flooded with sunlight. Jumping to his feet, he looked around for an explanation. If the morning bell failed to wake him, Grasos usually pounded on the door.

Then he saw Kara.

She was fast asleep, the sun warming her as she lay on her side, her hand gripping the pillow beneath her head as if the she held someone's hand in hers. He knelt beside the bed and watched her, studying her face. She smiled in her sleep and then, without warning, her eyes flew open. Using the bedclothes as a shield, she shrank away from him.

Tyre retreated to the center of the room.

"Kara, you don't know how much you frighten me." Her eyes widened, but she was prevented from speaking by his upraised palm. "I've never joined with a woman and it's hard for me to trust myself. I've been afraid for so long that . . . that . . ."

His throat closed. Unable to continue, his heart in his mouth, his knees shaking and his chest close to bursting, he waited for a sign. Slowly, more slowly than she had reached out to offer him the pear, she rose to her knees, her hands folded in her lap. Perusing him with solemn brown eyes, she nodded for him to continue. Encouraged, for he'd feared she wouldn't listen, he steadied his resolve.

"I said hurtful things that I can't unsay. But I can tell you this: that night, you filled me with such longing that not just my body but my soul yearned for you. I wanted to join with you, wanted to be truly inside you, wrapped in your arms, finally safe from harm and hurt. You gave that to me, Kara, something I've never felt for any woman, something that goes against everything I was taught to feel and think. That's why it's taken so long for me to . . . to come to you. That night, all the old fears came back. I never meant to hurt you—would die before I hurt you again."

As he spoke, she began to smile. Somewhere in the middle of his speech, she was standing before him, looking searchingly up at him, her eyes beginning to shine with hope. By the time he stammered to a halt, she was reaching down to the hem of her nightshift and drawing it over her head, letting it slide from her fingertips to melt on the floor in a cream-colored puddle. Not daring to move, he held his breath as her nimble fingers untied his loincloth. That, too, she let drift slowly to the floor.

Placing her hands directly over his heart, over the sunburst Belwyn had carved in his flesh, she ran her hands down until they reached his core. He closed his eyes at her touch, feeling himself rise into her hands. Her eyes never left his face; her smile was slow and full of passion.

He throbbed in her hands. Now she was kneeling, the pressure of her mouth and lips sending tremors through him, threatening his balance. Completely vulnerable, he braced himself, his fingers laced in her hair, his groans echoing against the stone walls. When he could endure it no longer, he lifted her up and swung her into his arms. There she lay warm and pliant, her breasts rubbing against his chest, her hair hanging off his arm in a waterfall of darkness.

"Can you forgive me?"

He saw her remember. The proof of his cruelty lay before his eyes—bruises marring the perfection of white shoulders, the crescents of his fingernails like tiny half-moons carved into her flesh. For a moment he despaired and looked away, but she turned his face toward her and held it between her palms. Her fathomless eyes looked into his soul, accepting what they found there.

She had forgiven him; now he lowered her onto the bed and made her forget. With hands and mouth he paid homage to her, worshipping her until her moans filled the cell and her skin burned like molten silver. With exquisite care, he lowered himself between her legs, finding the warm, liquid place she rubbed so longingly against him. Pushing forward, he reached a barrier. Almost senseless now, she fought her way back up to him, giving him the permission he longed for.

"Come into me, Tyre. Let us be one."

He pushed forward, feeling her fight against him for a moment, then broke through to find himself inside her. Everything in him urged him to move, but he held himself motionless, his arms trembling with effort, and looked down at her face. Her eyes wide with wonder, she tightened herself around him. He groaned with pleasure, his head thrown back, and she was moving under him, inviting him to move as well. They moved slowly for awhile, luxuriating in the sensation of oneness. Their leisurely rhythm increased its tempo and soon he was grimacing in his effort to hold back, not knowing how to take her with him. Lifting her hips, she wrapped her legs around his flanks so he could move more quickly now, driving deep inside her. Her eyes were half-closed, her breathing rapid, her cries rich and sweet-voiced. Suddenly, she arched her back, crying out her victory. With a glad shout, he answered with his own release.

Her kisses brought him slowly back to the cell, no longer a prison since Kara had freed him. He turned them over on their sides, not removing himself from her, still feeling the receding waves of her passion. They lay with legs entangled, her cheek against his heart, his golden head resting against her midnight mass of curls.

As they watched the sun reach its zenith, Kara hummed her love song to the beat of Tyre's heart.

Chapter 15

Stratagems

GRASOS LUMBERED PAST parallel ranks of iron doors. Coming to an abrupt halt where three hallways converged, he selected the right fork, ascended a steep staircase, executed a sharp ninety-degree turn at the top of the landing and continued relentlessly forward, down more torch lit hallways flanked by more identical doors. As usual, Tyre lagged a few paces behind. His body might be in motion, propelling him forward by sheer force of habit; his thoughts lay elsewhere.

Opening his eyes on the sun-drenched cell, feeling the play of Kara's fingers over his chest, he dreamed they'd been forgotten by everyone in the Maze. Here they would live forever, locked safely away amongst rumpled bedclothes, the cell lit in a perpetual amber haze, her skin turned to porcelain, his to bronze. They might never have risen had not Kara's stomach growled.

Lazily he watched the rising tide of color move from the tips of her breasts to her cheeks.

"I've come to admire your blushes," he observed, amused when she blushed an even deeper shade of pink. "My favorite was the evening we met, when your gaze stripped me of my loincloth."

Grinning broadly, he warded off a blow aimed squarely at his mid-section. She fired back an immediate retort.

"And my favorite was yours when you stepped out of the bath." Her expression softened. "You were so beautiful, standing in front of the fireplace, your skin rosy from the heat of the water and the warmth of the fire."

"Beautiful?" he snorted, anxious to conceal how much her opinion mattered, feeling betrayed when she laughed outright, ignoring his chagrin.

"What word would you prefer?" She paused for effect, peeking slyly at him through her hair. "Handsome, well-endowed . . .?"

He tickled her until her giggles filled the cell. Finally, giving in to her cries for mercy, he left the bed, announcing his intention to warm water for a bath, wondering to himself if she, too, would like to linger here forever.

They washed one another thoroughly, an adventure which left Tyre wondering if he would ever become used to her charms and their affect on him. Her hair full of suds, her eyes brilliant with laughter, she insisted on washing behind his ears, scolding him when she found an imagined speck of dirt. Kara made him play, something he had not done since he left his mother's tent. Even his years with Hourn were not truly play, for their escapades taught the skills necessary for one who would be a future warrior of Lapith; every game, every race, conducted with those thoughts in mind. Kara's games were ones of lighthearted joy which grow out of true intimacy, and Tyre recognized their seductive power. He had seen the loveliness of Kara's appearance by the light of the fire he kindled two moons ago. In the time that followed he had discovered the loveliness of her soul. Until today he had seen these things merely as a spectator. Having become a participant, his honesty demanded that he examine a new fear and one he had never foreseen.

A moon ago, by the time of the Instructor's last session with the men, Tyre formed a plan. Despite his reluctance, he would join with the woman they assigned him. He would learn their ways and give the gifts they demanded as quickly as he could, no matter how they filled him with loathing. If there was no other way to free himself from slavery, he would persevere regardless of the cost to his honor and self-esteem.

He had not counted on meeting Kara.

And then Grasos arrived.

Kara ran to the door just as Tyre crossed the threshold. As she smiled up at Grasos, Tyre watched in disbelief as the normally expressionless guard regarded her with unmistakable affection.

"Grasos, please return for me. I need to speak with the Fifteenth Mother."

"As you wish, lady."

Grasos turned to Tyre.

"Present your wrists, ernani."

Unthinkingly, obeying a command he heard numerous times everyday, Tyre held out his arms for the manacles. And then he heard Kara's indrawn breath. As the cold metal locked around his wrists, she averted her eyes and retreated back into the cell. The door swung shut, the bolt slid shut, but nothing could erase the picture of Kara, her expression full of sadness and worst of all, pity. Since the night they met, it was her first sight of him in chains. The sweet euphoria of the cell died at that moment, extinguished by the sound of metal links clinking down the dim passageways of the Maze.

"Try these on for size."

A piece of cloth was thrown at him. Holding it up for inspection, he recognized loose breeches such as the guards wore.

"Hurry up. You're the last one to be fitted and Zelor is spitting mad at the delay. Pick out a blouse and some boots and go. You've still got to be fed before training begins."

Tyre's relief as he donned the breeches must have amused the supply guard, because he loosed a laugh that almost bent him double.

"If I were you, I wouldn't be so quick to rejoice. The others weren't too happy when they found out. If truth be told, most of them looked like they'd rather take a return trip to Agave."

Tyre chanced a question to the most talkative guard he'd ever encountered.

"Found out what?"

"Zelor's decided you need to learn to ride."

Zelor strutted around the group of men huddled by the gates of the arena. It took two corps of Legionnaires half a morning, but the work went well and the transformation pleased him. A training corral was newly erected in the center of the track with a makeshift stable still being constructed at the far end. Fifteen horses were haltered and tied to fifteen posts sunk into the ground with riding tack stacked neatly in front of each post. Examining the men who faced him with emotions ranging from irritation to outright fear, he noticed Tyre had no eyes for anything except the horses.

"Ernani, the schedule changes today. Everything is to proceed as usual, with the exception that the morning session will focus on conditioning and arms training. You'll have your lessons after midday meal, clothe yourselves, and proceed here for riding lessons."

A muted curse greeted his pronouncement. Zelor turned immediately to its source. With a great show of pleasantry, he addressed the provocateur.

"Samos. There's something you'd like to share with us concerning my decision?"

Hearing the trainer's silky tone Samos fought the impulse to back down. Squaring the considerable expanse of his shoulders, he decided to stand his ground.

"I can't speak for anyone else, but I wasn't born on a farm. I wouldn't mind wrestling a horse, but I've no desire to break my neck learning to ride a beast with four legs and no brain to speak of."

A loud rumble of agreement rose from his fellow ernani. Zelor leapt at the challenge.

"That's not what I hear. The guards say you've been riding pretty regularly these days, or, more accurately, these nights."

He hit the last word hard and to a man, they froze. No one, not a trainer or guard, had ever commented on their lives within the cells. Samos, wanting desperately to punch Zelor in the mouth, held his temper and focused on counting pebbles on the ground.

Marking Samos' self-control, Zelor continued his rant.

"Each of you will learn to ride. Lessons commence today. You will master this skill, as obediently and quickly as you can, or all riding privileges will be cancelled and you can walk back from whence you came."

With that, he strolled away from the wall of hatred rising up around him, asking himself why he had ever agreed to accept such a thankless task.

Zelor looked over his shoulder. Grudius was already at work, familiarizing the ernani with equine anatomy. Some of the men could barely manage to touch their horses. Tyre, on the other hand, was making the acquaintance of the bay gelding assigned to him. After running a practiced hand over the delicate skin, he inspected each hoof and opened the mouth, checking teeth for wear and signs of age. Zelor was no horseman, although he knew enough to recognize an expert when he saw one. As Beal promised, Tyre showed every indication of ease and familiarity with his new mount, who was already rubbing his head against Tyre's chest. Not even Beal's promise prepared Zelor for the sight of Tyre on horseback.

The other men struggled through the ordeal of bridles and saddles, and after checking every bit and girth strap, Grudius gave a demonstration of mounting. At his command, "Riders, mount!" fifteen men left the ground. To Zelor's surprise, all fifteen landed in the saddle, although two went off the other side almost immediately. Ladon was beside them in a moment, tightening his lips at the roughness of the falls and the danger posed by the dancing hooves of nervous horses. Zelor's attention was brought up short by a mental call from Grasos. Following the direction of Grasos' gaze, Zelor swore softly under his breath.

With a sword, Tyre had agility and power, although he came too late to training to achieve Rama's mastery. On a horse, that same body came alive with grace and control. Strong thighs gripped the sides of the bay, the long frame balancing effortlessly on its broad back. Quickly, he put the bay through his paces, the horse responding instantly to each command. The reins hung loosely now, Tyre leaning over the arched neck, black tail swishing nervously to and fro, black-tipped ears flicking back to listen. In the next moment the bay was flying around the arena, black-stocking legs pumping in answer to his master's commands.

Half-heartedly, Zelor decided they must be stopped. Before he could signal Grudius, the bay slowed, Tyre working him now at an easy trot, asking him to reverse directions and leads. The gelding rose to each challenge, shaking his head in confusion at signals he didn't know, learning as Tyre communicated what was necessary through shifts of his weight and changes in knee and thigh pressure.

Grudius, old horse soldier that he was, stood transfixed, shaking his head as if to clear his vision, his seamed face twisted into what Zelor could only interpret as a beatific smile. Tyre was asking the gelding to back up now, unaware of the crowd of men gathered to watch. The bay fought him a bit, unused to such a maneuver, but the hands on the reins were firm and allowed no mutiny. The command executed to his satisfaction, Tyre rewarded his sweating mount with a firm pat on his thickly muscled neck. At the sound of raucous cheers and applause which greeted the completion of this maneuver, the bay started and shied, eyes rolling back in his head, his flailing hooves sending the crowd scattering. Zelor decided it was time to break the spell.

"Did Grudius give you permission to remove yourself from the training group?"

Blue eyes turned icy, narrowing in revolt.

"No, trainer."

"Then as punishment for proceeding without permission, you'll groom and feed all fifteen horses at the end of the session. After witnessing your exhibition, I've no doubt you've the skills to perform the task, although I fear you won't return to your cell for many hours past the evening trumpet."

Zelor could barely sustain a chuckle at Tyre's look of pure delight, although the blonde head merely nodded acceptance.

As he moved away from the group and Grudius called for a remount, Zelor wondered if Tyre would ever know that this day was a gift arranged especially for him, a reward for his first voluntary step toward Preparation.

The women gathered in the center of the dayroom, eager for Nerissa's arrival, their excited conversations more high-pitched than usual. Their lessons cancelled for the afternoon, plus the previously unknown experience of spending the morning with their ernani, had left them understandably giddy.

Kara stood by a window, paying little attention to the others, looking out thoughtfully at the watchtowers scattered along the outer walls of the Maze. Having just returned from her meeting with the Fifteenth Mother, the noise and general high spirits of the other women seemed especially unwelcome.

"So, my child, the choice is yours. Will you continue the term of the three moon contract or leave the Maze?"

Kara almost laughed aloud at the picture of her former misery.

"I will stay."

Keen grey eyes regarded her for what seemed to be an eternity.

"I remind you of your purpose here. This marks a great step for both of you and I'm pleased with your happiness. But it is only a first step. Remember, Kara, you will not be released a second time from your promise."

Shivering, Kara tried to dismiss her feelings of foreboding. Surely the Fifteenth Mother had not meant to sound so ominous . . . .

Nerissa's arrival ended her reverie.

"Beginning today, the rule of privacy no longer applies. Its purpose was to safeguard each of you from unsolicited and unnecessary advice from your sisters. In the future, you are free to seek out your friends for help and guidance. I caution you, however, to trust your feelings and instincts concerning your situation before you trust those of another."

The women, who had grown quiet as Nerissa began to speak, started to whisper to one another. With a single raised eyebrow, she brought them back to silence.

"In addition, beginning tomorrow, you may bring your ernani to this room after the evening meal. You are not required to come, nor should you feel any pressure to come. These are simply gatherings, times during which you may meet with one another for purposes of conversation, reading, music, games, study—anything you choose to devise."

Hearing the growing hum around her, Nerissa raised her voice.

"These gatherings have a single rule which must be obeyed. Any kind of fighting or argument is prohibited, whether it is between you and your mate, or between the ernani. Use your cell for scenes of disagreement, for I know you will have them. This room must remain inviolate."

By the time she finished, the room was hushed. Each woman had registered the images of violence Nerissa sent them as she spoke. Their partners had survived the outside world through daring and ruthlessness. None of the women believed that a few moons in the Maze had cured them of their proclivity for solving problems with their fists. They accepted their responsibility as a group. The women of Pelion would guard the sanctity of the gatherings.

Nerissa sent them her love and appreciation.

"You may come anytime after tomorrow evening's trumpet and stay until the torches are put out. I wish you happiness, my daughters, and success on the Path you have chosen."

". . . just as Beal promised. Grudius says he's never seen anything like it!"

Nerissa's sharp eyes noticed that for once the Fifteenth Mother didn't flinch at the mention of Beal's name. She also noticed Ladon's exhaustion and guessed it was not due to the sprained ankle suffered by one of the ernani in a fall from horseback. Something had transpired last night, something to do with Kara's private session with the Fifteenth Mother. Nerissa ended her speculations to concentrate on the discussion underway.

"How do you plan to keep him interested, son, if his abilities make training an unnecessary enterprise?"

Having worked long and hard on this problem since seeing Tyre on horseback, Zelor announced his solution with no small amount of pride.

"I'll use him as I did Rama. He'll teach the others."

Before Luxor could interrupt, Zelor shot his father a warning glance and continued.

"If he gets bored, we'll hold a contest, many contests if we have to, to keep him interested."

"What kind of contest, son?"

Zelor was becoming annoyed, but managed to keep it out of his voice.

"Something with a prize like no other: a ride outside the city gates."

Before anyone could object, Zelor provided information that proved how carefully he had considered the matter.

"We pick the day. We mark off a course to the southeast, where there's no cover to speak of. Rhacius posts his best men on our best horses along the course in plain sight. If Tyre runs, he'll be doing it over unfamiliar ground, whereas our men know every ditch, every hedgerow. He's far too smart to try it."

Luxor nodded. He could find no flaw in Zelor's plan.

Suddenly, a bass voice spoke inside their minds. Stanis rarely communicated in Council. When he did, heads shot up all around the table.

"What of the beast chosen for him?"

Zelor hurried to reply.

"He's a four-year-old bay gelding Grudius trained himself. He's bred out of a Lapith mare we were able to buy for a small fortune, and more closely matches the size and temperament of Tyre's previous mounts. Grudius is the only one who's ever ridden him, and he seems gentle enough."

Stanis nodded, seemingly reassured, but the Fifteenth Mother remained unconvinced. Her Master of Mysteries never spoke without a reason.

"What troubles you, Stanis?"

"The cook's helper has disappeared."

Everyone looked to the Fifteenth Mother, who repeated blankly,

"The cook's helper?"

A ruined face appeared before their eyes.

"Eris, the man Tyre attacked inside the Maze. He left the House of Healing before he was truly healed, insistent that he go back to work in the Maze. Since we agreed he must be kept far away from the Golden One, he returned to his previous assignment in the laundry. Now he is gone and we cannot be certain as to how long he has been missing."

Nerissa sensed Stanis' concern but was unable to pinpoint the reason for his uneasiness.

"Do you have reason to suspect that Tyre might have harmed him in some way?"

The cropped head moved from side to side in rapid negation. Another image rose before them, this one of a man dressed in robes of a distinctive leaf-green hue, sitting in the atrium of the House of Healing. His expression was vacant, his eyes those of someone struck blind. Spittle dribbled from his mouth, to be cleaned away by a woman whose face was ravaged by sorrow.

As the vision faded, the Fifteenth Mother was grimmer than Nerissa had ever seen her.

"This was the servant's healer, Cydon, brother to Ladon. He worked without his healing partner since shared attunement was deemed unnecessary in such a simple case. There was no sign of difficulty to serve as warning. The servant left and Cydon's mind began to slip away. His mate works with him, but there is little hope."

Ladon rose shakily and headed for the door. A voice like the tolling of a great bronze bell stopped him.

"I, too, love your brother, and mourn for him and his mate. But members of my council are required to put aside personal considerations to concentrate on the general good. That is your vow, Ladon, and I hold you to it."

Resuming his place at the table, each step more reluctant than the last, Ladon buried his head in his arms. The old woman lowered a blue-veined hand to rest on his shoulder.

"It is a life against nature, Ladon, yet each of us has chosen. Luxor sends men to their death every time a patrol passes through the northern gates.

Stanis endured unimaginable horrors outside these walls. And I," she sighed heavily, "I gave up my healing partner and the mate of my heart. You're not alone in your grief—it's shared by those who understand better than any the cost of your sacrifice."

Calmed by her touch as much as by the words she spoke, Ladon quieted. Now she turned on Stanis with a fierce look, daring him to add to Ladon's sorrow.

"Where is your evidence that the servant is the cause of Cydon's illness?"

Again, Stanis shook his head from side to side, his brown eyes black with mourning although it was not clear for whom he mourned.

"You must find that proof, Stanis. Too much is at stake to give up without a fight. I, for one, refuse to battle ghosts who lurk among the shadows. We must gather our forces in the light!"

Her voice rang out against the stones of the tower walls, each head around the table lifting in answer to her summons. For an instant they saw her transfigured, clothed in radiant white, holding a staff hung with a silver pennant. The vision shimmered for a moment before dissolving to reveal a gaunt old woman in pitch-black robes.

"Continue your work in the Maze. It is our highest priority. I bid you good night."

As she made her way slowly back to her sleeping chamber, Nerissa's flesh prickled on the nape of her neck. Her name had not been mentioned in the Fifteenth Mother's litany of personal sacrifice. With a sudden leap of intuition, intuition which had not failed her in forty years, Nerissa knew the time of her sacrifice would soon be upon her.

When that time came, she could only hope that she, like Ladon, would have the Fifteenth Mother's help.

Grudius' stallion whickered softly in the cool night air.

With a jerk and a snort, the guard awoke, his eyelids lifting sleepily to survey his charges. They seemed content enough, munching on their evening rations, tossing their heads from time to time as they pulled hay from their mangers.

The guard yawned, pulling his cloak more closely about his shoulders and settling his backside more comfortably on the wooden crate. The stallion moved restlessly about the box stall, iron-shod hooves beating time on the hard-packed earth. Deciding he really must investigate, the guard smothered another yawn. Odd, he thought to himself, how sleepy I am tonight . . . .

The stallion pawed the ground, his shrill whinny echoing hollowly in the empty arena.

The sleeping guard never heard the welcome in the stallion's cry, nor did he spy the shadowy figure picking its way deftly around crates and barrels in the near darkness of the stable. Ducking under a row of newly-polished saddles, the figure paused to grab a fistful of dried clover from an open bale. The guard's snores came regularly now, the stallion suddenly quiet, nostrils flared, ears trained forward, registering the sound and smell of the visitor.

"Softly, my beauty, softly," the figure whispered into the darkness, "You remember me, don't you?"

A single hoof pawed the ground in answer, the stallion's nostrils flaring at the sweet scent of clover. The stall door swung open.

"Take it, great-heart."

Moleskin lips nibbled at the withered pink flowers, a single dark eye glowing down benignly on the bearer of this welcome offering. Without protest, the stallion accepted the bit, bending his neck as a firm hand passed over his mane and down his withers, tracing the curve of his ribs, his skin quivering slightly at the pleasure of the touch, at the gentleness of his handler as he was led out of the stall, past the slumped figure of the sleeping guard, and into the arena.

The stars were mere pinpricks in the immense vault of the heavens, the moon so high, so shrunken in size and blue-white in color as to resemble a star—especially when a line of high-moving clouds raced across its surface, causing it to disappear, then reappear in the rapid blink of a celestial eye.

The stallion pranced restlessly under the tight rein, his breath turned to steam in the frigid night air. He wanted to run. He wanted to fly over the broad, sunlit plains of his birth, past shallow lakes where long-necked geese nest each spring, through belly-high grasses nodding their heads lazily in the summer breeze.

The man on his back wanted to run as well. The stallion sensed it, had sensed it with the first welcome trace of his scent on the night air. He had visited the stable before, this soft-spoken man who whispered to him in a language he first heard as a colt running at his dam's side. He rode as those other men did, those bright-haired men who smelt of oiled leather, smoke and sweat, the ones who taught him to obey the iron bit. This man smelled differently—of wet earth and moldy grain—but his hands and knees were the same, the lightness of his body belying the strength of his hold on the reins.

They were far from the stables now, far from the other horses and the box stall and the man breathing noisily through his nose. The stallion tensed, anticipating the next command. It came almost immediately. Rearing up onto his hindquarters as he had been taught on the wind-blasted plains of his birth, the stallion heard the man loose the war cry, the high-pitched scream heralding a battle. Gathering his legs beneath him, the stallion plunged forward into the night.

"This is life!" Eris exulted, as the stallion tore around the track. Having once ridden this prince of horses, long of leg, deep of chest, with the arched neck of a swan and the enormous liquid eyes of a wild deer, Eris vowed to ride no other.

How the stallion came to be here remained a mystery. That he was pure Lapithian stock was unquestionable, his confirmation and temperament the result of generations of careful breeding by the greatest horsemen in the world. To sell such a magnificent animal would be unthinkable to any self-respecting Lapithian, be he warrior, huntsman, or herder; such a horse would only be owned by the chieftain of a wealthy tribe. As the stallion flew about the track, Eris imagined his forearms thick with bronze and copper bracelets, his brow crowned by a circlet of hammered gold, his saddle bedecked with tassels of scarlet-dyed wool, a throwing spear balanced over his right shoulder, bearing down on an enemy of the tribe. They would quail, would they not? Quail at the sight of this fearsome warrior astride a stallion out of legend, two devotees of Sturm united against a common foe, their destiny a glorious victory or an even more glorious death.

The stallion settled into a smooth canter, breathing easily, his tension gone, worn away by his first mad dash around the track. Cruel to keep him here, Eris thought angrily, trapped in a makeshift stable, trotting in circles, unable to stretch his legs or roll in the sand. Cruel to waste his talents among this bunch of amateurs, this so-called Cavalry, none of them worthy enough to put a brush to his gleaming hide. Not to mention the scrub stock with whom he was stabled. The bay gelding was the single exception in that rag-tag bunch of over-fed, flea-bitten nags. Yet compared to the black stallion, the bay seemed a mere shadow of true greatness.

They were both trapped, he and the stallion of Lapith, who was slowing now, gliding seamlessly into a brisk trot, as reluctant as Eris for the ride to end. Eris had thought the healing house a refuge, a place to rest while he planned a more permanent escape from the Maze. Instead, it became a place of horror, a place where random thoughts came unbidden into his head, where voices called to him from the past, returning him against his will to dreadful places he could not bear to remember. Frightened at first, he grew angrier as nail after nail was driven into his brain, hating the healer with his searching eyes and troubled frown, wishing him blank-faced and staring, an idiot among idiots, a clown among clowns.

They were all clowns, mawkish fools and imbeciles, swearing good intentions yet sending him back to sweat in the laundry, scrubbing the belongings of slaves and whores. Each bundle of stained sheets was a studied insult, each lace-trimmed shift a reminder of the woman he did not have, each mud-stained loincloth that of the horse-boy, the one who left him gap-toothed and crooked-nosed, the snot running in a continual stream down his ruined face.

Finally, he escaped, not into the city, as he had planned, but deep into the belly of the Maze, down tunnels uninhabited for more centuries than he could imagine, silent but for the dripping of water through the grate. Forced to hide during the daylight hours, the night brought freedom. Like the stallion, Eris lived for the night, for these all too brief gallops around the deserted arena, for the sight of moon and stars and the feel of the wind in his face, for memories of starlit plains and moonlit lakes.

The stallion was tiring now, the exaltation of the race fading, the blood pounding in the veins, the breath coming in shorter and shorter gasps, the proud neck lowering, the elegantly muscled legs slowing to a sedate walk. Eris had asked nothing of him, yet he had given his all, running for the sheer joy of it as only a horse of Lapith could run. If asked, he would run until he died, his great heart bursting inside his chest, racing the wind for no other reward than to feel the harmony of earth and horse and rider. So ran the sun-steeds of Sturm, the darlings of Lapith, the beloved horse-kin of the northern plains.

"So, my beauty, have you done?" Eris murmured into a coal-black ear, stroking a sweat-darkened flank as he dismounted. Tying on a lead, he headed for the stable, the stallion following obediently, childlike in his devotion, sure of a long walk under a warm blanket and the meticulous grooming to follow.

Slowly, and oh so unwillingly, they traveled forward in time, leaving behind shared memories of dimly-recalled happiness, the horse plodding resolutely behind his master, resolved as only beasts can be to existence in an unimagined future. But men, it seems, possessing the benefit (or burden) of forethought, can imagine almost anything; anything, that is, save the moment of their death. So it was that the man stalked resentfully toward a hated future, since, having hated his past, he could imagine nothing better.

Two silhouettes moved across a vacant landscape that seemed, in the quivering shafts of silver-tipped moonlight, to shift and rearrange itself, resembling at one moment a wind-swept plain under a star-laden sky, and in the next, the desolate training ground of a fortress known as the Maze.

Chapter 16

The Gathering

"ARE YOU COMING to the gathering tonight?"

Brimus peered over the back of the roan mare he was currying. Next to Brimus, his shoulder wedged firmly against the bay's flank, Tyre worked methodically over the massive hindquarters, brushing until the hide shone. Several moments passed, moments during which Brimus decided he was being ignored.

"What business is it of yours?" Tyre finally responded.

Brimus stifled a grin. Rude as Tyre's reply might be, it was more than he'd expected. Long after the end of the rule of privacy, Tyre maintained a discreet distance from the other ernani. Today, at long last, Brimus decided it was time to break through that cool reserve, for Tyre had become not only his idol, but someone Brimus wanted to call friend.

From the day Tyre put the bay gelding through his paces in the arena, Brimus vowed to put aside his fears and learn to ride. In the past few weeks he'd improved rapidly, due, he knew, to the dedication of his teachers. Grudius had passed him on to Tyre a few days ago. Brimus and four other men (who either possessed previous riding experience or had decided, as did Brimus, that this new challenge was more to their liking than the sessions with arms) trained exclusively with Tyre. He was a careful, but remote, taskmaster. He never cursed or swore at mistakes but could shame Brimus with a single eyebrow cocked over a disapproving eye. In these weeks of training, Tyre lost his temper a single time. After that incident, he had no further problems with discipline.

The explosion was triggered when Suda's mount refused a low fence and the burly man was thrown head over heels. Annoyed by the laughter of the other men, Suda grabbed the reins of his horse, jerking them with brutal force. As he did so, Tyre leapt off his horse, hit the ground at a dead run, and knocked Suda to the ground with a single, well-placed blow to the jaw. Ignoring his pupil, Tyre tended to the horse, calming it with a soft voice and gentle hands. By this time, all the ernani had gathered around the fallen man and the guards were moving in warily with cudgels drawn. Unbuckling the bridle and removing the bit, Tyre inspected the horse's mouth. Grim-faced, he approached Suda.

"The next time you treat a horse in my care with such ignorance and cruelty I'll put this bit in your mouth and drive you around the track on your knees."

Grudius stepped forward through the crowd.

"What's all this ruckus?"

Tyre snapped to attention, his respect for the older man readily apparent.

"The horse refused the jump because Suda didn't time the approach correctly. He was thrown, and punished the horse for his own stupidity. The mouth is torn and bleeding. I simply promised Suda the same treatment he gave his horse. I'm still waiting for his reply."

Grudius nodded and both men turned their attention to Suda, who rubbed his jaw with one hand while dusting himself off with the other. Confronted by two men with like minds, Suda stood his ground. The tension in the crowd increased.

"Well, ernani?"

Grudius' voice cracked like a whip. Suda swung his head toward him in alarm, fingering a red mark that had already begun to swell.

"What, uh, what Tyre said is true. Everybody laughed and it made me angry. I apologize, Horse Master."

"It's not me who needs an apology, but your teacher."

Suda regarded Tyre for a long moment, weighing the decision. With a sheepish grin, the burly man thrust out his right arm.

"I apologize, Tyre. You'll never have cause to put a bit in my mouth."

"I'll hold you to that promise."

Tyre clasped the proffered arm and the crowd relaxed. As the two men walked toward Suda's horse, it was Dino who had the last word.

"He's the last man I'd want to fight and the first I'd follow into battle."

Muttered agreement passed through the ernani. Even taciturn Rama grunted at the accuracy of Dino's appraisal. From that day forward, Brimus strove to join Tyre's class.

Roused from his daydream, Brimus explained, "It's just that tonight there's going to be something special. Everyone's coming, and I thought . . ."

"What's so special?"

Grasping the gelding's rear leg between his thighs, the hoof held securely in his lap, Tyre bent over to pick the shoe.

"My partner, Minthe, is planning something. When I question her, she just smiles and shakes her head."

Brimus knew his voice changed when he spoke of Minthe. Long ago he'd stopped worrying about what the other men thought. His relative youth made him a favorite butt of ridicule, but Minthe had given him such confidence that he no longer responded to their baiting. Recently he'd noticed that their jibes were less frequent.

Tyre grunted. Brimus tried again.

"Your partner's name is Kara, isn't it?"

Tyre lifted his head abruptly.

"Did Rama tell you that?"

Taken aback by Tyre's unexpected hostility, Brimus stammered out a denial.

"M . . . M . . . Minthe told me. She adores Kara and they often play m . . . m . . . music together."

Tyre put the hoof down carefully and straightened. Picking up a soft rag, he began putting the finishing touches on the gleaming bay, keeping his head down so as to avoid meeting Brimus' eyes.

"It's true we've never gone to a gathering." After a few more strokes, he asked, "What are they like?"

The younger man heard the curiosity and the hesitance with which the question was posed.

"It's strange, but they're more enjoyable than I ever thought they'd be. You see, before I came here I, uh, I didn't spend much time with women, especially this kind of woman . . ." to his dismay, his voice broke. "I didn't want to go at first," he hurried on, hoping to disguise the lapse, "but Minthe insisted. Since I have so little to give her, I don't begrudge what little she asks."

Brimus curried his roan with a vengeance, causing the beast to turn her head and nicker a protest. When he lightened his touch, she swung her head back around to the manger and continued munching hay.

"The room is large and airy, a different world from the passageways we always see. Sometimes there are only a few people and the evenings are passed in conversation or storytelling." Brimus smiled. "The other night Pandar read a story from beginning to end and we all applauded. Then Dino said we should have a reading contest and all the men started reading as loudly and quickly as they could. Dino played Zelor, swearing and cursing and giving out points until the women were helpless with laughter."

Aware that there had been no response to anything he'd said, Brimus stopped currying and looked over the roan's shining flank. Tyre was staring at him with the oddest expression. When Brimus caught his eyes, he looked away.

"Does anyone else attend?"

Brimus knew what Tyre was really asking. He'd seen the coldness with which the Instructor treated Tyre. Come to think of it, Tyre's guard was nastier than most. Maybe Tyre wasn't willing to trade the privacy of the cell for the chance of being treated badly in public.

"The Instructor came once, but only because the women issued a special invitation. The guards never enter except to announce that the torches are going to be put out."

The trumpet sounded. Giving the roan a farewell pat, Brimus shut the stall door. Tyre was finishing quickly now, as anxious as Brimus was to return to the cell. As Brimus headed for the stable door, a hand dropped on his shoulder. Looking up (for Tyre topped his height by more than a head) Brimus observed the warmest smile he had ever seen on that sternest of faces.

"Thanks, Brimus. Perhaps you'll meet Kara soon."

With that, Tyre was striding off toward his guard, his arms already outstretched to receive the waiting manacles. As Brimus watched him pass through the arena gates, he felt the pressure of that hand on his shoulder again. Dino was right. Brimus, for one, would follow Tyre anywhere.

Tyre had been alone in the cell for almost an hour. He sat dejectedly on the wooden stool and dried his hair. For the first time in weeks, the empty cell confined him as surely as it had the first lonely moon of Preparation. A fire blazed in the hearth and a stew bubbled in the iron pot, but Kara was nowhere to be found. As usual, she warmed the water for him and laid out drying cloths and clean loincloth, but he missed her presence as he bathed. Since the night he'd returned late from his work in the stables, reeking of horse, she'd laughingly insisted that she help him bathe, ". . . lest you miss a spot, and I forget it's you I'm kissing and not your horse." He acquiesced without regret, especially when he claimed (and received) the right to bathe her in return.

Now Kara was absent without any explanation and Tyre was moving from mild worry to real distress. His first thought was that she might be ill, although there had been no indication of any such complaint this morning. When he awakened her with feathery kisses on her porcelain shoulder, she purred like a contented cat and rubbed her cheek against his chest. There was no reason for her to rise at the morning bell but she insisted he wake her every morning so she could greet him before he left. With a wry smile, he remembered how one of her more lavish greetings barely left him time to leap from the bed and tie on a loincloth before Grasos slid the bolt.

A familiar trill of laughter in the passageway reassured him of her well-being. Relief was quickly replaced with irritation. The thickness of the door prevented a clear understanding of what was being said, but Grasos' low rumble could be heard, and then another warble of laughter as the door swung open.

"Did you think I'd been spirited away?"

Dark eyes laughed down at him. Pulling his head between her breasts and depositing a kiss on the crown of his head, she ran her fingers through his damp hair. His irritation vanished. Burying his head in the fragrant folds of her azure gown, he wrapped his arms around her waist and hugged her close.

"I knew you'd wonder at my absence, but I never meant you to worry," she said, surprised, perhaps, by the tightness of his grip.

He held her in silence for a long moment before pulling her down into his lap. She lifted her face, expecting a kiss, but he refused to be deterred from what was on his mind.

"I feared you were ill or somehow injured and there was nothing I could do; no way to find you or give you aid."

"No harm could come to me here!"

Suddenly he felt a fool. Indicating that she should get off his lap, he began to pace.

"What worries you, Tyre? It must be something more than my lateness. Tell me, please! Must you always hide things from me?"

As she pleaded with him, he remembered his conversation with Brimus. Like him, Tyre had nothing with which to repay this woman who began her giving with a ripe pear and continued to give him her care, her music, her laughter, and the delights of her body. The one thing she asked in return was that he share his thoughts and worries with her. It was small recompense, but for him, an almost impossible request. He stopped pacing, and facing the hearth, for he found he could not look at her, he pried open his heart.

"I was worried about you, but it wasn't the worry so much as the frustration of being trapped here. This place without you is . . ." he closed his eyes, ". . . unbearable." Opening his eyes, he stared at the mantelpiece for a long moment. "Sometimes I hate you, Kara, for you make slavery too easy," he found himself pounding his fist against the stones above the hearth, "for—I—will—not—live—as—a—slave!"

This was why he didn't talk about how he felt, why he avoided confession at all costs. It didn't help to say things out loud, it only made them worse. Acknowledging pain only made the pain worse. Exhausted, he rested his forehead against the mantle, wondering if this time he'd hurt her beyond repair.

"Do you think I don't know?" she asked quietly, "that I can't see your hatred of the manacles? That I can't sense it when you touch me sometimes as if bidding me farewell?"

She had known all along. His relief was so powerful it threatened to unman him.

"Who can know what the next hour will bring? We're joined together and we journey on the Path. I tell you this, Tyre: I'm thankful I was brought to your cell."

He turned to find silver drops on her cheeks as she stood waiting by the iron door. He held out his arms and she ran into them. Pressing her close against him, wishing he could absorb her flesh into his, he whispered his promise in her ear.

"We'll do as you say. We'll live as best we can, hour by hour, day by day. I will bear my slavery and you will bear my silence." When she looked up at him, a question in her eyes, he tried again to speak what was in his heart. "It's hard for me, Kara, to tell you things I've never shared with anyone. I . . . I've always been alone . . ."

She stopped him with her lips, her kiss sealing their pact. Their shared sorrow turning to hunger for one another and their loving was fierce, as though the joining of their bodies could push away the walls of the cell.

Tyre waited until their heartbeats slowed to wipe away the locks of hair covering Kara's flushed face. Smiling down at her, he watched as black eyelashes fluttered open to reveal brown eyes still smoky with passion.

"Have we another sheet for the bed?"

Kara stared at him blankly and nodded.

"Will you help me gather up the one underneath us?"

When recognition dawned, the joy of her reaction made him unaccountably shy. It was meager compensation for the tears she'd shed, but he had nothing else to give. Wordlessly, sensitive to his mood, she rose and together they stripped the bed. She cleaned him off gently with the sheet and used it to wipe his seed from her thighs. After wrapping the sheet into a tidy bundle, she held it out to him.

"Is this your first gift, Tyre?"

Blinking in surprise, remembering they had never discussed this subject, he answered simply, "I gave my hair on the day of my arrival."

"But not in gratitude."

"No," he admitted, surprised by the shrewdness of her guess.

"And this," she asked calmly enough, although not so calmly that he failed to sense the importance of his reply, "will this gift be given as it should be?"

He nodded, unable to speak, hoping she knew from whence his gratitude sprang.

There was little conversation between them over the meal. For once, Kara was grateful for Tyre's silence, needing time to regain her equilibrium. He retreated into himself again and ate without seeming to taste the food. Suddenly she couldn't bear the thought of spending another evening in the four walls that had rendered him so melancholy before her arrival. As he cleared away the dishes and began his customary chores, she remembered what had delayed her and clapped her hands with sudden glee. Startled by her unexpected outburst, he dropped a plate, his curse mingling with the sound of crockery crashing against the stone floor. Uttering a long-suffering sigh, he contemplated her with mock despair.

"Are you trying to shame my household skills by making me break all the dishes? I thought you'd forgiven me for being the better cook."

Heartened by his reaction, Kara returned the jest.

"I thought warriors of Lapith were never taken unaware!"

He advanced with a playful growl, threatening her with lifted arms. Evading him, she ran toward the door to retrieve the package she'd dropped when she saw his mournful figure slumped on the wooden stool. Laughing at his antics, she held the package behind her back, teasing him as she had their first night together.

"I've brought you something that will make up for the broken dish. You can have it if you guess correctly."

After studying her for a moment he pointed to her left. When she held out the package for him to take, he retreated.

"What is it?"

Exasperated by his caution, she tossed the package into the air. He caught it easily, regarding her with a crooked grin.

"This isn't fair. I've nothing to give you in return."

Refusing to let him retreat into his former melancholy, she announced: "If you don't open it soon, I'll take it back."

He seemed strangely childlike to her in this moment, clearly wanting to open the package yet fearful of what it might contain.

"Very well, I'll open it; but only if you name your price."

She pursed her lips and maintained a stubborn silence, tapping her leather-shod foot against the stone floor. Totally bemused by her behavior, he lowered himself to the bed with a sigh and began to untie the knot.

As the cording and wrappings fell away, Kara moved closer, barely able to contain her excitement. She had worked long and hard on this gift, running back to the dayroom after preparing the evening meal in order to wrap it.

Long-fingered hands stroked the blue-grey, tightly-woven fabric, tracing the laces which ran from the neck opening to the middle of the tunic. It had taken Kara hours to embroider each opening for the laces to pass through, days for her to design and execute the emblem of the tiny running horses whose silvery threads circled the neck. Putting aside the tunic, he turned his attention to the breeches. They were cut much tighter than the ones he wore for riding sessions, with lacings along the waist opening instead of buttons. His hands ceased their examination and he sat motionless, looking down at the clothes in his lap.

Was it possible that he didn't want them? Kara dismissed the thought. He was ridiculously proud of the riding gear they issued him, and was only persuaded to remove them when she crinkled her nose at the strong odor of horse. It might be that he didn't care for the color or the style, but she'd been careful about selecting fabric from the merchants who called regularly at the Maze, trying to find something neither gaudy nor dull. The style was of her own devising, having guided the conversation toward clothing one evening when he spoke of his home and drafting a pattern as close to his description as was possible. Yet he sat there like a lump while she grew more bewildered with every passing moment.

"Doesn't it please you?"

He passed his hand over his face before looking up at her. His white teeth glistened in the firelight as he bestowed on her the widest grin she had ever seen. The grin disappeared soon after, his manner rough as he beckoned to her.

"Come here."

It was Kara who was cautious this time. Creeping forward, she was grabbed up in his arms and swung onto the bed with such force that she nearly lost her breath. He covered her face with kisses before kissing each of her fingers in turn.

"It pleases me very much."

With difficulty she pulled her hands free and hit him on the shoulder, enjoying his exaggerated grimace of pain.

"Then put them on!"

He executed a mock bow in acknowledgement of her command and started to pull on the breeches.

"You told me you didn't wear a loincloth before you came here. They won't fit over all that fabric."

Throwing her a raffish grin, he stripped off the offending loincloth, flushing as he felt her eyes upon him. He cocked an eyebrow at her, his light eyes darkening with amusement and desire.

"If you insist on staring at me, I may never get these breeches on."

Color washing over her face, Kara averted her eyes. He uttered a regretful sigh before turning back to the clothes. The breeches fit him snugly and she was relieved to see they were long enough. The tunic went over his head, and as the blonde head emerged from the neck opening, Kara rose to tighten the laces. He stood patiently as her slender fingers flew over his chest. When she moved back to admire her work, he read her delight in her eyes. There was no teasing in his voice this time.

"They're like a second skin. The fabric is as warm and soft as your hands as they pass over me. Tell me their price and I'll try to meet it no matter the cost."

His seriousness made her feel foolish. Her objective had been to tease him into accepting the gift. Now he insisted she name a price. Unfortunately, she knew him well enough to know his pride demanded an answer.

"The price is something we've never talked about, but it's often been in my thoughts. I'd like you to accompany me to the gathering tonight."

His eyes narrowed; otherwise, he revealed nothing. Kara forged on, choosing her words carefully, certain she was on dangerous ground. The few times she'd mentioned the gatherings in casual conversation, he'd retreated into stony silence. She had no idea why the thought of attending bothered him, but he demanded a reckoning and she could think of nothing else to ask.

"Minthe, Brimus' partner, asked me to come. She plans an evening of music and several people have offered to sing or play an instrument. Minthe wants me to sing some of the ancient songs of the city." She lifted her chin, proud of the invitation. "They're difficult, Tyre, and I'm the only one with enough training to master them. I told her I would attend, and so I will. It would please me greatly if you came with me."

He considered her a moment.

"Are the clothes a bribe, then?"

The accusation hurt until she realized how manipulative her refusal to name her price must seem to him.

"I've worked on them during our morning sessions for a fortnight—designing, cutting the pattern, sewing, and embroidering. Minthe asked me to sing three days ago. I admit I rushed to finish so you might have something to wear should you decide to attend. But they are not a bribe. They are yours no matter what you decide. And regardless of your decision, they remain a gift of love."

A shadow flew over his features—remorse, relief, she couldn't be sure. Giving no hint as to his decision, he drew closer to her, inspecting her critically from head to toe.

"Well, I'm dressed in my new finery, but you're in a sad state of disrepair. Your hair is mussed, your gown wrinkled, and there's a smudge of grease on your bodice. What do you have to wear to this gathering that won't shame me in front of the other ernani?"

Rewarding him with a quick kiss, she moved to the wardrobe. Tyre lounged against the mantelpiece, his arms crossed over his chest, watching her preparations from under hooded eyes.

As she brushed out her hair, she hummed one of the songs she'd been practicing. Tonight she would sing it as she had never sung it for her teachers. The formal title came from an old language known by a handful of scholars proficient in ancient tongues. To Kara, and to all the inhabitants of Pelion, it was simply known as the "Hymn to Harmony."

Sinking down into a chair positioned near a long trestle table piled with fruit, cheeses, and sweet pastries, Tyre picked up a pewter goblet. The liquid inside was unfamiliar to him, but catching the faint scent of honey he drank it with relish. Kara stayed by his side until a woman claimed her assistance at a platform lined with freshly-cut evergreen boughs near large windows draped with a dull red fabric. Kara introduced him to Minthe, a tiny creature who looked up at him with wide eyes.

"I knew you were tall, for I helped Kara cut the pattern for your clothes, but . . .!" she threw up her hands in wonder, her braids shaking merrily, her good humor easing his shyness. Her next comment took him off-guard. "Somehow I feel I know you already. Brimus talks of nothing but you and your skill with horses."

Kara's elbow in his ribs reminded him he was standing with his mouth hanging open. Regaining his composure, he returned the compliment.

"Brimus learns quickly and has a way with animals. Has he told you that his roan calls to him whenever we enter the stable?"

He could tell she was delighted and guessed every word would be repeated to Brimus when this night was over. Kara beamed approval at him before taking her leave. As she walked toward the platform, he admired her rounded hips beneath the rose-colored gown. She had left her hair unbound at his request, wrapping a creamy shawl around her shoulders. He'd met several beautiful women tonight; none compared to her. A dark-skinned hand reached for a goblet next to him, jolting him out of his musings.

Rama's ebony face split with a wide, white-toothed grin.

"Kara is indeed a lovely woman."

Sheepish at the thought that his feelings showed so clearly on his face, Tyre rose from the chair to retaliate in kind.

"And what of Varuna? Will I ever meet the one who took away your tongue for a full moon, letting me land blows a novice could have parried?"

"Here I am, Tyre. I welcomed you at the door."

The speaker was almost as tall as Rama and elegantly wrapped in an iridescent blue cloth edged in long black fringe. Her tightly curled hair was cut close to her head, a pink pearl gleaming in each of her tiny earlobes. Tyre recalled the strength of her smooth hand as she grasped his at the door. Her greeting was surprisingly formal:

"Welcome to the Hall of Gathering. Enter its doors for fellowship with others. There must be no violence here."

Tyre risked betraying his ignorance by asking Varuna the question that had been on his mind since entering the room.

"Is everyone greeted by you, Varuna, and in the same way?"

She took his question seriously, as he had intended.

"Each woman takes her turn at the door. Now that you have come, Kara will repeat the same words to each couple as they enter some other evening." Her eyes flicked to Rama and back to Tyre as she lightened the formality of the conversation. "I, for one, am glad you've come at last. I was beginning to think this fellow Tyre was a ruse devised to rouse my pity for Rama's sorry state."

When Rama growled something deep in his throat, Varuna slipped a slender arm around his waist.

"It's alright, wounded one. Now that I've met him, I promise to believe all your stories."

Their eyes met and Rama's growl died in his throat. A hearty slap on Tyre's back claimed his attention. Dino grinned broadly at him.

"I spied that hair of yours from clear across the room. Here, Tyre, I want you to meet someone."

Dino pushed a woman in front of him. Tyre looked down at a pink-cheeked face staring up at him with wide eyes. His greeting died on his lips as she pointed her finger at him, stammering in surprise and dismay.

"You . . . you . . . you're the one who was beaten for killing a servant!"

Tyre backed away, his throat dry and drawn. Her shrill voice cut through the hum of conversations and many heads turned to investigate the disturbance. His skin crawled underneath the new clothes. He had worn them with such pride. Now he cringed as surely as if he had been stripped of them, standing naked in front of all these prying eyes. This is what he dreaded about attending the gathering. Dino's partner confirmed his worst fears. Everyone in the room was remembering him hanging from the ropes, the belts cracking against his back and shoulders, a disobedient slave being disciplined in front of the entire population of the Maze.

A cool, dry voice broke through his humiliation.

"No one was killed, Dias. As to the punishment, Tyre accepted it freely and stood silently under the lash. Perhaps it would behoove you to study his silence, since your outburst brings discomfort to the entire room."

The grey-robed Instructor stood beside Tyre, eyes snapping with anger at the young woman who gasped at her rebuke. Backing away until she ran into Dino, Dias spun around to meet his matching look of disapproval, burst into loud sobs and ran from the room. Dino moved to follow her, but was detained by the Instructor.

"Like a child, she needs to cry out her misery alone. Let her be. I'll visit her later."

Dino rushed to his partner's defense.

"As you say, she's young. There's no malice in her, only confusion."

"It's not as simple as you suggest. The Fifteenth Mother said the incident was to be forgotten. Dias must learn to think before she blurts out the first thing that comes to mind."

The Instructor softened her judgment by patting Dino's shoulder, moving off in a slither of grey silk to greet another couple signaling for her attention. The conversations interrupted by Dias' outcry resumed and soon the room was buzzing again.

Rama and Varuna tried to engage Tyre in conversation, but nothing they said could pierce the haze of shame enveloping him. Not long after, they moved away. Oblivious to anything but his need to escape, Tyre surveyed the quickest route to the door. A pair of almond-shaped eyes claimed his attention. Kara stood on the platform, her brows drawn together in a troubled frown. He was thankful she'd been too far away to hear what happened. It was enough to be humiliated in front of strangers; to have it happen in front of her would have been intolerable. Another burden dropped on his shoulders. If he left, she might follow him, ruining the evening she'd looked forward to as a chance to perform for the others. Smiling weakly at her, he was relieved when she turned back to Minthe.

Trapped, he reached for another goblet. A servant in drab clothing stood behind the table, staring at him as if he'd grown another head. The servant was huge, with thinning locks of hair falling about his ears. Catching Tyre's eyes on him, he hurriedly refilled the goblets from a pitcher he held in his ham-like fists and moved to another table, looking back over his shoulder as if to imprint Tyre's face on a slow-working mind. With a defeated shrug, Tyre drained the goblet, certain the kitchen would soon be buzzing with gossip. Choosing a chair pulled off to the side of the room next to the wall, he locked his hands together in his lap and readied himself to endure the rest of the evening.

From the platform came the sound of a flute. Tyre barely registered its plaintive melody. The sound of furniture being dragged over the wooden floor made him look up from his hands. A middle-aged woman struggled with a chair while trying to maintain her hold on a large woven basket filled with multiple skeins of yarn. Without thinking, he rose to assist her.

"Where would you like it?"

She pointed gratefully to the space next to him.

"I've little liking for so many people gathered in one place. I'd join you if you've no objection."

Her accent was different than Kara's. Quaintly dressed in a striped skirt and wide-yoked blouse, a starched white apron tied neatly about her waist, her brown hair was tightly braided and pinned to the top of her head. Settling herself in the chair, she knitted away at a pair of enormous woolen socks. Tyre found himself mesmerized by her flying fingers, the socks growing longer by the minute. She lifted her eyes from her work to smile at him from time to time. From this he deduced she was willing to talk but content to let him begin.

"What are you making?"

"If you need to ask that, I'd best unravel and begin again." She chuckled to herself, enjoying her joke to the point that Tyre was forced to laugh with her. She winked at him.

"I'll put you to a test, laddie. Who do you think has the biggest feet in this room?"

Taken aback for a moment, Tyre thought she might be poking fun at him. But her eyes were kind as she observed him with barely contained merriment.

"Uh . . . Suda?"

She barked out a laugh.

"Right you are, laddie! That man goes through socks like food through a goat. I'm on the eighth pair as it is. Soon I'll be running out of yarn."

The numerous skeins of wool in the basket belied her words, her indulgent tone proof of her regard for her big-footed companion. Putting down her knitting, she held out a rough palm to Tyre.

"I'm Chione, partnered to Suda. Who might you be?"

Holding her horny hand in his, he realized he liked her enormously. She was funny and kind and made him feel like a boy again.

"I'm Tyre. My partner is Kara."

She nodded as she resumed her knitting.

"I guessed it was you who was joined to the singer. Ah, she's a lovely girl! I've missed her music. She used to sing every night in the women's quarters. Warbled like a skylark, she did. Reminded me of the songbirds I fed on my farm back home."

"You're not from Pelion?"

She laughed outright, her rosy cheeks abloom.

"The likes of me city born and bred? No, laddie. I come from the west country." Her face lit up with longing. Tyre guessed that she, too, was homesick. "I left the farm when my mate was killed by raiders who stole our stock and burned our crops. I had nothing but the clothes on my back and a heavy heart, for I loved my man . . ."

She knitted away for awhile, the rapid clicking of her needles seeming to restore her good humor.

"It was the Fifteenth Mother herself who suggested I come here. Everyday I bless her for her good advice."

"Are you content, Chione?"

She lowered her knitting and regarded him steadily, her expression softening a bit.

"I confess I miss my farm and my sheep and the sun on my face. For here and now, I'm as happy as I can be. Suda may seem harsh, but his heart is as solid as an old oak tree." She paused. "What of you?" To Tyre's relief, she took his reply for granted, never lifting her eyes from the ever-moving needles. "How could you not be happy, with such a lovely girl who thinks so highly of you?"

His curiosity was strong enough to overcome his shyness.

"What did she say about me, Chione?"

The farm woman clicked the needles as she clucked her tongue.

"I'm not one for repeating tales out of school." Chione raised her head toward the platform and tapped Tyre's knee. "Hush, now. She's about to sing."

The room quieted as Kara rose to take her place beside Minthe. Her dark hair reflecting the light of the torches mounted in the wall behind her, she stood composed and graceful before the assembly. Tyre sensed the anticipation of the crowd.

"Minthe and I have chosen a song far older than Pelion. Legend has it that it was sung in the years of before, handed down to us by one of the Makers who brought us to this world. Even though the language is unfamiliar, we hope the music will make the meaning clear."

This introduction was greeted by several sighs and a smattering of applause. Minthe began to play, cradling the lute in her arms, the sound of the plucked strings resounding off the high ceilings until they ended on a full chord. Out of the lingering sounds of the chord rose Kara's joyful soprano, repeating the soaring melody established by the lute. As she held the last note of the phrase, the lute joined her, the two sounds, one of wood and gut, the other of flesh and blood, melded together in perfect harmony. As Kara had promised, words were not necessary. The song was a dialogue between two perfectly matched voices echoing each other in a canon of such beauty that neither lute nor voice was distinguishable one from the other. The song ended as it began, with Kara's last note, low and throbbing, stretching endlessly over the vibrations of the lute.

During the applause and cries of appreciation which followed, Tyre turned to find Chione's weathered face wet with tears. She dabbed at them with a sock, a faraway look in her reddened eyes.

"What does the song mean, Chione?"

"I'm surprised you can't guess." Dropping her knitting, she looked him squarely in the eyes. "It was sung on the day of my mating, as it has been sung in the city and the country for as long as anyone can remember."

Tyre scanned the torch-lit room, finding Kara surrounded by a group of admirers. She was looking for him as well, searching through the crowd until she located him in the chair by the wall. Their eyes met, locked, and the room receded, the noise and bustle of the gathering forgotten.

Chione chattered on. Tyre heard nothing save the haunting melody of Kara's song, saw nothing but the heart-felt longing in Kara's face.

Grasos pushed open the tower door and strode over to the place at the table left empty for him. Lowering his frame into a chair, he clasped his brawny arms over his chest and regarded the others with a smug grin. Vena smothered a laugh at the change in his usually wooden expression.

"Grasos, everything about you promises good news! Tell us!"

"Well," he drawled, enjoying the fact that everyone around the table was leaning forward, "it seems I'm to accompany Tyre to the Sanctum tomorrow morning. He stopped me at the door of the cell this evening after the gathering. The lady went inside while I unlocked the manacles. He says he has a gift to give."

The old woman beamed. Nerissa relaxed, Zelor chuckled, and Luxor drummed his fingers on the table top. Even Ladon's mouth curved upward at the ends. After enjoying a moment of hard-won success, the Fifteenth Mother delved on with the subject at hand.

"Nerissa, you were telling us about the gathering. Continue, if you please."

"I stopped Dias as best I could but the damage was already done. When Tyre didn't respond to either Rama or Varuna, they left him alone. I hope you approve, Fifteenth Mother, but I sent Chione to him. It was a simple suggestion and she went immediately. She soon had him talking and listening, no doubt telling him all about her sheep farm."

Vena remembered the sturdy widow who had knocked boldly at her chamber door at dawn one day, demanding that she "be put to use somewhere."

"What of Dias?"

Nerissa frowned, shaking her head in dissatisfaction and defeat.

"I've tried so hard with her. This is the last in a long line of failures: her refusal to sleep on the bed even after Dino gave his word he wouldn't touch her, her refusal to bathe until I threatened her with dismissal, her inattention to rules and her seeming inability to understand their purpose. I blame myself, for I knew she was young and pampered. I thought Preparation would help her find her womanhood. Instead, she grows more childish. It saddens me, but I think we must send her home."

Everyone around the table understood Nerissa's bitterness since it was the hetaera's belief that Dias' inability to adapt to life in the Maze was directly related to the prudery of her family.

"What's to become of Dino?"

Zelor broke in without missing a beat.

"I speak for Dino. If the council votes to dismiss his partner, so be it. Just bear in mind that Dino's both a leader and a valuable man on a team. Once he stops joking and settles down to work, there isn't a better all-round man-at-arms among them."

"Can you suggest a solution, Nerissa?"

For the Fifteenth Mother to ask Nerissa's opinion so quickly and without revealing her own mind was a rarity. Nerissa rose to the challenge.

"We might offer Dino a choice. He can either join the Legion with Zelor as his sponsor, or stay here in the Maze until the next class is formed. In truth, I don't know the depth of his feelings for Dias. Without that information, it's impossible to know if he'll be willing to undergo Preparation again."

Nodding her approval, Vena turned her thoughts to Luxor and Ladon, who added their support to Nerissa's plan.

"We have consensus. Dias will be removed tomorrow after the morning bell. Nerissa will speak to Dino in private counsel." Vena turned to Zelor. "What have you to report?"

"Three ernani have qualified to leave the Maze for cross-country work on the cavalry training grounds. Grudius insists on being present. Rhacius has mapped out a route, devised a rotating guard detail, and assigned his best men to duty." Zelor paused for good effect. "I suggested he put most of our strength to the north but the cracked rib Tyre gave him seems to have convinced him that Tyre's crafty enough to run south just to confuse us."

Luxor slapped the table in delight, father and son enjoying a good laugh at Rhacius' expense. As Luxor wiped away his tears, he addressed the Head Trainer with unaccustomed respect.

"Who else qualified, son, and how good are they?"

"No one comes close to Tyre. Brimus shows considerable promise; he's lean and wiry, built for riding, and attempts anything Tyre asks of him. Suda is the surprise in the group. I thought he might bear a grudge but Tyre's blow seems to have knocked some sense into him. He's trained hard in the past few weeks—a good man, slow but steady, someone to depend on when the going gets rough."

Luxor considered the information, chewing thoughtfully on the ends of his moustache.

"Ladon, can you free yourself from your duties in the Maze that afternoon? The Legion healer will be on duty but I'd feel better if you were there as well."

Ladon nodded distractedly, his mind on other matters.

"Where's Stanis?"

Ladon had not uttered a word in Council other than in direct reference to a healing matter or to execute his vote. There was no hint of sullenness or resentment as he carried out his tasks, only heart-wrenching grief at the condition of his brother's mind. Vena grieved with him, having attempted to use her healing powers on Cydon, but to no avail.

"Since it's impossible to link the two events without more information, Stanis searches for clues. He's gathered every bit of information available concerning the missing man—his selection and purchase in Agave, the journey to Pelion, the ceremony of Blessing, as well as interviewing every person who ever worked with him down below."

Stanis was at work even as they spoke, reading and re-reading the ancient books of lore that had once been the province of Beal.

"We go to visit Phylas in the city tomorrow. Pray that we find some shred of information to lead us to this man."

Clearly and cleanly, Ladon's call opened their minds, lifting their thoughts through the rafters of the high ceiling and out into the cool night air. There was no moon. Outside the window the stars blinked at the intensity of their need. As they had for time out of mind, the Council of Pelion kept watch against the gathering darkness.

Chapter 17

Strife

THE BABE SUCKED noisily at Nomia's over-flowing breast, tiny hands clenching and unclenching as he strove to satisfy a seemingly insatiable hunger, a hunger which made the act of sleeping an unheard of luxury for his parents. Phylas was home on short leave, attempting to relieve his distracted mate of the household chores. From time to time Phylas found himself wishing he could give suck, not just because of the pleasure it seemed to give both mother and child, but to let Nomia rest in the early hours before dawn when their rest was shattered by a piteous cry. Despite her exhaustion, the satisfaction on Nomia's down-turned face as she rocked the child, now fast asleep, mirrored his own. When she slid from his arms this morning, laughing at his grumbles and complaints, she reminded him that their son had inherited his father's grumpy disposition when he wasn't regularly fed. Chastened, he rose with her and kindled a fire, content to enjoy the coming of dawn.

That he was more blissful than he deserved caused Phylas to give thanks daily to those who made it possible. He returned from Agave to find Nomia waiting for him by the northern gate. Keeping her pledge to the Fifteenth Mother, she had not even looked at him as he passed by. Later, much later, when he was groomed and fed and lying with her rounded stomach pressed against his loins, her cheek pressed against the thatch of hair covering his chest, she confessed how much she missed him. Her fingers stroked his beardless face and shorn head, seeking reassurance that he was unhurt and truly restored to her. As the Fifteenth Mother promised, his trip to Agave changed nothing between them, except for the fact that there had been no nightmares since his return.

His contemplation of mother and child was broken by a rap at the door. Swinging it open, he beheld a tall woman dressed entirely in black with an even taller man beside her.

"Welcome, Mother! I thought only birds and babes were up at this hour! Enter and warm yourselves by the fire. I was about to prepare our morning meal. Will you break bread with us?"

He herded them inside, watching proudly as the Fifteenth Mother headed directly for Nomia and the child to begin the ageless ritual of exclaiming over the size and obvious superiority of this particular babe over any babe born of woman. Phylas, recognizing the black man who purchased him in Agave, gave him a friendly nod which was readily returned. The men stood side by side, watching the nativity scene before them, the elderly woman bending over to inspect mother and child, her withered hand resting lightly on the brow of the sleeping infant. Phylas had not seen her since the afternoon of the child's birth, when she officiated at the ceremony of Blessing.

"Phylas, you've met Stanis before but Nomia has not. Nomia, this is Stanis, a Searcher of Souls, who returned to us recently from the outside world. Stanis has no tongue, so you will understand why he does not greet you with words."

With the infinite grace and hospitality of a trained hetaera, Nomia held out a lightly freckled hand. It was immediately grasped in two enormous palms and lifted to Stanis' lips. Clearly, Nomia was enchanted. Phylas resolved to kiss her hand more regularly in the future.

When the Fifteenth Mother spoke again, the room seemed to grow chillier.

"Thank you for your offer of food and drink, but we've come on other matters. May we sit now and talk to you again of the march from Agave?"

Phylas couldn't imagine what could have been overlooked in the grueling interview held with the Council upon his return, but he offered chairs to both of them. Placing her palm lightly on his forearm, the old woman began.

"Phylas, we must go deep into your memory. Your words, your impressions, anything said by anyone, in word or gesture, must be recalled. Breathe deeply, emptying your mind of everything except the afternoon under the trees."

The power of the Fifteenth Mother was such that by his third breath, Phylas was in chains.

"Dino told the others you were bound for Pelion. Eris was the only one among the group who had ever heard of it. Were you surprised by that?"

With a start, Phylas recalled he was not, although he should have been. Pelion guarded its privacy well. Those who entered its gates rarely returned to the outside world. As a Legionnaire, his training included study of various dialects and methods of camouflage and disguise, for the Legion's first rule was that of secrecy outside the walls of Pelion. One of the reasons the Legionnaires played the role of slavers so successfully was their ability to hide any trace of their origins.

"I never gave it a thought. Since I knew something of the mission, I concentrated on what Eris might reveal to Tyre." Phylas frowned. "I was worried he might tell Tyre things he should not hear."

The grey eyes squinted and Phylas quailed at their intensity. Her voice was no longer soothing.

"Repeat for me word for word what the slave said of Pelion. No detail is too small."

Phylas obeyed. As he spoke, her eyes flickered in shock, but he could not recall what was different from his former report. Making no comment, she turned to Stanis. As the black man regarded her with an unwavering gaze, Phylas imagined he could hear his unspoken question. The Fifteenth Mother shifted uneasily in her chair.

"This is no reflection on your abilities, Phylas, but you might take offense at my asking."

Phylas couldn't prevent the grin spreading over his face.

"You've given me everything I value in this world and you rule the city I proudly claim as mine. What could you possibly ask me that could give offense?"

There was relief in her answering smile.

"It concerns the moment the slave attacked you. You were a mercenary and an assassin in your former life. In addition to your training in the Maze, you've spent two years in the Legion. In all that time, has anyone ever been able to defeat you in a surprise attack?"

Again, Phylas was rocked at the ramifications of her question. He heard himself threatening the slave again, just as he'd threatened countless men in his years as thief, cutpurse, and hired killer, but the chain the slave wrapped around his neck caught him completely off guard. He could remember no warning signs—no tension, no sudden breath—nothing about the man had warned Phylas of his intent. In fact, strive as he might, his memory remained a blank until the moment the metal links encircled his throat. There was no indignity in his reply.

"Now that you put it that way, I realize he jumped me without any of the signs of a would-be attacker."

Bowing his head, he cursed his stupidity, as he had cursed himself these many moons. What a mess he'd made of things, not to mention letting the old woman down. A chair creaked and someone knelt by his side. Lifting his head, he looked directly into Nomia's eyes, his self-hatred mitigated by her steady gaze. He could never think himself worthless as long as this woman could look on him with such tenderness.

The visitors rose to their feet, seemingly anxious to take their leave. Taking Nomia's hand in his, Phylas hurried to open the door for them.

"Mother, I know it's not my business, but how goes Tyre's Preparation?"

She considered him for a moment.

"Do you care so much for him, then?"

A vision rose before Phylas' eyes: Tyre standing over him, his hands wrapped around another man's throat, risking everything to protect someone with whom he'd shared but a few weeks of slavery.

"I do."

The corners of her mouth curved upward.

"We, too, care for him. It's difficult for him, more difficult than you might imagine. He is helped, though, as you were helped, for he has found his Nomia."

The freckled hand he held squeezed his. The lines in the old woman's face settled into a smile.

"You must not blame yourself for Tyre's attack. I tell you with a full heart, you helped us then, and help us now, as no one else could." A note of prophecy came into her voice, deepening the tones to the sound of a muted bell. "You will suffer no more nightmares. Rest easy with your mate, this child, and those who will follow, and continue your service to the city."

Phylas closed the door, feeling rather than seeing Nomia's proud eyes upon him. Momentarily embarrassed, he patted her rounded bottom, pushing her toward their sleeping chamber.

"Just keep reminding yourself that your bed is graced with the presence of a remarkable soldier of Pelion."

Her eyes crinkling at his jest, she pulled him as eagerly as he had pushed her.

"As long as you remember that you must prove yourself likewise as remarkable in bed."

And their joining was as tempestuous as it had ever been and remarkable enough to satisfy them both.

Stanis walked beside her, his broad features drawn in thought, his hands clasped behind his back. Vena matched him stride for stride. Together they walked through streets still empty of people save where small groups gathered around an occasional food stall offering fresh-baked goods and steaming pots of hot milk and tea. A sudden gust of wind brought Vena's eyes up from the street, where she had been counting paving stones, to observe the morning sky. There, on the battlements of the northern wall, the blazoned banner of the city snapped and furled in the dew-heavy air. On a field of sable stood a many-pointed golden sun conjoined with a silver crescent moon. Its heraldic origins might be lost in the years of before, but its message seemed as clear to her this morning as it had the day she first arrived at the walled city, an orphan lass of ten, barefoot and starving.

Once she passed over the threshold of the northern gate, solemn-faced soldiers escorted her to a place where she was given clothes and shoes and food in abundance, not to mention the learning she craved. When she discovered children younger than herself could read books aloud, she was determined to surpass them, and did so in record time.

Laboring over the mysteries of reading, writing, and figuring (for literacy was required if she was to become a citizen), Vena found herself comforted by the sight of the banner billowing outside the high windows under which she studied. Facing her final examination for citizenship, she was confident of her success, having memorized every text set before her, the suppleness of her mind delighting her instructors. Alone in the chamber of high-backed chairs and long tables, she greeted her examiner with ill-concealed dismay. Never had she anticipated being questioned by the Thirteenth Mother herself! This black-shrouded creature frightened her more than her first hesitant step through the northern gate.

"What do you seek, stranger to the city?"

The question itself was not surprising in itself since it was asked of every outsider seeking citizenship. Vena expected it, indeed, counted on it. But the manner in which it was posed gave her pause, for surely no one had ever addressed her more seriously, or with such earnest fervor.

Suddenly, the answer Vena planned to give seemed trite, even boastful. Flustered, she searched for something to say, and in doing so, spoke from her heart.

"I seek a home."

Immediately, she wished she could call back her words. She'd intended to offer her talent for scholarship, her skill at learning languages, anything except a picture of herself as a lonely orphan. Eyes downcast, she waited for correction.

It never came. Instead, she heard the movement of cloth brushing against wood, the creak of a chair, and a heavy sigh echoing in the dusty air of the Lesser Library.

"You are frightened, child, and without reason. Raise your eyes to me."

Obeying the undeniable power of the speaker, Vena lifted her eyes to meet a face lined with untold years of worry. It was not the wrinkled skin around eyes and mouth that shocked her (for she had never seen a woman so old), but the fact that the eyes regarding her were blank, their natural darkness overcast with a milky glaze.

Again, she heard a sigh, and the Thirteenth Mother continued.

"I've seen you many times at your studies. Always, your attention strays to the banner of our city. And always, it brings comfort to your heart. Tell me, Vena, what do you see when you behold the banner?"

Sometime during the posing of this question, Vena realized that the Thirteenth Mother had indeed seen her at her studies, and that she was not referring to actual vision, but to inner sight. Freed of the burden of her secret, her continuing fear that others might learn about her powers and punish her for seeing as they could not, Vena's heart thumped noisily in her chest. This woman, blind as she might be, shared Vena's ability to see into other's hearts and minds, to touch objects and understand their history, to touch flesh and understand the cause of illness and suffering.

A glad cry burst from Vena's throat, her reply unedited:

"The banner brought me here from the north! I've seen it inside my mind ever since I can remember, floating above castle walls. It drew me here with a promise of home, of belonging. I understood its power, but not its meaning. Since I've been here, it's become something more. The banner," Vena paused, "the banner is you."

This last admission came slowly, the silence that followed it seeming to exist outside of time, as if the world hushed at the boldness of Vena's reply.

"How am I the banner?" the Thirteenth Mother asked quietly. "Come, child. Show me. We'll go together."

Vena took a deep breath of dusty air, closed her eyes, and pushed herself into the inner world that had frightened her up to this moment, beckoning to her as it always did with promises she feared to explore. This time she crossed over with confidence born of the knowledge of companionship within its unknown lands.

The Thirteenth Mother's mind met hers easily, wrapping her thoughts in swaddling clothes.

"Gently, child, gently. Remember, we come to view the banner."

At the mention of the word, Vena concentrated on that familiar image, seeing as she did so a pitch-dark field glimmering to reveal a line of dark-robed figures stepping out of the enveloping darkness to greet their guests. The robed figures stood on a broad plain, windswept and barren, their voices raised in a chant whose words Vena heard but could not understand.

The sky above them was starless and empty. As the chant continued, a fire began to kindle on the ground before them. From its flames, gleaming red against a background of total darkness emerged two figures. As they were revealed, unscathed from the conflagration that begot them, they turned to face one another, their silhouettes announcing them male and female. The crescendo of the chant began to pulse in the air around them, a many-pointed sun and a crescent slip of moon appearing above their heads. The figures moved toward one another, slowly at first, then more rapidly, until, without warning, the darkness through which they moved exploded into a brilliant white light of unbelievable splendor.

As the vision left her, Vena heard the chant again, and then there was only the musty smell of the deserted library and the quiet presence of the mind enfolding hers.

"I have watched and waited for you these many years. You are accepted, child-of-light. From this day you enter the service of the city, which will be your hearth and home."

"Stanis, this man, this former slave, he mentioned the banner!"

It had taken enormous effort not to reveal her reaction to the responses Phylas gave to her questions. His mind was more pliant today than when he was newly-arrived from Agave. Three moons ago, the anxiety of the upcoming birth of his child had colored every thought and feeling. Today, he was relaxed, fulfilled, and able to concentrate as she demanded.

Vena was thankful for Stanis' presence since she would never have thought to question Phylas so closely about the attack. During the moments in which Phylas relived the chain choking off his breath, she, too, had struggled to breathe, trusting Stanis to end the memory before she and Phylas lost consciousness. Now, sensing Stanis' turmoil, she waited to return the favor. They strode quickly through the still-deserted streets. At the door of the Greater Library, he paused.

"We must continue to tread carefully. Here is the evidence you require, proof that the events are linked. Only an adept could have taken someone as skilled as Phylas so completely by surprise. Not only that, but the blank space in Phylas' memory resembles Cydon's injury. Thus, Eris is the source of the danger signs which have troubled me since my return trip from Agave."

His tumultuous thoughts slowed, almost overpowering her with their guilt and shame.

"It's my fault. I chose him for the line, missing every clue as to his identity. I brought the wolf into the fold."

"Stanis, you can hardly blame yourself. I, too, examined him during the ceremony of Blessing. He spat on me, disturbing me enough to deny him entry into Preparation, but I felt no sickness, no darkness within him, or I would have denied him work within the Maze." She mused over this for a moment, sensing a paradox. "It may be that his abilities are different than ours. My session with Cydon revealed no signs of tampering. His mind has not been changed, but emptied."

Vena shuddered at the thought.

Stanis was already in motion.

Her farewell to his retreating form floated on the morning breeze. *"Find him, Searcher of Souls. Find the one who eludes us."*

Tyre sat easily on the big bay, waiting for Brimus and Suda to finish their practice turns on the small track near the cavalry stable. The gelding, having given Tyre his usual perfect round, was cropping the dry grass hungrily, lifting up his head from time to time to catch an unfamiliar scent, his nostrils sending out jets of steam on the chilly afternoon air. His black-tipped ears flickered back and forth continuously and every few minutes a ripple passed over his skin. Tyre noticed his nervousness the moment he entered the stable, registering it as a reflection of his own, for in a short time he would be able to ride without walls hampering him, free to gallop straight over the hard ground rather than following the monotonous circles of the track.

Zelor announced the session at the morning meal. Twelve heads swung in unison toward the three men who would be the first to leave the Maze. Zelor was as severe as usual, seemingly unaware of the envy and longing with which Tyre, Brimus, and Suda were regarded by their peers.

". . . for cross-country work. The course has been marked, and takes you for a twenty mile run over diverse types of ground, including low hedges, water crossings, gravel patches, and hills." He paused for effect. "There will be no divergence from the course for any reason. You will begin ten minutes apart in this order: Suda, Brimus, Tyre." His delivery was like a knife being honed, grating over the sharpening stone. "Cavalry soldiers are posted throughout the area. They are fully armed and have orders to pursue anyone who leaves the course for any reason. Be clear on this point, ernani, you will be severely punished if you attempt an escape."

His point made, Zelor turned to administrative details.

"You'll be chained until you reach the cavalry training grounds outside the northern gate. Guards will accompany you, as will Ladon. Grudius will watch the course in order to critique your skills. A cloak will be issued as you pass out of the Maze."

With announcements over, the men finished the meal in silence. Passing out of the dining hall, Dino gave Tyre's shoulder a mighty whack. Tyre stiffened at the unexpected blow, then relaxed when he saw Dino's self-satisfied smirk.

"Pandar said if they ever let you out, you'd make a run for it the first chance you got. After I saw Kara at the gathering, I bet him three horse groomings that you'll come running back as fast as your horse can carry you."

Dino's laughing face became serious. That night had been his last with Dias and the cell was lonely. The Instructor promised him another mate in time; still, he grieved for the young girl, especially at the gatherings. The other women fussed and made much of him, but they left with their ernani, while he walked the dim passageways back to the cell with no one but a guard for company. Refusing to give in to melancholy, he hit Tyre again, forcing a grin.

"Maybe I should hope Pandar's right! Yes, go ahead and run, Tyre! Once you're gone, maybe the Instructor will put in a good word for me to Kara."

Dino's grin faded as two cobalt eyes burned into his, bloodless lips spitting out words so low-pitched he struggled to hear them.

"Keep your eyes off Kara if you value your life."

Turning abruptly on his heel, Tyre strode down the hall behind his ever present guard. When Dino was able to breathe again, he sent up a fervent prayer that Zelor be prevented from pairing him with Tyre. If Tyre had held a weapon in that moment, Dino would have been dead. Cursing himself for his mouth and his stupidity, Dino walked dispiritedly down the hall toward the healer's chamber. He'd much rather be lonely than dead.

Freed of the manacles and astride the bay, Tyre's first look at the horizon since his interment in the Maze beckoned him to gather his horse underneath him and flee in any direction that led away from the walled city. He could breathe again and the late winter air held the promise of spring. It would still be cold in the north, the ice frozen in the shallow lake, the tribe lean and hungry after a hard winter. If he was careful with the bay, he could be at his father's tent in less than a moon. His sessions with the teachers in the library included careful study of maps both ancient and modern, allowing him to check and re-check the most direct route north. One chart in particular drew his attention since it mapped the exact location of his father's tribe, the surrounding terrain, the site of the Harvest celebration, and several caravan routes crossing between east and west. There was no date or signature, just the marks of a careful hand detailing lakes, ravines, plains, and low mountain ranges. No map of such accuracy was known to Tyre, but what little he knew of map-making convinced him that the maker must have spent many years in Lapith to record its territories in such detail. He was puzzled by this, for why should someone in Pelion be interested in the land of the Lapith? Still, the map served his purpose.

After careful thought, he selected a route due east from the walled city, a trip over hill country that would be rough going for the bay but equally difficult for any who chose to follow. Once clear of his pursuers, he would head northeast until he reached the banks of the great river Tellas. He could hunt along its shores and avoid spending time looking for watering places as he followed it north. Once it brought him to the boundaries of the farthest eastern edge of Lapith, he would turn west and fly on the smooth dry plains toward home.

His father's weather-beaten face rose before him, reminding him of the duties for which he had been bred. Ariod had been alone since early autumn, a chieftain without an heir, a proud man whose son had led twenty-four warriors to slavery and death. How had the tribe survived without those men, the core of the warrior clan?

He was determined to return, to take the place for which Belwyn had trained him, to regain his honor and care for the tribe. Yet even as he hardened his resolve to go, Kara wrapped her hand around his heart, pulling him inexorably toward her. What would become of her if he left, no matter if it was today or in the future when he had been mysteriously "prepared" for some cause or mission or plan that was always intimated, but never discussed? Trying to put aside his pride and his feelings for her, he decided she would survive. Instinctively, he knew she would continue on the path toward Preparation, which would mean another ernani, another joining with a stranger in a cell.

And what would become of him? He would lead raids, settle disputes, attend the yearly Harvest celebrations . . . and everything would be done without Kara. Her dark eyes would not glow at his arrival into her tent, her songs would not resound within its leather walls, her laughter would not allow him to forget his cares and lose himself in her abundant joy in life and living. And worst of all, he would be forced to mate with another woman to beget a son and future leader of the tribe. There would be no pleasure in that joining, could be none, for how could he know another woman as he had come to know Kara when custom demanded that he visit her only during the nights of his need? A lump rose in his throat at the thought of the cheerless existence that would be his . . . yet he must return.

The bay jolted forward and Tyre almost lost his seat. Raucous laughter greeted his near upset as Suda rode up beside him, his mount steaming from the trial run over a small track that was to prepare them for the rigors of the cross-country event.

"Hey, Tyre, were you napping? It does me good to see you taken unaware for once!"

Tyre frowned and settled the bay, patting the muscled shoulder and bringing away a hand wet with sweat. His attention was diverted by young Brimus, whose roan danced lightly in the dust, eager to be off.

"It's nearly time, Tyre! Look, Grudius, is coming!"

The Horse Master arrived on the black stallion he always rode, the only horse that surpassed Tyre's gelding in size and breeding. The scarred face of the old veteran puckered in disapproval.

"Settle yourselves and your horses. This is not a game. Suda, you took the last jump without a careful approach and it's your horse's skill, and not your own, that kept you out of trouble. And you, Tyre, since when does a horse practically unseat you from a standstill?"

Suda sulked while Brimus smirked. Tyre frowned again, noticing that the bay's ears had not stopped their constant twitching. Something nagged at him, some memory he couldn't quite recall. Grudius brought him back to the present.

"Suda, off you go. Be careful, ernani. It's unfamiliar ground. Follow the red markers and they'll bring you back here."

With a glad shout, Suda was off, moving due east toward the first flag.

Tyre scanned the eastern horizon, following the burly form on the equally burly gelding. Then he saw the guards. Zelor had warned them, but Tyre had been too busy with the bay and his private worries to analyze the territory. Now, his hunter's eyes, schooled to pick out the slightest movement from a seemingly empty landscape, registered the unmistakable forms of men and riders posted along the route of Suda's departure. As all hope of flight vanished, Grudius spoke.

"They're everywhere, and mounted on the best horses in the cavalry stable. The bay might be able to take them in a flat race, but they've trained in these hills for years. Most of them could manage it blindfolded."

Tyre flinched at the pity in those growled words. He turned to the old soldier whose love for horses equaled that of any tribesman of Lapith.

"I will learn."

"We know you will."

Tyre returned his attention to the course. His decision was irrevocable. The presence of the guards put off the inevitable. If not now, then later. Having tasted freedom again, he would not give it up. No matter if the cost ripped him in half. He would live on memories of what had been, but he would live free.

On a high ridge overlooking the most northern edge of the course, Ladon shifted uncomfortably on the mare Grudius had chosen for him. It had been years since he sat a horse and he cursed himself for allowing Luxor to persuade him that his services were necessary. The Legion healer, Idas, was a former student, a competent healer, and more to the point, an excellent rider. Rhacius having deposited him here hours ago, Ladon was growing impatient with the entire plan.

"I'll leave you here, healer. You're at the farthest point from the beginning of the course, so if there's trouble this far out, you can be there quicker than Idas."

"Do you expect trouble, Commander?"

Leather creaked as Rhacius eased himself in the saddle and absentmindedly patted his horse.

"You forget I've been trained by Luxor. His rule is to always expect trouble and then be thankful if it doesn't come to pass." His hard profile regarded the vista beneath them. "I laid out the course especially for him. It starts in wooded hills with tough approaches and dangerous descents. He'll have to pace his horse and jump a few gullies in the bargain." Rhacius pointed south along the ridge where they stood. "The course levels out there. He can pick up speed and have a good run across flat land. He'll like that."

Ladon studied Rhacius closely. This was the man Tyre had injured, an incident Luxor and Zelor enjoyed without malice, yet one that must certainly have wounded his pride. Yet here he was, purposely designing a course to give Tyre pleasure.

"You honor him, Commander."

Rhascius' rugged face lifted from the course to regard Ladon. No trace of humor lightened his words.

"He's as wild and high-strung as the horses he was raised with. The thought of him caged in the Maze has haunted me. This course is my gift to him. I helped trap and chain him; I owe him nothing less." When Ladon thought to protest, Rhacius cut him off with a gloved hand. "I don't question the rightness of what I did. If the Fifteenth Mother wanted him, that's all I need to know." He shifted his weight in the saddle. "You didn't see him in Agave, healer. I did."

Unable to respond, Ladon mused over what he had just learned, surprised by the depth of Rhacius' guilt, even more surprised that this somber, grim-faced man would admit it to a total stranger. Rhacius' attention returned to the course, gesturing toward a red flag almost directly below them.

"This is where they'll have to slow. The sudden rise will force them to pull up and turn west and south again." Rhacius gathered up his reins. "I'm off to inspect my men. Grudius will come cross-country to join you as soon as Tyre's safely begun. You'll see my men from time to time since they'll be pacing the ernani from along this ridge."

Grudius arrived in a cloud of dust, his stallion breathing easily as he picked his way confidently up the graveled path leading from the red flag to the top of the ridge. Ladon sensed his proud excitement as Grudius watched Suda pass below them.

"He rides surprisingly well for as heavy a man as he is. Stanis told me he was a farmer who lost his land and sold himself to some mercenaries. They taught him to ride although he didn't learn much more than the bare essentials. Tyre's teaching him the finer points." The mention of Tyre's name brought a sudden glow to the cavalry veteran's eyes. "Have you ever seen Tyre ride, healer?"

"I was in the arena the first day, although I must confess my attention was claimed by the fallen ones."

"He's a wonder and no mistake. I've never seen anything like him in forty years. Just wait until you see him in action." Grudius hawked and spat. "I just hope he doesn't try anything foolish."

Grudius gave Ladon no hint as to his actual meaning. Was he afraid Tyre might try to escape, or afraid he might attempt some dangerous escapade with the horse? Ladon never had a chance to ask.

"Here comes Brimus!"

Horse and rider proceeded at a frolicsome canter, the roan's natural high-spirits making her toss her head, her hooves barely seeming to touch the ground. And then, far behind them, a dark shape moving swiftly over the hard-packed clay, gaining on Brimus with each pounding stride came Tyre.

The bay flew low to the ground, racing the wind at a dead run. His rider hugged his neck, the black mane streaming backward, mingling with one of gold. Uneasy with horses as he was, Ladon could appreciate the mastery of the man who seemed a part of his mount. As they drew closer to Brimus, who remained unaware of the speed of their approach, Tyre straightened in the saddle, gathering up the reins lying slack over the animal's neck. They were close enough now that Ladon could see the white foam covering the bay's neck, chest, and shoulders. Tyre was leaning back now, his weight positioned far back in the saddle, arms straining as he pulled at the reins.

Grudius spoke up, his worry evident, "Something's wrong. The bay isn't responding."

Tyre was close enough now for Ladon to see horse and rider in some detail. Foam issued from the horse's mouth, white foam flecked with crimson.

"Is that blood, Grudius?"

Without shifting his gaze, mesmerized by Tyre's progress over the course below them, Grudius explained:

"He's trying to turn him. It's standard procedure with a runaway. Turn his head and force him to break stride and slow. It's cruel, though. Drives the edges of the bit into the soft flesh of the mouth and tongue."

Grudius paused in his explanation to curse softly under his breath.

Almost on top of Brimus now, the bay gave no sign of slowing. Sides heaving, ears flattened against his head, he was a bay no longer, his hide turned black with sweat. Perhaps Brimus heard Tyre's cry of warning, for he seemed to shout at that moment, his words lost on the breeze. Perhaps Brimus heard the rapid tattoo of the bay's hooves on the hard-packed earth. Ladon heard it, like a drumbeat answering the pounding in his chest. Whatever the cause, Brimus turned in the saddle, gauged the situation, and kicked his horse into a gallop. Tyre waved Brimus away, shouting at him, gesturing toward the ridge rising up in front of them, its eroded surfaces littered with gravel and rocks.

The sound of his tortured breathing punctuating the sound of hoof beats, the bay overtook the roan on the right. Now they were matching each other stride for stride, the bay heaving badly, heading straight for the rise, blind to the dangers looming in front of him. Ladon held his breath. All at once, Tyre was kicking off his stirrups, freeing his legs but still gripping with his knees, his upper body leaning out to the left, his arms outstretched toward Brimus.

"He's not going to jump, is he? Ladon cried. "Jump from a running horse?"

Grudius was screaming now.

"Turn her, Brimus! Turn her or you'll run onto the rocks!"

As though he heard Grudius, Brimus pulled the roan off to the left at the exact moment Tyre jumped from the saddle. Ladon closed his eyes, certain Tyre must have missed his target, only to open them and catch sight of a blonde head level with Brimus' right thigh. Tyre struggled to maintain his grip on the saddle as his body hung below, his legs being dragged across the ground. Brimus reached down, offering a hand to pull Tyre up behind him, but either because of her rider's inexperience or the unaccustomed weight hanging off her right side, the roan bucked and bolted, catapulting Brimus out of the saddle.

The last thing Ladon saw before following Grudius' breakneck rush down the ridge, was one man clutching desperately to an empty saddle, while another lay still on the ground.

Panting, every muscle straining to maintain his hold on the saddle at the same time he strove to avoid the flying hooves, Tyre took a deep breath to steady his nerve, bounced his feet on the ground to gain momentum, and swung himself up onto the roan's hindquarters. She was riderless. Edging himself up her rump and into the saddle, he found the reins and pulled her up as quickly as he dared. Shuddering and badly blown, favoring her right foreleg, she shook her head in alarm, ears flat against her head and eyes rolling back toward him in fear and panic. Turning her, he saw the bay laid out on the ground, his legs flailing helplessly even as he gasped out his life on the rocky hillside. And then he saw Brimus.

Lying motionless, face-down on the hard clay, Brimus' rough brown cloak hid the outline of his body. One arm was thrown up over his head, suggesting he had tried to protect himself during the fall. Tyre jumped off the roan to crouch beside him, afraid to disturb him, yet frantic to discover if he still breathed. Reaching out to touch the shoulder nearest him, he heard a low moan, and leaned back on his haunches in relief.

"Stay as you are, Brimus. There may be some injury inside you. I'll go for a healer."

Tyre picked up the reins hanging from the exhausted horse, who stood with legs splayed and head down, considering the fastest route back to the stable. The sounds of hooves and shouting brought his head up, and he was no longer alone.

Grudius led the pack, his long-legged stallion charging down the ridge, gravel and dirt tumbling down to spray over Brimus' unmoving form. Behind him streamed four cavalry riders, Ladon bringing up the rear.

In an instant, they were off their horses, the cavalry guards surrounding Tyre, Ladon on his knees beside Brimus, busily unstrapping a pouch from his waist.

"Did you touch him?" he asked curtly, pulling away Brimus' cloak as he did so.

"No. I heard him sigh and knew he lived."

"Are you hurt?"

Tyre looked down at his blouse, speckled with the dark blood of the bay. Although his shoulders and back ached from pulling himself up onto the roan, compared to Brimus, he was unharmed.

"No."

"Grudius, leave us alone. Make sure Tyre sits down, give him some water and keep him warm. I don't want another patient."

As Ladon spoke, Tyre began trembling. A soldier threw a saddle blanket over his shoulders and a strong arm went around his waist, pulling him away from the healer, who closed his eyes as he placed a palm on Brimus' outstretched arm. A tin cup was thrust into Tyre's hands and he drank deeply, tasting the bay's blood as it mingled with the water. Hands on his shoulders forced him down and he sank onto the ground.

The trembling lessened and he pulled the blanket tighter around him. His boots were scarred, his breeches ripped and torn from being dragged. Through the rents, he could see the scrapes and feel the promise of bruises on his knees and shins. Grudius crouched in front of him, his scars white against his darkly-tanned face.

"I saw most of it, but tell me what happened."

If it had been anyone else, Tyre wouldn't have cared what conclusions was drawn from his mad race and its awful consequences. But Grudius understood both horses and men. Tyre wanted him to know he had tried to protect Brimus.

"The bay was drugged. Myrrhine, from the smell of it. I should have known, all the signs were there: nervousness, the flicking ears, rippling skin, the stench of his sweat. I couldn't turn him nor could I jump off at that pace. I'd decided to ride him into the ground and hope I could jump clear when he foundered. I tried to warn Brimus away, but he . . ." Tyre swallowed hard, ". . . he wouldn't go. So, I tried an old trick I learned as a boy. It saved me, but Brimus . . ," he repeated slowly, "Brimus was not so lucky."

Grudius nodded, indicating agreement and grudging approval. Gradually, Tyre calmed. The soldiers hovered around him, although none seemed overtly hostile.

"What of the bay?"

"He breathes no more."

Tyre closed his eyes at the thought. He'd put horses down because of age or injury, but that such a beautiful animal, well-trained and well-mannered, should die in agony, filled him with sorrow. Grudius sounded as bereft as Tyre felt.

"I slit his throat. He'd suffered enough."

"Why would anyone want to poison him?"

"Why assume the victim was the horse and not yourself?"

Startled by the question, Tyre dismissed it with a rueful shrug.

"If someone wants me dead, why drug my horse? Why not kill me in the arena or during arms training, when it could be accomplished more easily and without undue suspicion?"

"Is there anyone who might wish your death?"

Tyre remembered his threat to Dino that morning.

"There's no one."

Grudius seemed unsatisfied with his answer but a call from Ladon ended the interrogation. Two soldiers helped Tyre to his feet. He waited for one of them to produce manacles. None appeared. Grudius led him over to the healer. Brimus, eyes open and surprisingly alert, rested with one cloak pillowed under his head, another draped over his body. The healer held a cloth to a nasty gash on the crown of Brimus' head. Despite his injury, a grin wobbled on the younger man's face as Tyre approached.

"I think we should practice before we try that again."

"Hush, Brimus. No more talking until the cart comes. You need stitches and you must not move."

Brimus looked up at the healer, who pulled away the bloodied cloth, re-folded it and placed it gently on the wound. He paled, his grin fading, and drew an unsteady breath. Ignoring the healer's command, Brimus asked, "Save the cloth for me, will you, Ladon?"

This time the healer didn't correct him. As Ladon nodded, a contented smile hovered around Brimus' lips.

When the cart arrived, the soldiers lifted Brimus, depositing him with surprising gentleness on the mattress-covered boards. Ladon gave Tyre a quick inspection, reassuring himself that he was indeed unharmed. Tyre limped toward the cart, his legs already beginning to stiffen as a result of their punishment against the hard ground. Soon after, they were jouncing along toward the cavalry stable in the weak light of the setting sun. Brimus was either asleep or unconscious, although Ladon seemed not as worried as he had been before. They were silent, Ladon checking and re-checking pulse and breathing; Tyre contemplating the bloodied cloth.

"Why did he ask you to save it for him?"

"I imagine he wants to offer it as a gift."

For once Tyre spoke without editing his words, not sure why he was angry, but angry all the same.

"It should have been me. By rights, my blood should be on that cloth. There was no reason for him to try to help me; no reason for him to be hurt."

After pulling up another blanket to cover his patient, Ladon turned to face Tyre.

"Yet of his own free will, he chose to do so. And through his choosing, you are alive and Brimus will give his last gift. What began in darkness finishes in the light."

"Must the blood come from injury and pain? Is that what this Maker of yours demands?"

Ladon shook his head.

"You fight against understanding. Brimus gives blood from an injury; another might offer a single drop from a pricked finger. It is the act of giving that matters, not the offering itself."

"And if Brimus gives this last gift, he's free?"

Brimus shifted and muttered something. Ladon stilled him by pulling the blanket more tightly across his chest. It was a long time before he spoke again.

"The Fifteenth Mother would be better able to answer that question."

Tyre knew he was being put off, and it infuriated him, especially since Ladon had always been frank with him.

"She said three gifts, Ladon."

"Three gifts from man and woman."

Startled, Tyre tried to remember everything Kara had said about her gifts. She'd given her hair during childhood and the blood of her first menses. She'd never mentioned another gift.

"What is a woman's third gift?"

This time Tyre knew there would be no appeal. Ladon was as remote as the evening star rising slowly above the eastern horizon.

"Only a woman may answer that question."

"Well?"

"I, uh, watched like you said."

"And?"

"They came in on a cart."

Baldor felt his worries calmed as that good feeling came over him again, the feeling he liked.

"You're a good watcher, one of the best. Sit down and rest yourself. No need to hurry, just tell me what you saw."

Baldor rested his back against the hard rock and slid down to the ground. It was nice here, dark and quiet. It had taken awhile for him to feel comfortable this far underground. A large brazier filled with coal warmed the air, sending large shadows leaping against the stone walls. There was water and food in abundance. He'd helped carry most of it down from the kitchens and nobody upstairs was the wiser. He'd been careful about that. A finger in his mind seemed to prod him, reminding him he was supposed to talk some more.

"They came in late and everyone was worried. I couldn't see much, there were too many people lined up at the main gate."

"Who was in the cart, Baldor? You're so tall, you must have been able to see over their heads."

"There was the healer, the one who inspects the food. And another man who was lying in the cart, all wrapped up in a blanket. There was a bandage around his head."

Baldor felt waves of pleasure ripple over him and basked in the happiness they gave him.

"Do you remember the man you told me about at the party in the big room upstairs? The one who drank from the goblet after you poured it?"

Certainly Baldor remembered him. Everyone had stared at him at the party. His friend was always interested in stories about the goings-on in the rooms upstairs.

"He was there, in the cart."

"So it was him wrapped up in the blanket?"

Baldor saw the blonde man lying on the pile of mattresses, the top of his head wrapped in a bloody bandage. Confused, he shook his head. No, that wasn't what he'd seen. Why was it so hard to remember what had happened only a few minutes ago?

"No, the one lying down was a different man. The blonde man was sitting across from the healer. When they pulled him out of the cart, he was limping."

The pleasure stopped. Baldor braced himself for the pain that sometimes followed its removal. There was no pain this time, but the loss of the good feelings made him feel bad. Tired from trying to remember, Baldor felt sleepy and closed his eyes.

When he opened them, his friend was staring into the fire, his hands working busily on slender strands of leather, braiding them into a sturdy rope. He looked up as Baldor woke and smiled.

"You're a good friend, Baldor. Did you see anything of interest today, anything that might amuse me?"

Baldor sifted through the events of the day. He'd risen long before the morning bell and worked the morning meal. He was the best pot washer the cook had ever seen. Then he helped carry the supplies for the midday meal to the kitchen. They liked him in the supply room, too, because he could carry so much, more than anyone else. After cleaning up, he'd gone out into the city and wandered through the shops, buying a few things his friend had asked for. Then he'd come down into the belly, being careful no one saw him. None of the other servants knew how to lift the grate in the laundry and climb down the steps into the secret, empty places below. He was sad he had no stories to tell his friend today. His friend loved stories.

"No, Eris. Nothing exciting happened today. Everything was just the same as always."

Eris smiled at him again. Baldor had grown used to the places in his mouth where there were no teeth anymore.

"You'd better leave now, Baldor. The laundry will start up again in an hour or so. Make sure you close the grate and dry your boots so you don't track any mud over the floors."

"I won't forget. I'll see you tomorrow."

"Oh, I nearly forgot. I need some more leather. This time get some wider, stronger strips as long as I am tall. Take this halter with you to use as barter."

Baldor fingered the halter with awe. His admiration was sincere. His friend could do anything.

"They always like what you make in the shops. One shopkeeper told me he'd give the highest price for anything you make. I always go to him last of all."

"That's good to hear. You're a sharp trader. Go now."

Baldor was half-way up the stairs when he remembered something he was supposed to tell his friend, something about being at the main gate at the evening trumpet. His thoughts were muddled, though, and he couldn't remember if he'd told Eris or not. It worried Baldor. These days there was so much he couldn't remember.

Chapter 18

Revelations

THE FINAL VISITOR dismissed, a lull fell over the Council. Taking advantage of this gap of inactivity after a long day of interviews, Vena observed her companions.

In some ways, the brunt of yesterday's events had been borne by Ladon. Returning late this morning from the House of Healing (where, after a sleepless night spent at Brimus' side, he reluctantly surrendered his patient to Maenon and Chloe), he arrived exhausted, nodding through most of the testimony. Yet Vena noted that his mind was less troubled than it had been of late. Ladon needed action around him to combat his tendency toward melancholy. He was at his best in an emergency. Yesterday, he'd proved his worth a hundredfold. Although Brimus' head injury was serious enough to merit constant attention, if there was no fever or complications, he would soon be back in the Maze. Wisely, Ladon left Tyre's scrapes and bruises to Kara, judging her better suited to the task considering his confrontation with Tyre in the cart. He was nodding again, now, the thinning brown hair showing grey at the temples, the fine-boned face drawn with weariness.

Her gaze drifted toward Luxor, her old wolf, who sat smug and self-satisfied throughout the proceedings. Giving credit where credit was due, that yesterday had not ended in disaster was a tribute to Luxor's theories of discipline, security, and planning. Ladon had been placed in exactly the right spot and the adept guards working the course were able to call the stables for the cart before Grudius could traverse the hill down to the site of the accident. Without these safeguards, Tyre would have been forced to wander in the gathering dusk on a badly limping horse, leaving Brimus exposed to the chill of the winter night after an afternoon whose events left Tyre trembling with shock. Luxor licked his lips and broke into a cavernous yawn, his yellowed teeth glistening in the candlelight. Luxor's exterior calm didn't fool Vena. The wolf had seen his den broached and every protective instinct was alerted.

Nerissa, her robes covered with a heavy shawl against the damp of the stone walls, listened attentively as was her habit. Her report was brief, yet revealed her upset. Acting on Vena's orders, she interrupted the women in the dayroom to announce the accident. Minthe, who had lost her mate a year earlier, heard Brimus' name and fainted before Nerissa could reassure her Brimus lived. Once revived, Minthe begged to accompany him to the House of Healing. Nerissa, this time working on Ladon's orders, was forced to refuse. Such was Nerissa's greatest trial, to obey when all her instincts fought against obedience. Vena had seen through Nerissa's cool demeanor early on. Her calm, austere manner protected a tender, giving heart. Nerissa could be remorseless when it came to self-criticism and she blamed herself for frightening Minthe. This honesty with self was her greatest virtue. Many people are honest with others; few can be as honest with themselves.

Stanis, the solid rock on which Vena built and tested the majority of her plans and resolutions, sat immobile, his face set into lines of concentration. He had been unusually active in council today, questioning Grudius repeatedly about the condition of the horse, his knowledge and familiarity with the poison, and the schedule of all guards and stable workers in the Maze. Each rider along the course was asked to describe what he had seen from his post, their testimonies agreeing on a single point: Brimus' courage and Tyre's skill prevented certain disaster.

A healer of animals confirmed Tyre's suspicions. The bay had been fed myrrhine, and must have been dosed during the midday meal. By the time the horse began the course he was in agony, his last desperate burst of speed the result of the poison's potency.

Once the visitors departed, Stanis retreated into his research. Vena could almost hear his mind ticking off entries of information against the records he'd memorized in past weeks. It saddened her that his muteness accentuated his natural isolation of spirit. Cut off from the easy communication of speech, his inner voice was equaled only by hers, but he remained aloof from others, a lone panther tracking his quarry, unaware of the other creatures with which he shared the wilderness.

Such were the strengths and weaknesses of Vena's Council. Now it was time to take stock of herself. She had spent the night reading and re-reading the prophecy she had committed to memory on the first morning of her ascension to this office. Summoned to the Fourteenth Mother's deathbed, she listened as She-Who-Was-Ilena, a parchment held against her laboring breasts, her words rasping out of diseased lungs, strove in her last minutes of life to hand over the wisdom of the ages.

"You are the one of the prophecy, Vena, the one who comes out of desolation, unknown and unknowing. Even without eyes, the Thirteenth Mother recognized you. You are unlike any who have gone before, brought here by the call of a Searcher in the north." The dying woman rested for a moment, continuing in inner speech, her message delivered with equal measures of longing and regret.

"As one not-born-of-the-city, you see the world differently than any who helped prepare the way. It seems fitting that you, an outsider, should tear down the walls of Pelion."

Reverently, her shriveled hand passed the parchment into Vena's waiting palm. Vena had thought her beyond speech, but She-Who-Was-Ilena's voice spoke in her mind.

"Remember: a prophecy is a voice from the past speaking to the future."

The old woman seemed to sleep, allowing Vena to move quietly toward an open window. Spring breezes brought with them the odor of freshly tilled soil and growing things. The cries of children in the streets below were combined with the high yapping of a pup that joined them in their play. Vena held the parchment up to the morning light and began to read . . . .

Refusing that memory, sending it back to live in the vast storage chambers of her mind, Vena wrestled her thoughts into the present, into the stone chamber where her Council sat waiting for enlightenment.

"We're ready to consider all we've heard. Stanis, we await your findings."

The Searcher of Souls acknowledged each face around the table as they joined their minds together. The swirling darkness surrounding Stanis since the trip to Agave vanished, replaced with rationality and order. The tale he wove for his listeners began in a past of nearly-forgotten memories.

"I speak of the days of the Searchers of old. The early hope of breeding adeptness had come to naught—our science could yield no promise of its gifts. The Councils of yore considered a different approach. If there were adepts in Pelion, there might be others beyond its walls. For the first time since its founding, Pelion looked to the outside world. The Tenth Mother began the search, sending the Searchers out with these watchwords: `Seek for any, no matter the strength of their vision. If they cannot be persuaded, mark them well. Our best hope lies in the children.'"

"And so the Searchers passed their lives in the world outside. Many were lost in the years that followed, but always their findings were sent back to Pelion and diligently recorded by the scribes of the Greater Library. As time passed, the need for secrecy increased. The world had grown smaller and Pelion was endangered by those who envied the city's wealth and power. The Searchers no longer persuaded with words. Instead, they implanted images in the adept minds they found, trusting their directions would reveal the path to Pelion. Each Searcher used certain images, a signature, if you will. When the adept reached Pelion, it was a simple matter to test them and reveal which Searcher had sent them to the city."

"The method was simple: after locating an adept, the Searcher sent them visions in their dreams. The images might differ, but the message never altered—help, home, safety, freedom, fortress, walled city, black banner, south, ever southward to the valley of the castle. It's difficult to judge the effectiveness of the plan. Yet many came, and nearly all were accepted."

Stanis shut them out for a moment. Vena found herself considering the images which had brought her here, planted by a Searcher whose face she had never seen, whose name she would never know. Yet those images lured her here, a brown-headed girl child with long thin legs, placing a dirty foot over the threshold of the northern gate, her grey eyes full of dreams . . . .

Vena started as Stanis continued, his inner voice colder, more brittle:

"There were failures as well. Some reached the city to reveal minds broken by the strain of their journey. Others were twisted, crippled by their gift—marked and hunted as witches and wizards, demons in human form. The records reveal that in almost every case, these failures were the strongest adepts, those who could alter the thoughts of the minds they touched or read the histories of objects, and thus, the ones who had the most difficulty shielding their thoughts from others, most of them unable to either control or understand the nature of their gift. To have such strength without guidance often ended in madness or self-destruction."

"In time, the Council turned their attention to the mission we continue today, and fewer Searchers of adepts roamed the world. The age of the Searchers for ernani began, the golden one looked for in the north and west; the silver one in the south and east. But this you know."

Stanis passed a dark hand over his tight curls while Vena readied herself for what would follow.

"The man we seek, Eris by name, must be one of the last adepts implanted by one of the last Searchers of old. His code was given to us by Phylas yesterday morning. The information was meager and so general that I despaired of finding his origins until I questioned Grudius and the animal healer. The clue is myrrhine, a poison whose symptoms Tyre recognized. It would have been unknown to us except that Beal recorded it in the book of herb lore he completed in Lapith and sent via a caravan trader who served us as a go-between. Beal was fascinated with its properties and knew he had found something important, something unique to Lapith. With few facilities for research, his findings were incomplete, yet, in a short message accompanying the manuscript, he asked that his notes and seed samples be forwarded to the herbalists in the House of Healing.

"Only someone who was native to Lapith, or spent time there, would know of the plant. Thus, we know two facts now: from Beal and Tyre we have learned his origin; from Phylas and Cydon we can ascertain that Eris is not only strongly adept, but dangerously so."

"How could he have brought the poison into the Maze? The ernani are stripped of every belonging and everything is burned on the day of their arrival."

Luxor was belligerent at the idea that his security measures might be found wanting. Ladon answered before Stanis could respond.

"He did not need to bring it. I'm acquainted with the book Beal sent us from the north. Many of the seeds within it were planted and tended by specialists in herb lore. This is only a guess on my part, but if Beal was fascinated with it, the respect he commands in his field would have encouraged others to study it more completely. Those gardens are contained in the House of Healing and patients and their healers often stroll within its peaceful avenues. My brother loved those gardens. Eris could easily have recognized the plant and plucked it without arousing suspicion."

Nerissa roused herself now, her face a study of confusion.

"If what you say is true, and I doubt it not, then this one called Eris has been read by you in Agave, by the Fifteenth Mother upon his arrival, and again by Zelor after Tyre's attack. Not only this, but Cydon must have touched his mind repeatedly even in the short time he spent in the House of Healing and would have immediately reported his patient as adept. Our early training teaches us to build barriers against would-be intruders, yet this man has had no such training. No barriers are completely safe, I know, yet he withstood the strongest of us. How can this be?"

"How can it be that an orphan found her way to a city that called to her in her dreams and was able to see a mystery reserved for the Mothers of Pelion? How could Stanis, untrained and under physical duress, break into a Mother's protected mind? Our own experiences prove that the strongest minds are often rogues of a sort, different from those born and trained to their gifts since childhood. Eris' abilities point to powers unlike ours. His advantage is that he can completely shield himself from other adepts. His disadvantage is that whoever he touches can lose their thoughts and memories to him. Cydon's mind is not hurt; it has, quite simply, been drained." Vena shook her head wearily, hating the waste that had come of such talents. "His gift might have enriched us. With training, he might have controlled the impulse to absorb."

Pragmatic Luxor was on the trail now, having leapt ahead of the others.

"Then it's impossible to search for him and dangerous to try. The next question concerns me the most, that of the reason behind his actions. We must assume he was angered by Tyre's attack on the road to Pelion. If so, then he purposefully goaded Tyre in the passageway during a time when Tyre was particularly vulnerable. This last attempt proves he has knowledge of the intricacies of the Maze, which horse Tyre rides and the times of the daily feedings. It makes no sense. This man could have easily escaped the Maze. Why does he risk capture and imprisonment so as to revenge himself on someone he doesn't even know?

Nerissa regarded Luxor thoughtfully.

"It would seem the reason is simply hatred."

"It's also possible," Vena interjected, "that he remains unconscious of what he does. He simply wishes something and it comes to pass. We assume he was brought to Pelion against his will and wonder why he didn't make Stanis release him. It may be that Pelion has always been his goal; that instead of Stanis choosing him, he chose Stanis."

Lips pulled tight over yellow teeth, Luxor pressed his point.

"Even so, why give up so much for the death of a mere stranger, someone who might have hurt his pride, but did no lasting harm? A broken nose, yes, and a few missing teeth, but all that might have been remedied had he stayed in the House of Healing. All this for hurt pride and vanity? As I said before, it makes no sense."

"I have no answer, Luxor. Some things remain hidden, although Stanis has linked him to the north and to a certain period of time spent in Lapith. I remind you, however, that we have discerned several important facts. We are probably free from his probing since he believes himself to be alone. We must not search for him lest we arouse his fears and invite him to retaliate as he did with Cydon. And somehow, in ways we can only imagine, he will try again to harm Tyre."

The Council meeting ended in silence. Vena thought she was alone until she felt the delicate question sent to her by Stanis.

"Tell me why you are not worried by this madman."

"Timing and coincidence. The three-moon contract draws to a close, at which time Tyre and Kara must face their most difficult choice. And what of Beal? He sent us both the means of Tyre's destruction and the clue that unmasked his attacker. Do you truly believe all this is random? Each time Eris aims for Tyre, he forces him to learn, to grow, to re-evaluate. I must believe the darkness makes the light possible. If I lose that belief, there is nothing left but despair."

"Then tell me why you were worried by Ladon's recital of his conversation with Tyre."

"Because the next few days are crucial to their union. He has turned his back on his customs, been initiated into a woman's mysteries, and has lost his belief in his god. Old habits die hard, especially for one raised in such an unforgiving atmosphere. He must let go of the past and embrace the future. And she, I fear, will have to forgive him one more time." Vena dropped her defenses. "I ache for them, Stanis. I see them as Beal and I were so long ago, only they are so much more alone."

"Yet you and Beal remain joined even though he has gone. Find your comfort in that. Few are allowed the chance at such a joining. We offer them the greatest of gifts."

"I know, Stanis. I know."

The women's energy and creativity had transformed the dayroom into a place of glittering light. After the rugs were rolled up and stacked against the walls, the wooden floors beneath were polished to reflect the glow of torches, braziers, and candles. It was still too early for the first flowers of spring, so they made do with pussy willows, placing long branches in huge pottery jars full of water. Some of them had sprouted, the pale yellow shoots framing the grey fur of the buds. The tables were laden with delicacies prepared in the kitchens over the past few days. Still no better at baking than she had ever been, Kara spent her time arranging music for the dance, selecting simple tunes with lively rhythms. When Nerissa offered her help, Kara asked her to find some local musicians who might volunteer to play for them. They were playing now: a fiddle, tin whistle, and tambora sending out a jolly invitation to all who gathered to join the dance.

Like the other women, Kara tapped her foot in time to the lively strains, eyeing the empty floor with longing. The men, on the other hand, were decidedly ill-at-ease. Certainly their social skills had improved in these weeks of gatherings, but dancing was not much called for in their former lives and none of them was willing to be the first volunteer. Off to Kara's right, Chione rose purposefully from her usual chair, placed her ever-present knitting in the basket, and reached out her hands for Suda. As she backed toward the cleared space, he resisted, dragging his feet and looking nervously about him. Undeterred, Chione favored him with a beguiling smile, pulled up her skirts to reveal sturdy legs encased in striped knitted stockings, and began to sashay in front of him. Kara nearly laughed out loud at the expression on Suda's face. Then, all at once, he was dancing, a brawny arm wrapped tightly around Chione's waist, promenading her around the room with his chin held high, daring the other ernani to match his abilities on the dance floor. The mood changed swiftly and soon the floor was full of dancing couples.

Dino swung by with Minthe, her dark braids flying around her thin face. His jollity soothed her anxiety for Brimus; since the accident, they sat together nightly at the gatherings. It occurred to Kara that Dino had been avoiding her lately. He greeted her with his usual warmth, but confined his attentions to Minthe and several of the other women.

Chiding herself for too vivid an imagination, Kara smoothed the folds of her new dress. She knew she looked well this evening. Tyre's attentive look as she pulled the richly-woven fabric of deep rose shot with silver threads over her head confirmed her hopes. His strong fingers had laced her tightly, the telltale signs of desire in his eyes and lightly-flushed skin. He protested when she pinned up her hair, giving way when she turned for his inspection, confidant that the upraised mass accentuated her long neck and that the escaping tendrils of curls framed her face.

A pair of long legs in tight-fitting breeches caused her to lift her eyes up from her skirt. Bright blue eyes regarded her mischievously. His golden mane touched his shoulders; a strip of leather tied horizontally around his forehead held it away from his face. Kara strained to hear him over the noise of the music and the stomping feet.

"It didn't seem possible that the loveliest woman here has no partner. I thought I'd rescue her from humiliation."

Kara flirted back at him, overjoyed that he was joining in the spirit of the dance.

"What makes you think I'll dance with you? I hear horsemen are hard on their partner's feet."

He threw back his head and laughed.

"And I've always heard that gently-bred women are short of breath and weak in the legs."

Kara pulled up her skirt and petticoat, displaying trim white legs and slender feet encased in leather slippers. When his eyes glowed a brighter blue she felt an answering rush of desire.

"I've never had any complaints about my legs."

He pulled her to him and whispered in her ear, causing shivers to course down her spine.

"You shall never have any from me."

With that, he swept her onto the floor to join the dance in progress.

Kara and Tyre had become frequent participants in the gatherings, missing only two evenings in the last few weeks. Kara's monthly flow prevented one visit, although as her mother and Nerissa predicted, the loss of her virginity seemed to lessen her discomfort. Even so, she spent the night surrounded by Tyre's strong arms as he regaled her with stories of his boyhood pranks. He spoke often of his life and family now and she opened her own life to him. The sole forbidden subject was his entry into slavery. He never mentioned it and she waited patiently for another wall of his privacy to crumble away.

The second evening was missed on the night the bay was poisoned and Brimus was injured. Forewarned by Nerissa, Kara waited anxiously for Tyre's return. Nothing prepared her for his entrance through the cell door. His shoulders slumped, his face drawn and spattered with blood, he stumbled into the room and dropped to the floor, his head drooping down, staring sightlessly at the floor. Kara didn't waste words. Stripping off the filthy blouse and shredded breeches, she gasped at the raw scrapes and angry bruises covering his knees and shins. Helping him into the bath, her heart wrenched when he winced at the heat of the water. She let him soak until he shivered, then dried him and wrapped him in their warmest blanket. A few swallows of soup were all he could manage, so she helped him into bed. She'd brought out her lotions, anticipating using them, but decided against it, fearful of adding to his hurts.

She thought him asleep, but he said with a tired smile, "Soothe me with your gentle hands, Kara. I ache all over and I . . . I've thought of nothing but your touch for hours."

She kissed him on his white, drawn lips, watching as his eyelids fluttered and closed. As she began to apply the lotion to his neck and shoulders, he heaved a contented sigh which touched her so deeply she blinked away tears. Finally his chest rose and fell in the regular rhythms of sleep. As she slid under the blankets to lie beside him, she curled up on her side, her arms aching from her exertions. Just as she closed her eyes, he drew her against him, nestling his face in her hair. His words were uttered close to her ear, so quietly spoken that his breath barely moved across her hair. It was to be the first and last time he ever referred to the events of that day.

"I faced death today. Saw it and recognized it for the second time. Brimus kept me safe today, just as Belwyn did the first time." His voice lowered, coming from some inner recess. "I've often yearned for death since my captivity, thinking it an honorable way to escape my wretchedness. Yet today, even as I looked it in the face, I rejected it, fighting against it with every skill I possess. The only reason for my fight was the impossibility of leaving you behind."

Kara turned into his arms, brushing away the golden silk of his hair. Torment was etched on his features, torment that had nothing to do with his injuries. She pulled his head onto her breast and continued to stroke his hair, holding him deep into the night, grateful that he had discovered what Kara had held in her heart for oh so many moons.

Despite her thankfulness, his admission of her power over him stunned her. Three moons ago, such a confession from him would have filled her with elation. Tonight, the responsibility of his need for her seemed overwhelming. She had thought love a charming pastime, an easy sharing of common interests and pursuits. Yet this man, who lay so trustingly in her arms, had made her the fixed star in his firmament. Tyre's love had nothing frivolous about it. Kara felt no doubt as to her capacity to love, but the totality of his devotion intimidated her.

Whether Tyre sensed her quandary or was immersed in his own worries was not clear, but for the last few evenings he had been withdrawn. Kara saw him cast several furtive glances at Minthe during the gatherings, confirming her suspicion that he was grieving over Brimus, blaming himself for what had happened. When the dance was mentioned one afternoon in the dayroom, Kara worried over Tyre's reaction, and even considered not attending. He surprised her with his insistence that they go.

Looking up at him as he twirled her around the room, guiding her dexterously around the other couples, moving with the sinewy grace which characterized everything he did, a laugh of pure joy escaped Kara. At his questioning gaze, she pulled him aside for a moment, trying to catch her breath.

"I cannot lie. Gently-bred women are short of breath." After her confession and the smug grin it elicited from him, she couldn't resist another dig. "But you, Tyre, when will you tell me all your secrets? Sometimes I think I know nothing about you."

All of a sudden he was wary, his eyes narrowing dangerously.

"What secrets?"

Taken aback by this rapid change of mood, she tried to recapture their former light-heartedness.

"Only that I must add dancing to your list of talents: first a cook, then a scholar, now a dancing master."

His obvious relief at her reply hurt her more than she could bring herself to admit. Looking around, hoping to find a diversion from this awkwardness, she noticed two guards enter the dayroom, supporting a man with a bandage wrapped around his head.

"Look! They've brought Brimus to the gathering. He must be well enough to leave the House of Healing."

Tyre's immediate departure to greet Brimus convinced her, not without some bitterness, that he was as glad to leave as she was glad to see him go. A joyous cry signaled that Minthe, too, had seen Brimus. Kara found herself standing next to Dino, a sidelong glance at his face revealing a mirror of her own as they witnessed Brimus' and Minthe's reunion. Reaching out her hand to grasp his, she felt a commiserating squeeze.

The musicians began another tune and soon they were surrounded by whirling couples.

"It seems we've both lost our dancing partners," said Kara. "Shall we make the best of it?"

Dino was strangely hesitant. Embarrassed at her effrontery, for it was obvious he would rather dance with anyone but her, Kara's lips trembled. A finger lifted her chin and warm brown eyes twinkled down at her.

"No one's ever wept at the thought of dancing with me before. I know I've one foot too many, but I try to conceal it by talking so much my partner never realizes her feet are being stepped on. Come, Kara!"

And with that they were off, gamboling about the dance floor like children freed from school, running into other couples with alarming frequency. It only took a few minutes for Kara to realize Dino had not been joking. His feet stepped on hers regularly, although, as he promised, he soon had her laughing at his expert observations on everyone moving about the dance floor.

"I've always suspected Tessa ruled the cell. Now I know it. She leads Pandar about like a bull with a nose ring."

The formidable Tessa flew by, her ringing voice never ceasing its careful critique of every move Pandar made. Kara dissolved into giggles, trying unsuccessfully to hush Dino, who waxed loud and long until the song ended. Her hand at her mouth, trying to stop the waves of merriment created by this good-hearted jester, she looked over Dino's shoulder and froze. Dino must have seen the change in her expression, for he turned and lifted his hand to his waist, reaching for the knife that should have been at his side. When his hand clutched empty air, he dropped it, his fingers clasped into a solid ball.

Tyre stood before them, his body tense and balanced on the balls of his feet. Fists clenched at his sides, his eyes burned blue-black with fury, the cords of his neck pulled tight against the opening of his tunic. Kara had seen him angry and cruel, but she had never seen him like this. With a flash of sudden insight, she realized he was prepared to kill. Stunned, she tried without success to imagine what could possibly have enraged him. He deserted her on the dance floor and she found another partner. Why, then, this inexplicable hatred of Dino? Or was this a result of something that had nothing to do with her? Had Tyre and Dino some grudge between them, something to do with their training? And then Tyre spoke, and with a sinking heart, all was revealed to her.

"I warned you, Dino. I told you plainly to keep away from her."

Kara backed away from Tyre's fury. Dino stepped forward, for he was no coward, and waited for Tyre to make the first move.

"There will be no violence in this place!"

Nerissa's command ripped through the dayroom, the force of its delivery stabbing into Kara's ears and mind.

"Both of you will leave immediately!"

Tyre's head whipped back as if he had been slapped. He moved slowly toward the door, looking back at Kara over his shoulder. When she made no move to join him, he bowed his head as he passed through the open threshold. Chains rattled outside the door. As if in a dream, Kara heard the music again, conversation beginning to fill the void Nerissa's voice had created. Dino slipped silently toward the door, and he, too, vanished.

"Come sit by me for a moment, Kara."

Woodenly, she followed Nerissa to some chairs on the fringe of the room. A light arm wrapped around her shoulders.

"You must recover yourself before you return to the cell."

Kara nodded, and they sat quietly for awhile. Her thoughts churning, confused and bereft, she struggled to understand.

"How could he be jealous? All the women feel sorry for Dino. All of us try to include him whenever we can. He's so funny, so full of cheer and good will."

"Perhaps that's the reason. Perhaps Tyre isn't jealous so much of Dino, but of his easiness with other people. Dino is everything Tyre is not. To see you laughing and happy in Dino's company reminds him he can't fulfill you in that way."

"But he can be charming and gentle, and often is inside the cell. Outside, he's stiff, reserved, pulling away from people."

"Yet Brimus risked his life for him."

Kara pondered this for a moment, tasting the truth of it. She knew from the women's comments that the other ernani were in awe of Tyre.

"What should I do, Nerissa?"

Her plea brought a look of loving confidence to the other woman's face.

"You know him better than anyone. In a few days you must decide your path. Will you give the third gift, extend this contract, or part? If these things are to be discussed, you must break through his silence. The time has come for you to know him whole, and for him to know your secrets as well."

Grasos appeared at Kara's side, his brow creased with worry.

"He asks for you, lady."

She rose and smoothed the silken folds of the dancing dress.

"Take me to him, Grasos."

Tyre must have paced the tiny perimeters of the cell a hundred times at least as he waited for her. Stopping to catch his breath and listen for her footsteps in the corridor, the clothes she had made for him were suddenly too binding. He ripped them off, wrapping the loincloth around his hips, resentful that he was more comfortable in this slave's garment than in the clothes of his homeland. Too much was changing too quickly and he was helpless to prevent it. The cell was too welcoming, Kara too dear, a different way of life too beckoning. He smashed his palm into the wooden mantle, grateful for the sting of pain. Now there was something to think about besides the picture of Kara in Dino's arms.

He knew, even as the Instructor's warning bludgeoned his brain, that he was wrong. He knew, with frightening surety, that Kara had no feelings for Dino. She had been utterly confused, neither coy nor guilty. She had no idea why he was angry, had never even suspected he was jealous to the point of madness. But now she knew, her regret and disappointment wounding him to the point that he welcomed Dino's defiance. In a single thoughtless moment, he had destroyed the gathering, Kara's respect for him, and what little peace he had ever known.

Leaving Brimus and Minthe to search for her, intending to apologize for his rudeness, he picked her out instantly from the surrounding crowd, dancing gracefully in her new dress, laughing merrily at Dino the way she had so recently laughed up at him. The skirt swayed around her like a bell and the candles made her white neck and throat shine like polished silver. Without warning, he was desperate to hide her away, to keep her from outsider's eyes, to have her be only his. And then his desperation turned to madness as he remembered what Dino said outside the dining hall.

That Kara didn't follow him out of the dayroom was the crux of his present anxiety. His last look found her standing by the Instructor's side, her eyes large and her expression wounded. Now he wondered if she would return at all. No pride left within him, he begged Grasos to bring her to the cell. Six moons ago he cared nothing for women; tonight he paced like a wild thing, tortured by the thought that one he had been taught to despise might despise him in return.

His ears caught Grasos' familiar tread and the light patter of leather slippers on stone. The iron door swung open and closed.

She took in his scattered clothing and panting breaths in one sweeping glance. Moving to the wardrobe, she removed her clothing, patiently unlacing the dress and lifting it over her head with her shift. Her back to him as she placed them on the pegs, her bare shoulders, back, and hips gleamed faintly in the firelight. A white nightshift fell over her slender form, shielding her from his gaze, and she began to unpin her hair. Freed from their prison, a wild mass of curls framed her face. Picking up the brush, she held it out to him.

"Would you brush out my hair?"

Wordlessly, he took it from her. It was a ritual between them, Tyre sitting on the bed, Kara perched on the edge of the mattress between his legs, her hips pressed against the inside of his thighs, leaning back, waiting for him to begin. As he pulled the brush through the dark heaviness of her hair, the repetitive motion of grooming her from the scalp to the end of each strand lulled his distress. She must have felt his tension ease, for she took the brush from his hand and turned to face him, searching his face with troubled eyes.

"Do you truly think I care for Dino as I care for you?"

"I . . . No." He paused. "I know I was wrong."

He had never seen her so concerned, so serious. There was no anger in her, only determination to unlock his secrets.

"I've told you of my life. Many men have been a part of it: my father, my childhood friends, my fellow students in the guild. Gelanor, the hetaera, taught me to give the gift of caring. Ladon, the healer, examines my body each moon. Dino, Rama, Suda, Pandar, Brimus, Samos —all the ernani are dear to me, each in his own way."

Tyre flinched at her recitation. Seeing his reaction, she bit her lips.

"It's . . . difficult for me to hear those things. I've been raised so differently. Here in the cell it's only us. I want," he finished in a rush, "I want it to always be like that."

Her brow furrowed as she spoke slowly and deliberately.

"Are you saying you want me to avoid the company of other men? See no man's face but yours, enjoy no conversation or exchange of ideas with anyone but you?"

Her rephrasing of his desire made him feel foolish. When he made no reply, she continued, refusing to retreat.

"From what you've told me, what you wish for me is not so different from the women of Lapith. They, too, live apart, isolated from everyone but a man who visits them occasionally under cover of night. Shall I wear veils as well?"

There was no contempt in her question, only disappointment as sad as it was profound. A lump in his throat prevented him from answering. With a sigh, she moved away from him. Replacing her brush, she walked to the wooden chair by the hearth and sat, wrapping the folds of her nightshift around her bare feet.

"What do you want, Tyre?" Sensing his confusion, she elaborated. "What do you want from life? If you were free, where would you go and what would you do?"

He had avoided this conversation for so long, it was almost a relief to begin.

"If I was free, I would ride north and take over my duties with my people."

"What duties?"

He had never told her of his position in the tribe, or anything about his capture or indoctrination into slavery. Momentarily surprised, he realized she had no idea of what he had been—to her he was simply a slave from the north, not a chieftain's son, not the heir to a position held by his family for generations. In Lapith, he was valuable for what he would become. To Kara, he was valuable for himself alone.

"I'm the chieftain's only son." Her eyes blinked in surprise. As he spoke, he saw her immediate understanding of the visions that had haunted him for so long. "I was captured when I led a raiding party against another tribe. We . . . I . . . lost many men. Those who survived were taken into slavery. Our captors marched us to Agave." When she shivered at the mention of that dreaded name, he felt the old horrors take hold of him. "My people were bought by a wealthy stable owner in the east. I was brought here."

It was her turn to be silent as he became intent on making her understand. He rose and began to pace, trying to choose the right words to express his dilemma, knowing she was weighing everything he said against what he'd said he felt for her.

"I must return. It's what I was born for, what I was raised and trained to be by my father, and most of all, by Belwyn." He knew he was losing control, but he couldn't stop the rush of words he'd held inside so long. "I must go, but I can't imagine my life without you. I would hunt and fight and lead my people as best I could, but my heart wouldn't be in it. And what of Belwyn, who trained me to lead, to be strong and just, to help my people? I don't know what he would say. I only know he thought my life more valuable than his own."

She lifted his head and held his face between her palms.

"What would you say if I told you I could ride?"

Struck dumb for a moment, he could only stare at her. She was searching his face closely now and he sensed her tension. He was slow to respond, trying to curb his growing excitement.

"Do you mean you would go with me?"

"I didn't say that. I asked if I would be welcome."

How could she possibly doubt her welcome? He'd never dared to dream she would leave this place, her family, her studies, and a life of comforts he could never offer her. Looking up into those dark, mesmerizing eyes, he gave her his heart.

"I would welcome you with everything I possess."

"And how would I live, if I went with you?"

All her earlier words came back, and with them, a wash of regret. She would be the caged one in Lapith, her beauty covered by veils, living alone in a tent he could only visit at night. His excitement died as he realized he could not, would not, ask it of her. Kara wouldn't sing for long in such a place and he couldn't bear the thought of Kara without her songs. He lowered his head and she removed her hands from his face, her breath catching in a long, ragged sigh.

Tyre pulled the wooden stool to her feet and they sat staring at each other, their heads at the same level. He took her hands and felt them tremble.

"And you, what do you want from life?"

There was no hesitation in her reply.

"I want to give my third gift."

Ladon's words reverberated in his ears.

"What is a woman's third gift?"

Her words were oddly chanted, as if she was reciting a litany of some kind.

"In the Place of Preparation, the gifts of man and woman are three: beauty, strength, and fertility. We both offer hair and blood and you offer your seed. My last gift must be given by both of us. . ," her eyes filled with tears, ". . . for it is the milk of my breasts."

Liquid rolled down her cheeks and sparkled in the firelight. A vision rose before his eyes, Kara with a child at her breast, a small mouth suckling her as she sang a wordless lullaby. And then there was only Kara, her tears, and the bitterness of their choice.

"The Instructor promised us there would be no children."

"There will be none unless we choose."

"What if we choose and still there is no child?"

"My mother could have no children, yet when I was brought to her, she offered the goat's milk which fed me. Not all can conceive, or wish to conceive. This is something I've come to long for in my time with you."

He asked the single question left unspoken.

"And if I choose not to give this gift with you?"

Kara's eyes swam in tears, but she lifted her chin, that simplest of gestures more eloquent than words. Belwyn had spoken of gentleness and caring, yet Kara was so much more than that—bravery, courage, strength of will; these things were as much a part of her as her music and her laughter.

"If you make that choice, I'll return for awhile to my home and live as before with my parents and my studies. When I can bear to . . ." her voice failed her, but she stumbled on, ". . . when I'm ready, I'll come back here, to the Maze, and walk the Path with another ernani."

No secrets remained. The walls between them dissolved, yet still there was no remedy. Every choice led them down a dimly lit corridor toward another kind of wall, one of countless layers of impenetrable stone, one which offered no doorway through which they could pass.

Tyre rose from the stool and pulled Kara up from the chair. Her head found its accustomed resting place beneath his breastbone. As he wrapped his arms around her, she clung to him. They shared each other's misery and hopelessness, taking solace from the joining of their sorrow. Her tears ended and she lifted her face to him, her lips parted, her eyes full of need. He untied the ribbon of her nightshift while she loosened the knot of his loincloth. The fabric fell off her gleaming shoulders, sliding to the floor and settling around her ankles like a pool of milk.

The firelight danced over them, throwing its panoply of light and shadow over gold and silver bodies entwined in the timeless ceremonial that tempers the loneliness of the night.

Chapter 19

Burial

THE PLACE WAS unknown, foreign; the air hung stale around her. No wind or breeze ever disturbed these moist, heavy layers; no light ever pierced this darkness. Squinting accomplished nothing; her eyes were useless. Palms held before her for protection, she stumbled forward over loose stones and rubble, the noise of their dislocation echoing eerily, suggesting the vastness of the place. Her ears, sharpened by the loss of sight, distinguished the drip of water and the answering splash of liquid meeting rock. The completeness of her isolation terrified her, for no minds met hers, even when she commanded them to attend her with the full force of her powers. Disoriented as she was, deprived of inner and outer sight, her other senses reinforced what her mind had difficulty accepting: she was deep in the bowels of the earth, wandering through a place of incalculable age.

Mustering her courage, she ventured forth into blackness, searching for whatever lay in wait. Tentatively, a mind touched hers. It groped for her, sharing her blindness, unable to identify her. With all her strength, she strove to reach it, sensing in its presence a lifeline, a deliverance from the soul-crushing loneliness of this place. Triumphantly, she latched onto it, rejoicing; her exultations ceasing when she experienced no welcome in return. Too exhausted by its efforts to continue the search, the presence detached itself from her and faded away, to be swallowed up by darkness. She had been judged and found unworthy. And now she was alone.

Fighting against the bedclothes, Vena struggled back into the world, pushing away the coverlet, tearing frantically at the cloths knotted around her throat. Breathing hard, her heart racing, she opened her eyes on her sleeping chamber. As the familiar forms of furniture helped her regain her bearings, she collapsed against the pillows. Lifting her hand to brush away coarse grey hairs from her eyes and mouth, a gnarled claw moved in front of her face. Obeying her will, the hand arrested its movement in mid-air. Was it possible this hand was connected to her in some way? Her hands were slim and supple, with oval nails and small knuckles. The hand that met her eyes belonged to a crone; the knuckles swollen, the fingernails ridged and yellowed, the ugly, bluish veins standing out in high relief against the loose covering of spotted skin. She tested the hand again, demanding it perform a task for her, and watched sadly as it accomplish what she willed.

Closing her eyes against the evidence of her decaying body, she chose instead to examine the abilities of her mind. Summoning her memories, they came to her effortlessly, accepting her invitation to swirl around her. Immersed in colors, textures, smells, and sounds, she was placated for the loss of youth and health. Then, uninvited, the memory of her dream invaded her reverie. She bolted upright in the bed, heedless of the protest of her ancient joints.

Alert, wide-eyed at last, the old woman suppressed the urge to waken each member of the Council and warn them of the significance of her dream. Voices swam inside her head—all of them cautionary: *"Gently, go gently"; "Resist the temptation"; "Accept all conditions."* Bowing to their wisdom, She-Who-Was-Vena turned her focus inward and repeated the prophecy, holding it staunchly within her, melting and forging it into a talisman to help her find her way through this day, the Day of Choice.

The morning bell found Nerissa awake and dressed, reviewing her notes and readying herself for the events of the day. The morning hours stretched before her, to be filled with clerical tasks and record-keeping. Now it was noon, and inexplicably, a strange reluctance overcame her. Troubled, she threw open the windows of the dayroom, inviting the first warm breeze of spring to wash over her cheeks. Grey veils fluttered around her like wings, causing her to spread her arms and wish she might join the doves that perched so casually on the outside ledge. She found herself being drawn closer and closer to the window, called by the clouds racing by, so free, so weightless, so alluring . . . and stopped at the brink of the window casement. What were these feelings of trepidation, these icy fingers of doubt? Where was her faith, both in her abilities and the city she served? This was the Day of Choice, the fruition of five moons of teaching, counseling, and planning. Having faced it a dozen times before, she harbored no illusions about what it would bring. She was prepared for the successes and the failures, and knew from experience that at least one couple would surprise her completely by their decision. It had always been so, even in the Novice class so many years ago.

Then why this foreboding? She worried at it, examining it from all perspectives, turning and twisting it about in her mind, casting away some conclusions, embracing others. As she discarded her emotional connections with each ernani, each woman, she made herself look unflinchingly at the source of her disturbance.

It lay in herself, in Nerissa. For eighteen years she had labored, first as a Master Teacher of the Hetaera Guild before being called by She-Who-Was-Vena to become Instructor of the Maze and Council member. Reading the prophecy, she had believed, her belief so strong, so sure, that in each of the hundreds of couples passing through Preparation, she searched for and found the qualities of what was promised, testing them in a crucible designed by the Fifteenth Mother and instrumented by Nerissa. Today, for the first time, her doubts surfaced, stunning her with their ferocity. What had they wrought here, in these dimly-lit avenues of locked cells and clinking chains? What right had they to threaten, punish, and frighten these daughters of Pelion and sons of the outside world? How had she been able to endure the tears of the wounded and the sorrowful, all on the grounds that some miracle, the nature of which they could only hope, might come to pass? In a few minutes, yet another group would gather in front of her, forcing her into the role of the cool, correct lecturer—restating the rules of a game which had no purpose, whose center was rotten and corrupt.

The breeze washed over her again, the fluttering silks becoming a plumage of feathers. She felt no fear at her transformation. With the strange, inflexible logic of a dream, her metamorphosis seemed natural, even welcome. Flexing her newly-made wings, Nerissa jumped lightly onto the sill to watch the flight of the doves as they circled the domed roof of the Sanctum. Shedding her cares, she joined them in the fresh spring air, circling the white stones whose surfaces bounced back the rays of the gleaming orb fixed at its zenith. An open window offered her rest from the novelty of flight. Landing daintily, she folded her wings against her sides and preened the grey down covering her breast. Cocking her head, she surveyed the vaulted ceilings, arches, and columns of the immense interior. The Sanctum stood empty, not a single soul in evidence.

As she rested, comforted by the symmetry and perfect peace of the interior, the great bronze doors swung open. A line of figures stumbled over the threshold, the clanking of iron chains and shuffling feet disrupting the stone-deep silence. She stared down unblinkingly on the faces of the ernani marching below her, hundreds of shaggy-headed, bearded, stinking slaves; their faces cruel, haggard, hopeless, old before their time. The women, too, passed by, the linen and wool of their gowns whispering against the paving stones: widows grieving for a mate they had known with such intimacy they despaired of ever finding another; wealthy women tired of being loved for their possessions; shy women who hid in corners, unable to express themselves; headstrong women in search of a challenge. Each one passed beneath Nerissa, marching forward to the pedestal, giving their gifts as best they could.

Their joint offerings burned in the sacred fire, crimson flames leaping joyfully into the air. On the fragile tendrils of its smoke Nerissa floated, the beating of her wings unnecessary as she was carried back to the dayroom and deposited on the carpeted floor. The vision faded, and she was as she had been, her aging beauty clad in simple grey, the wisps of her silver hair floating beneath the gauzy textures of her waist-length veil.

She raised her arms to the open sky in gratitude, for the desire to flee her destiny vanished with the covering of feathers and down. Nothing came without a price. She saw again and again that brutality could yield kindness; fear, confidence; and pain, healing. The Makers were not gods, but beings from another world; perhaps from another time. Sowers, they called themelves, who planted seeds across a universe whose vastness was unimaginable. Even so, they had a plan, of that Nerissa was certain. And her life's work was not in vain because it was a part of that plan.

The door behind her opened. Fourteen couples streamed over the threshold. Gathering around her in a semi-circle, they blinked at the sunlight illuminating a room they frequented every evening, a room usually lit by tapers and torches. Opening herself to the souls in her care, Nerissa accepted them all; rejoicing with those whose minds shone with decision, sympathizing with those still plagued by doubts.

"This is the Day of Choice. Today the decision must be made by each of you. For this reason, there will be no afternoon training or evening gathering. Each couple will be interviewed in the library. You may spend the time together or alone; in conversation or meditation. I will proceed by the combined age of each couple; you will find the order posted in this room. Your guard will escort you at the proper time."

They swarmed and buzzed around her, claiming her attention, and she ministered to each as she was able. Out of the corner of her ever-watchful eyes, she saw Suda clasp Chione's hand in his and stroll confidently toward the doorway. They knew without looking that their names led the list. Nerissa was grateful that her first session would be a successful one. She scanned the others, watching as Kara stood on tip-toe to whisper something to a down-turned face hidden by golden hair. Tyre nodded slowly, and Nerissa thought, a trifle reluctantly. As he turned to go, his long-fingered hand reached out to caress Kara's dark waves in farewell.

Nerissa watched as Kara scanned the list, marking her relief as she reached the last two names. Given the Fifteenth Mother's request that they be last, Nerissa settled on this solution. Minthe was Kara's elder by two years, while Tyre and Brimus were a single year apart. Kara said a fleeting word to Rama and Varuna, and slipped out the door. Without any need for inner sight, Nerissa knew her destination.

Hearing footsteps in the passageway, Tyre shut the book he had been trying to read without much success. Kara had been gone longer than he expected, although, for once, he didn't begrudge her absence. She had such faith in the powers of the room she had told him about, and he waited, hoping against hope, for her to return and reveal to him some pathway they had not explored. He needed no list to tell him theirs would be one of the last sessions. His only regret was that these few remaining hours could not be spent together. Tyre had made his choice last night in the long hours between midnight and dawn, holding her lithe, sleeping body against him as she lay dreaming in the moonlight.

In the past few days they had spent every minute allowed them in the cell. Shunning the gatherings, they requested that their evening meals be provided so they need not spend time cooking or cleaning. Tyre had even asked Grudius privately if he could leave his pupils an hour early each evening. Every request was granted without comment or question.

Their hours together were dream-like, completely removed from the realities they faced. They sang and bathed and played like children, heedless of time, sleeping when they were tired, rising at midnight to read and talk, dozing together by the fire until dawn. They memorized each other's body, tasting and savoring each scent and texture, joining together until they were exhausted only to begin again at the least hint of desire. They talked of everything—of childhood fears, the loss of Tyre's mother, and the difficulties of adulthood. Kara spoke of the wonders of Pelion, its ancient heritage of knowledge and culture, its fountains and gardens, the libraries, schools, and galleries. Tyre made her large eyes larger with tales of horse herds thundering over open plains, of storms turning rivulets into swollen streams, of stalking deer and elk and sleeping under a roof of stars. They reveled in their differences; delighted themselves with their similarities.

And through it all, they never mentioned the day fast approaching. Everything had been said. Rather than relive that agonizing evening, they chose instead to celebrate their freedom from long-held restraints.

Holding Kara, whose heartbeat matched his, whose sleeping body fitted every line and contour of his own, Tyre decided he must leave her. He could stay another three moons and prolong their happiness, but these last few days proved the cruelty of that solution. Even the thought of a return march to Agave had become acceptable to the thought of staying with her another day when he knew he could not stay forever. The wound caused by their parting would never heal within him. Even so, he found himself wishing that Kara might find another mate of her heart. It helped to think she would not be alone, as he would be alone until the end of his days.

He could near footsteps clearly now, their heaviness denying him Kara's presence for a little while longer. The bolt slid back. Expecting Grasos' form to fill the doorway, he looked up to find a stranger surveying him, someone who almost matched Grasos' height and girth, but a stranger all the same. Frowning, Tyre shut the book and laid it on the mantle. Not until he took a second look did he recognize the servant at the gathering who had stared at him so intently. His hair was even dirtier now, his eyes dull and staring. His enormous hands, red and chapped, held the key ring Grasos used daily on Tyre's manacles. Tyre shifted his weight, uncomfortable with this break in routine on a day already fraught with difficulties. The servant's eyes seemed to focus.

"Your woman needs you," he blurted out all at once, startling Tyre into a state of immediate alarm.

"Where's Grasos?"

The servant blinked rapidly.

"He's with your woman. He sent me to bring you."

Tyre considered the possibilities. The key ring verified that Grasos had indeed sent the man to him. He had also seen evidence of Grasos' regard for Kara. For some reason, Kara's need was more pressing than Grasos' responsibility for Tyre. All of a sudden, he was frightened. Somehow, Kara had been hurt. The old dream of not being able to reach her was coming true.

"Where is she?"

"I'll take you to her."

The servant lumbered out the door, Tyre following at his heels, mentally urging him to move faster, dogging his footsteps along the deserted corridor. Even after five moons in this warren of doors, corridors, and dead ends, Tyre was quickly lost. He had no idea where the solarium lay and had never thought to ask. It seemed they were moving downhill, which confused him, although the Maze had fooled him many times before. He had no choice but to follow, trusting the servant to take him on the swiftest path to Kara.

The air grew moister, heavier, causing his nostrils to flare at the smell of lye. The servant pushed open two swinging doors, leading him into a kind of antechamber. As the door swung shut behind them, a form flashed across Tyre's field of vision. Turning to investigate, a stunning blow on the right side of his head sent Tyre crashing forward into darkness.

The ernani slumped to his knees then toppled forward onto the tile floor. Blood oozed out of a deep gash on his temple.

"He's bleeding. Why did you hit him?"

Baldor was troubled. Eris hadn't said anything about hurting anyone when he'd asked for Baldor's help.

"I didn't want him to know where we were taking him in case he told someone after we bring him back upstairs."

"Why did you hit him so hard?"

"It was a mistake. I'm not used to your club and I swung too hard. It's such a strong, heavy club. Don't worry, I'll wrap up his head and he'll be fine."

Baldor was proud of his club. He'd carved it himself out of an old log he'd found in a woodpile. He kept it for killing rats and other vermin, carving a notch in it for every one he killed. Baldor didn't have very many things and it pleased him when Eris wanted to borrow one. He still didn't understand why Eris wanted to talk to this man. Eris explained something about old gambling debts; Baldor wasn't too sure about the details. Eris was afraid the man might not want to come, so he'd asked Baldor to play a game and trick him. It had been hard to learn all the answers for the different questions Eris said the man might ask.

Eris was pulling up one of the grates that served as drains when water overflowed the laundry tubs.

"Pick him up and carry him down the stairs. I'll hold the grate and follow you in a minute."

Nodding, Baldor picked up the limp body, heaving it up and over his shoulder. As he started down the narrow staircase, Eris wiped up the blood on the floor and threw the stained cloth into a basket of dirty laundry. Then he pulled the grate down over their heads. Baldor knew his way so well he didn't need a light. The man was heavy, but not any heavier than the carcasses of beef Baldor carried from the supply room to the kitchen. He wondered if the man would be cold in just a loincloth until he remembered that Eris had many clothes and blankets in the room where he kept his food and water.

Eris went in front of him now, holding a torch to lead the way. It was always dark here. Baldor could hear the echo of their footsteps and sometimes the drip of water falling from the ceiling. Eris told him all about this place, and Baldor grew to like it. You could see where the people who built the city had carved out the rock and where they'd fitted the stones for the foundation of the outside walls. There were big chunks of rocks everywhere; Eris said it was rubble they hadn't bothered to cart away. It was also old, the oldest part of Pelion, according to his friend.

They were nearing the place where Eris lived. Baldor was glad they were almost there since the man was getting heavier. Every so often he moaned. Baldor stopped in front of a blanket hung between two supporting walls that marked Eris' living space.

"Not here, Baldor. I don't want him to know where I live. I've found another place a little farther on. After you've carried him there, you can come back here and sleep while he and I talk."

After a long time of walking, Eris stopped to wedge the torch into a large chink that had been dug out between the stones. Baldor put the man down.

"Now, my friend, you can go."

For some reason, Baldor didn't want to go. Something about Eris bothered him. His eyes were different than they usually were, bloodshot and staring. Eris turned him around and pushed him back the way they had come. Baldor looked over his shoulder, seeing Eris crouch down beside the man, his shadow huge against the wall.

"I know you're awake."

Trying to ignore the throbbing of his head, Tyre was baffled by those words, teased by the riddle held within them. They had drawn him into consciousness and now he couldn't decipher them. Frustrated, he tried to push away the darkness in front of his eyes. He could not move, nor could he see or speak. Blindfolded and gagged, he was immobilized; his hands were pulled over his head and tightly bound together at the wrists. His feet were bound as well, his ankles tied together and anchored to something that didn't give against his struggles. Hating the restraints, cursing the darkness, he struggled silently, furiously, making no progress at loosening the tightness of his bonds.

"It's no use, horse boy. I learned my trade from the finest leather workers in the world."

Someone was speaking to him in Lapithian! The familiar sounds spoke to him of home, but brought no sense of comfort. Harsh laughter followed his initial jerk of recognition.

"So it surprises you that I speak your tongue, does it? Does it also surprise you that I know you're the son of Ariod?"

The hatred contained in that last phrase was unmistakable.

"I knew you were from Lapith when we were chained together, but I never imagined you were the great chieftain's only son. If I'd known, I would have killed you there and then instead of wasting time on your friend."

Hands reached around to untie the blindfold. Darkness fell away. In the dim light of a single torch, bloodshot eyes stared down at him. The face was broken, smashed—the nose askew, the open mouth revealing gaps in the gums where teeth should have been. Tyre blinked rapidly, trying to clear away the fuzziness plaguing his vision. The face receded from his view, to be replaced by an object held within inches of his face.

"You've seen one like it before, haven't you? Your father always carries one when he rides."

Recognition came slowly. It was a quirt. The stock was braided; hanging from its end was a loop that fitted around a rider's wrist. His father's was more worn than this one, having been used to discipline many a horse.

"Did he ever tell you who gave it to him, horse boy? Did he tell you that a slave made it for him?

Tyre turned his head slowly from side to side. The quirt was withdrawn. The torch flickered as a shadowy form pacing around him. As Tyre followed that form with his eyes, he saw himself for the first time. The leather straps binding his ankles were tied around a large chunk of quarried stone. From the tension in his arms, he guessed that another stone was situated above his head. He lay on stone as well, rough pebbles biting into his back and shoulders.

"I was young, maybe eleven or twelve, and making my way south with a group of fellow-travelers when slavers caught us and herded us north. They met up with some caravan traders and sold us as a group. When the caravan traders decided they needed right-of-passage across your tribal lands, they thought a gift might sweeten the deal. I was skinny and not much use, so they gave me to your father."

As that word was spoken, the quirt slammed down on a nearby stone. Tyre's stomach knotted. So this was the slave his father had once owned—the same man who had threatened Phylas and taunted Tyre that day in the corridor.

"Your grandfather had just died and your father was new to his position." The fervor of the speaker's reminiscence softened his harshness for a moment. "He was good to me at first. He was busy all the time, but others taught me how to be useful, how to strip a carcass and stretch a hide, how to scrape and tan, how to braid and stitch. Once I proved myself useful and trustworthy, he had them teach me how to ride. I picked it up fast, so fast it impressed him, I think. Not long after, he took me hunting and even said something about training me as a warrior."

The longing after happiness once felt faded.

"But you see, I made a mistake, a mistake that couldn't be forgiven." The quirt reappeared, touching Tyre's forehead and tracing its way down the bridge of his nose until it lodged under his chin.

"My mistake was that I told your father I loved him." The voice thickened. "I loved him and wanted to be his son. That I'd train day and night to be the best warrior in the clan so he could be proud of me."

The quirt was moving down his body now. Goose-flesh rose where it passed.

"Do you know what your father said?"

Tyre closed his eyes, readying himself for what was promised by the flicking quirt and unforgiving eyes.

"He told me he already had a son, a boy named Tyre, a child with the golden hair of one favored by Sturm." Tyre's eyes flew open as the quirt lifted a loose strand of his hair. "Not only did he have a son, but he would never consider allowing an outsider to come near this blessed child." The voice trembled and the quirt shook. "It was almost time to bring you into his tent and he'd decided that I must leave. He wanted to free me and send me to another tribe. He even offered to help me gain entry into the tanners' clan. That's all he thought I was good for."

Mirthless laughter echoed eerily in the cavernous space.

"When I protested, when I told him I would come back even if he sent me away, he picked up the quirt I made for him and beat me with it."

Suddenly, the voice was perfectly calm. Tyre clenched his fists in anticipation of what would come.

"Today I settle all my debts, son of Ariod. First I'm going to repay you for my broken nose and missing teeth. Then I'm going to repay your father by helping his blessed son Tyre die a long and painful death."

The quirt sang as it flew through the air, landing on Tyre's flesh and leaving in its wake a welt thick with blood. The second stroke came immediately after, and the third, and the fourth, each one leaving a bloody ridge. By the fifth stroke Tyre was in agony, his moans changing to screams as the quirt hit faster and harder.

Baldor couldn't listen anymore. He couldn't fall asleep either, not with the sounds of a beating ringing in his ears. He'd been beaten before, and it hurt. Hurrying back to the spot where he'd left the man, he found Eris standing over the bleeding man and called out his name.

"Eris!"

When Eris swung around, Baldor could hardly recognize his friend. His eyes were glassy with hatred, his breath coming in deep, sobbing gasps.

"I told you to stay away!"

He took a step toward Baldor, brandishing a thing made of leather and covered with blood.

"You said he was a friend."

"I said you were to obey me!"

As much as it hurt to disobey that voice, Baldor stood firm.

"Let him go."

Eris' voice rose in volume and pitch, echoing madly against the stone walls and inside Baldor's head.

"Let him go? You idiot, I've already killed to bring him here! Do you think I'll let him go just because you feel sorry for him? Anyway, you're the one who told me his name. You're just as much to blame."

"I didn't know you were going to hurt him."

"I haven't begun to hurt him!"

Eris turned his back and stood over the man, who was looking at Baldor now. His eyes were so sad, thought Baldor. He remembered how worried the man had been when he'd told him his woman needed him. It was true that he'd given Eris the name and description of the man after the girl had pointed at him at the party. And it was Baldor's club that had given him the gash on his head. He was to blame for this; he, Baldor, who had never hurt anything but rats and mice.

Baldor saw the hilt of the knife that stuck up out of the sheath that Eris always wore on the back of his belt. He'd stop Eris, no matter how much his head pained him. He snatched the knife in one quick move and grabbed Eris around the neck. He wouldn't hurt his friend; just frighten him into letting the man go.

Tyre was at the point of unconsciousness when the blows ceased. Blinking away tears of pain, he heard two voices lifted in argument and guessed that he was the subject of debate. He struggled to understand, but was unable to concentrate until he heard a phrase that awoke in him a fear so horrible in its implications that his lacerated flesh no longer mattered. His captor had killed. Kara's lateness, Grasos' disappearance, the keys grasped in the servant's fist—all the evidence supported a conclusion the madman's boast confirmed. Kara was dead, killed by the one who had imprisoned him in this underground cavern of dripping walls and stale air. Somehow, he could not fathom the idea of her claimed by death, but she lay somewhere in the Maze next to Grasos' inert form, for Tyre knew the devotion of his jailor. No one could have harmed Kara unless Grasos fell first.

A gurgling cry interrupted his thoughts. The servant was reaching helplessly for his neck, which had been neatly slit from ear to ear. A waterfall of blood streamed down the front of his tunic, his huge body crumpling, then crashing onto the ground. The madman clutched his right shoulder with his left hand, the bloodied knife blade still held in his right hand. Slowly, ominously, he approached Tyre, staring down at him not with the burning, bloodshot eyes of the man who had beaten him, but the flat, cold stare of a serpent testing the distance before its next strike. Seemingly satisfied with what he beheld, he crouched down close enough for Tyre to see blood leaking from a wound in his right shoulder. His coarse brown shirt was stained with a slowly-spreading blotch of crimson gore.

"I meant to draw out your last hours, horse boy. I was even going to take out the gag so I could hear you beg for mercy. That fool has changed my plans. I can't wield a quirt, but I can still use a knife."

The eyes never lost their cold deliberateness, flickering over him, gauging him, experimenting with all the possible cruelties he could inflict. Tyre had been frightened of the quirt and the pain it promised. He faced the knife without a qualm. He had feared it as it lay on the table in the Sanctum, but now it offered blessed relief from the vision of a woman who lay in a deserted passageway, her eyelashes resting against a creamy cheek.

"You've guessed right. I killed the guard first, then the woman. They'll think you did it. When they discover you're missing, they'll think you killed them in order to escape."

Tyre invited the knife, wanting it encased in him as surely as it had cut into her soft, yielding flesh. The madman's eyes glittered insanely as they read his dearest wish. The ghastly mouth twisted into a smile.

"So you welcome the knife, do you? Nothing too easy, I think, nothing too quick. A slow death. Bleeding to death in this hole that has been my home, yes, that will content me."

His smile vanished, to be replaced by a look of grim hatred.

"They'll never find you, horse boy. You'll be dead long before the stench of decay reaches upstairs."

The knife flashed downward. A burning flame was kindled between his ribs. The blade's withdrawal was more lingering than its entry. The outlines of the face leering down at him grew fuzzy as the fire between his ribs continued to burn.

"It's a fitting tomb for Ariod's son, for the blessed child of Sturm. The sunlight has never touched this place. Think of that as the damp and darkness close in on you. You are my legacy, Tyre of Lapith. My gift to the tribe of Ariod."

The light of the torch receded and disappeared. Blackness enveloped him, the coldness of the stone on which he lay reaching deep into his bones. The only warmth was the burning wound and the blood trickling down his ribs. In the ensuing silence, he could hear water dripping against stone. Time passed; how much time, he could not be sure. He moved in and out of consciousness, growing colder all the while, the pain becoming a dull ache, a general numbness spreading out like the cold fingers of approaching winter.

There was not much longer to wait. There was nothing to regret or even grieve for. He would join Kara soon. Wrapping memories of her around him, he felt the coldness lessen, the thought of her pushing away the growing darkness. His success in calling her forth encouraged him. Grateful at being able to escape this tomb, he ventured further into memory. She appeared before him in countless visions of love—Kara handing him the pear, the leather-bound book, the package of clothes, the hairbrush. She laughed at him with suds in her hair. Her hands held high, her fingers spread wide, she promised to cure his aches and pains. She lay beneath him, stroking him, urging him on, her cries filling the cell as he lost himself within her.

The intensity of his vision wavered for a moment, as if something shifted inside his head, allowing him to see her in a place he didn't recognize, her form crystal clear and outlined by the light. She sat on a cushioned bench against an open window; her rose-colored dress dyed a rich ruby by the rays of the setting sun. She had drawn her knees up under her chin and seemed to be dreaming, her eyes focused on a distant point beyond the window. He wanted nothing more than to enter her dream, to experience it through her eyes. Again, his vision wavered. Again, something shifted inside his head, almost as if someone had opened a door through which light streamed, blinding him with its intensity. Plunging forward, drawn forward by the light, he found he could no longer see her, but it didn't matter, nothing mattered, because she was all around him, and her thoughts were only of him.

"You're leaving me, Tyre. I see it clearly, this new secret you keep from me. It was in your eyes when I awoke and you kissed me so tenderly, your lips trembling against mine. In the dayroom, you stroked my hair as if your hands would never touch me again. How can you go and say nothing? Do you believe my brave

words, my boasts that some stranger will replace you in my heart? Don't you know there will never be another?"

Her longing encompassed him. Testing the measure of her love, he found it boundless. What did it matter that this bright vision was the creation of a dying man's imagination? He reached out to her, an effort demanding that he spend the last of his hoarded strength, intent that he, too, express the measure of his devotion.

"I will never leave you."

It seemed to him he was drifting now, floating away on a river of pain, unable to fight against the current. Memories faded, the vision of Kara receding, its light dimming, until, at last, he was alone in the silent tomb, hearing the systematic drip of water against stone. Once he had been drifting, drifting and floating; now he was sinking, an abyss opening up beneath him, sucking him down, down into darkness, hearing as he fell a faint cry echoing against the stone walls of his tomb.

It was a woman's cry, a woman crying a single name over and over again, a name he had once known, but now could not recall.

The Council of Pelion sat in the tower chamber, minds linked, heads bowed, waiting.

A furious pounding on the door broke the circle of concentration. Five heads rose as one. Ten hands loosed their grip. At Vena's signal, Luxor strode to the door.

Kara burst into the room and knelt beside the wearer of the black robes.

Vena searched her upraised face.

"What brings you to my chamber, child?"

"Something's wrong. I can't find Tyre."

"Where have you looked for him? And where is Grasos?"

"I went to the solarium after Nerissa posted the list. I told Grasos to come get me in three hours, but he never came. Finally, I asked Echetus to take me to the cell. It was empty."

Vena forced a calmness she did not feel. Where was Grasos? She fought the temptation to search for him, forcing herself to concentrate solely on the girl.

"I understand your worry that you cannot find Tyre. But why are you so distraught? Surely his absence can be explained. Perhaps Grasos took him to the arena so he could ride this afternoon."

Kara hesitated.

"I . . . I have this feeling. It's so strong. I can't put it aside."

Vena struggled to still the sudden leap of her heart.

"Tell me about this feeling."

The dark head at her side bowed, then lifted, Kara's expression troubled, unsure.

"I was sitting in the solarium and . . . and it was so strange, but I was thinking of Tyre, and suddenly, it was as if he entered my thoughts."

"Yes, my child. Go on."

"He told me he would never leave me." She fought to hold back her tears, then, giving up, let them slide slowly down her cheeks. "It wasn't what he said that alarmed me, but the way I heard what he was saying." She shook her head, as if to clear it. "He was inside me, inside my mind."

The minds linked with Vena reeled. Nerissa's reaction was purely one of shock, Stanis' one of joy. Ladon was thankful, while Luxor sat lost in wonder.

"So it seemed that Tyre was inside your mind. This, in itself, does not seem to worry you, yet still you are afraid. What is the source of your fear?"

Kara registered relief that she had been believed. Now she struggled to express in words something completely novel, completely unknown.

"It wasn't what he said that frightened me, but the way he felt inside my mind. He's hurt, I think, and cold, but it's more than that." Her lips were bloodless now, her cheeks the color of ashes. "He's dying. Tyre's dying, and for some reason, he longs for death."

Vena fell back against her chair as Luxor took over, helping the girl up from where she knelt and offering her a chair.

"I'm Luxor, the Commander of the Legion. Tell me anything that could help us find him."

Upset by his request, she shook her head.

"There's nothing more to add. He said nothing else."

A brief smile touched Luxor's heavily-lined mouth.

"I understand that," he said quietly, intent on gaining her trust as quickly as he could. "I also understand that even though Tyre said nothing about being cold, you sensed that he was. You must have sensed other things as well. I want you to think back now, and answer my questions. Close your eyes. It will help you concentrate."

Thick lashes rested against porcelain skin.

"Can you tell me the position of his body?"

Her forehead creased.

"He's lying on his back. I think he's bound in some way."

"Can you sense what kind of surface he's lying on?"

"It's hard. Also cold and slightly damp. Stone, I think."

"What can he see?"

Her reply was a wail of fear.

"Nothing! There's no light, no sound except dripping water. He doesn't know where he is—its someplace he's never been before." The fringed eyelashes flew open, the anguish in their depths accusing them all. "He's frightened of closed spaces, of places without sky and wind and sun. And now he's dead or dying in a tomb of some kind, a place buried in the earth."

Her gaze came to rest on the woman in black.

"You must find him or he'll surely die."

Vena rose to her feet.

"And so we shall. You will go with Nerissa to the solarium and keep yourself open to Tyre's call. Nerissa will instruct you in how this can be accomplished."

The girl's fear turned to bewilderment. A wash of love came over Vena for this youngest of ernani. She saw her again as a child, being rocked in Beal's arms, and in memory of him, gave Kara what hope she could.

"We will find him. I can tell you this—he's not dead. May that thought comfort you and give you strength to begin your vigil."

Nerissa rose to escort Kara to the door. As it closed behind them, Vena sent out a beacon to guide her helpers in their search.

"He is in the place of my dream, deep in the belly of the Maze. There is a trail to follow, a trail of blood."

They rose as one and left her. Her wolf, her panther, and her faithful hound had been given the scent. Now, she must wait, listening for their mingled voices raised in pursuit as they tracked a quarry lost somewhere in the lair of darkness.

Vena closed her eyes and continued her battle against Tyre. She had fought against him since the moment she realized the significance of her dream. Her barricades had been strengthened by the Council, but now they had left her and she struggled on alone. Some moments were overpowering. For a second time, she felt a knife enter her body, leaving her gasping in pain, but so far she had resisted the overwhelming urge to reach out and help him. Weakening now, she worked desperately against the pull of one who had been a part of her for so long. How had Beal, alone and unaided, been able to keep his vow?

At the simple thought of her mate, Beal was with her.

"You call for me at last! Come, Vena, and we'll wait and watch together."

Vena leaned back into his arms, held snug against his slender frame, his chin resting on her shoulder, his breath moving across her long brown tresses. He, too, was fighting against Tyre, and he shared with her his fears for the son of his heart.

"He has come so far, Vena, so far from what he was. The promise has always been there. Today he reached out to her with the last fragment of his strength before surrendering to the pain. The Golden One has broken through the barrier. Will she join him?"

The burden of the prophecy rested on the frail shoulders of the tiny girl child Beal brought Vena long ago, the first fruit of their separation.

"She, too, has grown during her time here. She stood up to him, refusing to make things easy for him, as she has always done before. Even when she wanted nothing more than to go, she swore she would stay. It was a bitter night, Beal, as bitter as ours." His arms tightened around her. *"She will be frightened. Her bravery is not that of the body. We will try to ease her entry, but it will take every portion of her courage and her love . . ."*

"As it took every measure of mine to let you go . . ."

". . . and every fiber of mine to cast you away."

The gathering twilight swiftly darkened the tower room. Two brown-haired heads bent towards each other, their slim, youthful bodies clothed in the leaf-green robes of healing, their minds attuned to their children, lost and crying in the shadows.

Chapter 20

The House of Healing

THE WOLF LED the pack through the corridors, heading downward, ever downward, through passageways rarely used by any except those who labored beneath the surface of the Maze. As they traversed the stairs and hallways, Stanis maintained a wordless commentary with Luxor about each byway and dead end they passed, tracing their journey against the ancient maps stored in his memory. The wolf hunted by scent, his burly frame bent low to the floor, his short legs moving with deceptive speed over unfamiliar ground.

Ladon loped behind them, his legs propelling his body onward while he reviewed every skill of healing known to him. This was his test, and he faced it with foreboding. Forbidden entrance to Tyre's mind, he would be forced to heal without the reassuring certainty his inner sight offered him. He never understood why Beal chose him as High Healer. There were others more learned, more skilled in research and the preparation of medicines. There were also practitioners, Maenon and Chloe among them, whose inner sight was clearer, more vivid than his. Yet out of all his students, Beal chose Ladon, whose greatest gift was that of diagnosis, to be his successor. Hurrying down the passageways, Ladon felt the burden of his mentor's choice, for he knew that it was for this moment he had been chosen.

The pack came to more inhabited corridors, the smells of the sewers growing stronger. They passed onlookers now, men working in the storage chambers, stacking wood and coal. To each inquiry, they shook their heads, wondering at the sight of three grim-faced men striding through a place that received few visitors. Luxor paused in front of two wide-swinging wooden doors that lacked any bolt or key hole. To Stanis' raised eyebrow, he shook his head.

"My eyes tell me little, old friend. Feet passed this way this afternoon. Look, here the dust is disturbed." He wandered several more paces down the hallway before turning back. "The laundry is active from the second watch until midday. They prefer the cool hours of morning for their work. And this door has no lock, in case there is a need for clean linens."

When he pushed open the doors, their nostrils were assailed by the heavy scent of soap and cleaning solutions. As Luxor predicted, the room was empty. Stacked linens lined the walls. Enormous vats of copper rested near iron grates resting flush against the stone floor. While Ladon waited, Luxor and Stanis stalked about the room. A bellow of triumph reverberated off the tiles as Luxor waved a stained cloth high in the air.

"Ladon, quickly, were there any injuries or accidents today? Anything that might explain this?"

Ladon responded to Luxor's urgency with quick deliberation.

"None, yet it could be the result of a woman's flow." He examined the fabric closely, speaking without lifting his eyes. "The blood is too wet, too recent."

Another cry from Luxor.

"More here," he pointed toward the floor, "and here," and stopped in his tracks. Frowning, he knelt by a grate and lifted it up. "Torch," he ordered, and Stanis pulled one from the wall. Not one to travel without a knife and a tinderbox secreted somewhere on his person, Luxor lit the torch and peered down into darkness.

"A staircase." He considered his companions. "It's a long way down. We'll each need a torch. It will be wet," he warned them, "and cold."

Torches found and lit, they made their way past the grate. Water ran underneath their feet as they descended the narrow staircase to reach the lower level. The torches they held were unable to dispel the gloom of this place. The panther took the lead now, Luxor bringing up the rear, swinging his torch from side to side, intent on every detail. Stanis padded soundlessly in the shadows, the whites of his eyes the only visible feature on his face.

The Searcher of Souls trod warily over the rough, uneven stones, negotiating the labyrinth. Counting his paces, he checked their progress against the charts of the city-builders. They were moving steadily downward, well below recent construction sites of the Maze, down into the bedrock of the escarpment that the First Mother chose as the resting place for her flock, a ragged bunch of wayfarers bound together by their unique talents, bringing with them volumes of forgotten knowledge, the remnants of a former world or worlds, no one knew for sure. Finding shelter and protection in the rocks, they built a small community around a stone altar carved into the rocks that thrust upward from the valley floor. The records from those times were crude affairs, written on scraped sheepskins using ink made of plant juice. Stanis led them toward a destination that was little more than a circle penned on a map more than five centuries ago.

"Stanis, look to your left."

Luxor spoke quietly, but his voiced boomed in the hush of the vast emptiness. Stanis pulled aside a blanket that served as a crude door, his torch illuminating an inhabited place, the walls lined with baskets and jars. Hoisting an enormous club found leaning against a wall, he held it toward Ladon's torch. The healer bent his head over the carved wooden surface, studying it for a long moment before lifting a worried face to his companions.

"It's been notched on the end with a knife. The notches are caked with blood, some of it old, most of it fresh, certainly within the past few hours."

Since their descent into darkness, Luxor followed Stanis' lead without a challenge. What doubts he had, he kept hidden. With this discovery, he was exultant, all faith restored.

"Lead on, Searcher!"

Stanis picked up the pace. On they went, the soft padding of Stanis' sandals followed by a measured tread, a heavy boot sole bringing up the rear. Without warning, Stanis stumbled over something in his path, Ladon's quick reflexes helping keep him upright. The Searcher lowered his torch, revealing a dead man slumped across the floor, his eyes wide and staring. Luxor crouched beside him, examining the slash that had slit open his throat.

And then they heard Ladon whisper, "We have found him."

Ladon looked down on an inert body bound like an animal readied for slaughter. Two more torches added light to his. Pools of blood, most of them already congealing, stood between a score of grooves cut into the chest. More blood dripped steadily down his ribs to form a shallow puddle on the broken stones. What looked to be a deep gash in the right temple bled sluggishly, staining the golden hair with gore. Even in the ruddy light of the torches, his skin was like that of a corpse, bloodless, waxy, his lips blue and his eyes sunken into his skull. Only the slow throb of vein in his neck served as witness that Tyre lived.

The High Healer of Pelion stood with his torch extended, aghast at the cost of the miracle he had so lately celebrated in the tower chamber. How dare they congratulate themselves on an event wrung from such torment? Rebellion rose within him, he, Ladon, the one chosen because of his lesser talents, the one raised to a position he had never coveted, never deserved. He dismissed his vow without remorse. He would enter Tyre and heal him from within. Anything less might imperil his patient. Kneeling beside the broken body, he reached out his hand—

"Healer, weigh it carefully."

Ladon rocked back onto his heels at the power of Stanis' inner voice.

"We see only a tiny part of the mystery. Are you sure your version of the truth is correct? You see the mutilation of his flesh, the proof of his suffering. Yet what else came to pass here? He was bound and helpless, but found enough strength to reach out to the Silver One. He was tortured, but another seems to have died in his place. Is it possible that he has not been punished, but spared from certain death? You are confident that you can touch his mind and heal his wounds, yet he has been with the twisted adept for hours. Can you heal the wounds in his mind as well? Could it be that we must wait for one who can truly restore him to health?"

The High Healer of Pelion bowed his head.

"Contrition is unnecessary. All of us are to be tested. Your trial begins now. Tell us what we can do."

A great river of peace running through him, Ladon settled to his work, blessing Beal as he did so for his meticulous teaching. Running his hands over his patient, he was grateful Tyre would feel nothing. Then he began to give orders, his voice firm and controlled in the cavernous silence surrounding them.

"Remove the gag, cut loose the bonds, and begin massaging his ankles and wrists. The circulation in his hands and feet must be nearly gone. Luxor, find some way to group the torches together. I must be able to see."

As his helpers went about their chores, Ladon began to take stock. Finding Tyre's skin cold and clammy to the touch, Ladon unfastened the clasp at his throat and threw his cloak over Tyre's lower body, tucking it around his hips and legs, rubbing him with its rough texture. Having cut him free, Stanis knelt at his feet, working the bluish skin marked by deep indentations. At Ladon's request, Luxor's cloak joined his as a blanket, while Stanis' was folded into a pillow and placed beneath Tyre's head. As the torches were arranged, Ladon began to see the injuries in more detail.

"Luxor, start on his wrists while Stanis continues with his ankles. Keep an eye on his face and tell me if you see him flinch or react in any way to what I'm doing."

The grizzled head nodded and set to work.

Taking a clean white square of cloth from one of his pockets, Ladon began to wipe away the blood. The cuts on Tyre's chest were many and deep, but he was suspicious and puzzled by the amount of blood. As the cloth turned from white to red in his hands, he found the stab wound and felt his stomach lurch. The light was bad, but after dabbing away to clear the field of the wound, he found the edges of the incision and guessed they signified a deep thrust. Lowering his head to the ribs, he could hear no hiss that would indicate a punctured lung. By the time he lifted his head, the wound had already refilled with blood.

"Luxor, take a torch and search for a knife. I need to see the length of the blade."

Working quickly, he took clean linen bandages from his pouch and formed a pad, pressing it tightly to the lips of the wound. As he'd feared, the pad was soaked through in a matter of minutes. Despairing, he cursing himself for not being better prepared, knowing that none of his bottles and packets held a remedy for this unrelenting flow of blood. Pressure did not work, nor could he attempt surgery in these primitive conditions. In any case, with a wound this deep, sutures would accomplish nothing. Unless he could stop the bleeding, Tyre would die before they could get him up the stairs. Then, he heard Beal's voice in the lecture hall:

"We must never forget the legacy we hold in trust from our ancestors. The lure of the new encourages us to dismiss techniques that were used with great success in the past. They were simple remedies and available to everyone. Search through the old volumes and you will find proof of the democracy of healing."

"Stanis, what do you know of this place? I know it's old, but was it ever inhabited?"

Stanis disappeared into the surrounding shadows without explanation. Ladon shrugged and tripled his efforts, holding the pad firmly over the wound while he used his free hand to rub life and warmth into the stiffened limbs. Luxor appeared over his shoulder, disappointment written clearly on his rugged face.

"There's no knife, healer. I did find this."

He held up a braided quirt stained with congealed blood. Ladon shuddered and made no answer. Stanis emerged from the darkness, his hand clenched and outstretched toward Ladon; a waterfall of silver ash fell into Ladon's open palm. Stanis' inner voice quivered with barely controlled emotion.

"Sacred ash from the first fire. The ancient altar lies directly under the one in the Sanctum. From its flame the new one was kindled."

Swiftly, Ladon pulled away the pad and sprinkled the silvery ash over the exposed wound. Packing it firmly, he bandaged it with fresh strips of cloth. Finally, he turned his attention to the head wound, cleaning away the gore, most of which was caked and crusted over the abrasion. Finding the skin around the gash angry and swollen, he spread an oily salve over it and applied yet another strip of cloth, tying it loosely to avoid any pressure. Leaning down to check the knife wound, he almost laughed, so relieved was he to see the whiteness of the bandages.

Not long after, Tyre's fingers flexed.

"He wakes."

At Ladon's silent warning, Stanis and Luxor retreated into the shadows. Ladon edged closer to Tyre's head. His eyelids were fluttering now, his fists clenched against the agony of returning consciousness. Reaching for his pouch, Ladon pulled from it a tiny flask.

Twin pools of bottomless pain regarded him, the pupils so enormous there was little trace of blue. His breathing was rapid and shallow now as he tried to move his torn chest as little as possible. Ladon held his finger to the drawn mouth before Tyre could speak.

"Say nothing and try not to move. We've found you and I've stopped the bleeding. Now, take a drop of this."

Ladon raised the heavy head as gently as he could so as to cradle it in his lap.

"You must open your mouth," Ladon repeated quietly, wondering if he was being understood. Eyes closed, Tyre seemed to rest for awhile. Then, slowly, obediently, his lips parted, and a stream of blood leaked out of the corners of his mouth. Horrified, Ladon reached for another cloth, wiping away the blood from his bitten mouth and tongue. Satisfied that this was not a sign of internal bleeding, he poured a drop of clear liquid into Tyre's mouth and watched him swallow. His pulse grew stronger as the fiery restorative coursed through his veins.

". . . cold . . ."

Ladon pulled the second cloak up over Tyre's chest, seeing him flinch as the rough fabric settled over the open cuts. The pulse in his throat grew more regular, and in time, the golden lashes fluttered open again. His eyes were more focused this time; a question was forming in their depths. As he struggled to speak, Ladon lifted his fingers to the cracked lips again. But Tyre would not be silenced. His voice was low and ragged, his speech slurred and difficult to understand.

"Belwyn . . . told . . ."

"I remember. Your friend, Belwyn, was a healer. He told you something. Something about healing?"

It was only a guess, but it seemed to satisfy Tyre. His eyes closed in gratitude for the translation, then flickered open again, intent on Ladon.

". . . an . . . easy . . . death . . ."

Startled, Ladon knew exactly what those eyes were asking him. Surely Beal had not told his pupil that a healer killed . . . until he recalled the painful honesty of his teacher in the House of Healing and remembered the first time he had been forced to offer a painless death to a victim of the bone-eating sickness. He couldn't gainsay Beal's teachings, but he could deny the request.

"What your friend said is true, but only for those who have no chance of recovery. I know you are in pain, but if you don't develop a fever, there is every chance that you'll recover both health and strength. My vows forbid me to offer you an easy death."

As he spoke, Tyre's eyes grew dull and cloudy. Ladon read in them a hopelessness that bewildered him. He thought his explanation would comfort Tyre; instead, it brought him grief. Confused, he set about work again, and after checking the head wound, decided to replace the bandage. As he lifted way the bloodied cloth, Tyre's tormented eyes latched onto it. Again, the dry, cracked lips framed words, so softly this time that Ladon was forced to bend his ear within an inch of Tyre's mouth.

". . . save . . . gift . . ."

Touched, Ladon smiled his understanding. Folding the cloth in a careful square, he placed it in his pouch for safekeeping and withdrew a small bottle containing an emerald elixir.

"Drink again, Tyre, and rest. When you're strong enough, we'll move you to the House of Healing. I'll give the cloth to Kara so she can keep it safe for you."

Tyre's lips trembled as he drank. As Ladon lowered the blonde head onto the makeshift pillow, his eyelids closed. In the wavering light of the torches, the golden lashes glittered with tears.

Ladon spoke silently to his companions.

"The second drug is a strong opiate. He'll fall into a deep sleep and will not awaken for hours. I've called for a litter to meet us in the laundry. We'll have to carry him up the stairs. Stanis, you'll support his upper body while Luxor lifts his legs and I hold his head."

Two strong hands descended on Ladon's shoulders, one of them black-skinned and pink-palmed, the other brown and horny with calluses. Not until that moment did Ladon realize he had not been tempted to use his gifts and had functioned as efficiently as he had ever done with all his powers intact.

The faithful hound, together with the panther and the wolf, lifted up their thoughts to the tower chamber to receive the Fifteenth Mother's fervent benediction.

The House of Healing lay in the heart of the city, surrounded by terraced gardens and fruit trees, many of which were beginning to blossom in the early spring of the new year. Constructed at the same time as the Sanctum, it was built of the same white stone. Red tiles topped the gently sloping roofs. The passages that led to different parts of its interior were open to the air and ornamented with graceful arches supported by slender, fluted columns. Built in a large square, a garden lay at the center, onto which each interior door and window opened. There, on its broad avenues and benches, children played, invalids sunned themselves, and visitors held the hands of loved ones. The green-garbed healers were a constant presence, greeting new patients and counseling others; sitting patiently beside those who could not express their hurts and fears; speaking quietly to those who needed affirmation and consolation.

Vena passed through avenues that sang to her of bygone days; of her long tenure there as apprentice, Master, and High Healer; of all-night vigils spent with Beal as they struggled over the arrival or departure of a soul of Pelion; of patients and friends, teachers and students. This was the close-knit community on which she turned her back almost twenty years ago, choosing instead a life that offered little companionship and less tangible rewards.

Today Vena limped slowly along the manicured pathways, feeling rather than seeing Kara, who walked silently by her side, unsmiling, eyes downcast, everything about her evidencing discontent and deep, abiding, dread.

Hoping a stroll through the gardens might restore Kara's spirits, Vena abandoned the idea as the girl grew paler with each step. Seeing a honey-colored head of hair before her, Vena steered Kara toward Chloe's beckoning hand and together they passed into a counseling chamber. After nodding to those assembled around the circular table, Vena motioned for Kara to sit beside her. The room was warm from the heat of the sun spilling into the atrium, yet Vena noted that Kara pulled her woolen cloak tightly around her. Sighing, Vena lowered herself into the only cushioned chair at the table, sending a thankful glance to Ladon, whose never-failing thoughtfulness extended to her aching bones and swollen joints.

As everyone settled into their chairs, Vena took inventory: Chloe and Maenon were holding hands, not unusual unless one considered the tightness of their grips. They are afraid, Vena realized, but of what? Ladon claimed her attention as he introduced the man sitting beside him.

"Kara," he indicated a hawk-nosed man wearing the uniform of a Legionnaire, "this is Idas, a healer who works with the sick and injured among the Legion."

Before he could continue, a concerned Maenon sent a silent query to Vena, who answered with words spoken so sharply they startled Kara and caused Maenon to lift his eyebrows in surprise.

"We will withhold nothing from Kara. She has tended Tyre these three days and knows this meeting concerns how we may best help him. I urge you to speak plainly, sparing no truth"

Sweet-voiced Chloe sent Kara a compassionate look.

"You mustn't worry, Kara. Tyre is so very strong. "

Vena's patience was nearing its limit. If she was interpreting the healers' behavior correctly, they were running out of time. Three days in the House of Healing and Tyre was no better. This was no time for Chloe to mouth pleasantries. Vena intervened.

"I assume you invited Idas because he's an expert in sword and knife wounds."

"For that reason, I brought him here yesterday to probe the wound."

Ladon behaved in his usually calm, cool manner, but Vena knew better. The triumph of finding Tyre alive and transporting him to the House of Healing had been the climax of Ladon's career. Now he worried over the possibility of losing Tyre entirely, a triumph turned to tragedy.

"Tyre ran a slight fever the first day, a natural reaction to the shock and the beating, but the lacerations on his upper body appeared to be clean and free from infection. There was no sign of trouble until yesterday."

After a few minutes of uncomfortable silence, during which Kara's lips tightened into a thin line, Maenon spoke up, his light, calm voice in startling contrast to what it described. He addressed Vena only, avoiding eye contact with Kara.

"He woke yesterday morning, raving, pulling at the bandages over the knife wound. He actually succeeded in removing them before we could restrain him. The violence of his actions caused the bleeding to begin again. It was at that time that Ladon contacted Idas. We thought it possible that we might have overlooked something and that Idas should assist."

"Was Kara asked to leave Tyre's room during the procedure?"

"Yes," Ladon said. "We thought it best."

Clearly, Vena noted, Kara did not agree.

Next, Vena turned her attention to Idas, impatient for him to begin. When his eyes darted nervously about the room, Vena was reminded of her first oral examination in front of her teachers. Idas sat at table with four of the most experienced healers in Pelion and was understandably tongue-tied. Vena took pity on him.

"Describe the wound, healer."

Responding to her tone of command, Idas cleared his throat and was off, reporting with the crisp clarity ingrained in each student by the Master Teachers of the House. His earnestness and intensity pleased Vena, although his observations were troubling.

"He was unconscious again by the time I arrived, so I was able to examine him thoroughly without adding to his pain." After a quick glance in Kara's direction, Idas turned his attention to Vena, gaining confidence as he spoke. This was his specialty, after all, having spent five years working for the Legion and rarely losing a patient. "The wound is not a slash, but a puncture. Judging from the incision, the weapon was extremely sharp, a skinning knife, perhaps, with a blade of between five and six inches. No vital organs were touched, which is something of a miracle. There is no sign of infection or other complications."

Idas looked around the table for a moment, took a deep breath, and forged on.

"I have little else to offer, except this observation." At this, Vena's eyes narrowed. "That wound was not made in the heat of anger. It was a cool, calculated incision made by someone who knew exactly what he was doing. Whoever stabbed Tyre intended for him to bleed to death. I would guess that the person who did this uses a knife as competently as a surgeon," he paused, "or a butcher."

"Were you able to halt the bleeding after the wound was re-opened?"

Idas deferred to Ladon, whose careworn face was bleak.

"Yes, Mother."

Annoyed at Ladon's slowness, not to mention his obvious reticence to explain the reason for this emergency meeting, Vena turned to Maenon, only to meet another set of mournful eyes. At last, Chloe disengaged her hand from her mate to turn her chair so she could look directly at Vena and Kara. The musical rise and fall of her voice blunted the harshness of the message she conveyed.

"Understand this: Idas was our last hope." When the Legion healer shifted uncomfortably in his chair, Chloe encompassed him in her gaze as well. "The fault is not yours, Idas. We had hoped," she paused as if refreshing her memory; ". . . we had hoped that something could be learned from the nature of the incision. You see, there is no infection, no internal damage, the bleeding has stopped, his fever has broken; yet Tyre is dying."

Kara lowered her head into her hands. She knows, thought Vena, but has been avoiding the truth, putting all her faith in the healers, her resentment building as she watches Tyre grow weaker despite their care. Sensing that words would bring no comfort, Vena sat quietly in the sun-filled room. The voices of children playing in the atrium rose on the breeze. Upon hearing them, Vena tested her fortitude, found it sufficient to the task, and began the course of action she had feared was unavoidable since the moment Kara had beaten on the tower door.

"If you have exhausted the possibilities for explaining his inability to respond to treatment, then you must believe the sickness lies in his mind. Tell us the evidence of your diagnosis and your recommendations."

Perhaps it was the shrewdness of Vena's guess, or perhaps the healers were simply relieved at hearing their suspicions voiced. Whatever the reason, her refusal to admit defeat heartened them. Ladon rushed to answer.

"The first few times he woke, he was so weak and feverish he could barely lift his head. Even with Kara beside him, encouraging him to take nourishment, he resisted our efforts. We were finally reduced to using restraints to enable us to force liquid and drugs down his throat." Ladon frowned in distaste. "Then, yesterday morning, he seemed to be stronger, his eyes more focused. We were hopeful, weren't we, Kara?" Ladon asked, receiving a short nod by way of a reply. "After standing vigil all that time, Kara left the room for rest and a meal. When Tyre woke in the afternoon, Chloe was with him." With a swift gesture, Ladon passed the telling to her.

"We felt it unwise to bind him when he slept. His resistance to our efforts was so intense, so violent, that we feared such an action would destroy what little regard he holds for Ladon and me. For him to wake, bound as he was in that awful place," Chloe shivered, "was distasteful to us all."

"Ladon was exhausted and I insisted he rest. I stayed with Tyre, who seemed to be resting comfortably. All of a sudden, he," Chloe's voice broke, "he went mad. He pulled himself up somehow and ripped at the bandages, moaning at the pain of movement, but working at the cloths like someone deranged. I went to him immediately, trying to calm him, calling his name over and over. He seemed to see me for a moment and paused, his face troubled, his eyes searching me as if he had a question he couldn't quite remember. At first I thought he recognized me from the journey to Pelion, but then he," Chloe turned her full attention to the pale girl by Vena's side, "he called me 'Kara.' We look nothing alike, but the drugs and the pain must have made my voice sound like yours. I told him that I was not Kara, that you would soon return, and he grew more frantic than ever. Ladon and Maenon answered my call, and soon we had him in restraints. That was yesterday evening. Since that time he has not returned to consciousness, but moves further and further away from us."

As Chloe finished, Maenon began. As he spoke, Vena saw for herself the accuracy of Luxor's and Stanis' report concerning his mystical ability to sense both Tyre and Beal. She knew Maenon still obeyed her command that Tyre not be read, yet somehow he was attuned to Tyre. This was a new and entirely unsuspected variation of adept powers, and one that called for further study. Hiding that thought away for another day, Vena turned her attention to Maenon.

"Chloe's voice brought Tyre back to consciousness, but when she told him you were not there, he tried to achieve what Ladon denied him in the tunnels. Luxor found Grasos' keys on the dead man, so we must assume that Tyre was lured from the cell, perhaps by a tale that you were ill or injured."

The light, reasonable voice stilled, and Maenon's eyes grew dreamy, as if he looked at a far horizon that remained hidden from view.

"He holds you in his arms, Kara, but it's not you he holds. His grief is such that he has closed the door behind him. Another has locked the door, trapping him within . . ."

When his musings caused him to drift away, Chloe's touch called him back to the table. Maenon started, blinked, and completed his diagnosis with his usual composure.

"Since there is no physical reason for his illness, it is my belief, and that of Ladon and Chloe, that Tyre believes Kara to be dead. For this reason, he has decided to die as well."

The clear voices of the children ceased as a healer called them inside. A single robin chirped in the stillness of the garden. Kara turned to Vena.

"What can I do?"

"The healers make your course clear. If Tyre could return to consciousness, if only for a moment, he could see you and know that you live. Since he has turned away from life, you will have to go to him."

Kara's furrowed brow revealed her perplexity.

"But I've been with him from the beginning!"

Vena went to work, hoping that Nerissa's single session with Kara concerning the nature of adept abilities had been worthwhile.

"Nerissa explained to you that Tyre called you by reaching into your mind." Kara nodded. "We are asking that you save him by calling for him as he called for you."

"She also told me others share this gift, and that she and all the members of the Council have this ability. Why can't you do this for Tyre?"

Kara's voice rose to plead with her other mother, the one who had never failed her.

Slowly, with growing force, Vena shook her head.

"It cannot be. Any of us might try this thing, yet how could we convince Tyre that you live? If he nears the end of his strength, as Maenon believes, there might be only one opportunity to reach him."

"But I know nothing about . . ."

"This has nothing to do with knowledge. This has to do with faith—your faith in what I tell you—and most of all, faith in your love for Tyre." Vena shifted in her chair, shutting out the others gathered around the table, talking solely to the one who was silently begging Vena to rescue her. "Do you remember when you came to me?" Kara blinked, her lips trembling. "I warned you that if you chose to stay with Tyre, you would not be released from your vow a second time. It is time for you to fulfill that vow."

Kara said nothing, but sat enveloped in the dread Vena had sensed earlier. She's more than afraid, Vena realized. She's terrified, as anyone would be if asked to attempt something that has never been done by anyone living in this world. Adept children were introduced to their gifts by family members in well-known surroundings. Kara's thoughts were touched by Tyre calling to her from the ice-cold belly of the Maze, his body broken, his whole being intent on seeing her one last time. What must that mean to Kara? Did she associate this opening of her mind with gladness and hope, as Vena did when the Thirteenth Mother took her on her first mental journey? Or was it something to be dreaded because of its associations with the pain and loneliness Tyre was experiencing when he called out for her? If this was the case, Vena must ease Kara's fears as she had done on a chilly autumn evening when she visited Kara for the purpose of bringing her into the Maze. That girl, too, had been frightened, but even so, she had done what Vena asked.

"Tell me your fears, child."

"Nerissa says that an adept," Kara stumbled over the unfamiliar word, "feels everything in the mind they contact." She glanced quickly at the faces of the healers gathered around her. "All of you say he is in pain, even agony. How can I be of use if I, too, am in pain?"

Chloe answered before Vena could intervene.

"What Nerissa says is true. One of the most difficult things a healer must do is experience their patient's pain so they may learn of it and thus chose the best way to cure it. The healers of Pelion have been using their gifts in this way for five hundred years. Nerissa is a hetaera and so not trained as a healer. What she does not tell you is that at the same time you feel Tyre's pain, a part of your mind always knows that it is his pain and not yours. That does not make the hurting any less, but it ensures that you will not lose your ability to focus on your task."

Maenon continued as if he and his mate spoke from the same mouth.

"You must also consider that Tyre has retreated from his body. When this happens, a patient is often hiding from the pain, buried deep somewhere in their mind to escape it. As you draw closer to the center of his being, the pain will lessen."

Kara listened closely, her eyes shut tight so as to allow no tears to escape. When Maenon finished, she spoke in a voice no louder than a whisper.

"How will I find him? And if I find him, how can I unlock this door you speak of, this door that someone else has shut?" Her voice broke, and she was sobbing. "What if I fail and I am the cause of his death?"

The old woman made no answer. Sensing Vena's inability to fulfill the role she had always played in her life, Kara stiffened in disbelief. Then, in the face of utter abandonment, Beal's littlest ernani stood true.

"I love him, and I love us together more than I love myself. I will do what you ask, but if," Kara swallowed hard, ". . . if I lose him, I'll join him in death."

Vena resisted the urge to stroke the fine mass of dark curls away from the heart-shaped face that gazed at her so fiercely. The woman who faced her, proudly announcing her ability to choose, was no longer the winsome, pliable girl of the garden.

"The time has come for you to test your courage and your love."

Vena gestured for Kara to rise.

"Go with Chloe. Soon I'll join you and we'll go to Tyre."

Kara followed Chloe out of the room.

Vena felt a pang in the region of her heart. Her hand lifted instinctively toward her breast, its palsy transformed to violent tremors. Vena tried to steady it, but for the first time, the rebellious hand would not obey. Troubled by its refusal to do her will, she used her other hand to draw it back into her lap, catching the frown on Ladon's face. Shrugging off his concern, she matched him frown for frown as she debated her next duty. Upon being dismissed, Maenon and Idas rose and left her alone with the High Healer.

"You have not been to Council these three days. Luxor reports that a horse was stolen from the Calvary stables two nights ago. It is his belief that the twisted adept has fled the city, although we've no proof of it. Also, Stanis found Grasos yesterday. As we feared, he is dead, stabbed repeatedly in the back and dragged to a forgotten corridor. I said the rite of passing at dawn."

Ladon nodded and looked off into the atrium.

Vena's vision was a different one.

Grasos' hulking form bent over her as she sat at a table in crisp black robes, interviewing candidates to serve as personal bodyguards for the novice class of ernani. Vena described the duties firmly and dispassionately: bodyguards were ultimately responsible for the physical well-being of their charges. They must protect the ernani from any injury while in their care, but they must hide their duties under the guise of brutish jailers. She was careful to emphasize the fact that there would be no rewards of trust or friendship with their charges. No one could know the truth of their loving concern. Grasos gazed down at her from his incredible height and spoke the halting words that had comforted her for nearly two decades.

"I will know."

In the early morning hours she said farewell to Grasos. Now she ushered him into a part of her, confident that his essence had not truly passed away.

"It's time, Ladon. Call the others here and wait with them. I will join you as soon as she's settled. We may not interfere, but we can help her cross over and shield her as much as we can against the pain. I . . . I will need your help, for I reach the end of my strength."

Ladon was at her side in a moment, reaching out to touch her with a healing hand. She struck it away with a cry.

"I forbid you to touch me! I passed the point of remedy long ago. I cannot allow the distraction."

Sensing Ladon's hurt, she strove to make him understand.

"Don't you see? My age brings with it wisdom; my failing body makes me treasure the possibilities of the mind; my discomfort ensures that I remain continually sensitive to my humanity, my mortality. Everything exists in balance; two parts create the whole. Without these things, I would wield my powers unhindered—an empress, or worse, a goddess, with no one able to match my limitless abilities."

She spoke of mysteries that were beyond him. He took her arm without comment and helped her into the garden, still lit by the last rays of the setting sun. Spring's promise lingered in the rapidly cooling air. At her feet, pale green shoots of narcissus pushed out of the loamy soil. In another day, free of the soil's hindrance, they would begin their gradual unfolding of leaf and flower, sending their sharp, unmistakable scent onto the skirts of the wind.

Clearing her mind, Vena lifted her eyes to the sky, choosing, one last time, to serve the light.

Chapter 21

Resurgam

A STRAND OF burnished hair fell across his brow. A bandage covered his right temple, a match to his alabaster skin. His chest and ribs were tightly wrapped in bands of soft linen while a cloth covered him below the waist. He seemed a pale stranger, his usually firm lips slack and slightly open as he breathed. Her mind rebelled, refusing to translate this idle creature into Tyre. Relief spread through her. She need participate in this farce no longer. Confident of her discovery, she turned to go, eager to flee this place, hating the smells and sights of disease, knowing what no one else seemed to understand—that this was not a House of Healing, but a House of Death.

"It's Tyre, Kara. Your Tyre."

Looking into piercing grey eyes she had trusted and obeyed since childhood, her elation vanished. Uttering a sound between a sob and a sigh, she turned back to observe the long, still body awaiting her approach. The healers had kept her away from him, their concern for him outweighing any thoughts they might have for Kara's needs. She was placed in a corner and allowed to watch, growing angrier and angrier at all of them, especially Ladon, who she thought truly cared about her well-being.

"Touch him, Kara."

Reaching out, her fingers tensed, she brushed aside the stray lock, restoring the square symmetry of his forehead. As her skin came into contact with those silken strands, she recognized the texture and color of hair that could only be Tyre's. Encouraged, she leaned over so as to run her hands over him, refreshing her memory of his shape and form despite the alien bandages. It was disquieting to touch him intimately, yet receive no welcome response; even when her palms lingered over his thighs and groin, there was no reaction. Running her hands back up to his chest, her fingers lingered over the sunburst scar peeking over the top of the bandages. As she did so, Tyre's lips moved. Exultant that he responded to her touch, she looked down and, for the first time, saw the restraints. She'd heard what the healers said, but hadn't grasped their full meaning. That Tyre, her Tyre, who hated the manacles, was wrapped up tight by multiple leather bands angered her to the point that she missed the first few words of what Chloe was saying.

". . . and hold his hand to make entry. Once that is accomplished . . ."

"I will hold him as he has held me every night since the first moon of our joining!"

Kara plunged on, removing hairpins from the knot at the back of her neck and throwing them against the stones beneath her feet.

"All the restraints must be removed. And you must give me your word that if he returns with me, no one will ever chain him again."

The last hairpin fell and she shook her head to release her hair. Luminous grey eyes blinked once in acquiescence to her request. Chloe moved to the bed and loosed the restraints.

"I also want your promise that we'll be left alone." When Chloe seemed to protest, Kara turned on her with nostrils flaring. "You've told me repeatedly that this task is mine alone. What help can you possibly offer?"

Her sarcasm was cruel, and the honey-haired woman blanched, but the Fifteenth Mother nodded assent. Kara stretched out her hand.

"And you must give me a knife."

At this, Chloe gasped, looking beseechingly at the Fifteenth Mother, but again, the old woman nodded, patting the healer's shoulder to allay her fears, and went to a large oaken chest standing against the far wall of the chamber. Pulling open a drawer, she removed a small silver knife and pressed its handle firmly into Kara's waiting palm.

"This is a surgeon's knife that cuts deep so quickly there will be little pain. Everything will be as you require; you have my word. Let us help you lie beside him, and then we will be gone."

The Fifteenth Mother pulled aside the sheet and Kara slid beside Tyre. Chloe helped position him so that his head rested on her breast and her left arm could slip easily around his shoulder. She held his right hand in hers. The Fifteenth Mother floated the sheet over them. A lined, drooping face regarded Kara. With a pang of guilt, Kara decided she had never seen the Fifteenth Mother look so weary. Her palm touched Kara's forehead in blessing and she turned away, her voice coming back to Kara as she moved toward the open door.

"You will be alone now, but not abandoned. Remember that, Kara. Never abandoned." The tall figure in black paused with her hand resting on the door handle. For a moment Kara thought her narrow shoulders stooped. Then she was as erect and self-possessed as ever.

"You are angry with me, and in many ways I deserve your contempt. I make no excuses for my actions. No matter what happens, I forgive you, as I hope you will someday forgive me."

Without a backward glance, the Fifteenth Mother passed over the threshold and closed the door quietly behind her.

The room was warm from the many braziers lining the walls. The bed was soft, the bedclothes wonderfully clean and fresh-smelling. She had not slept the night through since the Day of Choice. Tyre's head was heavy on her breast, his hand limp and lifeless in hers. Even so, she held him gratefully, kissing his hair and smelling his scent that lingered over the smell of salves and herbs. She removed her hand from his for a moment to check the placement of the knife beneath the pillow. Comforted, she took a deep cleansing breath and began the concentration exercise Nerissa taught her that first awful day when she waited in the dayroom while others went in search of Tyre. It took time for her to find a peaceful place amongst the jumble of her thoughts, but at last she was ready. Closing her eyes, she drew a picture in her mind and stepped forward into blackness . . . .

A wall of pain hit her as she crossed over the void, almost causing her immediate retreat. Never had she experienced such unremitting agony; her head throbbed mercilessly, her breasts and stomach ached under tightly wound bandages, every breath was an effort that renewed the stabbing fire of a wound between her ribs. Gasping, she tried to remember everything the healers advised, and gradually found the part of her that was unhurt, retreating as much as she dared into that corner of her mind. The pain receded somewhat, though it clung stubbornly to her, wrapping around her like a shroud. Resting for a moment, she regained her equilibrium before taking a tentative first step toward familiarizing herself with her surroundings.

As she began to explore, she was shaken by the realization that this place was not unlike the Maze. The pathways and corridors were lined with doors, most of which stood open and inviting, the light from within streaming out into the hallway and illuminating her way. Soon she was over her initial shock and relieved to find that what she had dreaded was well-known, even ordinary. Once, she looked around for Grasos, half-expecting his massive form to turn a corner and lead her to Tyre. Chiding herself for her momentary lapse, she heard Nerissa's parting words.

"Each adept begins as you will, entering a mind well-known to them. With natives of Pelion, it is usually a parent; sometimes a sibling or grandparent. With those not native born, the Fifteenth Mother makes the first contact, taking them with her until their fears are lessened."

Nerissa's eyes had glowed, a flame glimmering in their usually placid depths.

"It will be strange, although not truly frightening, for you will be with one you love and who loves you in return. The joining of bodies is one kind of union; there, you will experience another. Go carefully at first, learning your way, remembering that much of what you see will be but shadows of the past."

Heartened, Kara moved toward a shaft of sunlight emanating from a door flung wide open. Crossing the threshold, she found herself on a broad plain covered in waist-high grass; the sky a flat, cloudless blue. Nothing moved on its vast emptiness except the heads of the grasses as they bent with the wind. Unaccustomed to such open spaces, she was almost overpowered by the fierce wildness of this untamed landscape. Shielding her eyes from the sun, she could see a mounted figure approaching her, riding at a breakneck pace. In the next moment she recognized who was hugging the horse's neck and waved wildly at Tyre, expecting every moment for him to look up and see her. Yet he rode past her without a glance, his eyes slitted against the wind in his face. Disappointed, she withdrew, wondering why he had ignored her, until she realized that this memory belonged to a Tyre she had never known.

In another room, a smaller version of Tyre, a boy of twelve, she thought, sat on the bank of a shallow lake, laughing up into the face of a small man with short brown curls. "Belwyn!" she thought, recognizing Tyre's tutor. Eager to see more, she was interrupted by the sound of music. A woman's voice lifted in song came from a door down the hall, this door, too, standing open and inviting.

As she drew closer, she recognized the song and the singer. Pushing her head inside, her hands wrapped around the door frame, she saw an eerie vision of herself sitting on the wooden chair in the cell, her head thrown back as she sang a song celebrating spring planting—the first song she ever sang for Tyre. He was in his accustomed place, lounging on the floor by the hearth, his skin turned bronze by the brightly-burning fire, his attention locked on her double. With a tightening in her throat, Kara observed his open adoration of her, something she was never able to see in that first moon of joining. The song ended, and she saw herself laughing, responding to his applause, but oblivious to the kindling of love in those piercing eyes. Unable to bear this reminder of her blindness, she retreated into the hallway.

She traveled more quickly now, glancing right and left as she went, finding herself in almost every room. In one of them, she stood naked, the moonlight streaming down over her head and shoulders, her skin turned to silver as she reached for her nightshift. Tyre stood in the opposite corner, his back to her, but his head turned over his shoulder, stealing covert glimpses of her nakedness. The air around her was heavy with sensuality yet again she had been insensible to it, persuading herself that he felt nothing for her.

As she moved deeper into the labyrinth, more doors were half-shut or only slightly ajar. Sensing that these were difficult memories, reluctance to invade his privacy kept her from investigating. Still, one door called again with the sound of music, and curiosity drew her on. She peered through the narrow aperture, flinching as she saw herself twirling in the rose and silver dress, laughing up into Dino's face. The other dancing figures were mere shadows; only her form, held tightly in Dino's arms, was illuminated. The air was almost unbreathable, so thick was it with jealousy and fear of betrayal. Unwilling to endure this moment a second time, she retreated, her image continuing its ghostly twirl amongst the swaying figures of the Gathering.

As Maenon predicted, the further away she moved from the point of entry, the less pain she felt, and that truth soon became her compass, her only way of negotiating this maze of interlocking corridors. Often she would choose one path, feel the pain increasing, and turn back, searching for a different route. Her travels took her increasingly toward passageways that were dim, lit by an occasional torch, rather than the sunlit passages that had characterized the early stages of her journey.

One door was especially forbidding—its iron door slightly ajar, and seemingly guarded by two silhouettes. As she came closer her confusion grew, for she recognized the shadows as those of the Fifteenth Mother and the man she'd identified earlier as Belwyn. At her approach, they moved closer together, preventing her entry or so much as a glance at what lay within. When a small boy with wildly tangled hair and tear-stained cheeks appeared from behind the door, the two guardians reached out for him, holding him firmly between them. Solemn-faced, he looked up at them, wiped away his tears, then reentered the room from whence he'd come. Calmed by the boy's new-found serenity, Kara moved on, looking backward over her shoulder at the two figures who now held each other's hand with, Kara decided, the intensity of lovers.

The hallway began to narrow until it was barely wide enough for her to pass. She held her hands in front of her for protection, for there was no light now, and she feared she would stumble. The darkness was a solid presence, her sense of panic at being unable to see forestalled because there was no longer any pain. Once freed of its weight, she felt stronger, more confident. Finally, she reached the last door.

Unlike the others, it was not situated on the side of a wall, but loomed directly in front of her, its sturdy timbers promising her either victory, or total defeat, for there was nowhere else to search. Tyre, her Tyre, lived somewhere beyond it, and she yearned for him, tired of the likenesses that filled the other rooms, that looked and sounded and moved as he did, but were mere phantoms. Testing the latch, she found it bolted. Maenon had mentioned the difficulty of entering, but provided no clue, no charm with which she could open this solid oaken barrier. She pushed against it with all her strength, knowing as she did so it would never yield. Hopeless, and wretchedly tired, she slid down the rough boards and curled up on the floor.

Leaning her head against the planks, she faced defeat. At that moment, the sound of whispering voices preceded the arrival of a presence entirely new to her, yet one which inspired no fear. The murmurings were indistinguishable, reminding her of wind rustling through dry leaves, or the trickling of water in one of the many fountains of Pelion. At one moment she could hear the sound of a child laughing fearlessly at the unknown; at another she heard the melody of a half-familiar lullaby. Comforted, she let the presence encompass her. The door was no longer so formidable. It became, instead, a puzzle, a riddle whose solution lay within her.

"Count your gifts, moonchild."

Startled, Kara obeyed the chorus of voices emerging from the chanted murmurs, answering by rote with the response drilled into her since childhood.

"My gifts are three: beauty, strength, fertility."

The chorus reprimanded her, not unkindly.

"These are gifts that all are given and all may give. Ask instead what is uniquely yours, what no one may give save you."

"My music is my greatest gift."

Again she was chided, forced to look deeper within herself.

"Many are given the gift of music. Ask instead what you alone bring the Golden One."

Baffled, Kara tried to understand the question. The golden one must be Tyre. As to the uniqueness of what she brought him, that was more difficult, especially since it demanded that she consider the question from his perspective rather than her own.

"I bring him refuge from loneliness, laughter that lifts his spirit, and forgiveness of things he cannot forgive himself."

Now came the most difficult question of all.

"What gift does he offer the Moonchild, whose silver orb balances nightly the daily journey of the sun?"

What did Tyre give her? She was ready to blurt out a thousand things, sure of his love, his desire, and his respect, each of them hard-won in days of heartache and compromise. But her voice was stilled with the sudden knowledge that these things were due to her from any man who received the gift of her love. The question demanded that she provide the balance, the harmonious interchange that bonded them together. What did Tyre offer her that none had offered her before?

She began slowly, working through the puzzle.

"He challenges me."

It sounded too simple, too pat. She must make herself clearer.

"I've always been loved and cherished because I yearned to please, because I couldn't bear to bring discord to anyone. Tyre dares me to be strong, to differ with him, to have my own opinions rather than adopting his for mine."

She was closer to the answer now, the words tumbling out effortlessly.

"He teaches me to risk, to dare, to endure, even when there is no hope."

Kara waited for judgment without fear. The door might block her way, but the possibility of defeat could not lessen the solid core of calm her answers gave her.

A fire began to glimmer on the ground before her, yet it was like no fire she had ever known, for its white flames burned without heat. All around her, the murmurings became a chorus of voices rising to a magnificent crescendo, pulsing in her ears until they became her heartbeats. Rising to her feet, she added her voice to theirs, singing the Hymn to Harmony, accompanied by the magnificent full chords of the unseen choir. Her voice was the voice of her love, rising high and clear until it was free of earthly things, and floated above all other sounds. Her last note hung pulsating in pure white light, its force radiating outward toward the door, the vibrations of the sound causing the timbers to quiver, rock, and finally splinter in an explosion that shattered all light and sound.

Picking her way through the wrecked debris of the door, she was drawn inside by the familiar sight of a long, lean, body lying stretched out on the well-worn coverlet of their bed in the cell. He seemed to sleep soundly, one arm flung over his head, the other hidden under a blue woolen cloak covering what appeared to be a lump in the bed. Her curiosity aroused, she spied a dark curl threading its way across the pillow beneath Tyre's head. Pulling away the cloak, she found her corpse.

The bodice of her favorite rose-colored dress was covered with rusty stains of dried blood leaking from a wound beneath her left breast. The corpse's face was ghastly, a skull with skin, the eyes open and staring, the hair dull and lifeless, although a great mass of it was held in Tyre's hand, his fingers laced through its curls. Kara stood unmoving for a long time, horrified at the sight of the corpse, yet touched by the depth of his devotion.

Stung into action, her first instinct was to bring light into the cell. Unfamiliar draperies hung over the high window. Once she pulled them aside, sunlight streamed in, pushing back the shadows. At the first touch of the sunlight on the corpse, it began to melt, a cloud of steam rising as it thawed, evaporating in front of her eyes until nothing was left, not even a damp stain on the coverlet.

Kneeling beside him on the stone floor, she began to stroke him, immediately sensing the difference between this Tyre and the one covered in bandages inside the House of Healing. His skin was warm, smooth-textured, and responsive. Recalling her success in the healing chamber, she traced the sunburst on his chest. He awoke slowly, muttering something she could not understand, his brow creased in a troubled frown, eyelids fluttering open, until, at last, he regarded her with an expression of growing confusion.

"I . . . I'm dreaming again . . ."

"I am no dream."

Obviously disoriented, he pulled himself into a sitting position, pushing his hair from his shoulders to his back. As he did so, that familiar gesture caused Kara's throat to constrict. How could she convince him she wasn't a dream?

"Touch me." She proffered her hand, palm upraised. "Touch me and you'll know that I live."

She put every morsel of love and longing for him into that plea. Widely-spaced blue eyes blinked once, twice, then looked away, refusing to meet her gaze.

"You are very like my Kara, but none of you are truly her."

Suddenly she knew that he, too, had searched those corridors, finding phantom after phantom and discarding them in turn. Where had he found the corpse?

"Why are you so sure that I'm not the real Kara?"

For the first time, she noticed how haggard his face was. When he replied, she caught a glimpse of the horror through which he'd lived.

"He beat me. Beat me with my father's quirt."

A shudder ran through him, causing him to reach for the bed frame, as if he needed its support to remain upright.

"None of it mattered, nothing mattered, because he said he killed her. And then," his voice broke, ". . . I found her body in a passageway nearby. I carried her here, thinking I would stay with her, but she was horrible, a horrible thing that couldn't be my Kara."

Noticeably weaker than when he began, he rested for a moment, sinking back to lean against the headboard.

"I tried to leave but the door was locked. And I . . . I was so tired . . ."

Kara was nearly ill with frustration. How could she prove herself to him?

"Do you remember when you lay in the tunnels, Tyre?"

He frowned before nodding, unwilling to remember and too exhausted to form a reply.

"Do you remember finding me in the solarium?"

Startled, he frowned and nodded.

"I was sitting in a window seat, dreaming of you, and suddenly you were there, promising never to leave me."

Slowly, so slowly that it barely seemed to move, his long-fingered hand reached toward her. She made herself wait as it lingered in mid-air and then drifted toward her, a forefinger tracing the line of her cheek. As it was removed, a single tear glistened on its tip.

"Kara . . .!"

His cry was cut off as she threw herself in his arms. He ran his hands through her hair, rocking her back and forth, whispering words of love. She could understand little of what he said, her relief so great that only gradually did she realize that his arms were shaking from the effort of holding her. Worried, she pulled away to see his hand tremble as he pushed away a lock of hair that had fallen into her eyes. An eyebrow cocked over a rueful blue eye.

"It seems I can't hold you as tightly as I wish."

Kara was instantly contrite. There wasn't time to enjoy one another's company. He lay white and cold in the healing chamber and she must bring him back.

"Come, Tyre. Rest your head on my breast."

She positioned herself as she lay on the bed in the healing chamber, holding her arms out to him as he moved toward her, seeking her warmth. Sighing, he relaxed as she began to hum under her breath, watching his eyelids grow heavy, his lashes almost touching the purple smudges of exhaustion that lay like bruises underneath each eye.

Kara closed her eyes against the cell. Focusing on the healing chamber, she drew a picture of it in her mind as Nerissa had taught her, taking care to make its outlines clearer, more distinct. Her lips grazed his ear as she whispered to him.

"We must go together into the darkness. Here is my promise: when we wake there will be no cell, no chains, and no slavery. We will wake together, or not at all."

Not until Kara stepped forward into the void did she remember the pain.

Tyre heard her scream a split-second before a like one was ripped from his throat. She held him tightly, but as she moved forward into the void, her grip loosened, forcing Tyre to rouse himself as the waves of pain sought to separate them. Realizing that she must have come through this to find him, his courage rose to meet hers. It was too easy to slip back into the place they left; they must go forward or be trapped forever in this tomb.

Together they pushed forward toward sanctuary, sensing its nearness. A pinprick of light danced before their eyes, urging them on. Kara was tiring, her energy sapped, the pain closing about her like a vise. Hearing her despairing cry, a great fury rose in Tyre. He was losing her for a second time, losing Kara, who had risked everything to answer his call, her daring spirit sound and true. The loss of her, the waste of the gifts she would not give to him, to others, to the world she gloried in, was not to be borne.

This could not be allowed. He, Tyre of Lapith, would not allow it.

"Help us!" he cried out to the world in general even as he readied himself to fall with Kara into the abyss.

"Help always comes when you least expect it!" Belwyn cried. *"We hear your call, young lord!"*

"Come, stripling," a gruff voice interrupted. *"It seems I must deny you death today as well."* Lycus' meaty hands found their way around Tyre's waist.

"Why must you always do things the hard way, long-hair?" Rhacius complained as he took hold of Tyre's right shoulder while Carmanor steadied him from the left.

As the honey-haired healer began her silver-tongued song, Nerissa spoke out of the darkness, calling to Kara, *"It's time! Time for the union I told you of!"*

Kara was growing stronger now, the pain dispersed by Chloe's song of healing. As she struggled forward, Tyre strove to help her across the abyss that separated them from the light.

Zelor urged him on, barking orders as usual.

"Strength and stamina are their own rewards. Put your back into it, ernani!"

Kara was so close that he could smell the fragrance of her hair. With one last joint effort, their minds met, and they were One.

A resonant bass voice Tyre had never heard before turned them away from the darkness, speeding them joyously toward the light.

"It is accomplished! For the first time, two have crossed over!"

Tyre was surrounded by the faces and voices of all who brought him here and all who tended him in the Maze. Each face brought with it memories, yet as he moved closer to the light, those memories were relived and rethought, every perception fine-tuned, as if his mind, now linked to the woman beside him, was re-forged. He had not been punished, but cherished, brought here for a grand experiment, one they had been perfecting long before he was born.

And Tyre fought them every step of the way; refusing to choose the innate goodness of Belwyn over the cruel demands of a blood-thirsty god, refusing to honor Hourn's love for his Nephele over a mindless tradition. They schooled him gently, this band of teachers. The sessions with Nerissa in the library were not meant to intimidate him, but to ease his ignorance of what was possible between a man and a woman. Rather than a jailor, Grasos was his protector, keeping him safe and preventing him from committing murder. The beating at the ropes was not their doing, but the result of his temper. Even then, his caretakers rose to the challenge, punishing him without leaving a mark and giving him Ladon to help him through the hours of misery and self-hatred. Zelor's arena was not a torture chamber, but a place to release his aggression and hostility. In the training room his body was changed from a youth to a man, giving him the strength necessary to pull himself up onto the back of a running horse and by doing so, save his own life. The beautiful bay was their gift to him, bred and trained for him years before his arrival, kept in reserve to reward him as soon as he turned toward the Path.

And the Sanctum was neither a place of emasculation and terror nor a house of worship. Instead, it was built as a place where the populous of Pelion could give their gifts. There, grateful citizens remembered forebears who were transported from a dying world to this one by the Makers, the Sowers of Seed, who asked of them a single favor in return, that they continue the cycle of giving, a request the First Mother honored even as she lit the first flame on the first altar.

The flame beckoned, kindled by generations of hope and planning. Kara and Tyre moved toward it in unison. From the source of that light could be heard the prophetic voice of the Fifteenth Mother:

"The covenant is fulfilled! In time, humanity will be as One, speaking mind to mind and heart to heart, until all who live on this new world of ours will inhabit the Realm of the Gift."

Chapter 22

Renaissance

"SO, LAZY ONE, you've finally awakened from your nap!"

Tyre looked up into a heart-shaped face. While he fought an impulse to grab a curl that had escaped the hairpins, Kara disappeared from view. A heap of clothes were thrown at him. A shower of giggles answered his muttered curse as he untangled the breeches, tunic, and riding boots she had dumped on top of the bed.

"Hurry up, ernani! Ladon says you may ride today! I've already been to the stable to warn Grudius of our arrival."

He dressed hurriedly, turning away from her as he did so, unwilling for her to see the scars and bandages still covering him after these long weeks of recuperation. Pulling up the breeches, sensing that she watched him, he grew awkward with the laces. By the time he'd finished, she was pulling away the draperies that darkened the healing chamber, allowing the bright afternoon sunshine to pour in from the atrium. Her back to him as she gazed out the window, beams of light seemed to emanate from her rather than the sun. His gaze lingered over her, only to stop in dismay.

"What are you wearing?"

Swinging around to face him, she pranced as daintily as a filly, brimming with barely contained laughter at his reaction. A silky blouse, cut full and open at the neck, revealed the slender column of her throat. Its cream-colored fabric was tucked neatly into a pair of loose breeches not unlike those Tyre had been issued in the Maze. Her feet were encased in leather riding boots that reached her knees, displaying her shapely calves. When she pivoted, allowing him to view her from all sides, Tyre felt a twinge of desire at the sight of her trim hips now freed from the enveloping folds of heavy skirts. Cursing his body, which could hardly obey the simplest of his commands, but was immediately responsive to her, he was just recovering his equanimity when her eyes, twinkling with mischief, caught his.

"I thought you, of all people, would appreciate my riding gear. I brought everything from home on my last visit, hoping that we'd be able to ride together at last."

Faced with the prospect of trying to conceal the affect of her loveliness on him for a full afternoon, it was difficult to muster much enthusiasm.

"It's just that I've always seen you in a dress. Breeches must be comfortable," he added lamely, "as well as practical."

Her laughter died and she dropped her eyes, hurt by his reluctance to join her high spirits. Tyre gave himself a mental shake. These weeks had been difficult for both of them. It was impossible for Kara to stay with him in the beginning with the healers working over him, keeping him drugged against the pain. Alone and immobile on the enormous bed, too weak to move without assistance, he slept almost continually, waking to eat a few mouthfuls of broth, relieve himself and take more drugs, then fell asleep again, too exhausted even to converse with her. Throughout it all, she remained in the women's quarters at the Maze despite her parents' wish that she return home so as to resume her studies. The healers were compassionate, but firm, allowing her a single visit each day. He tried to be alert when she came, but often their time together consisted of no more than exchanged glances and a few whispered words.

In the last few weeks, he gradually regained his strength and appetite. Ladon started him on a rehabilitation program of simple exercises and walks in the atrium. Kara joined him every afternoon, and there had been more time to talk, yet no true intimacy was possible, surrounded as they were with healers and patients. In the beginning he was too occupied with his first experience as an invalid to be concerned. Then, as time passed, he realized he was increasingly, and mystifyingly, ill at ease with her. He considered consulting Ladon, but shyness won out and he said nothing. He did his best to hide it from Kara, knowing that the blame was his, but witnessed her hurt every time he evaded one of her caresses. Despite her hurt, Kara never pushed him, never complained, and her visits remained the single focus of his monotonous, tiresome days.

There was also the matter of their newly acquired gift. Inside him, locked away like a treasure for which he had no key, Tyre held the memory of their strange and exhilarating union, a union that ended the moment they awoke in the healing chamber and the healers began their work. Confused, deeply frightened at how close he was to death, he had neither the skill nor the knowledge to explore it. As time passed, he began to doubt that it had happened at all. Kara never spoke of it, nor did any of the healers. The sense of having lost something precious continued to haunt him.

Only Kara's presence could abate the gloom that hung about him. As he grew stronger, their walks lengthened, and for the first time, he saw Pelion. Its enormity both impressed and daunted him. Kara was the perfect guide, showing him everything and renewing her delight in her city of cascading fountains and broad promenades. On rainy afternoons she read and sang to him, making the impersonal healing chamber as cozy as their cell. She must have planned today's ride with care, cajoling Ladon until she received his approval. Tyre regarded her with a surge of tenderness and pride.

"You're lovely in your riding clothes. I told you once I would never question the beauty of your legs, and I never break a promise."

Having intended to tease her, he was surprised when she didn't laugh.

"Then come with me and prove that you're a Master of the Horse. If you fall off, Ladon will never forgive me."

He tried his best to lighten the mood, working for animation, humor, anything to restore her good spirits.

"I'm not worried about falling off. It's mounting that has me worried. I'm not very bendable."

The hurt in her face was replaced by fear.

"If you're still too weak, don't let me bully you into going. We can always ride another day."

"I was teasing. You know how much I've longed to ride again."

She put out her hand, he took it, and they walked out of the House of Healing and on until they found themselves at the northern gate. Tyre looked out on the fields and orchards of the verdant valley surrounding the escarpment. People came and went through the gates, accompanied by carts, dogs, and children. A few Legionnaires lounged at the entry; no one paid Tyre the slightest attention. The past assaulted him: twin lines of townspeople gathered at daybreak, silent and thoughtful as a pathetic band of strangers passed into their immaculate, well-ordered city.

"Kara?" She looked up immediately, sensing his seriousness. "Did you know what kind of man you would meet in the Maze?"

She took her time in replying.

"I'm not sure what you're asking. The Fifteenth Mother came for me one evening, explaining that I would be joined to an ernani."

"I've been called 'ernani' since I arrived, but no one told me what the word means."

"It's our word for someone who is lost,"

He nodded, accepting the aptness of the term.

"You'd never seen an ernani before. What did you expect?"

Her gaze never wavered. "That's not quite true. I saw a group of ernani enter at this very gate a year before I entered the Maze."

Tyre visualized himself at the end of the chain, filthy, footsore, and frightened out of his wits.

"You saw them and still you agreed to come?"

She stood on tiptoe to pull his head down, her eyes searching his, comforting him as no one else could.

"Will you ever understand? Ernani are not slaves. Yes, I saw them—dirty, defeated, wretched—and yes, I was frightened. But ernani have always been special, set apart, because they represent a potential for us. For the city, they say, and even the world. That potential was realized in you. And me."

She'd explained it, the looks on the people's faces as the group of chained men marched past them on the way to the forge. Even those unsure as to the exact purpose of the Maze, all those unknowing, unsuspecting residents of this great city, had gathered to welcome him, and he had not known it until today. The gates were fearful no longer. On impulse, he leaned down and kissed her cheek. A crimson tide rose from her neck to her forehead. With a quick intake of breath, she was off and running through the gate and down the road toward cavalry headquarters, her laughter trailing after her as he took up the chase.

For once, Kara hadn't told Tyre the whole truth. She'd told him that she'd already visited the stable, but she'd hidden the fact that she'd been going there regularly every morning for the past three weeks. Ever since her conference with Nerissa, Ladon, and Gelanor, she'd planned this day down to the final detail. The last thing she wanted was to embarrass herself with her rusty riding skills. Grudius, overjoyed at her request, offered to put aside his duties to help her brush up her horsemanship, assuring her that Henna would be waiting for her at the cavalry stables. They worked together in the ring for the first week, then headed for the hills, Grudius riding beside her on the trails, talking endlessly of Tyre's wondrous ability with horses. Satisfied that she could keep her seat if they kept to the well-worn paths, Kara prayed for fine weather. Her reward came this morning, when the sun broke through early-morning clouds, promising a bright, breezy day.

Besides the fact that regular exercise had brought roses to her cheeks and new firmness to her legs and thighs, she was thankful for anything that prevented her from worrying about Tyre. The euphoria of waking beside his conscious, living body faded as she realized how weak he was. Although the healers were unfailingly optimistic, she saw Ladon's concern. Surprisingly, Tyre was a good patient; obeying orders, swallowing doses of medicines (some whose odor made Kara nauseous) without complaint, and overcoming his natural modesty as he was handled hourly by all number of strangers. Granted, Ladon was his primary healer, but Tyre accepted them all. All, that is, save Kara.

She sensed it long before Tyre did, his rejection wounding her so deeply that all she wanted to do was retreat to her parents' house and mourn. She did so the fourth week of his stay at the House of Healing.

Speechless with emotion, crushing her hands in his hard, leathery grip, her father searched her face, drinking in her features like a desert traveler drinks from a well. Megara's greeting was almost pathetic in its fervor; she seemed unable to let her daughter out of her sight, following her from room to room like a faithful spaniel. Having arrived that morning without warning, Kara avoided committing herself to any particular time for departure. By afternoon, she was seated in her garden, listening to the loom in her father's workroom while her mother hummed tunelessly to herself as she copied out lesson plans for the morrow. Kara had missed the crocus and the narcissus, but the tulips were in full bloom, their bold, showy colors gleaming against the evergreen hedges. Evander must have taken over her duties with the birds. Robins, sparrows, and an occasional jay, crunched on grain and seeds sprinkled on the ground, unafraid of the stranger who sat quietly under the trellis. Her peace was almost complete when her father answered a knock at the door and Kara learned, with a heavy heart, the identity of the visitors who had come to call.

"Three people from the Maze ask to see you. Shall I tell them they are welcome?"

Her father's meaning was clear. Sensing her trouble, he assumed the role of protector. If she chose, he would deny them entry. Touched by his concern, she put him at ease.

"They're friends of mine, Father. Ask them to join me in the garden." She paused. "Perhaps it would be best if you took mother for a walk. She asked to see the flowering cherry trees in the park."

He nodded his understanding.

"We will not disturb you." He wasn't finished, and even after a six moon separation, she knew exactly what he would say. "You are always welcome here, and you may stay as long as you wish. But don't use us as an excuse or an escape. We love you too much to allow you to hide from your destiny, whatever that might be."

Her eyes filled at her father's steady faith in the role chosen for her. He was a man of his word, his pledge to the Fifteenth Mother as strong as it had been twenty years ago. Nodding at her with an expression of encouragement, he ushered in the visitors, and after a few moments of pleasantries, left them alone.

Nerissa seated herself on the bench next to Kara. Ladon chose a small gardening stool nearby. Much more at ease than his companions, Gelanor wandered around the garden, seeming to drink in the colors and scents, finally settling in a crouch on the ground, his fingers tracing designs in the gravel. For once, Kara felt no desire to play hostess. They had tracked her here; let them make the first move. She was tired of being manipulated, tired of having people tell her what to do. She had done as they asked and it came to naught. Tyre was alive, but couldn't bear her touch. A miracle had occurred, but Kara had seen no proof of it since the moment she woke in the healing chamber. She wondered for a moment if they were reading her thoughts. Suddenly angry, she decided to take the initiative.

"Nerissa, are you reading my mind?"

It was impossible to judge whether her question or her brittle tone upset Nerissa more. Clearly, she was shaken.

"I am not. And I want to make it clear to you that I've only read you twice in all your time in the Maze: on the evening of your arrival and after you saw Tyre beaten in the arena."

"Why haven't you done so, if you have the ability?"

A fond smile rose on the Instructor's lips.

"Ah, Kara, you are so new to this—I forget how difficult it must be. The first lesson we learn is that our gift must be used sparingly; if it isn't, it becomes too easy to depend on it for information our other senses can provide. Also, we respect the privacy of others, and only enter a mind by invitation, or in the case of emergency or distress. Neither of your parents is adept. I would guess that with the exception of their healers, Evander and Megara have never been read by anyone other than the Fifteenth Mother."

"Could you read me if I chose not to be read?"

Ladon spoke up.

"We learn to erect barriers, both to protect our privacy from other adepts, and in my case, to allow me to enter a mind that is not adept and begin the healing process without frightening my patient. The question is not could I read you, but would I read you, and the answer is no."

"And you, Gelanor, are you part of this conspiracy?"

All three were taken aback, but when Gelanor's answer came, Kara was humbled.

"I'm not so gifted as Nerissa or Ladon. I'm a limited adept, which means I can only share my thoughts with other adepts. It's impossible for me to read a non-adept. As to being part of the conspiracy, as you call it, I suppose I must plead guilty."

He flashed a winning smile.

"I teach at the Maze by the Fifteenth Mother's request. If you're hurt or embarrassed by anything I did or said, I beg your pardon."

Mollified, Kara looked down at her hands. Gelanor's apology soothed her, but brought no happiness. Nerissa picked up the conversation again.

"I knew you were unhappy, yet you never came to me for counsel. When Ladon told me you didn't appear at the House of Healing for your daily visit, Echteus told us where you'd gone. We've come to help you if we can."

Kara made no pretense of hiding her hopelessness.

"No one can help."

The normally serene Instructor surprised Kara by the vehemence of her distress.

"I blame myself for your misery. How lonely you must have been! We've been so concerned about Tyre; we didn't realize how troubled you were. Forgive me, Kara, forgive me for my thoughtlessness."

"Tyre missed you today," Ladon interjected. "He depends on your visits and plans his days around the moments he shares with you. He was upset and restless all afternoon, asked repeatedly for you, and didn't fall asleep until an hour ago, when I asked Chloe to sing to him." Protective of his patient, the healer's reproach changed to outright accusation. "I know it's tedious to tend a bed-ridden patient, but how could you leave without a word of explanation?"

None of them understood what was happening. It was so clear to her, so unavoidably clear, yet they were blaming her for everything. Her anguished wail made the birds take flight.

"Can't you see what's happened? The Fifteenth Mother called it a miracle, but all I see and feel tells me that something is wrong, terribly wrong! You say he misses me, but when I visit him, there's always a distance between us. He lets the healers, complete strangers, assist him with the most private functions of his body, yet he can't bear for me to lay my hand on his arm!"

She stopped, out of breath, and saw them exchange glances. Ladon cleared his throat, compassion in his dark, weary eyes.

"I was afraid of this, although I had no idea you sensed it so strongly." He smiled weakly. "I should have known that you would know more quickly than any of us."

He looked to Gelanor, who moved to Kara's side and knelt in front of her, lacing his fingers together in his lap like a schoolboy readying himself for a test.

"Do you believe me when I say I had never met Tyre when I spoke to you in the Maze?"

Kara nodded. Gelanor seemed unsure how to proceed. She could see an idea forming, and once more, he was transformed into a Master Teacher.

"Describe him for me."

Kara responded without thinking.

"He's very tall; my head comes only to his breast. His hair is blonde and he wears it long and unbound." She paused, momentarily embarrassed, but Gelanor offered no escape. "His eyes are blue, and change colors when he's angry, or teasing, or aroused." She lingered over that thought for a moment before continuing. "He has large hands, with long tapered fingers."

Gelanor wasn't satisfied.

"Tell me about his body."

Struck speechless, Kara stared at him.

"Trust me. Close your eyes if it helps, and describe his body as if you lay beside him."

Remembering his wisdom and good counsel, she closed her eyes, describing the vision she mourned over every night.

"Even though he's long and lean, his chest and arms are firm and molded. When he holds me, I can see muscles slide under the skin, and his skin is beautiful. Golden, almost hairless, and so smooth to the touch that it's nearly as silky as his hair. His stomach is firm with hard muscles. . ." She felt her lips trembling. "Gelanor, don't make me go on."

He nodded slowly.

"I saw Tyre an hour ago, after he had fallen asleep. Shall I tell you what I saw?"

Mystified, she gave her assent. As he looked beyond her, the wry-faced clown was nowhere in evidence.

"When Ladon removed the sheet, I saw some of the things you describe—a tall man, with blonde hair and tapered fingers. His eyes were shut, so I could not see their color. I saw an invalid who is not golden, but pale and painfully thin. His wrists and ankles are ringed with purple bruises and there's an ugly gash over his right temple. His skin is smooth from his shoulders to a small scar on his chest, but from there to his navel he's covered with ugly ridges and grooves cut deep into his flesh. Scabs have formed over the lacerations and a thick bandage cuts across his ribs, which stick out plainly from underneath his skin." His gaze shifted to her now. "I am no healer, but I guess that he will be badly scarred on his body, and may be scarred on his face."

Ladon broke the silence following Gelanor's description.

"He asked me about the scars a few days ago, which is why I suspected you sensed his trouble. I tried to put him off, but Tyre is stubborn, as you know." Ladon's shoulders drooped. "He asked for a mirror, and after denying him until I saw he would never rest until I agreed, I gave him one." A shadow crossed the healer's face. "He is not a vain man, Kara, yet he was greatly shocked. He still can't move without pain, and we have kept him bandaged up to now, so he has never seen the full extent of the scarring, nor has he seen his face. He asked me if they would fade. I told him the truth—that even though the redness will eventually disappear, the scars will always mark him. He took it calmly, handed me the mirror, and never mentioned it again."

Three faces looked at her expectantly.

"Are you telling me that he thinks he's suddenly grown ugly or unattractive to me? That he thinks I will love him or desire him less because he's scarred?"

Their silence was her answer.

"Then why does he allow everyone else to touch him?"

Gelanor smiled.

"That's the point. No one's touch matters except yours. The question is: do you still desire him? Have you seen the scars and do they repulse you?"

Kara was incensed at his suggestion.

"Of course I've seen them, although he's always careful to keep them hidden when he's awake. And no, I'm not repulsed by them. I want him so badly I ache!"

"Does he know that you've seen them?"

"No," Kara admitted, beginning to understand what Gelanor was asking. "I knew they bothered him, so I looked at them while he slept."

Gelanor's face lit up. Nerissa and Ladon relaxed.

"Then our course is clear and all will be well. We'll let him heal, and you'll continue to visit him, understanding how difficult this is for him. When he's better, we'll be ready." Gelanor looked over to Ladon. "How long before he can join with Kara?"

Kara felt a twinge of shyness but the healer took no notice.

"In three more weeks most of the scabs should be gone and the knife wound will be safely closed."

His smile turning into a grin, Gelanor rose to his feet.

Nerissa remained seated. Somehow Kara knew the interview was far from over.

"And what of your other union? Have you tried to reach Tyre with your new gift?

"I . . . I don't know how."

"Don't you want to, Kara?"

Nerissa's expression of dismay brought Kara to the boiling point. She regarded the Instructor with anger mixed with scorn. Kara was tired of being the sweet one, the nice one, of always doing the right thing, the thing everyone expected.

"You talk of miracles and transformations, but it was terrible going in and worse coming out. Why should I want to do that ever again? What good is it, this gift, if you're not a healer or a hetaera?"

Bowing her head, Nerissa sat unmoving for several long minutes. When at last she lifted her eyes to Kara, her expression was that of a person who returns from a long journey. Where did Nerissa go, wondered Kara.

"To have so little regard for what you and Tyre achieved is difficult for me to hear, but I am reminded by the Council of Pelion that you must be schooled as no one has been schooled before. "

Kara frowned.

"Are you saying you just had a conversation with the Council of Pelion?

"I did."

"The Fifteenth Mother . . .?"

". . . in her tower chamber, Stanis in the Great Library, Luxor on field patrol in the old forest to the west, and Ladon, sitting here beside me."

Kara held her breath, trying to imagine what such a gift would mean to her and to Tyre.

Nerissa stood.

"We begin your lessons tomorrow. In time, I'll teach Tyre as well."

Ladon and Gelanor rose also, waiting for Kara to pass in front of them. When she made no move to do so, Ladon's confusion was clearly written on his face.

"Aren't you coming with us?"

"I'll stay here tonight. Tell Tyre where I am and he'll understand. I'll see him tomorrow at my appointed time."

They let themselves out, Gelanor turning at the last moment to wink at her.

Kara stood alone in her garden. A lone sparrow hopped on the grass, searching for a tidbit everyone else had overlooked. Her pluckiness cheered Kara. Reaching up to the shelf that held the grain, she tossed a few seeds in her direction and watched her grab one and take wing, hurrying home, no doubt, to her family.

A sound behind her made her turn. Her mother and father stood hand in hand, regarding her with love and pride.

"Let's celebrate tonight! I'll return to the Maze tomorrow, but I'll spend the night here with you. You must tell me everything you've done this winter and what your plans are for spring!"

Reining in the stallion from a canter, Tyre braced himself for the trot, relaxing as the stallion settled swiftly into an easy walk. Tyre had coveted this horse since the day he first saw him in the arena, for even in Lapith he would have been extraordinary and much sought after for purposes of breeding. Coal black, long-legged and deep-chested, with elegant lines and a shapely head, he was clearly the pride of the cavalry stables. Despite his admiration, Tyre eyed him with apprehension today, even though Grudius assured him that he was extremely smooth-gaited. The effort of mounting made him grimace, but once in the saddle, all memories of the last seven weeks faded in the pure joy of riding. A breathless voice called his name and he turned in the saddle.

"Why must you go so fast?"

Kara pulled up the bay mare beside him with obvious relief, her hair coming loose from its pins and floating around her flushed face. Dropping the reins, she set about repairing the damage. The bay lowered her head and began to graze.

"I looked away for a moment and you had disappeared! If I hadn't come this way before, I might have gotten lost. Henna and I tend to walk, although we break into a trot from time to time, especially when I turn her for home."

Not only was she not angry, Tyre could see her admiration shining in her eyes. He hadn't meant to flaunt his abilities, but the urge to gallop was insurmountable. He shifted in the saddle, considering her for a moment.

"I didn't know you were familiar with these trails. You said you never left the ring before entering the Maze."

Despite her rosy skin, her blush was unmistakable. Tyre smothered a laugh. He'd guessed she was up to something for the past few weeks. Her skin glowed with unaccustomed color and he'd caught her wincing more than once when she sat down on a bench in the atrium.

"I . . . well . . . perhaps I forgot to tell you that I've been coming here in the mornings."

"Perhaps?"

She was growing pinker by the moment. Charmed by her chagrin, he couldn't resist waiting to see if she had anything else to confess. She must have seen the laughter in his eyes, because she started scolding him, brandishing a hairpin for emphasis.

"You knew all the time, didn't you? Well, I'm not sorry for not telling you! I wasn't born in a saddle and I needed to practice!"

"Are you going to throw that hairpin at me?"

Huffiness changed to cool disregard as she gathered up the reins.

"You may do as you like. Henna and I are going to find a place to rest. Not everyone can ride for hours . . ."

Her grumble faded away as she turned the bay and headed in an easterly direction. Amused by her stiff back and obvious indignation, he nudged the stallion forward at a meek walk. Soon he was judging her critically, noting her good posture, tight-gripping knees, and light hands on the reins. Someone had taught her well. Then he remembered Grudius helping her mount and the proud smile that had pulled his seamed face into one enormous pucker. Another mystery solved, Tyre let the steady gait of the big black soothe away his earlier misgivings, thankful that he was alive, free, and riding beside Kara.

She chose a clearing near a small brook for their rest. A stand of birch and willows provided shade, the sunlight filtering through the brilliant yellow-green leaves, dappling the grass beneath their trunks. Kara was off the bay in an instant and unfastening a saddlebag before he could dismount. He swung his leg over slowly, the stallion standing rock-still, and hardly felt a twinge as his feet touched the ground. Taking the bay's reins in his other hand, he tied both horses loosely to the trees, leaving them to graze on the new grass. He patted the mare, running a curious hand over her, her ears flicking toward him as he cooed to her.

"I always suspected you talked to me the way you talk to horses. Now I've proof."

Startled, he found Kara laughing up at him. Disconcerted for a moment, he realized she was right, and laughed with her, shaking his head at her powers of observation.

"What do you think of her?"

Highly entertained by her professional tone, Tyre watched Kara stroke the rough black mane much as she used to stroke his hair. The memory hurt and he pulled his attention back to her question.

"She's a trifle fat and out of condition. Her lines are good, though, and she moves neatly. She'd be good breeding stock."

"Do you think she'd be strong enough for a long journey?"

Kara hadn't moved her eyes away from the mare, but her hand had ceased its stroking and clutched a piece of the mane. Noting her tension, he answered cautiously.

"That would depend. How long a journey?"

"A trip far to the north of here; I'm not sure how many days."

He lowered his hands to her shoulders and turned her toward him. She kept her eyes stubbornly downcast.

"What are you saying, Kara?"

As she lifted her eyes, he read a tumult of emotions in their depths. "I'm saying that if you decide to return, I want to go with you, if . . . if your welcome still holds."

Letting out his breath, he released her. Her offer was unexpected and he was unprepared for it. In all the talks and walks of the past weeks, they had left the subject of the future strictly alone. He walked over toward the brook, noticing that she had laid out a blanket and unwrapped some fruit and cheese. More tired than he wanted to admit, he lowered himself onto the striped wool. His thighs and backside were sore after a mere hour in the saddle.

Kara stood where he had left her, her hand still wrapped in the coarse mane.

"Nothing has changed. You are still welcome, but the old problems remain. I can't ask you to share a life that will hold no happiness for you."

"Then we must change that life so we can find happiness together."

"What?"

She was moving toward him now, her body graceful, her chin high, her expression brimming with confidence.

"Why are you so sure of failure without at least attempting to change what is? You, who are so brave and who have endured so much?" The words poured out of her, proof that she had planned her appeal as carefully as she had planned this outing. "Why not try to change the tribe? I accept that it will be difficult. But you are your father's only son and your people need you."

He envisioned them riding up to his father's tent, Kara on Henna, himself on the black stallion. Kara; unveiled, her dark hair and exotic eyes almost as much a novelty as her strange clothing. What would they think of her, a woman unlike any they had ever known? He harbored no doubts as to his own welcome, but he was frightened for her.

"I know we'll have to make compromises. Perhaps we'll take a cart so I can ride in that until they accept the fact that a woman can ride a horse as well as a man. I can wear dark-colored dresses and hide my hair at first. But you will have to compromise as well. We will live together—day and night—in our own tent. And we won't be alone. We'll have friends!"

"What friends?"

"Our friends from the Maze, of course! They want new challenges, new lives outside the city. Most of all, Brimus and Minthe, Chione and Suda, want to find a place for themselves that's free of old memories, old ways of doing things. And then there's Hourn. You can find him, yes?" she asked, and when Tyre nodded in agreement, added quickly, "This is what Dino wants as well."

Tyre flinched. If Kara noted his reaction, it didn't prevent her from continuing.

"The next class is being assembled. In a few moons, he'll be joined with another woman of Pelion. He's spoken to Nerissa, asking that the one chosen for him be a woman willing to leave the city. He wants to join us, Tyre. Shall I tell him he and his mate will be welcome?"

She left the decision to him. How could he ever have doubted her? And in that same moment, he knew that he had never doubted Kara, but himself, and his worthiness of her love. She left the mare and stood in front of him, her expression intent.

"Tell Dino he is welcome."

Her eyes glowed. Suddenly, Tyre was irritated. Why hadn't she included him in all these plans? What did she know of Lapith or the immense problems they would face? He made no attempt to hide the sarcasm of his next question.

"So, it seems you've arranged everything. May I ask how you think four couples, and perhaps a fifth, will be able to overcome generations of traditions and custom? You think I'm stubborn, but you've never met my father."

She refused to let him dampen her enthusiasm.

"We will prove ourselves through our actions, prove it through our care for each other and for everyone in the tribe."

His disbelieving snort made her stop her head-long rush. She shook her head and sighed, not in defeat, but in disgust.

"Sometimes you are a great fool, Tyre of Lapith!"

When he bristled, she sat on the blanket and pointed her finger at his chest.

"Look at yourself, and at Brimus, Suda, Dino, and your friend, Hourn! You are men to be reckoned with, trained to fight and protect what you believe in. You'll bring all these skills with you, along with your knowledge of the world outside Lapith. Do you think slavers will be able to withstand your swords and strategies? Do you think your tribe will remain dependent on caravans to take their trade goods, and with them, half the profits, to places that don't understand your tongue?"

"And what of us, the women who accompany you? We know it will take longer for us to be accepted, but within our tents we'll ply our crafts as we've been taught. We'll take seeds and bulbs to root in the soil, and soon there will be fruits, vegetables, grains, and herbs blossoming on the plains. All of us have knowledge of crafts that will benefit the tribe. Chione is an expert in carding, spinning, dyeing and preparing wool for weaving or knitting. I am skilled at the loom and Minthe is learning. In time, we'll be able to provide something more than leather as a product for trade."

"In addition, we'll teach the people how to read and write. Some may resist at first, but who will persist when we prove that figures and sums make for better estimation of profits and written agreements prevent feuds between clans? Do you believe that good food throughout the long winter, literacy, and more products for trading won't persuade your people that we are good for something beyond the getting of children?"

Now she considered his most pressing question.

"As to your father, I concede that I don't know him. But from your description, I know he has placed all his hopes in you and will welcome you, regardless of the manner of your return. I also suspect that he's not as close-minded as you suggest. Why else would he have hired a tutor for you but to bring new ideas to you, and thus, to the people? Besides," she turned away from him, contemplating the tiny brook, "I doubt he will avoid our tent for long once his grandchildren play within its walls."

As she continued her steady contemplation of the water, Tyre considered the wonder that was Kara. And he thought she knew nothing of Lapith! He was the fool she named him, underestimating her again, blind to her insights, thinking her attention to his descriptions was meant to flatter or merely polite. Instead, she'd memorized everything he'd ever said about his home, creating a picture in her mind more truthful than the one he carried in his heart. He'd thought only to return and continue his family's tradition of leadership; Kara wanted to change the nature of the tribe's existence through sharing the accumulated knowledge of this remarkable city of Pelion. Her dreams were so much greater than his that it shamed him. Once in Lapith, she would continue her giving of gifts, to him, to his people, and to all who came into contact with her generous spirit. Always, Kara offered herself freely and without reservation. Then Tyre remembered something which made his newly-kindled hope fade.

"What of Sturm? And Stheno?"

She sat beside him, overriding his fears with scorn and a steely eye.

"I doubt that Stheno could convince the tribe to reject your father's heir, and from what you've said of your father, I doubt he would allow Stheno to attempt such a thing. You are the hope of your people," she paused, her eyes shining up at him, "and we will have fine sons and daughters. Your family has led your people for generations. Do you think one old man will be able to change that?"

She saw it all so clearly, and was willing to give up her glorious city, her studies, her family, everything she held dear.

"You spoke of compromise, yet it seems that you give everything, and I, nothing. What do you ask of me in return?"

Her attention wandered away from him again to settle on the placid landscape around them.

"I will go with you if you promise me two things. When our child grows within me, you must leave Lapith and bring me back to Pelion. Our child must be born here so it may be blessed and we may give the third gift. We must return for the birth of each child so my parents can know their grandchildren, if only for a little while." Her answer revealed how difficult she found it to imagine being separated from her parents. "You must also promise that once you become the chieftain, every year we will send a man and woman of the tribe to undergo Preparation."

"A woman?"

"Nerissa says that now they will open the gates to all who come. A prophecy told them that the male would not be of Pelion, so they brought only men to the city. Since the miracle, all will be accepted. In time, many of the tribe will be as we are."

He reached out his hand, pulling away a dark curl that separated them.

"And how are we?"

She met his eyes.

"In agreement, I hope," she said, then switched her attention to her saddlebag. Rooting around in it, she extracted a small jar and held it up for him to inspect. Recognizing its shape, Tyre pulled away, causing Kara to regard him as if he were a wayward child.

"Ladon let you go today because I promised I would care for you. He gave me careful instructions that I must spread this salve over your scars to keep them soft." Her eyebrows rose like dark wings. "Doesn't a healer do this for you several times each day?"

His protestation died in his throat. He couldn't explain that the healers weren't shocked by his wounds but that Kara might turn away in horror. He'd seen the scars and they were nothing short of hideous. The stitches on his forehead were partially hidden by his hair, but nothing could hide the deep indentations left by the madman's quirt.

She reached out and stroked his cheek.

"I won't hurt you, I promise. Don't fear me, beloved."

Her last endearment, together with her touch, gave him courage. He struggled out of the tunic, Kara helping him lift it over his head. She placed the saddlebag behind him, and with a firm grip on his shoulders, pushed him down so that he rested his head on it. Through half-lowered lids, he watched her spread the salve over the scabs, working quietly and competently over his body, bringing that special sense of calm he always experienced when Kara touched him. Relaxing, he closed his eyes and breathed in the scent of Kara.

Slowly, gradually, he became aware that her touch had changed and that she was caressing him as if . . . His eyes flew open. She was smiling down at him with a look he couldn't mistake. She wanted him. He could feel it in her hands and read it clearly in her flushed face. Unbelieving, he started to speak, but she placed a finger over his lips.

"Hush. Don't say a word. Let me finish."

Her hands touched each ridge and groove, familiarizing herself with him. As each stripe was covered with salve, his fears lessened. A shadow separated him from the sun. She was leaning over him, her face so close he could feel her breath on his cheek.

"Unpin my hair."

Reaching up, he did as she requested. Her lips wandered softly over his neck and shoulders, causing him to fumble with the pins as he hurried to release her hair and feel it against him once more.

"You needn't rush. We're not expected back until the trumpet sounds."

Her voice was languorous, provocative, and he slowed his fingers as she began to kiss him again, her lips warm and sensuous. The last pin removed, he was caught in the net of her hair. Sighing, he buried his face in it, smelling the fragrance of Kara. She lowered her lips to his and he took her offering willingly, longingly. After a time, she moved her head away, smiling down at him from where she knelt.

"Help me with my blouse."

He nodded, and she pulled it from the waistband, drawing it slowly over her head. He reached up to slide his hands over her breasts, feeling their ripeness fill his palms. She closed her eyes at his touch and leaned toward him, bringing their satiny whiteness closer to his lips. He was hungry for her now, his fears forgotten, her sighs ringing in his ears as he suckled her.

He was losing all sense of time with this languid, gentle joining. As the breeze moved through the leaves, the continual flow of water was like the current of their loving, meandering down the slope, heedless of rocks and logs, gaining speed as it swept down the hillside in an endless flow.

Her hands were at his waist now, untying the laces, and eventually his breeches were added to the pile with her own. Her mouth moved over him, avoiding the tender scars, his pleasure all the greater because of her acceptance of their presence. Each caress of her hands repeated the same refrain: "We are One."

Sliding her hands up from his loins to his shoulders, she leaned over him, kissed his mouth and eyelids, and brushing away his hair from his forehead, ran her lips lightly over the final evidence of the night of screams. With that touch, the memory faded as he knew the scars would fade, leaving pale traces to remind him of the time he called for her, and, true to her promise, she came.

"I need you."

They were the same words he had said to another. This time, he had no doubt of the response. Belwyn had placed him on the path to Kara; this was the culmination of his journey.

"My need is as great as yours."

"We'll go together then?"

"Always together. Always one. Now, lie still and let me love you."

She rode astride him, her hair billowing off her shoulders, her head thrown back in abandon. Stroking her thighs, he watched her graceful form dance above him as she reached higher and higher for what she sought. The pulse in the hollow of her throat throbbed rhythmically, and she held out her hands for his.

"Let us share the miracle again."

And so he opened himself at last to the greatest gift, held in reserve for this moment of surrender. His hands and mind met hers and their union was complete.

Their souls faced each other in the clear, quivering light. Moving beneath her, inside her, around her, feeling everything she felt, sure that her ecstasy equaled his, he joined her dance, and together they reached up and touched the sky.

To the west, the sun sank behind the battlements of the city, the last few rays dyeing the walls pale orange. In the east, a yellow moon rose over the rolling hills. Silhouetted against the gathering dusk, two riders on horseback faced north, a single star on the horizon burning steadily before them. The man sat tall, his head tilted toward a slender woman whose hair tumbled wildly over her back. At the man's full-voiced cry, the horses plunged forward as one, running on the evening breeze. As they vanished into the distance, strains of the woman's voice raised in song floated back toward the sacred city.

Chapter 23

On the Wings of a Dove

HE'D ASKED NOT to be disturbed, but the insistent rapping on the door demanded some kind of response. The servants, grown accustomed to his ways, usually pushed open the door a crack to ask if he could be interrupted. When the rapping continued unabated, Stanis pushed away the sea of paper surrounding him, heaved himself to his feet, and padded soundlessly to the door. Letting irritation over being interrupted override his manners, he swung the door open with a mighty heave.

Tyre stared back at him, whatever he had been about to say forgotten as he registered Stanis' identity. Incredulity and alarm washed over his face, his eyes widening in panic. Seemingly unable to turn and run, he backed away, stopping when his back came to rest against the stone wall of the hallway. Stanis thought hard, wondering how they were to communicate. Cursing his muteness, fearful that this unexpected visitor might vanish, never to be seen again, Stanis leapt into Tyre's unprotected mind.

What resulted was similar to being transported into the midst of a raging battle, of moving from a state of casual calm to gut-wrenching terror in the blink of an internal eye. Stanis did his best to maintain mental balance as Tyre's memories assaulted his senses, his nostrils flaring at the scent of vomit and human excrement, his ears ringing with the screams and mindless babble of the city of madness, his wrists aching from the pressure of the manacles, their metal edges cutting deep into his flesh. Burning hands ran down his body, shame and humiliation bringing his gorge to the back of his throat.

Against Stanis' will, the force of Tyre's memories triggered his own, exploding out of his control. Stanis was gagging now, his jaws being pried open, a hand reaching inside his mouth to pull out his tongue, the knife descending . . . until, locating the cold, hard, center of his reason, the kernel of his mind that kept him sane that wretched day, Stanis wrenched both of them away from the chaos of Agave, tasting as he did so the river of his blood even as he broke the connection and staggered backward, panting, to lean against the tapestry-covered wall of his chamber.

The air around him had vibrated with a riot of colors; now it cleared, the tapestries and rugs assuming their proper positions on walls and floors. As Stanis regained inner balance, his heartbeat slowed and his breathing returned to normal.

And then he remembered Tyre.

He was standing stock-still, eyes tightly shut, hands clenched into tight fists. Blaming himself for his lack of forethought, Stanis waited as Tyre shook his head from side to side as if to clear it. His eyes opened slowly as he recovered from an invasion for which there was no excuse. Reluctantly, Stanis entered again, keeping the contact light and as brief as possible, choosing to communicate with words rather than images.

"I am called Stanis and I have no tongue. Because I sought some means of speaking with you, I entered without invitation. No excuse validates such an action. I can only apologize for invading your privacy."

He broke the connection immediately and turned away, expecting to be left with the guilt that still permeated every thought concerning Tyre. His had been the cruelest role of all. Even though he understood its necessity, acceptance brought with it no absolution.

"What . . . what happened?"

Tyre took a tentative step over the threshold, his back still to the door like an animal protecting its sole means of escape. Stanis sank into his leather chair and stared at his hands.

"It was as if . . ." Tyre groped for a description, ". . . as if I was in Agave again, but in someone else's body."

Any other adept, born and trained to their gifts, would have run screaming down the hall after such an ordeal, yet Tyre was already trying to understand what had transpired. We know so little of what our labors have wrought, Stanis thought. This one, and all who follow, may surpass everything we have ever known. He looked up into eyes full of questions, yet he refused to break the rules again. Instead, he stared steadily at Tyre, lifting his hands in supplication. His visitor took another step forward.

"You have my leave to enter," Tyre said, adding, "although it seems a bit awkward to actually say it out loud." He regarded Stanis thoughtfully for a moment. "You're the first person I've ever said it to."

Something about him, the seriousness of his manner, the curiosity with which he regarded the man who had so recently invaded his thoughts, caused Stanis to see him for a moment as the boy Beal told him of, rather than the self-possessed man he had become.

Tyre was acting quite oddly now, frowning in what Stanis decided must be an intense effort of concentration. Stanis could do nothing but stare, more puzzled than ever about this newest of adepts. Opening his eyes to find himself the object of Stanis' inquiry, Tyre smiled somewhat shyly.

"Nerissa works with me everyday, drilling me in adept ethics at the same time she teaches me how to build barriers. After you left me, I put up a wall to keep you out. Now I've taken it away. She says I should be able to do it without closing my eyes, but it's still difficult for me." This explanation was punctuated with a short laugh. "Kara says my problems result from lack of practice, but the days are full of plans for our journey, and the nights," he flushed, adding lamely, "the nights grow shorter."

Stanis waited until he had controlled and locked away his mirth at his visitor's slip before entering, choosing to continue using words rather than images since he judged that the easiest way to begin.

"When I came into your thoughts, you were remembering Agave. I was unprepared for the strength of what you felt, with the result that your memories became mingled with mine. In a way, we were in Agave together; both of us slaves, both of us helpless . . ."

Stanis tried to maintain the tones of teaching, but the shudder running through his thoughts became uncontrollable. Unwilling to continue, he retreated. To his surprise, Tyre went on with the lesson, refusing to allow his escape, demanding his assistance.

"But you were not helpless. Somehow you were able to remove us, to return us here."

Blue eyes bored into him, determined, insistent. Beal, you are behind this quest for truth, thought Stanis.

"Much of it is experience. To free us," Stanis continued, *"I found the place inside me that was not Agave and took us there."*

Tyre absorbed his explanation. As his next question formed, Stanis' admiration grew.

"Could I achieve that level of skill?"

"You ask the unanswerable. What you and Kara accomplished as you crossed over is impossible for me to imagine since I have always been adept. No one knows the limitations of your gift, or even if any limitations exist."

The next question came more slowly, taking shape and form from thoughts that whirled with images of a dark-haired woman holding a child to her breast, the sweet notes of her lullaby echoing around them, the scent of wildflowers wafting on the air.

"We do not know if your children will inherit the gift. I am the child of non-adepts while Ladon was raised in a family adept for many generations. Sometimes children born of the same parents have greater or lesser gifts, while others have none."

Impulsively, he opened another door to Tyre, showing him the magnitude of the miracle he was just beginning to explore.

"This is what you have achieved, you and Kara, for it makes no difference if your child, or any child, is gifted from birth. All who desire it, who come to the Maze and offer up their gifts, will become as you are."

Stanis paused, letting those thoughts dissipate, allowing them both time to adjust to a new line of inquiry.

"Why did you come?"

"To find the owner of the black stallion. Grudius sent me to Zelor, who provided directions to your chamber. I wanted to ask you if . . ."

Stanis interrupted, suddenly intent on teaching this adaptable, inquisitive mind.

"You needn't use words, Tyre. Show me what you desire. Build the images slowly and carefully and I will understand."

As Tyre struggled to comply, Stanis was intrigued by the power of his voice. There was no subtlety, none of the shadings found in the greatest practitioners, but the images were clear, bright and highly focused. That's because they're new, Stanis realized in a private part of himself hidden away from Tyre's mind. Only a few moons old, this newest adept . . . .

The black stallion moved beneath him, his gait fluid and effortless as he sped over the ground. The picture grew more distinct as Tyre conveyed not only the horse's speed, but his love of speed, of a need to run that matched that of his rider. Still unsatisfied, Tyre filled in more details. The stallion was needed not only as a mount, but as a breeder of long-legged colts and fillies. His progeny would run wild and free on the grassy plains of the north, frolicking with tails uplifted, rolling on the sandy banks, splashing through shallow streams, grazing contentedly over endless miles of unfenced terrain.

Losing himself in the joy of Tyre's creation, Stanis joined his vision, supplying details from his own vast memories, and felt an answering jolt run through Tyre's mind. Exiting quickly, Stanis waited for him to recover.

"You've been to Lapith!" Tyre said aloud. "Not once, but several times." It took some time for him to make sense of all he had seen in the outpouring of memories supplied by Stanis. "You attended a Harvest celebration as a caravan trader and . . ." he was trembling now, shaking with disbelief, ". . . and you knew Belwyn, knew him well! His memory is strong within you, although you know him by a different name."

Beal's face rose in front of Stanis' eyes.

"Come with me, Tyre, and I'll show you how I came to know your lands."

A troubled Tyre considered the merits of his offer. Swallowing hard, he nodded.

Stanis wrapped the fledgling mind in his and thrust them both into the past.

A fair-haired boy lay dreaming near a dying campfire. His long, thin frame was wrapped snugly in a blanket, a bracelet-covered arm flung out toward the fire, the bronze links reflecting its light.

A slight, curly-headed man stared into the fire, at his side a figure wrapped in a bulky cloak, a hood concealing his face from curious eyes. Any passerby would see two men lost in private contemplations of the dying embers. No one would suspect that the outsider from Ariod's tribe was busily persuading his companion to a course of action first envisioned five centuries ago.

"You must convince her I've found him. Urge her to put things into readiness. The map is as complete as I can make it. I've spoken to every caravan trader who crosses the plains, traveled whenever Ariod allowed it, and recorded the tales of the elders as they teach the young ones the game trails and watering places."

Delicately, Stanis formed a question, receiving a strong negative response from his fellow Searcher.

"I cannot leave him, if only for a few moons. The time for that will come soon enough. He begins to put his trust in me. If I go, that trust will founder and fail."

Stanis wanted to accept Beal's findings without question. But belief came hard, especially after so many years of searching. They had found so many, only to be disappointed with each one during the course of Preparation.

"How can you be so certain? Doubtless he is golden-haired and comes from the north. But what of the west?"

Beal's enthusiasm slowed, his visage clouded. Stanis thought his question had dampened Beal's confidence. He should have guessed that Beal had already leapt ten years into the future.

"I ask myself, how shall we bring him to Pelion? He must know nothing, suspect nothing, and be stripped of all he holds dear. Loving him as I do, I hoped an easier way might be found." Beal paused to contemplate the sleeping face of the boy beside him, his lips tightening as he continued. *"But he is stubborn beyond belief, a half-broken colt who will become a rigid and unforgiving man unless he is forced to re-evaluate everything he takes for granted."*

Beal's gaze shifted back to his companion.

"We must enslave him, Stanis. Everyday I become more convinced that we must bring him through Agave."

Beal shared Stanis' wordless horror, his voice rising above the screams of the crowd and the crack of the whip.

"Agave lies in the west, old friend."

Stanis snapped to attention, his memories forgotten in a swift surge of hope. As his interest grew, Beal directed his gaze to the dreaming child.

"I can see only dimly into the mists before us, but I know that when the time comes, I will not be with him. Already I am too close; everyday I struggle to let him grow up free and untouched. I will prepare him as best I can, but it will be your task to strip him of all pretenses and vain beliefs that keep his eyes blind and his mind closed. You will test him in the place that tested you."

Stanis regarded the boy, reaching out a dusky hand to the outstretched arm covered elbow-deep in bracelets that announced his tribe, clan, and parentage. Before his hand could touch the gleaming metal, the boy moaned in his sleep, his forehead furrowed, his limbs twisting underneath the blanket. Quickly retracting his hand, Stanis watched as Beal moved closer to the boy, placed his palm on his shoulder, and soothed away the dream that disturbed his rest. Gradually the boy quieted, turning from his back to his side, nestling his cheek against the saddle that served as his pillow.

"What will happen if I do as you wish? What will be left when he is stripped?"

A soft smile played around the healer's lips, his eyes gleaming with secrets better left untold.

"Even naked he will be a formidable man. Having passed through Agave, he will pass into Pelion, and then . . . then . . .!"

Beal pointed wordlessly to the stars of the far north.

"I never saw him again. The next morning he gave me a saddle at parting. It was a token of his faith in me; a reminder of my pledge to help his princeling of the north pass through Agave. That saddle is the one you use when you ride my stallion."

Stanis left Tyre as the memory faded, wondering if what he had done would help heal the wound of Belwyn's passing or open it afresh. Tyre revealed no hint as to his reaction, but paced around the chamber, his long legs eating up the distance between the walls. Pausing, he turned a radiant face to Stanis.

"I've always yearned for Belwyn's approval. You've just given it to me."

Puzzled, Stanis searched back hurriedly through what they had just relived, sifting through the conversation for clues without success. Tyre raised an eyebrow, blue eyes gleaming as he enjoyed Stanis' perplexity.

"It seems that though you've traveled to Lapith, you know little of our lore. Our night skies are our maps, rather than the charts I've studied in your libraries. The stars tell us everything we need to know about the shift of seasons and the movement of game. I've not seen my native skies for seven moons, yet I can close my eyes and see the sky that is right for this season, this moon, this day."

"Belwyn was my tutor, yet I taught him as well. One of the things I taught him was the sky-lore, for all stars have their stories and we pass them down from father to son. Ten years ago, Beal sat with you facing south on the last eve of Harvest. When he lifted his face to the stars, he pointed to the Ring of Lapith."

Tyre's voice deepened as he began a kind of chant, the rhythms rolling easily off his tongue as he recited a story translated from the Lapithian tongue. Stanis knew he was hearing the same tale Beal had heard so many years ago from the mouth of a boy.

"For legend has it that the ring was placed in the sky by a woman wanderer. She was nameless, this woman, and manless as well, with feet of earth and hair of fire. Upon seeing her, the clansmen scoffed, jeering at her manless state, for woman is not woman without man. The woman bent to earth, gathering five stones heavier than any man could lift. As she threw the stones up into the heavens, they passed through her burning hair, turning to stars before their eyes. When the clansmen cowered in fear, she pointed to the blazing ring of stars, saying, `Man shall never touch the stars without the help of woman.'"

The child had spoken purely by rote; the man spoke from the truth of his own experience.

Stanis proffered his arm. Tyre grasped it tightly.

"Good journey. The stallion is yours. You return him to the place he was bred."

"We leave in ten days time from the northern gate at dawn."

Tyre hesitated at the door.

"You've never met Kara, have you?" At the quick shake of Stanis' head, Tyre beamed. "Then you must meet her before we leave. When I tell her everything I've learned today, she'll be jealous. I know her well," he uttered a playful sigh, "and she'll never be content until she meets you for herself."

In the short pause which followed, a single brow cocked over a measuring eye.

"May I come back tomorrow with Kara?"

Stanis nodded.

"We'll return to Pelion from time to time. When we come, would you teach us?"

Stanis' answer burst outward—joyous, triumphant—to be met with a spirit of exuberance that matched and then surpassed his own.

Tyre's promise floated over his shoulder as he strode out of the chamber.

"We'll touch the stars, Stanis."

Stanis walked slowly to the door and shut it. He had not recalled his last night with Beal in ten years, nor had he ever had any intention of allowing Tyre so deeply into his memories. The Fifteenth Mother was his closest friend, yet she had never plumbed the depths of his mind, nor did he want her to. Yet on a whim he had taken Tyre to the place it had all begun, when he responded to Beal's summons, dropping his duties in the east to hurry to him.

What moved Zelor to send Tyre to him in the first place? A simple request would have assured Stanis' immediate cooperation. He had surrendered the horse and saddle to Grudius with only a brief moment of regret, for as the Fifteenth Mother promised, his traveling days were over.

The room seemed empty after Tyre's departure, yet Stanis had his suspicions.

"He sees clearly now, old friend, and all is as it should be. Your task is ended."

Outside the window, a cloud passed over the sun, sending a shadow flitting across the room. Stanis smiled, white teeth ablaze in his dark-skinned face, as he lowered his gaze to his studies.

From Vena's high perch, the valley seemed a child's puzzle, its fields and borders broken into hundreds of tiny pieces, each one of a slightly different shape and coloration. A lush green was the primary color, shaded and textured by the passage of a few high clouds gliding swiftly over the valley. A wedge of geese flew due north, their unique shadow adding another variation to the landscape below. Envying them their route, she watched as they beat their enormous wings, their long necks extended toward their goal, intent on the lakes and breeding grounds in the far north. In a short time they would overtake the tiny band of wanderers who followed in a like direction. Vena corrected herself. Not wanderers, for wanderers lack a destination, while the contingent from Pelion navigated a route charted on a precious map, its details traced by Beal's steady hand. The map reached her four years after his tenure began with Tyre, so positive was he that he had finally found the promised one, just as he was convinced that the tiny girl-child brought from the east was a part of the plan.

For nearly twenty years she watched and waited, helpless to intervene lest she thoughtlessly ruin what had taken centuries to create, depending on others to serve as her hands, legs, and eyes. The waiting was nearly over. Clinging to the battlements for support, her hands ached as she gripped the stones in an effort to still the palsy that never left her now.

Awake and asleep, her hands shook incessantly and her fingers could barely hold a pen. With clinical acumen, she regarded the rebellious hands, certain that all too soon her entire body would vibrate with continual tremors. That there was a certain irony inherent to her demise did not surprise her. Her boisterous predecessor had gradually lost the ability to talk or breathe without pain. The Thirteenth Mother, a trained architect, lost her precious eyesight, and with it, her will to live. She, Vena, who delighted in control, was unable to manage the simplest movement. Sighing, she released her grip, surrendering herself to the involuntary movements of her hands. Balance was everything. This was the price she paid for twenty years of power.

This was her last watch. She had stood her post every morning since the miracle. Distracted for a moment, she lifted a hand to her breast. Upon hearing the crinkle of parchment hidden beneath the black folds of her robe, she was consoled. Each day at dawn, she trudged up the hundred steps that led from her chamber to this watchtower. Her hopes had been especially high this morning, but it was nearly noon, and again, no one had answered her call.

The soft slap of leather on stone drew her attention. Her ears caught the sound of wind against silk.

"Excuse my interruption, Mother, but I was in the Maze and it . . . it seemed to me you called."

Vena understood her uneasiness. This call had been different from any in Nerissa's experience for the simple reason that it was the first time Vena had used it. Having passed into her at the moment of the Fourteenth Mother's passing, it remained buried inside her, ready to emerge near the moment of her death. Now her old friend regarded her with confusion, her body poised for flight, her grey robes fluttering in the ever-present breeze that marked this lonely tower.

Vena returned to her steady observation of the valley floor.

"This is my favorite place in Pelion. Have you visited here before?"

"Never."

"I find it to be a place where all things are put into perspective. Here, I have a bird's eye view of the world, and things of seemingly great consequence assume correct proportion when compared to the beauty and order I perceive around me."

Vena expected no answer and Nerissa offered none. Now that the moment had arrived, Vena felt an enormous reservoir of patience fill her. She would approach her last task as she had approached her first, planting each seed carefully in the fertile ground, tending and watering with hope and love; her patience that of the farmer who plants and replants in the face of flood, drought, and infestation.

"Kara asked for you this morning."

When Vena failed to respond, Nerissa questioned her.

"Why do you avoid her? You've been so close for so long."

"She's no longer the child I cared for. She must make a new life for herself. I've freed her to do just that."

"She's so young . . ."

". . . and so full of energy and plans. This is her time. She's blossomed like the flowers she carries with her to transplant into different soil. Some will not survive the journey or adapt to the cruel winters. Others will bloom for a single year and then refuse to lift their heads above the soil. But some of them," Vena said, relishing this vision of the future, "some of them will become all the more beautiful and varied because of their transplantation. Thus it will be for Kara, for Tyre, and for all of them."

Vena decided it was time to change the subject.

"Did you see them safely off?"

There was no need for Nerissa to know that Vena had risen even earlier than usual to witness their departure.

"Since you could not be found, I blessed their venture." Her training took over and she began to report the morning's happenings. "Tyre, Kara, and Brimus were on horseback. Suda and Chione drove the carts that carry Minthe and their supplies. Tyre wasn't happy about Kara riding, but she just smiled up at him and waited for him to help her mount."

Nerissa's enjoyment grew.

"He let loose a string of profanities that turned Minthe quite pink with wonder. When Kara didn't budge, he gave in and threw her up on the mare, predicting dire consequences with a thunderous look on his face. He sulked until Chione spoke up in that understated way of hers: "And I thought my Suda was stubborn! Cheer up, laddie, she's won and you've lost."

Chuckling at the thought of Tyre's rout at the hands of the women, Nerissa approached the battlement, her eyes following the road that led beyond the northern gate. They shared a long moment of reflection; both women's eyes squinted against the glare.

"I worry for them, especially since they have no healer. They're all so new to their gifts. Minthe seems to show some promise in that direction, but there's been little time for training."

"Soon they will have a healer."

Nerissa met her eyes for the first time.

"Tell me what you see, Mother."

"In this place, at this time, you must call me Vena."

Nerissa's eyes widened at the oddness of the request.

"Tell me what you see, Vena."

Vena began handing over information to her successor.

"Ladon is weary past the point of recovery. When he has not been with Tyre, he has been with Cydon, undertaking the long process of filling his brother's emptied mind. Soon he will resign as High Healer, asking if he, like Beal, can become a Searcher of Souls. You will guide his choice, convincing him that his path lies to the north. There he will find rest and purpose, continuing his teacher's work in herb lore and healing."

Nerissa stiffened as Vena continued, resisting what she feared might follow, but listening carefully to every word.

"Luxor, too, will soon pass away; the old warrior will put down his arms at last. Three are fit to take his place—Rhacius, Carmanor, and Zelor. Choose as you will, remembering that one must love peace to effectively wage war."

Now she turned to the gist of Nerissa's mission in this new world, a world in which Vena would play no part.

"The pilgrimages to Pelion will begin slowly, giving you years to plan and prepare for the days to come. Gather your helpers wisely, watching for those who excel, no matter their training or talent. Some additions to the legislation of the Maze will be necessary and Stanis will be of great use to you. He knows the ways of the outside world and the people who inhabit it."

"Remember as well that you must include Pelion and its people in the miracle. There will be resistance to many of your plans, but in this you will fare better than I, for you are native born and bred. Despite my years here, I remain an outsider, and the people have never taken me to their hearts. I have their respect. You will have their love."

Unable to contain herself any longer, Nerissa broke her silence.

"It cannot be! Surely you're mistaken. I come from the Hetaera Guild. There has never been a Mother . . ."

"Know this, old friend. I have sent out my call daily since the transformation. You alone have answered."

Nerissa gasped, struck speechless as her worst fear was confirmed. Vena regarded her with pity. The Fourteenth Mother had given Vena warning; Nerissa's call caught her unaware.

"There is no formula for selecting a Mother, and this is the last and greatest Mystery. Fifteen of us have foretold our deaths, and in each case, sent out a call. For five hundred years, that call has been answered by a single woman. In the past, we have been artisans, teachers, scholars, farmers, architects, and healers. Today a hetaera answers the call."

"But I lack the proper skills!" Nerissa searched frantically for a way out of the trap. "Chloe would be a much better choice."

Vena mustered what little was left of her skills of persuasion.

"Chloe could never make the decision I made and leave Maenon behind. You are stronger than you realize. Here in the Maze you have made responsible decisions based on sound judgments. Who better than a hetaera could undertake the joining of hundreds, even thousands of ernani? Who else could put them safely on the Path? You reported yesterday that all who chose to give the third gift are newly adept. Here is the proof you long for, for out of all those couples, only one was joined by me."

"But yours was the choice that yielded the miracle!"

Vena shrugged, an uncharacteristic gesture for her and a bitter one at that.

"Apply your unequalled honesty and tell me I was instrumental in their joining. I worked in total ignorance with a few scribbled words to guide me. At every moment of choice, I doubted. And many of my choices were wrong."

Nerissa's support for her old friend was fierce.

"I see nothing wrong with your choices. In every case, you kept your vows and fulfilled your mission."

Vena's eyes filled.

"On the contrary, the cost was high. Too high. The price of my mistakes begins with twenty-eight men whose ashes lie in a ravine and the death of Beal. Add to this the loss of Grasos, one of the gentlest souls I have ever known, the mind of a gifted healer, and the murder of a simple servant called Baldor."

Her voice hardened.

"And then there is the terror of the thought that the twisted adept is still at large, having eluded us at every turn, playing us for fools and incompetents."

She sighed, lowering her voice to the tones of confession.

"As to keeping vows, I tell you a secret that, with the death of Grasos, only Ladon shares. I broke a vow, broke it without a second thought to save the child Beal brought me so many years ago. It was the most difficult thing I have ever done. Since that night, my body has steadily betrayed me."

Nerissa was obdurate.

"Yet the miracle came to pass."

"And with it, my time comes to an end. Another must don the black robes."

Vena extended her hand palm up in a formal gesture of offering. This was the last step, the act of transference that would make Nerissa the next Mother of Pelion.

"Must I?" Nerissa asked, her reluctance clear.

"Would you end what has been more than fifteen generations in the making?"

"What will happen?"

"You will possess the memories of those who came before you."

"All of them?"

"Even unto the First Mother on the First Day."

Nerissa posed what Vena sensed would be her last question.

"Will it hurt?"

Vena considered her answer carefully.

"It will come to you in a jumble of sounds and images in no order, making no sense until you undertake the task of sorting out the voices, the sights and sounds, smells and tastes. Accept it without question. Let it wash over you like a stream. In time, over the course of years, you will learn how it may best be used."

Nerissa placed her palm over Vena's and closed her eyes.

Their minds met, and it was accomplished.

She-Who-Was-Nerissa opened her eyes on a new world. Even as she struggled to understand what had just happened to her, she watched Vena struggle with the ties on her cloak.

"How old she is," Nerissa thought, *"older than anyone I have ever known."*

With palsied hands, Vena unpinned her veil, her long grey hair escaping and flying wildly about her. Nerissa watched her disrobe in silence, eyes bright with unshed tears. As Vena began to unlace her gown, two white hands descended on her swollen ones.

"Stay with us, Vena. I can't imagine Pelion without you."

Nerissa's invitation wrenched Vena's heart, for the strength of her decision was weakening. Life was dear to her and the valley whispered a seductive promise of fertility and growth. Perhaps she should reconsider. Perhaps she had misread the signs.

The black banner unfurled and snapped in the breeze. Vena had her answer.

Fighting her way up onto the battlement, clutching with almost useless hands, her fingers bleeding from the effort, Vena pulled her aged body onto the ledge. She was breathing heavily by the time she reached the top and struggled to her feet, balancing precariously on the ancient stones.

With her earthly eyes, she saw Nerissa's tears. With her inner eyes, she saw the roof of the Sanctum shining like a beacon to all who would give their gifts. The castle gleamed its farewell in the late spring air. All that she had been passed away and she held out her arms to what she would become. Her silent cry pierced the void surrounding her.

"Beal, Beal, I come to you at last!"

"Vena, my Vena, how I have longed for you!"

She leapt out into space and into the arms of her beloved.

Nerissa stood transfixed, her arms holding the limp black robes, her hand clutching the folded parchment to her breast. There was no cry and no answering sound of a body crashing onto the rocks a hundred feet below the battlements. Gradually, life returning to her frozen limbs, she moved forward cautiously to peer out over the ledge, bracing herself for the sight of a broken body and a blood-smeared shift.

A white rag fluttered in the air, drifting downward in a lazy spiral to the floor of the valley.

A gust of wind brought new tears to her eyes. The banner snapped and curled overhead. Impulsively, she looked up, expecting to find the familiar sable pennant, finding instead a brilliant white field blazoned with a golden many-pointed sun and a silver crescent moon.

Nerissa unfolded the parchment and read:

". . . And the elder days will pass away, and that which was black will be white, and that which has been will be no more, and that which has never been, will be."

Here was the final proof of Vena's success, yet her friend would never see her beloved banner transformed.

Voices floated on the wind.

"We see, Nerissa. We see."

Peace filled Nerissa. Taking up Vena's post on the watchtower, she surveyed the fields below her, noting the tiny figures of men and women who went about their routine tasks without the slightest awareness of the passing of the Fifteenth Mother. This would be her responsibility, to make sure they lived free and unafraid. These were her people. She would make the necessary sacrifice to keep them safe and secure in a perilous world.

With that thought, a vision rose before her, much like the one she experienced in the dayroom on the Day of Choice. Two lines of men and women marched along the roads that led to Pelion. From all points of the compass they came, each one filled with a yearning to receive the gift, the news of which the Searchers were spreading even now. Some were like her ernani of old—tired, beaten, full of despair, yet others were free-born and proud—courageous, ambitious, eager to claim the treasure awaiting all who journeyed to Pelion. Even as her vision shimmered and faded around her, she witnessed the departures of the newly-adept couples, their faces shining as they left the gates and dispersed into the wide world, taking with them their new-found gift, using their abilities to heal the wounds of slavery, war, ignorance, poverty, and famine. Pelion had been founded to this end, that all would share this gift, the single blessing to emerge from their migration from one world to another, something the Sowers gave them, perhaps as recompense for the loss of their civilization as they abandoned their dying world.

Nerissa fingered the black cloth lovingly. She would have it refashioned to fit her smaller form. Everyday she wore it, she would be clad in the raiment of She-Who-Was-Vena. Humbled, she wiped away her tears and rearranged her veil.

She was unworthy, but she would try.

The Sixteenth Mother of Pelion, Legislator of Preparation and Keeper of the Flame, lifted her arms to begin her first task of office. Raising her voice to the skies, She-Who-Was-Nerissa recited the opening phrase of the rite of passing.

About the Author

Anna LaForge read Tolkien's *The Lord of the Rings* at fourteen, Asimov's *Foundation Trilogy* at sixteen, and LeGuin's *The Left Hand of Darkness* at eighteen, at which time she decided that she, too, wanted to create new worlds. Born in Philadelphia, she has lived throughout the country, from urban centers in the Midwest and Northeast to tiny Andrews,Texas. A former executive director of several not-for-profit arts organizations, she divides her time between teaching and writing.

Connect with Anna LaForge online:

Twitter: #annalaforge
Facebook: facebook.com/annalaforge
Goodreads: goodreads.com/annalaforge
Her website and blog: annalaforge.com

Appendix I

Commentary on the Marcella Fragment

The source of this manuscript fragment is *The Book of the Mothers*. According to legend (which is now being challenged by experts in the field of antiquity), these records were chronicled by the scribes of the Great Library of Pelion. It is now believed by scholars specializing in the Elder Days (Before Transformation, B.T.) that many of the early entries are written in the actual hands of the Mothers. Rowra/Crosus of Endlin, in their extensive study, *Assigning Authors: "The Book of the Mothers"* (Great Library of Endlin, 1040) suggest that sometime before Transformation, the duty for transcription fell to the hands of the Head Scribes, many of whom were members of the Council. Rowra/Crosus also suggest that *The Book of the Mothers* was used exclusively by The Mothers of All, a tradition unbroken until the founding of The Council of Pelion in 237 B.T. After that time, Rowra/Crosus theorize that Council Members and the Head Scribe were granted limited access to *The Book of the Mothers*. The Marcella Fragment upholds Rowra/Crosus' work in this field, since it is one of the few signed entries. According to Rowra/Crosus, this particular prophecy was either revealed and/or first recorded after the ascension of the Twelfth Mother (ca. 130 B.T.), whose reputation for mysticism is still unequalled among her sisters.

An opposing interpretation is proposed by Nyra/Heliod of Lapith, in their influential study, *Vision of the Whispering Plain* (Great Library of Lapith, 1057). Rather than focusing purely on the Marcella Fragment, Nyra/Heliod consider the entire development of Elder Day Pelion as a series of deliberate actions taken by the Mothers to hasten and assure the moment of Transformation. Support for this interpretation rests primarily on two events: (1) the failure of Surnan's attempts to achieve adeptness through selective breeding, and (2) the Riot of 237 B.T. According to Nyra/Heliod, Surnan's inability to breed adeptness, coupled with the rapid dwindling of both sending and receiving adepts, brought about the inclusion of non-adepts in Pelion, a step necessary for the ongoing process of Pelion's expansion and development and one which put an end to the isolationist policies which had been unchallenged up to that time. The Riot of 237 B.T. (the devastation of which was unparalleled in the history of Pelion) demanded that the Eighth Mother devise a system whereby non-adepts and adepts could live and work together peaceably. Her great work on the subject, *Ethics*, laid the groundwork for the First Wave of Searchers for adepts and the Second Wave of Searchers for ernani. Nyra/Heliod argue that the Twelfth Mother may have revealed the prophecy regarding transformation, but her action came about as the result of her predecessors' efforts in preparing Pelion for the next step of the transformation process, namely, the building of the Maze. Thus, in the opinion of Nyra/Heliod, The Marcella Fragment may have been transcribed in 110 B.T., but was a guiding force to the leadership of Pelion from the time of the city's founding.

The Nyra/Heliod theory is corroborated by Varnia/Clytus of Pelion in *The Maze-Builders* (Great Library of Pelion, 1068). Basing their theses on archeological findings, they propose that although the vast majority of the Maze was probably designed by the Thirteenth Mother and begun around 70 B.T., a solarium was designed and constructed by her successor around 20 B.T., and that later additions thought to be the work of the Sixteenth Mother and completed around 20 After Transformation (A.T.) prove the collaborative nature of the venture. In an unprecedented finding (which is still being examined by scholars), Varnia/Clytus announced the location of the original site of the sacred flame of Pelion, and propose that The Marcella Fragment's phrase "at the place of the sacred fire" has been incorrectly interpreted as a metaphor for Pelion, and should be read literally since it indicates the exact location of the first Transformation.

Although it was written a century before the current wave of scholarly interest in The Elder Days, another important theory related to The Marcella Fragment is that of the Thirty-Fourth Mother's *The Outsider* (Great Library of Pelion, 962). Working from the opening phrases of The Marcella Fragment, the Thirty-Fourth Mother was the first to propose that the Fifteenth Mother was most probably not a native of Pelion. Her revolutionary approach to one of the more puzzling aspects of the fragment, (i.e. the identity of the "She" and "her") ties the identity of the Fifteenth Mother to the "one [who] shall come from desolation, unknown and unknowing." While scholars have always acknowledged the presence of non-native born adepts in Pelion after The First Wave circa 190 B.T., it was thought unlikely that the highly insular community of Pre-Transformation Pelion would accept an outsider in such a position of power. Working from the vast reservoirs of the Great Library of Pelion, the Thirty-Fourth Mother assembled a series of seemingly unassociated works from that period (ca.47 B.T. - ca.34 A.T.) to support her view. Among those manuscripts consulted are: *The Record of Searchers*, (Anon., ca.192-29 B.T.), an explanatory note prefacing Beal of Pelion's *Herb Lore of Lapith* (3 B.T.), Stanis of Pelion's *The Search for Ernani* (14 A.T.), and the Sixteenth Mother's entries in *The Book of Mothers*.

The most recent work on the subject can be found in Ilyia/Menas of Lapith's *The Settlement at Lapith* (Great Library of Lapith, 1082). Having trained under Varnia/Clytus in the School of Antiquity in Pelion, this couple has begun archeological digs on several sites near the fabled location of the first settlement of adepts in Lapith. Their most recent find is a gold and silver throat amulet which has been dated as ca. 10 A.T., which features an eight-pointed golden sun in conjunction with a silver crescent moon, with an inscription in the old tongue of Lapith which reads "We are One." Although the workmanship is purely Lapithian in style, its similarity to the heraldry of Pelion is unquestionable. Just as unquestionable is the inscription, which has long been associated with the newly adept couples who left Pelion for neighboring environs, and in the early days of Transformation, became a watchword among them which allowed immediate identification. Ilyia/Menas have theorized that this evidence supports the oral tradition of Lapith (long thought to be apocryphal) which purports that the original couple who underwent Transformation (the so-called "Ur" couple) founded the first settlement of adepts in Lapith.

[Commentary abridged from Astia/Royce, *The Critical Legacy of The Elder Days*, Volume I, Great Library of Pelion, 1093.]

Appendix II

Chronology of the Elder Days of Pelion

[Excerpted and reprinted here from Lazuli/Beorn of Agave's *A Short History of the Founders* (Great Library of Agave, 1089). They note in their preface the difficulties of establishing dates for this early period, a primary consideration being the lack of knowledge concerning the years immediately following the arrival of the First Ones. This reconstruction is based primarily on archeological excavations and the dating of texts catalogued in The Great Library of Pelion, beginning in the fifth century.]

Before Transformation (B.T.)

480—The First Mother, accompanied by her fellow adept practitioners, establishes the city of Pelion. The sacred flame is lit on a stone outcropping.

447—The ascension of the Second Mother.

433—An attack of southern marauders devastates half the population of Pelion.

432—The Legion of Pelion founded by Golax.

431—Construction of the city walls begins. Anara (also known as Anawra) affixes her handprint and name to the southwest cornerstone.

425—*The Legion Manual* (Anon.) is written.

410—The Ascension of the Third Mother. The Legion institutes regular patrols of Pelion's borders.

395—The first epidemic of the bone-eating sickness.

380—The outer walls of Pelion are completed. Construction of The Sanctum and The House of Healing begins.

375—Ascension of the Fourth Mother.

360—Establishment of the Guilds of Pelion. Houras, Master of the Forge, institutes the Guild Council and writes its constitution.

355—Construction of the Great Library begins.

345—Ascension of the Fifth Mother.

340—The Sanctum and The House of Healing are completed.

325—The Great Library is completed.

315—Ascension of the Sixth Mother. A search for surviving manuscripts and documents from Old Earth is instituted. The First Searchers leave Pelion on their quest.

309—A voluntary breeding program for adeptness is instituted as a result of Surnan's book, *On Inheriting Adeptness*.

293—Ascension of the Seventh Mother, who commissions Mycene to found the Chartists of Pelion.

291—Mycene leaves Pelion.

274—Mycene's *Cartography of Pelion and Its Environs* is catalogued in The Great Library.

263—Ascension of the Eighth Mother.

249—Iolas, daughter of Surnan, writes the first study of adept melancholia. As a direct result of this lost work (only fragments remain) the Eighth Mother opens the gates of Pelion to immigrants.

238—The second epidemic of the bone-eating disease.

237—Unrest develops as a result of the epidemic. A riot between native and immigrant factions results in many deaths and acts of violence. The first Council of Pelion is instituted by the Eighth Mother.

225—The Eighth Mother's *Ethics* is catalogued in The Great Library.

226—Ascension of the Ninth Mother. The fountains and parks of Pelion are designed and construction begins.

215—Phoras's *Musica Antiqua* is catalogued in The Great Library.

192—Ascension of the Tenth Mother. The Council of Pelion institutes the Searchers of Souls in an attempt to locate other adepts.

161—Ascension of the Eleventh Mother

156—Construction begins on The Lesser Library

145—The Eleventh Mother commissions the Forge to cast the bronze doors of the Sanctum. Designed by Corina, they portray the founding of Pelion by the First Mother.

130—Ascension of the Twelfth Mother.[1]

125—The Lesser Library is completed and the 200th anniversary of the building of the Great Library is celebrated with a city-wide festival.

100—The formation of the League of Independent Traders is approved by the Twelfth Mother.

87—Ascension of the Thirteenth Mother.[2]

69—Ground is broken for the construction of the Maze

47—Ascension of the Fourteenth Mother.

32—The third epidemic of the bone-eating disease. Work is halted on the Maze for several years.

29—The Fourteenth Mother recalls the Searchers of Souls.

23—The original design for the Maze is completed. Construction begins on the solarium of the Maze.

22—The Fourteenth Mother's *Legislation for Preparation* is catalogued in the Great Library.

20—The solarium is completed.

19—Ascension of The Fifteenth Mother.[3]

18—The Novice class begins the Path of Preparation. The Search for Ernani is instigated by Stanis.[4]

13—Beal of Pelion journeys to Lapith.

3—Beal's *Herb Lore of Lapith* is catalogued in the Great Library.

After Transformation (A.T.)

1—Transformation occurs. The Sixteenth Mother[5] ascends. The first colony of adepts is founded in Lapith.

[1] Also known as "The Mystic."

[2] Also known as "The Architect." Designer of the Maze.

[3] Also known as "The Outsider."

[4] Author of *The Search For Ernani.*

[5] Also known as "The Beloved."

CPSIA information can be obtained at www.ICGtesting.com
Printed in the USA
LVOW12s0507231113

362531LV00005B/97/P